THE MAN WHO LAUGHS

SOMETIMES CALLED

BY ORDER OF THE KING

THE

MAN WHO LAUGHS

BY

VICTOR HUGO

WITH ONE HUNDRED AND FORTY ILLUSTRATIONS FROM DESIGNS BY
D. VIERGE AND G. ROCHEGROSSE

IN TWO VOLUMES

VOL. II

GEORGE ROUTLEDGE AND SONS
LONDON AND NEW-YORK
1889

By the Same Author,
In Uniform Style.

LES MISÉRABLES, ... 5 VOLS.
TOILERS OF THE SEA, . . . 2 VOLS.
NÔTRE-DAME, ... 2 VOLS.
THE MAN WHO LAUGHS. . 2 VOLS.
NINETY-THREE, ... 2 VOLS.

GEORGE ROUTLEDGE & SONS,
LONDON AND NEW-YORK.

DRESSING DEA.

TABLE OF CONTENTS

VOLUME II

BOOK III

THE BEGINNING OF THE FISSURE

BOOK IV

THE CELL OF TORTURE

BOOK IX

IN RUINS

CONCLUSION

THE NIGHT AND THE SEA

LIST OF ILLUSTRATIONS

VOLUME II

LORD CLANCHARLIE'S SPEECH.

THE MAN WHO LAUGHS

BOOK III

THE BEGINNING OF THE FISSURE

CHAPTER I

THE TADCASTER INN

AT that period London had but one bridge—London-bridge, with houses built upon it. This bridge united London to Southwark, a suburb which was paved with flint pebbles taken from the Thames, divided into small streets and alleys, like the city, with a great number of buildings, houses, dwellings, and wooden huts jammed together, a pell-mell mixture of combustible matter, amidst which fire might take its pleasure, as 1666 had proved.

Southwark was then pronounced Soudric, it is now pronounced Sousouorc, or near it; indeed, an excellent way of pronouncing English names, is not to pronounce them. Thus, for Southampton, say, Stpntn.

It was the time when "Chatham" was pronounced *je t'aime*.

The Southwark of those days resembles the Southwark of to-day about as much as Vaugirard resembles Marseilles. It was a village—it is a city. Nevertheless, a considerable trade was carried on there. The long old Cyclopean wall by the Thames was studded with rings, to which were anchored the river barges.

1

This wall was called the Effroc Wall, or Effroc Stone. York, in Saxon times, was called Effroc. The legend related that a Duke of Effroc had been drowned at the foot of the wall. Certainly the water there was deep enough to drown a duke. At low water it was six good fathoms. The excellence of this little anchorage attracted sea vessels, and the old Dutch tub, called the *Vograat*, came to anchor at the Effroc Stone. The *Vograat* made the crossing from London to Rotterdam, and from Rotterdam to London, punctually once a week. Other barges started twice a day, either for Deptford, Greenwich, or Gravesend, going down with one tide and returning with the next. The voyage to Gravesend, though twenty miles, was performed in six hours.

The *Vograat* was of a model now no longer to be seen, except in naval museums. It was almost a junk. At that time, while France copied Greece, Holland copied China. The *Vograat*, a heavy hull with two masts, was partitioned perpendicularly, so as to be water-tight, having a narrow hold in the middle, and two decks, one fore and the other aft. The decks were flush, as in the iron turret-vessels of the present day, the advantage of which is that in foul weather, the force of the wave is diminished, and the inconvenience of which is that the crew is exposed to the action of the sea, owing to there being no bulwarks. There was nothing to save any one on board from falling over. Hence the frequent falls overboard and the losses of men, which have caused the model to fall into disuse. The *Vograat* went to Holland direct, and did not even call at Gravesend.

An old ridge of stones, rock as much as masonry, ran along the bottom of the Effroc Stone, and being passable at all tides, was used as a passage to board the ships moored to the wall. This wall was, at intervals, furnished with steps. It marked the southern point of Southwark. An embankment at the top allowed the passers-by to rest their elbows on the Effroc Stone, as on the parapet of a quay. Thence they could look down on the Thames; on the other side of the water London dwindled away into fields.

Up the river from the Effroc Stone, at the bend of the Thames which is nearly opposite St. James's Palace, behind Lambeth House, not far from the walk then called Foxhall (Vauxhall, probably), there was, between a pottery in which they made porcelain, and a glassblower's, where they made ornamental bottles, one of those large unenclosed spaces covered with grass, called formerly in France *cultures* and *mails*, and in England bowling-greens. Of bowling-green, a green on which to roll a ball, the French have made *boulingrin*. Folks have this green inside their houses nowadays, only it is put on the table, is a cloth instead of turf, and is called billiards.

It is difficult to see why, having boulevard (boule-vert), which is the same word as bowling-green, the French should have adopted *boulingrin.* It is surprising that a person so grave as the Dictionary should indulge in useless luxuries.

The bowling-green of Southwark was called Tarrinzeau Field, because it had belonged to the Barons Hastings, who are also Barons Tarrinzeau and Mauchline. From the Lords Hastings the Tarrinzeau

Field passed to the Lords Tadcaster, who had made a speculation of it, just as, at a later date, a Duke of Orleans made a speculation of the Palais Royal. Tarrinzeau Field afterwards became waste ground and parochial property.

Tarrinzeau Field was a kind of permanent fair ground, covered with jugglers, athletes, mountebanks, and music on platforms; and always full of "fools going to look at the devil," as Archbishop Sharpe said. To look at the devil means to go to the play.

Several inns, which harbored the public and sent them to these outlandish exhibitions, were established in this place, which kept holiday all the year round, and thereby prospered. These inns were simply stalls, inhabited only during the day. In the evening the tavern-keeper put into his pocket the key of the tavern and went away.

One only of these inns was a house, the only dwelling in the whole bowling-green, the caravans of the fair ground having the power of disappearing at any moment, considering the absence of any ties in the vagabond life of all mountebanks.

Mountebanks have no roots to their lives.

This inn, called the Tadcaster, after the former owners of the ground, was an inn rather than a tavern, an hotel rather than an inn, and had a carriage entrance and a large yard.

The carriage entrance, opening from the court on the field, was the legitimate door of the Tadcaster inn, which had, beside it, a small bastard door, by which people entered. To call it bastard, is to mean preferred. This lower door was the only one used. It opened into the tavern, properly so called, which was a large tap-room, full of tobacco smoke, furnished with tables and low in the ceiling. Over it was a window on the first floor, to the iron bars of which was fastened and hung the sign of the inn. The principal door was barred and bolted, and always remained closed.

It was thus necessary to cross the tavern to enter the court-yard.

At the Tadcaster inn there was a landlord and a boy. The landlord was called Master Nicless, the boy Govicum. Master Nicless—Nicholas, doubtless, which the English habit of contraction had made Nicless—was a miserly widower, and one who respected and feared the laws. As to his appearance, he had bushy eyebrows and hairy hands. The boy, aged fourteen, who poured out drink, and answered to the name of Govicum, wore a merry face, and an apron. His hair was cropped close, a sign of servitude.

He slept on the ground floor, in a nook in which they formerly kept a dog. This nook had for window a bull's-eye looking on the bowling-green.

CHAPTER II

NE very cold and windy evening, on which there was every reason why folks should hasten on their way along the street, a man who was walking in Tarrinzeau Field close under the walls of the tavern, stopped suddenly. It was during the last months of winter between 1704 and 1705. This man, whose dress indicated a sailor, was of good mien and fine figure, things imperative to courtiers, and not forbidden to common folk.

Why did he stop? To listen. What to? To a voice apparently speaking in the court on the other side of the wall, a voice a little weakened by age, but so powerful, notwithstanding, that it reached the passer-by in the street. At the same time might be heard in the enclosure, from which the voice came, the hubbub of a crowd.

This voice said:

"Men and women of London, here I am! I cordially wish you joy of being English. You are a great people. I say more: you are a great populace. Your fisticuffs are even better than your sword thrusts. You have an appetite. You are the nation which eats other nations—a magnificent function! This suction of the world makes England preeminent. As politicians and philosophers, in the management of colonies, populations, and industry, and in the desire to do others any harm which may turn to your own good, you stand alone. The hour will come when two boards will be put up on earth—inscribed on one side, *Men;* on the other, *Englishmen.* I mention this to your glory, I, who am neither English nor human, having the honor to be a bear. Still more—I am a doctor. That follows. Gentlemen, I teach. What? Two kinds of things—things which I know, and things which I do not. I sell my drugs and I sell my ideas. Approach and listen. Science invites you. Open your ear; if it is small, it will hold but little truth; if large,

5

a great deal of folly will find its way in. Now, then, attention! I teach the Pseudoxia Epidemica. I have a comrade who will make you laugh, but I can make you think. We live in the same box, laughter being of quite as old a family as thought. When people asked Democritus, 'How do you know?' he answered, 'I laugh.' And if I am asked, ' Why do you laugh?' I shall answer, 'I know.' However, I am not laughing. I am the rectifier of popular errors. I take upon myself the task of cleaning your intellects. They require it. Heaven permits people to deceive themselves, and to be deceived. It is useless to be absurdly modest. I frankly avow that I believe in Providence, even where it is wrong. Only when I see filth—errors are filth—I sweep them away. How am I sure of what I know? That concerns only myself. Every one catches wisdom as he can. Lactantius asked questions of, and received answers from, a bronze head of Virgil. Sylvester II. conversed with birds. Did the birds speak? Did the Pope twitter? That is a question. The dead child of the Rabbi Eleazer talked to Saint Augustin. Between ourselves, I doubt all these facts except the last. The dead child might perhaps talk, because under its tongue it had a gold plate, on which were engraved divers constellations. Thus he deceived people. The fact explains itself. You see my moderation. I separate the true from the false. See! here are other errors in which, no doubt, you partake, poor ignorant folks that you are, and from which I wish to free you. Dioscorides believed that there was a god in the henbane; Chrysippus in the cynopaste; Josephus in the root bauras; Homer in the plant moly. They were all wrong. The spirits in herbs are not gods but devils. I have tested this fact. It is not true that the serpent which tempted Eve had a human face, as Cadmus relates. Garcias de Horto, Cadamosto, and John Hugo, Archbishop of Trèves, deny that it is sufficient to saw down a tree to catch an elephant. I incline to their opinion. Citizens, the efforts of Lucifer are the cause of all false impressions. Under the reign of such a prince, it is natural that meteors of error and of perdition should arise. My friends, Claudius Pulcher did not die because the fowls refused to come out of the fowl house. The fact is, that Lucifer, having foreseen the death of Claudius Pulcher, took care to prevent the birds feeding. That Belzebub gave the Emperor Vespasian the virtue of curing the lame and giving sight to the blind, by his touch, was an act praiseworthy in itself, but of which the motive was culpable. Gentlemen, distrust those false doctors, who sell the root of the briony and the white snake, and who make washes with honey and the blood of a cock. See clearly through that which is false. It is not quite true that Orion was the result of a natural function of Jupiter. The truth is that it was Mercury who produced this star in that way. It is not true that Adam had a navel. When St. George killed the dragon he had not the daughter of a saint standing by his side. St. Jerome had not a clock on the chimney-piece of his study; first, because living in a cave, he had no study; secondly, because he had no chimney-piece; thirdly, because clocks were not yet

invented. Let us put these things right. Put them right. O gentle-folks, who listen to me, if any one tells you that a lizard will be born in your head if you smell the herb valerian—that the rotting carcass of the ox changes into bees, and that of the horse into hornets,—that a man weighs more when dead than when alive,—that the blood of the he-goat dissolves emeralds,— that a caterpillar, a fly, and a spider, seen on the same tree, announces famine, war, and pestilence,—that the falling sickness is to be cured by a worm found in the head of a buck, do not believe him. These things are errors. But now listen to truths. The skin of a sea-calf is a safeguard against thunder. The toad feeds upon earth, which causes a stone to come into his head. The rose of Jericho blooms on Christmas-eve. Serpents cannot endure the shadow of the ash tree. The elephant has no joints, and sleeps resting upright against a tree. Make a toad sit upon a cock's egg, and he will hatch a scorpion which will become a salamander. A blind person will recover sight by putting one hand on the left side of the altar and the other on his eyes. Virginity does not hinder maternity. Honest people, lay these truths to heart. Above all, you can believe in Providence in either of two ways, either as thirst believes in the orange, or as the ass believes in the whip. Now I am going to introduce you to my family."

Here a violent gust of wind shook the window-frames and shutters of the inn, which stood detached. It was like a prolonged murmur of the sky. The orator paused a moment, and then resumed:

"An interruption; very good. Speak, north wind. Gentlemen, I am not angry. The wind is loquacious, like all solitary creatures. There is no one to keep him company up there, so he jabbers. I resume the thread of my discourse. Here you see associated artists. We are four—*a lupo principium.* I begin by my friend, who is a wolf. He does not conceal it. See him! He is educated, grave, and sagacious. Providence, perhaps, entertained for a moment the idea of making him a doctor of the university; but for that one must be rather stupid, and that he is not. I may add that he has no prejudices, and is not aristocratic. He chats sometimes with bitches; he who, by right, should consort only with she-wolves. His heirs, if he have any, will no doubt gracefully combine the yap of their mother with the howl of their father. Because he does howl. He howls in sympathy with men. He barks as well, in condescension to civilization—a magnanimous concession. Homo is a dog made perfect. Let us venerate the dog. The dog—curious animal! sweats with its tongue and smiles with its tail. Gentlemen, Homo equals in wisdom, and surpasses in cordiality, the hairless wolf of Mexico, the wonderful xoloïtzeniski. I may add that he is humble. He has the modesty of a wolf who is useful to men. He is helpful and charitable, and says nothing about it. His left paw knows not the good which his right paw does. These are his merits. Of the other, my second friend, I have but one word to say. He is a monster. You will admire him. He was formerly abandoned by pirates on the shores of the wild ocean. This third one is blind. Is she an exception? No, we are all blind. The miser is blind; he sees gold, and he does not see riches. The prodigal is blind; he sees the beginning, and does not see the end. The coquette is blind; she does not see her wrinkles. The learned man is blind; he does not see his own ignorance. The honest man is blind; he does not see the thief. The thief is blind; he does not see God. God is blind; the day that he created the world, he did not see the devil manage to creep into it. I myself am blind; I speak, and do not see that you are deaf. This blind girl who accompanies us is a mysterious priestess. Vesta has confided to her her torch. She has in her character depths as soft as a division in the wool of a sheep. I believe her to be a king's daughter, though I do not assert it as a fact. A laudable distrust is the attribute of wisdom For my own part, I reason and I doctor, I think and I heal. *Chirurgus sum.* I cure fevers, miasmas, and plagues. Almost all our melancholy and sufferings are issues, which if carefully treated relieve us quietly from other evils which might be worse. All the same I do not recommend you to have an anthrax, otherwise called carbuncle. It is a stupid malady, and serves no good end. One dies of it—that is all. I am neither uncultivated nor rustic. I honor eloquence and poetry, and live in an innocent union with these goddesses. I conclude by a piece of advice. Ladies and gentlemen—on the sunny side of your dispositions, cultivate virtue, modesty, honesty, probity, justice and love. Each one here below may thus have his little pot of flowers on his window-sill. My lords and gentlemen, I have spoken. The play is about to begin."

The man, who was apparently a sailor, and who had been listening outside, entered the lower room of the inn, crossed it, paid the necessary entrance money, reached the court-yard, which was full of people, saw at the bottom of it a caravan on wheels, wide open, and on the platform an old man dressed in a bear-skin, a young man looking like a mast, a blind girl, and a wolf.

"Gracious heaven!" he cried, "what delightful people!"

CHAPTER III

WHERE THE PASSER·BY RE·APPEARS

THE Green Box, as we have just seen, had arrived in London. It was established at Southwark. Ursus had been tempted by the bowling-green, which had one great recommendation, that it was always fair-day there, even in winter.

The dome of St. Paul's was a delight to Ursus.

London, take it all in all, has some good in it. It was a brave thing to dedicate a cathedral to St. Paul. The real cathedral saint is St. Peter. St. Paul is suspected of imagination, and in matters ecclesiastical imagination means heresy St. Paul is a saint only with extenuating circumstances. He entered heaven only by the artists' door.

A cathedral is a sign. St. Peter is the sign of Rome, the city of the dogma; St. Paul that of London, the city of schism.

Ursus, whose philosophy had arms so long that it embraced everything, was a man who appreciated these shades of difference, and his attraction towards London arose, perhaps, from a certain taste of his for St. Paul.

The yard of the Tadcaster Inn had taken the fancy of Ursus. It might have been ordered for the Green Box. It was a theatre ready-made. It was square, with three sides built round, and a wall forming the fourth. Against this wall was placed the Green Box, which they were able to draw into the yard, owing to the height of the gate. A large wooden balcony, roofed over, and supported on posts, on which the rooms of the first story opened, ran round the three fronts of the interior façade of the house, making two right angles. The windows of the ground floor made boxes, the pavement of the court the pit, and the balcony the gallery. The Green Box, reared against the wall, was thus in front of a theatre. It was very like the Globe, where they played " Othello," " King Lear," and " The Tempest."

10

In a corner behind the Green Box was a stable.

Ursus had made his arrangements with the tavern-keeper, Master Nicless, who, owing to his respect for the law, would not admit the wolf without charging him extra.

The placard, " GWYNPLAINE, THE LAUGHING MAN," taken from its nail in the Green Box, was hung up close to the sign of the inn. The sitting-room of the tavern had, as we have seen, an inside door, which opened into the court. By the side of the door was constructed off-hand, by means of an empty barrel, a box for the money-taker, who was sometimes Fibi, and sometimes Vinos. This was managed much as at present. Pay and pass in. Under the placard announcing the LAUGHING MAN was a piece of wood, painted white, hung on two nails, on which was written in charcoal in large letters the title of Ursus' grand piece, " *Chaos Vanquished.*"

In the centre of the balcony, precisely opposite the Green Box, and in a compartment having for entrance a window reaching to the ground, there had been partitioned off a space "for the nobility." It was large enough to hold, in two rows, ten spectators.

"We are in London," said Ursus. " We must be prepared for the gentry."

He had furnished this box with the best chairs in the inn, and had placed in the centre a grand arm-chair of yellow Utrecht velvet, with a cherry-colored pattern, in case some alderman's wife should come.

They began their performances. The crowd immediately flocked to them, but the compartment for the nobility remained empty. With that exception their success became so great, that no mountebank memory could recall its parallel. All Southwark ran in crowds to admire the Laughing Man.

The merry-andrews and mountebanks of Tarrinzeau Field were aghast at Gwynplaine. The effect he caused was as that of a sparrow-hawk flapping his wings in a cage of goldfinches, and feeding in their seed-trough. Gwynplaine ate up their public.

Besides the small fry, the swallowers of swords and the grimace makers, real performances took place on the green. There was a circus of women, ringing from morning till night with a magnificent peal of all sorts of instruments,—psalteries, drums, rebecks, micamons, timbrels, reeds, dulcimers, gongs, chevrettes, bagpipes, German horns, English eschaqueils, pipes, flutes, and flageolets.

In a large round tent were some tumblers, who could not have equaled our present climbers of the Pyrenees—Dulma, Bordenave, and Meylonga—who from the peak of Pierrefitte descend to the plateau of Limaçon, an almost perpendicular height. There was a traveling menagerie, where was to be seen a performing tiger, who, lashed by the keeper, snapped at the whip and tried to swallow the lash. Even this comedian of jaws and claws was eclipsed in success.

Curiosity, applause, receipts, crowds, the Laughing Man monopolized everything. It happened in the twinkling of an eye. Nothing was thought of but the Green Box.

"'Chaos Vanquished' is 'Chaos Victor,'" said Ursus, appropriating half Gwynplaine's success, and taking the wind out of his sails, as they say at sea. That success was prodigious. Still it remained local. Fame does not cross the sea easily. It took a hundred and thirty years for the name of Shakspeare to penetrate from England into France. The sea is a wall; and if Voltaire—a thing which he very much regretted when it was too late—had not thrown a bridge over to Shakspeare, Shakspeare might still be in England, on the other side of the wall, a captive in insular glory.

The glory of Gwynplaine had not passed London Bridge. It was not great enough yet to re-echo throughout the city. At least not at first. But Southwark ought to have sufficed to satisfy the ambition of a clown. Ursus said :

"The money bag grows palpably bigger."

They played " *Ursus Rursus* " and " *Chaos Vanquished.*"

Between the acts Ursus exhibited his power as an engastrimythist, and executed marvels of ventriloquism. He imitated every cry which occurred in the audience—a song, a cry, enough to startle, so exact the imitation, the singer or the crier himself; and now and then he copied the hubbub of the public, and whistled as if there were a crowd of people within him. These were remarkable talents. Besides this, he harangued like Cicero, as we have just seen, sold his drugs, attended sickness, and even healed the sick.

Southwark was enthralled.

Ursus was satisfied with the applause of Southwark, but by no means astonished.

"They are the ancient Trinobantes," he said.

Then he added, "I must not mistake them, for delicacy of taste, for the Atrobates, who people Berkshire, or the Belgians, who inhabited Somersetshire, nor for the Parisians, who founded York."

At every performance the yard of the inn, transformed into a pit, was filled with a ragged and enthusiastic audience. It was composed of watermen, chairmen, coachmen, and bargemen, and sailors, just ashore, spending their wages in feasting and women. In it there were felons, ruffians, and blackguards, who were soldiers condemned for some crime against discipline to wear their red coats, which were lined with black, inside out, and from thence the name of blackguard, which the French turn into *blagueurs.* All these flowed from the street into the theatre, and poured back from the theatre into the tap. The emptying of tankards did not decrease their success.

Amidst what it is usual to call the scum, there was one taller than the rest, bigger, stronger, less poverty-stricken, broader in the shoulders; dressed like the common people, but not ragged.

Admiring and applauding everything to the skies, clearing his way with his fists, wearing a disordered periwig, swearing, shouting, joking, never dirty, and, at need, ready to blacken an eye or pay for a bottle.

This frequenter was the passer-by whose cheer of enthusiasm has been recorded.

This connoisseur was suddenly fascinated, and had adopted the Laughing Man. He did not come every evening, but when he came he led the public—applause grew into acclamation—success rose not to the roof, for there was none, but to the clouds, for there were plenty of them. Which clouds (seeing that there was no roof) sometimes wept over the masterpiece of Ursus.

His enthusiasm caused Ursus to remark this man, and Gwynplaine to observe him.

They had a great friend in this unknown visitor.

Ursus and Gwynplaine wanted to know him; at least, to know who he was.

One evening, Ursus was in the side scene, which was the kitchen-door of the Green Box, seeing Master Nicless standing by him, showed him this man in the crowd, and asked him:

"Do you know that man?"

"Of course I do."

"Who is he?"

"A sailor."

"What is his name?" said Gwynplaine, interrupting.

"Tom-Jim-Jack," replied the inn-keeper.

Then, as he re-descended the steps at the back of the Green Box, to enter the inn, Master Nicless let fall this profound reflection, so deep as to be unintelligible:

"What a pity that he should not be a lord. He would make a famous scoundrel."

Otherwise, although established in the tavern, the group in the Green Box had in no way altered their manner of living, and held to their isolated habits. Except a few words exchanged now and then with the tavern-keeper, they held no communication with any of those who were living, either permanently or temporarily, in the inn; and continued to keep to themselves.

Since they had been at Southwark, Gwynplaine had made it his habit, after the performance and the supper of both family and horses —when Ursus and Dea had gone to bed in their respective compartments—to breathe a little the fresh air of the bowling-green, between eleven o'clock and midnight. A certain vagrancy in our spirits impels us to take walks at night, and to saunter under the stars. There is a mysterious expectation in youth. Therefore it is that we are prone to wander out in the night, without an object. At that hour there was no one in the fair-ground, except, perhaps, some reeling drunkard, making staggering shadows in dark corners. The empty taverns were shut up, and the lower room in the Tadcaster Inn was dark, except where, in some corner, a solitary candle lighted a last reveler. An indistinct glow gleamed through the window-shutters of the half-closed tavern, as Gwynplaine, pensive, content, and dreaming, happy in a haze of divine joy, passed backwards and forwards in front of the half-open door.

Of what was he thinking? Of Dea—of nothing—of everything—of the depths.

He never wandered far from the Green Box, being held, as by a thread, to Dea. A few steps away from it was far enough for him.

Then he returned, found the whole Green Box asleep, and went to bed himself.

CHAPTER IV

CONTRARIES FRATERNIZE IN HATE

UCCESS is hateful, especially to those whom it overthrows. It is rare that the eaten adore the eaters.

The Laughing Man had decidedly made a hit. The mountebanks around were indignant. A theatrical success is a siphon—it pumps in the crowd and creates emptiness all round. The shop opposite is done for. The increased receipts of the Green Box caused a corresponding decrease in the receipts of the surrounding shows. Those entertainments, popular up to that time, suddenly collapsed. It was like a low-water mark, showing inversely, but in perfect concordance, the rise here, the fall there. Theatres experience the effect of tides: they rise in one only on condition of falling in another.

The swarming strollers who exhibited their talents and their trumpetings on the neighboring platforms, seeing themselves ruined by the Laughing Man, were despairing, yet dazzled. All the grimacers, all the clowns, all the merry-andrews envied Gwynplaine. How happy he must be with the snout of a wild beast! The buffoon mothers and dancers on the tight-rope, with pretty children, looked at them in anger, and pointing out Gwynplaine, would say, "What a pity you have not a face like that!" Some beat their babies savagely for being pretty.

More than one, had she known the secret, would have fashioned her son's face in the Gwynplaine style. The head of an angel, which brings no money in, is not as good as that of a lucrative devil. One day the mother of a little child who was a marvel of beauty, and who acted a cupid, exclaimed:

"Our children are failures! Gwynplaine is the sole success." And shaking her fist at her son, she added, "If I only knew your father, wouldn't he catch it!"

Gwynplaine was the goose with the golden eggs! What a marvelous phenomenon! There was an uproar through all the caravans. The mountebanks, enthusiastic and exasperated, looked at Gwynplaine and gnashed their teeth. Admiring anger is called envy. Then it howls! They tried to disturb "*Chaos Vanquished;*" made a cabal, hissed, scolded,

shouted! This was an excuse for Ursus to make out-of-door harangues to the populace, and for his friend Tom-Jim-Jack to use his fists to re-establish order. His pugilistic marks of friendship brought him still more under the notice and regard of Ursus and Gwynplaine. At a distance, however, for the group in the Green Box sufficed to themselves, and held aloof from the rest of the world, and because Tom-Jim-Jack, this leader of the mob, seemed a sort of supreme bully, without a tie, without a friend; a smasher of windows, a manager of men, now here, now gone, hail-fellow-well-met with every one, companion of none.

This raging envy against Gwynplaine did not give in for a few friendly hits from Tom-Jim-Jack. The outcries having miscarried, the mountebanks of Tarrinzeau Field fell back on a petition. They addressed to the authorities. This is the usual course. Against an unpleasant success we first try to stir up the crowd and then we petition the magistrate.

With the merry-andrews the reverends allied themselves. The Laughing Man had inflicted a blow on the preachers. There were empty places not only in the caravans, but in the churches. The congregations in the churches of the five parishes in Southwark had dwindled away. People left before the sermon to go to Gwynplaine. " *Chaos Vanquished*," the Green Box, the Laughing Man, all the abominations of Baal, eclipsed the eloquence of the pulpit. The voice crying in the desert, *vox clamantis in deserto*, is discontented, and is prone to call for the aid of the authorities. The clergy of the five parishes complained to the Bishop of London, who complained to her Majesty.

The complaint of the merry-andrews was based on religion. They declared it to be insulted. They described Gwynplaine as a sorcerer, and Ursus as an atheist.

The reverend gentlemen invoked social order. Setting orthodoxy aside, they took action on the fact that acts of parliament were violated. It was clever. Because it was the period of Mr. Locke, who had died but six months previously—28th October, 1704—and when skepticism, which Bolingbroke had instilled into Voltaire, was taking root. Later on Wesley came and restored the Bible, as Loyola restored the papacy.

Thus the Green Box was battered on both sides; by the merry-andrews, in the name of the Pentateuch, and by chaplains in the name of the police. In the name of heaven and of the inspectors of nuisances, the reverends holding to the nuisance, the mountebanks to heaven. The Green Box was denounced by the priests as an obstruction, and by the jugglers as sacrilegious.

Had they any pretext ? Was there any excuse ? Yes. What was the crime ? This : there was the wolf. A dog was allowable; a wolf forbidden. In England the wolf is an outlaw. England admits the dog which barks, but not the dog which howls,—a shade of difference between the yard and the woods.

The rectors and vicars of the five parishes of Southwark called attention in their petitions to numerous parliamentary and royal statutes putting the wolf beyond the protection of the law. They moved for something like the imprisonment of Gwynplaine and the execution of the wolf, or at any rate for their banishment. The question was one of public importance, the danger to persons passing, etc. And, on this point, they appealed to the Faculty. They cited the opinion of the Eighty physicians of London, a learned body which dates from Henry VIII., which has a seal like that of the State, which can raise sick people to the dignity of being amenable to their jurisdiction, which has the right to imprison those who infringe its law and contravene its ordinances, and which, amongst other useful regulations for the health of the citizens, put beyond doubt this fact acquired by science: that if a wolf sees a man first, the man becomes hoarse for life. Besides, he may be bitten.

Homo, then, was a pretext.

Ursus heard of these designs through the inn-keeper. He was uneasy. He was afraid of two claws—the police and the justices. To be afraid of the magistracy, it is sufficient to be afraid, there is no need to be guilty. Ursus had no desire for contact with sheriffs, provosts, bailiffs, and coroners. His eagerness to make their acquaintance amounted to nil. His curiosity to see the magistrates was about as great as the hare's to see the greyhound.

He began to regret that he had come to London.

"'Better' is the enemy of 'good,'" murmured he apart. 'I thought the proverb was ill-considered. I was wrong. Stupid truths are true truths."

Against the coalition of powers—merry-andrews taking in hand the cause of religion, and chaplains, indignant in the name of medicine, —the poor Green Box, suspected of sorcery in Gwynplaine and of hydrophobia in Homo, had only one thing in its favor (but a thing of great power in England), municipal inactivity. It is to the local authorities letting things take their own course that Englishmen owe their liberty. Liberty in England behaves very much as the sea around England. It is a tide. Little by little manners surmount the law. A cruel system of legislation drowned under the wave of custom; a savage code of laws still visible through the transparency of universal liberty: such is England.

The Laughing Man, "*Chaos Vanquished*," and Homo might have mountebanks, preachers, bishops, the House of Commons, the House of Lords, Her Majesty, London, and the whole of England against them, and remain undisturbed so long as Southwark permitted.

The Green Box was the favorite amusement of the suburb, and the local authorities seemed disinclined to interfere. In England, indifference is protection. So long as the sheriff of the county of Surrey, to the jurisdiction of which Southwark belongs, did not move in the matter, Ursus breathed freely, and Homo could sleep on his wolf's ears.

So long as the hatred which it excited did not occasion acts of violence, it increased success. The Green Box was none the worse for it, for the time. On the contrary, hints were scattered that it contained something mysterious. Hence the Laughing Man became more and more popular. The public follow with gusto the scent of anything contraband. To be suspected is a recommendation. The people adopt by instinct that at which the finger is pointed. The thing which is denounced is like the savor of forbidden fruit; we rush to eat it. Besides, applause which irritates some one, especially if that some one is in authority, is sweet. To perform, whilst passing a pleasant evening, both an act of kindness to the oppressed, and of opposition to the oppressor, is agreeable. You are protecting at the same time that you are being amused. So the theatrical caravans on the bowling-green continued to howl and to cabal against the Laughing Man. Nothing could be better calculated to enhance his success. The shouts of one's enemies are useful, and give point and vitality to one's triumph. A friend wearies sooner in praise than an enemy in abuse. To abuse does not hurt. Enemies are ignorant of this fact. They cannot help insulting us, and this constitutes their use. They cannot hold their tongues, and thus keep the public awake.

The crowds which flocked to "*Chaos Vanquished*" increased daily.

Ursus kept what Master Nicless had said of intriguers and complaints in high places to himself, and did not tell Gwynplaine, lest it should trouble the ease of his acting by creating anxiety. If evil was to come, he would be sure to know it soon enough.

CHAPTER V

NCE, however, he thought it his duty to derogate from this prudence, for prudence' sake, thinking that it might be well to make Gwynplaine uneasy. It is true that this idea arose from a circumstance much graver, in the opinion of Ursus, than the cabals of the fair or of the church.

Gwynplaine, as he picked up a farthing, which had fallen when counting the receipts, had, in the presence of the inn-keeper, drawn a contrast between the farthing, representing the misery of the people, and the die, representing, under the figure of Anne, the parasitical magnificence of the throne—an ill-sounding speech. This observation was repeated by Master Nicless, and had such a run, that it reached to Ursus through Fibi and Vinos. It put Ursus into a fever. Seditious words, lèse Majesté. He took Gwynplaine severely to task.

"Watch over your abominable jaws. There is a rule for the great —to do nothing; and a rule for the small—to say nothing. The poor man has but one friend, silence. He should only pronounce one syllable: 'yes.' To confess and to consent is all the right he has. 'Yes,' to the judge; 'yes,' to the king. Great people, if it pleases them to do so, beat us. I have received blows from them. It is their prerogative; and they lose nothing of their greatness by breaking our bones. The ossifrage is a species of eagle. Let us venerate the sceptre, which is the first of staves. Respect is prudence, and mediocrity is safety. To insult the king is to put one's self in the same danger as a girl rashly paring the nails of a lion. They tell me that you have been prattling about the farthing, which is the same thing as the liard, and that you have found fault with the august medallion, for which they sell us at market the eighth part of a salt herring. Take care; let us be serious. Consider the existence of pains and penalties. Suck in these legislative truths. You are in a country in which the man who cuts down a tree three years old, is quietly taken off to the gallows. As to swearers, their feet are put into the stocks. The drunkard is shut up in a barrel with the bottom out, so that he can walk, with a hole in the top, through which his head is passed, and with two in the bung for his hands, so that he cannot lie down. He who strikes another one in Westminster Hall is imprisoned for life and has his goods confiscated. Whoever strikes any one in the king's palace has his hand struck off. A fillip on the nose chances to bleed, and, behold! you are maimed for life. He who is convicted of heresy in the bishop's court is burnt alive. It was for no great matter that Cuthbert Simpson was quartered on a turnstile. Three years since, in 1702, which is not long ago, you see, they placed in the pillory a scoundrel, called Daniel Defoe, who had had the audacity to print the names of the Members of Parliament who had spoken on the previous evening. He who commits high treason is disemboweled alive, and they tear out his heart and buffet his cheeks with it. Impress on yourself notions of right and justice. Never allow yourself to speak a word, and at the first cause of anxiety, run for it. Such is the bravery which I counsel and which I practice. In the way of temerity, imitate the birds; in the way of talking, imitate the fishes. England has one admirable point in her favor, that her legislation is very mild."

His admonition over, Ursus remained uneasy for some time. Gwynplaine not at all. The intrepidity of youth arises from want of experience. However, it seemed that Gwynplaine had good reason for his easy mind, for the weeks flowed on peacefully, and no bad consequences seemed to have resulted from his observations about the queen.

Ursus, we know, lacked apathy, and, like a roebuck on the watch, kept a lookout in every direction. One day, a short time after his sermon to Gwynplaine, as he was looking out from the window in the wall which commanded the field, he became suddenly pale.

" Gwynplaine ? "

" What ? "

" Look."

" Where ? "

" In the field."

" Well ? "

" Do you see that passer-by ? "

" The man in black ? "

" Yes."

" Who has a kind of mace in his hand ? "

" Yes."

" Well ? "

" Well, Gwynplaine, that man is the wapentake."

" What is the wapentake ? "

" He is the bailiff of the hundred."

" What is the bailiff of the hundred ? "

" He is the *præpositus hundredi*."

" And what is the *præpositus hundredi* ? "

" He is a terrible officer."

" What has he got in his hand ? "

" The iron weapon."

" What is the iron weapon ? "

" A thing made of iron."

" What does he do with that ? "

" First of all, he swears upon it. It is for that reason that he is called the wapentake."

" And then ? "

" Then he touches you with it."

" With what ? "

" With the iron weapon."

" The wapentake touches you with the iron weapon ? "

" Yes."

" What does that mean ? "

" That means, follow me."

" And must you follow ? "

" Yes."

" Whither ? "

" How should I know ? "

" But he tells you where he is going to take you ? "

" No."

" How is that ? "

" He says nothing and you say nothing."

" But——"

" He touches you with the iron weapon. All is over then. You must go."

" But where ? "

" After him."

" But where ?

" Wherever he likes, Gwynplaine."

" And if you resist ? "

" You are hanged."

Ursus looked out of the window again, and drawing a long breath, said :

" Thank God ! He has passed. He was not coming here."

Ursus was perhaps unreasonably alarmed about the indiscreet remark, and the consequences likely to result from the unconsidered words of Gwynplaine.

Master Nicless, who had heard them, had no interest in compromising the poor inhabitants of the Green Box. He was amassing at the same time as the Laughing Man, a nice little fortune. "*Chaos Vanquished*" had succeeded in two ways. While it made art triumph on the stage, it made drunkenness prosper in the tavern.

CHAPTER VI

RSUS was soon afterwards startled by another alarming circumstance. This time it was he himself who was concerned. He was summoned to Bishopsgate before a commission composed of three disagreeable countenances. They belonged to three doctors, called overseers. One was a Doctor of Theology, delegated by the Dean of Westminster; another, a Doctor of Medicine, delegated by the College of Surgeons; the third, a Doctor in History and Civil Law, delegated by Gresham College. These three experts *in omne re scibili* had the censorship of everything said in public throughout the bounds of the hundred and thirty parishes of London, the seventy-three of Middlesex, and, by extension, the five of Southwark.

Such theological jurisdictions still subsist in England, and do good service. In December, 1868, by sentence of the Court of Arches, confirmed by the decision of the Privy Council, the Reverend Mackonochie was censured, besides being condemned in costs, for having placed lighted candles on a table. The liturgy allows no jokes.

Ursus, then, one fine day, received from the delegated doctors an order to appear before them, which was, luckily, given into his own hands, and which he was therefore enabled to keep secret. Without saying a word, he obeyed the citation, shuddering at the thought that he might be considered culpable to the extent of having the appearance of being suspected of a certain amount of rashness. He who had so recommended silence to others had here a rough lesson. *Garrule, sana teipsum.*

The three doctors, delegated and appointed overseers, sat at Bishopsgate, at the end of a room on the ground floor, in three armchairs covered with black leather, with three busts of Minos, Æacus,

25

and Rhadamanthus, in the wall above their heads, a table before them, and at their feet a form for the accused.

Ursus, introduced by a tipstaff, of placid but severe expression, entered, perceived the doctors, and immediately in his own mind, gave to each of them the name of the judge of the infernal regions represented by the bust placed above his head. Minos, the president, the representative of theology, made him a sign to sit down on the form.

Ursus made a proper bow—that is to say, bowed to the ground; and knowing that bears are charmed by honey, and doctors by Latin, he said, keeping his body still bent respectfully:

"*Tres faciunt capitulum!*"

Then, with head inclined (for modesty disarms), he sat down on the form.

Each of the three doctors had before him a bundle of papers, of which he was turning the leaves.

Minos began:

"You speak in public?"

"Yes," replied Ursus.

"By what right?"

"I am a philosopher."

"That gives no right."

"I am also a mountebank," said Ursus.

"That is a different thing."

Ursus breathed again, but with humility.

Minos resumed:

"As a mountebank, you may speak; as a philosopher, you must keep silence."

"I will try," said Ursus.

Then he thought to himself:

"I may speak, but I must be silent. How complicated."

He was much alarmed.

The same overseer continued:

"You say things which do not sound right. You insult religion. You deny the most evident truths. You propagate revolting errors. For instance, you have said that the fact of virginity excludes the possibility of maternity."

Ursus lifted his eyes meekly,—"I did not say that. I said that the fact of maternity excludes the possibility of virginity."

Minos was thoughtful, and mumbled: "True, that is the contrary."

It was really the same thing. But Ursus had parried the first blow.

Minos, meditating on the answer just given by Ursus, sank into the depths of his own imbecility, and kept silent.

The overseer of history, or, as Ursus called him, Rhadamanthus, covered the retreat of Minos by this interpolation:

"Accused! your audacity and your errors are of two sorts. You have denied that the battle of Pharsalia was lost because Brutus and Cassius had met a negro."

"I said," murmured Ursus, "that there was something in the fact that Cæsar was the better captain."

The man of history passed, without transition, to mythology.

"You have excused the infamous acts of Actæon."

"I think," said Ursus, insinuatingly, "that a man is not dishonored by having seen a naked woman."

"Then you are wrong," said the Judge, severely.

Rhadamanthus returned to history.

"Apropos of the accidents which happened to the cavalry of Mithridates, you have contested the virtues of herbs and plants. You have denied that a herb like the securiduca, could make the shoes of horses fall off."

"Pardon me," replied Ursus. "I said that the power existed only in the herb sferra cavallo. I never denied the virtue of any herb."

And he added, in a low voice:

"Nor of any woman."

By this extraneous addition to his answer Ursus proved to himself that, anxious as he was, he was not disheartened. Ursus was a compound of terror and presence of mind.

"To continue," resumed Rhadamanthus; "you have declared that it was folly in Scipio, when he wished to open the gates of Carthage, to use as a key the herb æthiopis, because the herb æthiopis has not the property of breaking locks."

"I merely said that he would have done better to have used the herb lunaria."

"That is a matter of opinion," murmured Rhadamanthus, touched in his turn.

And the man of history was silent.

The theologian, Minos, having returned to consciousness, questioned Ursus anew. He had had time to consult his notes.

"You have classed orpiment amongst the products of arsenic, and you have said that it is a poison. The Bible denies this."

"The Bible denies, but arsenic affirms it," sighed Ursus.

The man whom Ursus called Æacus, and who was the envoy of

medicine, had not yet spoken, but now looking down on Ursus, with proudly half-closed eyes, he said:

"The answer is not without some show of reason."

Ursus thanked him with his most cringing smile.

Minos frowned frightfully.

"I resume," said Minos. "You have said that it is false that the basilisk is the king of serpents, under the name of cockatrice."

"Very reverend sir," said Ursus, "so little did I desire to insult the basilisk that I have given out as certain that it has a man's head."

"Be it so," replied Minos, severely; "but you added that Poerius had seen one with the head of a falcon. Can you prove it?"

"Not easily," said Ursus.

Here he had lost a little ground.

Minos, seizing the advantage, pushed it.

"You have said that a converted Jew has not a nice smell."

"Yes. But I added that a Christian who becomes a Jew has a nasty one."

Minos lost his eyes over the accusing documents.

"You have affirmed and propagated things which are impossible. You have said that Ælian had seen an elephant write sentences."

"Nay, very reverend gentlemen! I simply said that Oppian had heard an hippopotamus discuss a philosophical problem."

"You have declared that it is not true that a dish made of beech-wood will become covered of itself with all the viands that one can desire."

"I said, that if it has this virtue, it must be that you received it from the devil."

"That I received it!"

"No, most reverend sir. I, nobody, everybody!"

Aside, Ursus thought, "I don't know what I am saying."

But his outward confusion, though extreme, was not distinctly visible. Ursus struggled with it.

"All this," Minos began again, "implies a certain belief in the devil."

Ursus held his own.

"Very reverend sir, I am not an unbeliever with regard to the devil. Belief in the devil is the reverse side of faith in God. The one proves the other. He who does not believe a little in the devil, does not believe much in God. He who believes in the sun must believe in the shadow. The devil is the night of God. What is night? The proof of day."

Ursus here extemporized a fathomless combination of philosophy and religion. Minos remained pensive, and relapsed into silence.

Ursus breathed afresh.

A sharp onslaught now took place. Æacus, the medical delegate, who had disdainfully protected Ursus against the theologian, now turned suddenly from auxiliary into assailant. He placed his closed fist on his

bundle of papers, which was large and heavy. Ursus received this apostrophe full in the breast:

"It is proved that crystal is sublimated ice, and that the diamond is sublimated crystal. It is averred that ice becomes crystal in a thousand years, and crystal diamond in a thousand ages. You have denied this."

"Nay," replied Ursus, with sadness. "I only said that in a thousand years ice had time to melt, and that a thousand ages were difficult to count."

The examination went on; questions and answers clashed like swords.

"You have denied that plants can talk."

"Not at all. But to do so they must grow under a gibbet."

"Do you own that the mandragora cries?"

"No; but it sings."

"You have denied that the fourth finger of the left hand has a cordial virtue."

"I only said that to sneeze to the left was a bad sign."

"You have spoken rashly and disrespectfully of the phœnix."

"Learned judge, I merely said that when he wrote that the brain of the phœnix was a delicate morsel, but that it produced headache, Plutarch was a little out of his reckoning, inasmuch as the phœnix never existed."

"A detestable speech! The cinnamalker which makes its nest with sticks of cinnamon, the rhintacus that Parysatis used in the manufacture of her poisons, the manucodiatas which is the bird of paradise, and the semenda, which has a beak with three holes, have been mistaken for the phœnix; but the phœnix has existed."

"I do not deny it."

"You are a stupid ass."

"I desire to be thought no better."

"You have confessed that the elder tree cures the quinsy, but you added that it was not because it has in its root a fairy excrescence."

"I said it was because Judas hung himself on an elder tree."

"A plausible opinion," growled the theologian, glad to strike his little blow at Æacus.

Arrogance repulsed soon turns to anger. Æacus was enraged.

"Wandering mountebank! you wander as much in mind as with your feet. Your tendencies are out of the way and suspicious. You approach the bounds of sorcery. You have dealings with unknown animals. You speak to the populace of things that exist but for you alone, and the nature of which is unknown, such as the hœmorrhoüs."

"The hœmorrhoüs is a viper which was seen by Tremellius."

This repartee produced a certain disorder in the irritated science of Doctor Æacus.

Ursus added :

"The existence of the hœmorrhoüs is quite as true as that of the odoriferous hyena, and of the civet described by Castellus."

Æacus got out of the difficulty by charging home.

"Here are your own words, and very diabolical words they are. Listen."

With his eye on his notes, Æacus read:

"Two plants, the thalagssigle and the aglaphotis, are luminous in the evening, flowers by day, stars by night."

And looking steadily at Ursus:

"What have you to say to that?"

Ursus answered:

"Every plant is a lamp. Its perfume is its light."

Æacus turned over other pages.

"You have denied that the vesicles of the otter are equivalent to castoreum."

"I merely said that perhaps it may be necessary to receive the teaching of Aëtius on this point with some reserve."

Æacus became furious.

"You practice medicine?"

"I practice medicine," sighed Ursus, timidly.

"On living things?"

"Rather than on dead ones," said Ursus.

Ursus defended himself stoutly, but dully; an admirable mixture, in which meekness predominated. He spoke with such gentleness, that Doctor Æacus felt that he must insult him.

"What are you murmuring there?" said he, rudely.

Ursus was amazed, and restricted himself to saying:

"Murmurings are for the young, and moans for the aged. Alas, I moan!"

Æacus replied:

"Be assured of this,—if you attend a sick person, and he dies, you will be punished by death."

Ursus hazarded a question.

"And if he gets well?"

"In that case," said the doctor, softening his voice, "you will be punished by death."

"There is little difference," said Ursus.

The doctor replied:

"If death ensues, we punish gross ignorance; if recovery, we punish presumption. The gibbet in either case."

"I was ignorant of the circumstance," murmured Ursus. "I thank you for teaching me. One does not know all the beauties of the law."

"Take care of yourself."

"Religiously," said Ursus.

"We know what you are about."

"As for me," thought Ursus, "that is more than I always know myself."

"We could send you to prison."

"I see that perfectly, gentlemen."

"You cannot deny your infractions nor your encroachments."

"My philosophy asks pardon."

"Great audacity has been attributed to you."

"That is quite a mistake."

"It is said that you have cured the sick."

"I am the victim of calumny."

The three pairs of eyebrows which were so horribly fixed on Ursus contracted. The three wise faces drew near to each other, and whispered. Ursus had the vision of a vague fool's cap sketched out above those three empowered heads. The low and requisite whispering of the trio was of some minutes' duration, during which time Ursus felt all the ice and all the scorch of agony. At length Minos, who was president, turned to him and said, angrily:

"Go away!"

Ursus felt something like Jonas when he was leaving the belly of the whale.

Minos continued:

"You are discharged."

Ursus said to himself:

"They won't catch me at this again. Good-bye, medicine

And he added, in his innermost heart:

"From henceforth I will carefully allow them to die."

Bent double, he bowed everywhere; to the doctors, to the busts, the tables, the walls, and retiring backwards through the door, disappeared almost as a shadow melting into air.

He left the hall slowly, like an innocent man, and rushed from the street rapidly, like a guilty one. The officers of justice are so singular and obscure in their ways, that even when acquitted, one flies from them.

As he fled he mumbled:

"I am well out of it. I am the savant untamed; they the savants civilized. Doctors cavil at the learned. False science is the excrement of the true, and is employed to the destruction of philosophers. Philosophers, as they produce sophists, produce their own scourge. Of the dung of the thrush is born the mistletoe, with which is made birdlime, with which the thrush is captured. *Turdus sibi malum cacat.*"

We do not represent Ursus as a refined man. He was imprudent enough to use words which expressed his thoughts. He had no more taste than Voltaire.

When Ursus returned to the Green Box, he told Master Nicless that he had been delayed by following a pretty woman, and let not a word escape him concerning his adventure.

Except in the evening when he said in a low voice to Homo:

"See here, I have vanquished the three heads of Cerberus."

CHAPTER VII

N event happened.

The Tadcaster Inn became more and more a furnace of
joy and laughter. Never was there more resonant gayety.
The landlord and his boy were become insufficient to draw
the ale, stout, and porter. In the evening in the lower room, with its
windows all aglow, there was not a vacant table. They sang, they
shouted; the great old hearth, vaulted like an oven, with its iron bars
piled with coals, shone out brightly. It was like a house of fire and
noise.

In the yard—that is to say, in the theatre—the crowd was greater
still.

Crowds as great as the suburb of Southwark could supply so
thronged the performances of "*Chaos Vanquished*," that directly the
curtain was raised—that is to say, the platform of the Green Box was
lowered—every place was filled. The windows were alive with spectators, the balcony was crammed. Not a single paving-stone in the
paved yard was to be seen. It seemed paved with faces.

Only the compartment for the nobility remained empty.

There was thus a space in the centre of the balcony, a black hole,
called in metaphorical slang, an oven. No one there. Crowds everywhere except in that one spot.

One evening it was occupied.

It was on a Saturday, a day on which the English make all haste
to amuse themselves before the *ennui* of Sunday. The hall was full.

We say *hall*. Shakespeare for a long time had to use the yard of
an inn for a theatre, and he called it *hall*.

Just as the curtain rose on the prologue of "*Chaos Vanquished*,"

34

with Ursus, Homo, and Gwynplaine on the stage, Ursus, from habit, cast a look at the audience, and felt a sensation.

The compartment for the nobility was occupied. A lady was sitting alone in the middle of the box, on the Utrecht velvet arm-chair. She was alone, and she filled the box. Certain beings seem to give out light. This lady, like Dea, had a light in herself, but a light of a different character.

Dea was pale, this lady was pink. Dea was the twilight, this lady, Aurora. Dea was beautiful, this lady was superb. Dea was innocence, candor, fairness, alabaster—this woman was of the purple, and one felt that she did not fear the blush. Her irradiation overflowed the box, she sat in the midst of it, immovable, in the spreading majesty of an idol.

Amidst the sordid crowd she shone out grandly, as with the radiance of a carbuncle. She inundated it with so much light that she drowned it in shadow, and all the mean faces in it underwent eclipse. Her splendor blotted out all else.

Every eye was turned towards her.

Tom-Jim-Jack was in the crowd. He was lost like the rest in the nimbus of this dazzling creature.

The lady at first absorbed the whole attention of the public, who had crowded to the performance, thus somewhat diminishing the opening effects of " *Chaos Vanquished.*"

Whatever might be the air of dreamland about her, for those who were near she was a woman ; perchance, too much a woman.

She was tall and amply formed, and showed as much as possible of her magnificent person. She wore heavy earrings of pearls, with which were mixed those whimsical jewels called "keys of England." Her upper dress was of Indian muslin, embroidered all over with gold—a great luxury, because those muslin dresses then cost six hundred crowns. A large diamond brooch closed her chemise, the which she wore so as to display her shoulders and bosom, in the immodest fashion of the time ; the chemisette was made of that lawn of which Anne of Austria had sheets so fine that they could be passed through a ring. She wore what seemed like a cuirass of rubies—some uncut, but polished, and precious stones were sewn all over the body of her dress. Then, her eyebrows were blackened with Indian ink ; and her arms, elbows, shoulders, chin, and nostrils, with the top of her eyelids, the lobes of her ears, the palms of her hands, the tips of her fingers, were tinted with a glowing and provoking touch of color. Above all, she wore an expression of implacable determination to be beautiful. This reached the point of ferocity. She was like a panther, with the power of turning cat at will, and caressing. One of her eyes was blue, the other black.

Gwynplaine, as well as Ursus, contemplated her.

The Green Box somewhat resembled a phantasmagoria in its representations. "*Chaos Vanquished*" was rather a dream than a piece; it generally produced on the audience the effect of a vision. Now, this effect was reflected on the actors. The house took the performers by surprise, and they were thunderstruck in their turn. It was a rebound of fascination.

The woman watched them, and they watched her.

At the distance at which they were placed, and in that luminous mist which is the half-light of a theatre, details were lost, and it was like an hallucination.

Of course it was a woman, but was it not a chimera as well? The penetration of her light into their obscurity stupefied them. It was like the appearance of an unknown planet. It came from a world of the happy. Her irradiation amplified her figure. The lady was covered with nocturnal glitterings, like a milky way. Her precious stones were stars. The diamond brooch was perhaps a pleiad. The splendid beauty of her bosom seemed supernatural. They felt, as they looked upon the star-like creature, the momentary but thrilling approach of the regions of felicity. It was out of the heights of a Paradise that she leant towards their mean-looking Green Box, and revealed to the gaze of its wretched audience her expression of inexorable serenity. As she satisfied her unbounded curiosity, she fed at the same time the curiosity of the public.

It was the Zenith permitting the Abyss to look at it.

Ursus, Gwynplaine, Vinos, Fibi, the crowd, every one had succumbed to her dazzling beauty, except Dea, ignorant in her darkness.

An apparition was indeed before them; but none of the ideas usually evoked by the word were realized in the lady's appearance. There was nothing about her diaphanous, nothing undecided, nothing floating, no mist. She was an apparition; rose-colored and fresh, and full of health. Yet, under the optical condition in which Ursus and Gwynplaine were placed, she looked like a vision. There are fleshy phantoms, called vampires. Such a queen as she, though a spirit to the crowd, consumes twelve hundred thousand a year, to keep her health.

Behind the lady, in the shadow, her page was to be perceived, *el mozo,* a little child-like man, fair and pretty, with a serious face. A very young and very grave servant, was the fashion of that period. This page was dressed from top to toe, in scarlet velvet, and had on his skull-cap, which was embroidered with gold, a bunch of curled feathers. This was the sign of a high class of service, and indicated attendance on a very great lady.

The lackey is part of the lord, and it was impossible not to remark, in the shadow of his mistress, the train-bearing page. Memory often takes notes unconsciously; and, without Gwynplaine's suspecting it, the round cheeks, the serious mien, the embroidered and plumed cap of the

lady's page left some trace on his mind. The page, however, did nothing to call attention to himself. To do so is to be wanting in respect. He held himself aloof and passive at the back of the box, retiring as far as the closed door permitted.

Notwithstanding the presence of her train-bearer, the lady was not the less alone in the compartment, since a valet counts for nothing.

However powerful a diversion had been produced by this person, who produced the effect of a personage, the dénouement of " *Chaos Vanquished*" was more powerful still. The impression which it made was, as usual, irresistible. Perhaps, even, there occurred in the hall, on account of the radiant spectator (for sometimes the spectator is part of the spectacle), an increase of electricity. The contagion of Gwynplaine's laugh was more triumphant than ever. The whole audience fell into an indescribable epilepsy of hilarity, through which could be distinguished the sonorous and magisterial ha! ha! of Tom-Jim-Jack.

Only the unknown lady looked at the performance with the immobility of a statue, and with her eyes, like those of a phantom, she laughed not. A spectre, but sun-born.

The performance over, the platform drawn up, and, the family reassembled in the Green Box, Ursus opened and emptied on the supper-table the bag of receipts. From a heap of pennies, there slid suddenly forth a Spanish gold onza.

"Hers!" cried Ursus.

The onza amidst the pence covered with verdigris was a type of the lady amidst the crowd.

"She has paid an onza for her seat," cried Ursus, with enthusiasm.

Just then, the hotel-keeper entered the Green Box, and passing his arm out of the window at the back of it, opened the loop-hole in the wall of which we have already spoken, which gave a view over the field, and which was level with the window, then he made a silent sign to Ursus to look out. A carriage, swarming with plumed footmen carrying torches and magnificently appointed, was driving off at a fast trot.

Ursus took the piece of gold between his forefinger and thumb respectfully, and, showing it to Master Nicless, said :

"She is a goddess."

Then, his eyes falling on the carriage which was about to turn the corner of the field, and on the imperial of which the footmen's torches lighted up a golden coronet, with eight strawberry leaves, he exclaimed :

"She is more. She is a duchess."

The carriage disappeared. The rumbling of its wheels died away in the distance.

Ursus remained some moments in an ecstasy, holding the gold piece between his finger and thumb, as in a monstrance, elevating it as the priest elevates the host.

Then he placed it on the table, and, as he contemplated it, began to talk of " Madam."

The inn-keeper replied :

"She was a duchess." Yes. They knew her title. But her name?

Of that they were ignorant. Master Nicless had been close to the carriage, and seen the coat of arms and the footmen covered with lace. The coachman had a wig on which might have belonged to a Lord Chancellor. The carriage was of that rare design called, in Spain,

cochetumbon, a splendid build, with a top like a tomb, which makes a magnificent support for a coronet. The page was a man in miniature, so small that he could sit on the step of the carriage outside the door. The duty of those pretty creatures was to bear the trains of their mistresses. They also bore their messages. And did you remark the plumed cap of the page? How grand it was! You pay a fine if you wear those plumes without the right of doing so. Master Nicless had seen the lady, too, quite close. A kind of queen. Such wealth gives beauty. The skin is whiter, the eye more proud, the gait more noble, and grace more insolent. Nothing can equal the elegant impertinence of hands which never work. Master Nicless told the story of all the magnificence of the white skin with the blue veins, the neck, the shoulders, the arms, the touch of paint everywhere, the pearl earrings, the head-dress, powdered with gold; the profusion of stones, the rubies, the diamonds.

"Less brilliant than her eyes," murmured Ursus.

Gwynplaine said nothing.

Dea listened.

"And do you know," said the tavern-keeper, "the most wonderful thing of all?"

"What?" said Ursus.

"I saw her get into her carriage."

"What then?"

"She did not get in alone."

"Nonsense!"

"Some one got in with her."

"Who?"

"Guess."

"The king," said Ursus.

"In the first place," said Master Nicless, "there is no king at present. We are not living under a king. Guess who got into the carriage with the duchess."

"Jupiter," said Ursus.

The hotel-keeper replied:

"Tom-Jim-Jack!"

Gwynplaine, who had not said a word, broke silence.

"Tom-Jim-Jack!" he cried.

There was a pause of astonishment, during which the low voice of Dea was heard to say:

"Cannot this woman be prevented coming?"

CHAPTER VIII

THE "apparition" did not return.

It did not re-appear in the theatre, but it re-appeared to the memory of Gwynplaine.

Gwynplaine was, to a certain degree, troubled.

It seemed to him that for the first time in his life he had seen a woman.

He made that first stumble, a strange dream. We should beware of the nature of the reveries that fasten on us. Reverie has in it the mystery and subtlety of an odor. It is to thought what perfume is to the tuberose. It is at times the exudation of a venomous idea, and it penetrates like a vapor. You may poison yourself with reveries, as with flowers. An intoxicating suicide, exquisite and malignant. The suicide of the soul is evil thought. In it is the poison. Reverie attracts, cajoles, lures, entwines, and then makes you its accomplice. It makes you bear your half in the trickeries which it plays on conscience. It charms; then it corrupts you. We may say of reverie as of play, one begins by being a dupe, and ends by being a cheat.

Gwynplaine dreamed.

He had never before seen Woman.

He had seen the shadow in the women of the populace, and he had seen the soul in Dea.

He had just seen the reality.

A warm and living skin, under which one felt the circulation of passionate blood; an outline with the precision of marble and the undulation of the wave; a high and impassive mien, mingling refusal with attraction, and summing itself up in its own glory; hair of the color of the reflection from a furnace; a gallantry of adornment producing in herself and in others a tremor of voluptuousness, the half-

41

revealed nudity betraying a disdainful desire to be coveted at a distance by the crowd; an irradicable coquetry; the charm of impenetrability, temptation seasoned by the glimpse of perdition, a promise to the senses and a menace to the mind; a double anxiety, the one desire, the other fear. He had just seen these things. He had just seen **Woman**.

He had seen more and less than a woman; he had seen a **female**.

And at the same time an Olympian. The female of a god.

The mystery of sex had just been revealed to him.

And where? On inaccesible heights.

At an infinite distance.

O mocking destiny! The soul, that celestial essence, he possessed; he held it in his hand. It was Dea. Sex, that terrestrial embodiment, he perceived in the heights of heaven. It was that woman.

A duchess!

"More than a goddess," Ursus had said.

What a precipice! Even dreams dissolved before such a perpendicular height to escalade.

Was he going to commit the folly of dreaming about the unknown beauty?

He debated with himself.

He recalled all that Ursus had said of high stations which are almost royal. The philosopher's disquisitions, which had hitherto seemed so useless, now became landmarks for his thoughts. A very thin layer of forgetfulness often lies over our memory, through which at times we catch a glimpse of all beneath it. His fancy ran on that august world, the peerage, to which the lady belonged, and which was so inexorably placed above the inferior world, the common people, of which he was one.

And was he even one of the people? Was not he, the mountebank, below the lowest of the low? For the first time since he had arrived at the age of reflection, he felt his heart vaguely contracted by a sense of his baseness, and of that which we nowadays call abasement. The paintings and the catalogues of Ursus, his lyrical inventories, his dithyrambics, of castles, parks, fountains, and colonnades, his catalogues of riches and of power, revived in the memory of Gwynplaine in the relief of reality mingled with mist. He was possessed with the image of this zenith. That a man should be a lord!—it seemed chimerical. It was so, however. Incredible thing! There were lords! But were they of flesh and blood, like ourselves? It seemed doubtful. He felt that he lay at the bottom of all darkness, encompassed by a wall, while he could just perceive in the far distance above his head, through the mouth of the pit, a dazzling confusion of azure, of figures, and of rays, which was

Olympus. In the midst of this glory the duchess shone out re-splendent.

He felt for this woman a strange, inexpressible longing, combined with a conviction of the impossibility of attainment.

This poignant contradiction returned to his mind again and again, notwithstanding every effort. He saw near to him, even within his reach, in close and tangible reality, the soul; and in the unattainable—in the depths of the ideal—the flesh. None of these thoughts attained to certain shape. They were as a vapor within him, changing every instant its form, and floating away. But the darkness which the vapor caused was intense.

He did not form even in his dreams any hope of reaching the heights where the duchess dwelt. Luckily for him.

The vibration of such ladders of fancy, if ever we put our foot upon them, may render our brains dizzy forever. Intending to scale Olympus, we reach Bedlam; any distinct feeling of actual desire would have terrified him. He entertained none of that nature.

Besides, was he likely ever to see the lady again ? Most probably not. To fall in love with a passing light on the horizon, madness cannot reach to that pitch. To make loving eyes at a star even, is not incomprehensible. It is seen again, it re-appears, it is fixed in the sky. But can any one be enamored of a flash of lightning ?

Dreams flowed and ebbed within him. The majestic and gallant idol at the back of the box had cast a light over his diffused ideas, then faded away. He thought, yet thought not of it; turned to other things —returned to it. It rocked about in his brain,—nothing more.

It broke his sleep for several nights. Sleeplessness is as full of dreams as sleep.

It is almost impossible to express in their exact limits the abstract evolutions of the brain. The inconvenience of words is that they are more marked in form than ideas. All ideas have indistinct boundary lines, words have not. A certain diffused phase of the soul ever escapes words. Expression has its frontiers, thought has none.

The depths of our secret souls are so vast that Gwynplaine's dreams scarcely touched Dea. Dea reigned sacred in the centre of his soul; nothing could approach her.

Still (for such contradictions make up the soul of man), there was a conflict within him. Was he conscious of it ? Scarcely.

In his heart of hearts he felt a collision of desires. We all have our weak points. Its nature would have been clear to Ursus; but to Gwynplaine it was not.

Two instincts—one the ideal, the other sexual—were struggling within him. Such contests occur between the angels of light and darkness on the edge of the abyss.

At length the angel of darkness was overthrown.

One day Gwynplaine suddenly thought no more of the unknown woman.

The struggle between two principles,—the duel between his earthly and his heavenly nature,—had taken place within his soul, and at such a depth that he had understood it but dimly.

One thing was certain, that he had never for one moment ceased to adore Dea.

He had been attacked by a violent disorder, his blood had been fevered; but it was over. Dea alone remained.

Gwynplaine would have been much astonished had any one told him that Dea had ever been, even for a moment, in danger; and in a week or two the phantom which had threatened the hearts of both their souls faded away.

Within Gwynplaine nothing remained but the heart, which was the hearth, and the love, which was its fire.

Besides, we have just said that " the duchess" did not return.

Ursus thought it all very natural. "The lady with the gold piece" is a phenomenon. She enters, pays, and vanishes. It would be too much joy were she to return.

As to Dea, she made no allusion to the woman who had come and passed away. She listened, perhaps, and was sufficiently enlightened by the sighs of Ursus, and now and then by some significant exclamation, such as:

"*One does not get ounces of gold every day!*"

She spoke no more of " the woman." This showed deep instinct. The soul takes obscure precautions, in the secrets of which it is not always admitted itself. To keep silence about any one seems to keep them afar off. One fears that questions may call them back. We put silence between us, as if we were shutting a door.

So the incident fell into oblivion.

Was it ever anything? Had it ever occurred? Could it be said that a shadow had floated between Gwynplaine and Dea? Dea did not know of it, nor Gwynplaine either. No; nothing had occurred. The duchess herself was blurred in the distant perspective like an illusion. It had been but a momentary dream passing over Gwynplaine, out of which he had awakened.

When it fades away, a reverie, like a mist, leaves no trace behind; and when the cloud has passed on, love shines out as brightly in the heart as the sun in the sky.

CHAPTER IX

ANOTHER face disappeared; Tom-Jim-Jack's. Suddenly he ceased to frequent the Tadcaster Inn.

Persons so situated as to be able to observe other phases of fashionable life in London, might have seen that about this time the Weekly Gazette, between two extracts from parish registers, announced the departure of Lord David Dirry-Moir, by order of her majesty, to take command of his frigate in the white squadron then cruising off the coast of Holland.

Ursus, perceiving that Tom-Jim-Jack did not return, was troubled by his absence. He had not seen Tom-Jim-Jack since the day on which he had driven off in the same carriage with the lady of the gold piece. It was, indeed, an enigma who this Tom-Jim-Jack could be, who carried off duchesses under his arm. What an interesting investigation! What questions to propound! What things to be said! Therefore Ursus said not a word.

Ursus, who had had experience, knew the smart caused by rash curiosity. Curiosity ought always to be proportioned to the curious. By listening, we risk our ear; by watching, we risk our eye. Prudent people neither hear nor see. Tom-Jim-Jack had got into a princely carriage. The tavern-keeper had seen him. It appeared so extraordinary that the sailor should sit by the lady that it made Ursus circumspect. The caprices of those in high life ought to be sacred to the lower orders. The reptiles called the poor had best squat in their holes when they see anything out of the way. Quiescence is a power. Shut your eyes, if you have not the luck to be blind; stop up your ears, if you have not the good fortune to be deaf; paralyze your tongue, if you have not the perfection of being mute. The great do what they like, the little what they can. Let the unknown pass unnoticed. Do not

45

importune mythology. Do not interrogate appearances. Have a profound respect for idols. Do not let us direct our gossiping towards the lessenings or increasings which take place in superior regions, of the motives of which we are ignorant. Such things are mostly optical delusions to us inferior creatures. Metamorphoses are the business of the gods: the transformations and the contingent disorders of great persons who float above us are clouds impossible to comprehend, and perilous to study. Too much attention irritates the Olympians engaged in their gyrations of amusement or fancy; and a thunderbolt may teach you that the bull you are too curiously examining is Jupiter. Do not lift the folds of the stone-colored mantles of those terrible powers. Indifference is intelligence. Do not stir and you will be safe. Feign death, and they will not kill you. Therein lies the wisdom of the insect. Ursus practiced it.

The tavern-keeper, who was puzzled as well, questioned Ursus one day.

"Do you observe that Tom-Jim-Jack never comes here now?"

"Indeed!" said Ursus. "I have not remarked it."

Master Nicless made an observation in an under tone, no doubt touching the intimacy between the ducal carriage and Tom-Jim-Jack; a remark which, as it might have been irreverent and dangerous, Ursus took care not to hear.

Still Ursus was too much of an artist not to regret Tom-Jim-Jack. He felt some disappointment. He told his feeling to Homo, of whose discretion alone he felt certain. He whispered into the ear of the wolf:

"Since Tom-Jim-Jack ceased to come, I feel a blank as a man, and a chill as a poet."

This pouring out of his heart to a friend relieved Ursus.

His lips were sealed before Gwynplaine, who, however, made no allusion to Tom-Jim-Jack. The fact was that Tom-Jim-Jack's presence or absence mattered not to Gwynplaine, absorbed as he was in Dea.

Forgetfulness fell more and more on Gwynplaine. As for Dea, she had not even suspected the existence of a vague trouble. At the same time, no more cabals or complaints against the Laughing Man were spoken of. Hate seemed to have let go its hold. All was tranquil in and around the Green Box. No more opposition from strollers, merry-andrews, nor priests; no more grumbling outside. Their success was unclouded. Destiny allows of such sudden serenity. The brilliant happiness of Gwynplaine and Dea was for the present absolutely cloudless. Little by little it had risen to a degree which admitted of no increase. There is one word which expresses the situation: apogee. Happiness, like the sea, has its high tide. The worst thing for the perfectly happy, is that it recedes.

There are two ways of being inaccessible; being too high and being too low. At least as much, perhaps, as the first, is the second to be desired. More surely than the eagle escapes the arrow, the animalcule escapes being crushed. This security of insignificance, if it had ever existed on earth, was enjoyed by Gwynplaine and Dea, and never before had it been so complete. They lived on, daily more and more ecstatically wrapt in each other. The heart saturates itself with love as with a divine salt that preserves it, and from this arises the incorruptible constancy of those who have loved each other from the dawn of their lives, and the affection which keeps its freshness in old age. There is such a thing as the embalmment of the heart. It is of Daphnis and Chloë that Philemon and Baucis are made. The old age, of which we speak, evening resembling morning, was evidently reserved for Gwynplaine and Dea. In the meantime they were young.

Ursus looked on this love as a doctor examines his case. He had what was in those days termed a hippocratical expression of face. He fixed his sagacious eyes on Dea, fragile and pale, and growled out:

"It is lucky that she is happy."

At other times he said, "She is lucky for her health's sake." He shook his head, and at times read attentively a portion treating of heart-disease in Avicenna, translated by Vopiscus Fortunatus, Louvain, 1650, an old worm-eaten book of his.

Dea, when fatigued, suffered from perspirations and drowsiness, and took a daily *siesta*, as we have already seen. One day, while she was lying asleep on the bear-skin, Gwynplaine was out, and Ursus bent down softly and applied his ear to Dea's heart. He seemed to listen for a few minutes, and then stood up, murmuring, "She must not have any shock. It would find out the weak place."

The crowd continued to flock to the performance of "*Chaos Vanquished.*" The success of the Laughing Man seemed inexhaustible. Every one rushed to see him; no longer from Southwark only, but even from other parts of London. The general public began to mingle with the usual audience, which no longer consisted of sailors and drivers only; in the opinion of Master Nicless, who was well acquainted with crowds, there were in the crowd gentlemen and baronets disguised as common people. Disguise is one of the pleasures of pride, and was much in fashion at that period. This mixing of the aristocratic element with the mob was a good sign, and showed that their popularity was extending to London. The fame of Gwynplaine has decidedly penetrated into the great world. Such was the fact. Nothing was talked of

but the Laughing Man. He was talked about even at the Mohawk
Club, frequented by noblemen.

In the Green Box they had no idea of all this. They were content
to be happy. It was intoxication to Dea to feel, as she did every evening, the crisp and tawny head of Gwynplaine. In love there is nothing
like habit. The whole of life is concentrated in it. The re-appearance
of the stars is the custom of the universe. Creation is nothing but a
mistress, and the sun is a lover. Light is a dazzling caryatide supporting the world. Each day, for a sublime minute, the earth covered by
night rests on the rising sun. Dea, blind, felt a like return of warmth
and hope within her when she placed her hand on the head of Gwynplaine.

To adore each other in the shadows, to love in the plenitude of
silence; who could not become reconciled to such an eternity?

One evening Gwynplaine, feeling within him that overflow of felicity, which, like the intoxication of perfumes, causes a sort of delicious
faintness, was strolling, as he usually did after the performance, in the
meadow some hundred paces from the Green Box. Sometimes in those
high tides of feeling in our souls we feel that we would fain pour out
the sensations of the overflowing heart. The night was dark but clear.
The stars were shining. The whole fair-ground was deserted. Sleep
and forgetfulness reigned in the caravans which were scattered over
Tarrinzeau Field.

One light alone was unextinguished. It was the lamp of the Tadcaster Inn, the door of which was left ajar to admit Gwynplaine on his
return.

Midnight had just struck in the five parishes of Southwark, with
the breaks and differences of tone of their various bells. Gwynplaine
was dreaming of Dea. Of whom else should he dream? But that
evening, feeling singularly troubled, and full of a charm which was at
the same time a pang, he thought of Dea as a man thinks of a woman.
He reproached himself for this. It seemed to be failing in respect to
her. Sweet and imperious impatience! He was crossing the invisible
frontier, on this side of which is the virgin, on the other, the wife. He
questioned himself anxiously. A blush, as it were, overspread his
mind. The Gwynplaine of long ago had been transformed by degrees,
unconsciously in a mysterious growth. His old modesty was becoming
misty and uneasy. We have an ear of light, into which speaks the
spirit; and an ear of darkness, into which speaks the instinct. Into the
latter strange voices were making their proposals. However pure-
minded may be the youth who dreams of love, a certain grossness of
the flesh eventually comes between his dream and him. Intentions lose

their transparency. The unavowed desire implanted by nature enters into his conscience. Gwynplaine felt an indescribable yearning of the flesh, which abounds in all temptation, and Dea was scarcely flesh. In this fever, which he knew to be unhealthy, he transfigured Dea into a

more material aspect, and tried to exaggerate her seraphic form into feminine loveliness. It is thou, O woman, that we require.

Love comes not to permit too much of paradise. It requires the fevered skin, the troubled life, the unbound hair, the kiss electrical and irreparable, the clasp of desire. The sidereal is embarrassing, the ethereal is heavy. Too much of the heavenly in love is like too much fuel

on a fire: the flame suffers from it. Gwynplaine fell into an exquisite
nightmare; Dea to be clasped in his arms—Dea clasped in them! He
heard nature in his heart crying out for a Woman. Like a Pygmalion
in a dream modeling a Galatea out of the azure, in the depth of his soul
he worked at the chaste contour of Dea; a contour with too much of
heaven, too little of Eden. For Eden is Eve, and Eve was a female, a
carnal mother, a terrestrial nurse; the sacred womb of generations;
the breast of unfailing milk; the rocker of the cradle of the new-born
world, and wings are incompatible with the bosom of woman. Virginity is but the hope of maternity.

Still, in Gwynplaine's dreams, Dea, until now, had been enthroned
above flesh. Now, however, he made wild efforts in thought to draw
her downwards by that thread, sex, which ties every girl to earth. Not
one of those birds is free. Dea, like all the rest, was within this law;
and Gwynplaine, though he scarcely acknowledged it, felt a vague
desire that she should submit to it. This desire possessed him in spite
of himself, and with an ever-recurring relapse. He pictured Dea as
woman. He came to the point of regarding her under a hitherto un-
heard-of form; as a creature no longer of ecstasy only, but of voluptuousness; as Dea, with her head resting on the pillow. He was
ashamed of this visionary desecration. It was like an attempt at prof-
anation. He resisted its assault. He turned from it, but it returned
again. He felt as if he were committing a criminal assault. To him,
Dea was encompassed by a cloud.

It was in April. The spine has its dreams.

He rambled at random with the uncertain step caused by solitude.
To have no one by is a provocative to wander. Whither flew his
thoughts? He would not have dared to own it to himself. To heaven?
No. To a bed. You were looking down upon him, O ye stars.

Why talk of a man in love? Rather say a man possessed. To be
possessed by the devil, is the exception; to be possessed by a woman,
the rule. Every man has to bear this alienation of himself. What a
sorceress is a pretty woman! The true name of love is captivity.

Man is made prisoner by the soul of a woman. By her flesh as
well, and sometimes even more by the flesh than by the soul. The soul
is the true-love, the flesh, the mistress.

We slander the devil. It was not he who tempted Eve. It was
Eve who tempted him. The woman began. Lucifer was passing by
quietly. He perceived the woman, and became Satan.

The flesh is the cover of the unknown. It is provocative (which is
strange) by its modesty. Nothing could be more distracting. It is full
of shame, the hussy!

It was the terrible love of the surface which was then agitating
Gwynplaine, and holding him in his power. Fearful the moment in
which man covets the nakedness of woman! What dark things lurk
beneath the fairness of Venus!

Something within him was calling aloud Dea, Dea the maiden, Dea

the other half of a man, Dea flesh and flame, Dea with uncovered bosom.
That cry was almost driving away the angel. Mysterious crisis through
which all love must pass and in which the Ideal is in danger! Therein
is the predestination of Creation. Moment of heavenly corruption!
Gwynplaine's love of Dea was becoming nuptial. Virgin love is but a
transition. The moment was come. Gwynplaine coveted the woman.

He coveted a woman!

Precipice of which one sees but the first gentle slope!

The indistinct summons of nature is inexorable. The whole of woman, what an abyss!

Luckily, there was no woman for Gwynplaine but Dea. The only one he desired. The only one who could desire him.

Gwynplaine felt that vague and mighty shudder which is the vital claim of infinity. Besides, there was the aggravation of the spring. He was breathing the nameless odors of the starry darkness. He walked forward in a wild feeling of delight. The wandering perfumes of the rising sap, the heady irradiations which float in shadow, the distant opening of nocturnal flowers, the complicity of little hidden nests, the murmurs of waters and of leaves, soft sighs rising from all things, the freshness, the warmth, and the mysterious awakening of April and May, is the vast diffusion of sex murmuring, in whispers, their proposals of voluptuousness, till the soul stammers in answer to the giddy provocation. The ideal no longer knows what it is saying.

Any one observing Gwynplaine walk, would have said, "See!—a drunken man!"

He almost staggered under the weight of his own heart, of spring and of the night.

The solitude in the bowling-green was so peaceful that at times he spoke aloud. The consciousness that there is no listener induces speech.

He walked with slow steps, his head bent down, his hands behind him, the left hand in the right, the fingers open.

Suddenly he felt something slipped between his fingers.

He turned round quickly.

In his hand was a paper, and in front of him a man.

It was the man who, coming behind him with the stealth of a cat, had placed the paper in his fingers.

The paper was a letter.

The man, as he appeared pretty clearly in the starlight, was small, chubby-cheeked, young, sedate, and dressed in a scarlet livery, exposed from top to toe through the opening of a long gray cloak, then called a capenoche, a Spanish word contracted; in French it was *cape-de-nuit.* His head was covered by a crimson cap, like the skull-cap of a cardinal, on which servitude was indicated by a strip of lace. On this cap was a plume of tisserin feathers. He stood motionless before Gwynplaine, like a dark outline in a dream.

Gwynplaine recognized the duchess's page.

Before Gwynplaine could utter an exclamation of surprise, he heard the thin voice of the page, at once child-like and feminine in its tone, saying to him:

"At this hour to-morrow, be at the corner of London Bridge. I will be there to conduct you——"

"Whither?" demanded Gwynplaine.

"Where you are expected."

Gwynplaine dropped his eyes on the letter, which he was holding mechanically in his hand.

When he looked up, the page was no longer with him.

He perceived a vague form lessening rapidly in the distance. It was the little valet. He turned the corner of the street, and solitude reigned again.

Gwynplaine saw the page vanish, then looked at the letter. There are moments in our lives when what happens seems not to happen. Stupor keeps us for a moment at a distance from the fact.

Gwynplaine raised the letter to his eyes, as if to read it, but soon perceived that he could not do so for two reasons—first, because he had not broken the seal; and, secondly, because it was too dark.

It was some minutes before he remembered that there was a lamp at the inn. He took a few steps sideways, as if he knew not whither he was going.

A somnambulist, to whom a phantom had given a letter, might walk as he did.

At last he made up his mind. He ran, rather than walked, towards the inn, stood in the light which broke through the half-open door, and by it again examined the closed letter. There was no design on the seal, and on the envelope was written, "*To Gwynplaine.*" He broke the seal, tore the envelope, unfolded the letter, put it directly under the light, and read as follows:

"You are hideous; I am beautiful. You are a player; I am a duchess. I am the highest; you are the lowest. I desire you! I love you! Come!"

BOOK IV

THE CELL OF TORTURE

CHAPTER I

THE TEMPTATION OF ST. GWYNPLAINE

ONE jet of flame hardly makes a prick in the darkness; another sets fire to a volcano.

Some sparks are gigantic.

Gwynplaine read the letter, then he read it over again. Yes, the words were there, "I love you!"

Terrors chased each other through his mind.

The first was, that he believed himself to be mad.

He was mad; that was certain. He had just seen what had no existence. The twilight spectres were making game of him, poor wretch! The little man in scarlet was the will-o'-the-wisp of a dream. Sometimes at night, nothings condensed into flame come and laugh at us. Having had his laugh out, the visionary being had disappeared, and left Gwynplaine behind him, mad.

Such are the freaks of darkness.

The second terror was, to find out that he was in his right senses.

54

A vision? Certainly not. How could that be? Had he not a letter in his hand? Did he not see an envelope, a seal, paper, and writing? Did he not know from whom that came? It was all clear enough. Some one took a pen and ink, and wrote. Some one lighted a taper, and sealed it with wax. Was not his name written on the letter,—" *To Gwynplaine?*" The paper was scented. All was clear. Gwynplaine knew the little man. The dwarf was a page. The gleam was a livery. The page had given him a rendezvous for the same hour on the morrow, at the corner of London Bridge. Was London Bridge an illusion?

No, no. All was clear. There was no delirium. All was reality. Gwynplaine was perfectly clear in his intellect. It was not a phantasmagoria, suddenly dissolving above his head, and fading into nothingness. It was something which had really happened to him. No, Gwynplaine was not mad, nor was he dreaming. Again he read the letter.

Well; yes. But then?

That then, was terror-striking.

There was a woman who desired him! If so, let no one ever again pronounce the word incredible! A woman desire him! A woman who had seen his face! A woman who was not blind! And who was this woman? An ugly one? No; a beauty. A gypsy? No; a duchess!

What was it all about; and what could it all mean? What peril in such a triumph! And how was he to help plunging into it headlong?

What! that woman! The siren, the apparition, the lady in the visionary box, the light in the darkness! It was she. Yes; it was she!

The crackling of the fire burst out in every part of his frame. It was the strange unknown lady, she who had previously so troubled his thoughts; and his first tumultuous feelings about this woman returned, heated by the evil fire. Forgetfulness is nothing but a palimpsest: an incident happens unexpectedly, and all that was effaced revives in the blanks of wondering memory.

Gwynplaine thought that he had dismissed that image from his remembrance, and he found that it was still there; and she had put her mark in his brain, unconsciously guilty of a dream. Without his suspecting it the lines of the engraving had been bitten deep by reverie. And now a certain amount of evil had been done, and this train of thought, thenceforth, perhaps, irreparable, he took up again eagerly.

What, she desired him! What! the princess descend from her throne, the idol from its shrine, the statue from its pedestal, the phantom from its cloud! What! From the depth of the impossible had this chimera come! This deity of the sky! This irradiation! This nereid all glistening with jewels! This proud and unattainable beauty, from the height of her radiant throne, was bending down to Gwynplaine! What! had she drawn up her chariot of the dawn, with its yoke of turtle-doves and dragons, before Gwynplaine, and said to him, "Come!" What, this terrible glory of being the object of such abasement from the empyrean, for Gwynplaine! This woman, if he could give that name to a form so starlike and majestic, this woman proposed herself, gave herself, delivered herself up to him! Wonder of wonders! A goddess prostituting herself for him! The arms of a courtesan opening in a cloud to clasp him to the bosom of a goddess, and that without degradation! Such majestic creatures cannot be sullied. The gods bathe themselves pure in light; and this goddess who came to him knew what she was doing. She was not ignorant of the incarnate hideousness of Gwynplaine. She had seen the mask which was his face; and that mask had not caused her to draw back. Gwynplaine was loved notwithstanding it!

Here was a thing surpassing all the extravagance of dreams. He was loved in consequence of his mask. Far from repulsing the goddess, the mask attracted her. Gwynplaine was not only loved, he was desired. He was more than accepted, he was chosen. He, chosen!

What! there, where this woman dwelt, in the regal region of irresponsible splendor, and in the power of full free will; where there were princes, and she could take a prince; nobles, and she could take a noble; where there were men handsome, charming, magnificent, and she could take an Adonis: whom did she take? Gnafron! She could choose from the midst of meteors and thunders, the mighty, six-winged seraphim, and she chose the larva crawling in the slime. On one side were highnesses and peers, all grandeur, all opulence, all glory. On the other, a mountebank. The mountebank carried it! What kind of scales could there be in the heart of this woman? By what measure did she weigh her love? She took off her ducal coronet, and flung it on the platform of a clown! She took from her brow the Olympian aureola, and placed it on the bristly head of a gnome! The world had turned topsy-turvy. The insects swarmed on high, the stars were scattered below, whilst the wonder-stricken Gwynplaine, overwhelmed by a falling ruin of light and lying in the dust, was enshrined in a glory. One all-powerful, revolting against beauty and splendor, gave herself to the damned of night; preferred Gwynplaine to Antinoüs; excited by curiosity, she entered the shadows, and descending within them, and from this abdication of goddess-ship was rising, crowned and prodigious, the royalty of the wretched. "You are hideous. I love you." These words touched Gwynplaine in the ugly spot of pride. Pride is the heel in which all heroes are vulnerable. Gwynplaine was flattered in his vanity as a monster. He was loved for his deformity. He, too, was the Exception, as much, and perhaps, more than the Jupiters and the Apollos. He felt superhuman, and so much a monster as to be a god. Fearful bewilderment!

Now, who was this woman? What did he know about her? Everything and nothing. She was a duchess, that he knew; he knew, also, that she was beautiful and rich; that she had liveries, lackeys, pages, and footmen running with torches by the side of her coroneted carriage. He knew that she was in love with him; at least she said so. Of everything else he was ignorant. He knew her title; but not her name. He knew her thought; he knew not her life. Was she married, widow, maiden? Was she free? Of what family was she? Were there snares, traps, dangers about her? Of the gallantry existing on the idle heights of society; the caves on those summits, in which savage charmers dream amid the scattered skeletons of the loves which they have already preyed on; of the extent of tragic cynicism to which the experiments of a woman may attain who believes herself to be beyond the reach of man; of things such as these Gwynplaine had no idea. Nor had he even in his mind materials out of which to build up a conjecture, information concerning such things being very scanty in the social depths in which he lived. Still he detected a shadow; he felt that a mist hung over all this brightness. Did he understand it? No. Could he guess at it? Still less. What was there behind that letter? One pair of folding-doors opening before him, another closing on him, and causing him a vague anxiety. On the one side an avowal; on the other an enigma.

Avowal and enigma, which, like two mouths, one tempting, the other threatening, pronounce the same word: Dare!

Never had perfidious chance taken its measures better, nor timed more fitly the moment of temptation. Gwynplaine, stirred by spring, and by the sap rising in all things, was prompt to dream the dream of the flesh. The old man who is not to be stamped out, and over whom none of us can triumph, was awaking in that backward youth, still a boy at twenty-four.

It was just then, at the most stormy moment of the crisis, that the offer was made him, and the naked bosom of the Sphinx appeared before his dazzled eyes. Youth is an inclined plane. Gwynplaine was stooping, and something pushed him forward. What? the season and the night. Who? the woman. Were there no month of April, man would be a great deal more virtuous. The budding plants are a set of accomplices! Love is the thief, Spring the receiver.

Gwynplaine was shaken.

There is a kind of smoke of evil, preceding sin, in which the conscience cannot breathe. The obscure nausea of hell comes over virtue in temptation. The yearning abyss discharges an exhalation which warns the strong and turns the weak giddy. Gwynplaine was suffering its mysterious attack.

Dilemmas, transient and at the same time stubborn, were floating before him. Sin, presenting itself obstinately again and again to his mind, was taking form. The morrow, midnight! London Bridge, the page! Should he go! "Yes," cried the flesh; "no," cried the soul.

Nevertheless, we must remark that, strange as it may appear at first sight, he never once put himself the question, "Should he go!" quite distinctly. Reprehensible actions are like over-strong brandies; you cannot swallow them at a draught. You put down your glass; you will see to it presently; there is a strange taste even about that first drop. One thing is certain; he felt something behind him pushing him forward towards the unknown. And he trembled. He could catch a glimpse of a crumbling precipice, and he drew back, stricken by the terror encircling him. He closed his eyes. He tried hard to deny to himself that the adventure had ever occurred, and to persuade himself into doubting his reason. This was evidently his best plan; the wisest thing he could do was to believe himself mad.

Fatal fever! Every man, surprised by the unexpected, has at times felt the throb of such tragic pulsations. The observer ever listens with anxiety to the echoes resounding from the dull strokes of the battering-ram of destiny striking against a conscience.

Alas! Gwynplaine put himself questions. Where duty is clear, to put one's self questions is to suffer defeat.

One detail, however, is noteworthy; the effrontery of the adventure, which might, perhaps, have shocked a depraved man, never struck him. He was utterly unconscious of what cynicism is composed. He had no idea of prostitution as referred to above. He had not the power to conceive it. He was too pure to admit complicated hypotheses. He saw but the grandeur of the woman. Alas! he felt flattered. His vanity assured him of victory only. To dream that he was the object of unchaste desire, rather than of love, would have required much greater wit than innocence possesses. Close to *I love you*, he could not perceive the frightful corrective, *I desire you.*

He could not grasp the animal side of the goddess's nature.

There are invasions which the mind may have to suffer. There are the Vandals of the soul, evil thoughts coming to devastate our virtue.

A thousand contrary ideas rushed into Gwynplaine's brain, now following each other singly, now crowding together. Then silence reigned
again, and he would lean his head on his hands, in a kind of mournful
attention, as of one who contemplates a landscape by night.

Suddenly he felt that he was no longer thinking. His reverie had
reached that point of utter darkness in which all things disappear.

He remembered, too, that he had not entered the inn. It might be
about two o'clock in the morning.

He placed the letter which the page had brought him in his side-
pocket, but perceiving that it was next his heart, he drew it out again,

crumpled it up, and placed it in a pocket of his hose. He then directed his steps towards the inn, which he entered stealthily, and without awaking little Govicum, who, while waiting up for him, had fallen asleep on the table, with his arms for a pillow. He closed the door, lighted a candle at the lamp, fastened the bolt, turned the key in the lock, taking, mechanically, all the precautions usual to a man returning home late, ascended the staircase of the Green Box, slipped into the old hovel which he used as a bedroom, looked at Ursus, who was asleep, blow out his candle, and did not go to bed.

Thus an hour passed away. Weary, at length, and fancying that bed and sleep were one, he laid his head upon the pillow without undressing, making darkness the concession of closing his eyes. But the storm of emotions which assailed him had not waned for an instant. Sleeplessness is a cruelty which night inflicts on man. Gwynplaine suffered greatly. For the first time in his life, he was not pleased with himself. Ache of heart mingled with gratified vanity. What was he to do ? Day broke at last; he heard Ursus get up, but did not raise his eyelids. No truce for him, however. The letter was ever in his mind. Every word of it came back to him in a kind of chaos. In certain violent storms within the soul, thought becomes a liquid. It is convulsed, it heaves, and something rises from it, like the dull roaring of the waves. Flood and flow, sudden shocks and whirls, the hesitation of the wave before the rock; hail and rain; clouds with the light shining through their breaks; the petty flights of useless foam; the wild swell broken in an instant; great efforts lost; wreck appearing all around ; darkness and universal dispersion; as these things are of the sea, so are they of man. Gwynplaine was a prey to such a storm.

At the acme of his agony, his eyes still closed, he heard an exquisite voice singing, " Are you asleep, Gwynplaine ?" He opened his eyes with a start and sat up. Dea was standing in the half-opened doorway. Her ineffable smile was in her eyes and on her lips. She was standing there, charming in the unconscious serenity of her radiance. Then came, as it were, a sacred moment. Gwynplaine watched her, startled, dazzled, awakened. Awakened from what ? from sleep ? no, from sleeplessness. It was she, it was Dea; and suddenly he felt in the depths of his being the indescribable wane of the storm and the sublime descent of good over evil; the miracle of the look from on high was accomplished; the blind girl, the sweet light-bearer, with no effort beyond her mere presence, dissipated all the darkness within him ; the curtain of cloud was dispersed from his soul as if drawn by an invisible hand, and a sky of azure, as though by celestial enchantment, again spread over Gwynplaine's conscience. In a moment he became, by the virtue of that angel, the great and good Gwynplaine, the innocent man. Such mysterious confrontations occur to the soul as they do to creation. Both were silent; she, who was the light; he, who was the abyss; she, who was divine; he, who was appeased; and over Gwynplaine's stormy heart Dea shone with the indescribable effect of a star shining on the Sea.

CHAPTER II

OW simple is a miracle! It was breakfast hour in the Green Box, and Dea had merely come to see why Gwynplaine had not joined their little breakfast table.

"It is you!" exclaimed Gwynplaine; and he had said everything. There was no other horizon, no vision for him now but the heaven where Dea was.

His mind was appeased; appeased in such a manner as he alone can understand, who has seen the smile spread swiftly over the sea when the hurricane has passed away. Over nothing does the calm come so quickly as over the whirlpool. This results from its power of absorption. And so it is with the human heart. Not always, however.

Dea had but to show herself, and all the light that was in Gwynplaine left him and went to her, and behind the dazzled Gwynplaine there was but a flight of phantoms. What a peace-maker is adoration!

A few minutes afterwards they were sitting opposite each other, Ursus between them, Homo at their feet. The teapot, hung over a little lamp, was on the table. Fibi and Vinos were outside, waiting.

They breakfasted as they supped, in the centre compartment. From the position in which the narrow table was placed, Dea's back was turned towards the aperture in the partition, which was opposite the entrance door of the Green Box.

Their knees were touching. Gwynplaine was pouring out tea for Dea. Dea blew gracefully on her cup. Suddenly she sneezed. Just at that moment a thin smoke rose above the flame of the lamp, and something like a piece of paper fell into ashes. It was the smoke which had caused Dea to sneeze.

"What was that?" she asked.

"Nothing," replied Gwynplaine.

62

And he smiled.

He had just burnt the Duchess's letter.

The conscience of the man who loves, is the guardian angel of the woman whom he loves.

Unburdened of the letter, his relief was wondrous, and Gwynplaine felt his integrity as the eagle feels its wings.

It seemed to him as if his temptation had evaporated with the smoke, and as if the duchess had crumbled into ashes with the paper.

Taking up their cups at random, and drinking one after the other from the same one, they talked, a babble of lovers, a chattering of sparrows! Child's talk, worthy of Mother Goose or of Homer! With two loving hearts, go no further for poetry : with two kisses for dialogue, go no further for music.

"Do you know something ?"

"No."

"Gwynplaine, I dreamt that we were animals, and had wings."

"Wings; that means birds," murmured Gwynplaine.

"Fools! it means angels," growled Ursus.

And their talk went on.

"If you did not exist, Gwynplaine ?"

"What then ?"

"It could only be because there was no God."

"The tea is too hot; you will burn yourself, Dea."

"Blow on my cup."

"How beautiful you are this morning !"

"Do you know that I have a great many things to say to you ?"

"Say them."

"I love you."

"I adore you."

And Ursus said aside : "By heaven, they are polite."

Exquisite to lovers are their moments of silence! In them they gather, as it were, masses of love, which afterwards explode into sweet fragments.

Then came a pause, and Dea cried:

"Do you know! In the evening, when we are playing our parts, at the moment when my hand touches your forehead—oh, what a noble head is yours, Gwynplaine!—at the moment when I feel your hair under my fingers, I shiver; a heavenly joy comes over me, and I say to myself, In all this world of darkness which encompasses me, in this universe of solitude, in this great obscurity of ruin in which I am, in this quaking fear of myself and of everything, I have one prop; and he is there. It is he. It is you."

"Oh! you love me," said Gwynplaine. "I, too, have but you on earth. You are all in all to me. Dea, what would you have me do ? What do you desire ? What do you want ?"

Dea answered:

"I do not know. I am happy."

"Oh," replied Gwynplaine, "we are happy."

Ursus raised his voice severely:

"Oh, you are happy, are you ? That's a crime. I have warned you already. You are happy! Then take care you aren't seen. Take up as little room as you can. Happiness ought to stuff itself into a hole. Make yourselves still less than you are, if that can be. God measures the greatness of happiness by the littleness of the happy. The happy should conceal themselves like malefactors. Oh, only shine out like the wretched glow-worms that you are, and you'll be trodden on; and quite right, too! What do you mean by all that love-making nonsense? I'm no duenna, whose business it is to watch lovers billing and cooing. I'm tired of it all, I tell you; and you may both go to the devil."

And, feeling that his harsh tones were melting into tenderness, he drowned his emotion in a loud grumble.

"Father," said Dea, "how roughly you scold."

"It's because I don't like to see people too happy."

Here Homo re-echoed Ursus. His growl was heard from beneath the lovers' feet.

Ursus stooped down, and placed his hand on Homo's head.

"That's right; you're in bad humor, too. You growl. The bristles are all on end on your wolf's pate. You don't like all this love-making. That's because you are wise. Hold your tongue all the same. You have had your say, and given your opinion; be it so. Now be silent."

The wolf growled again.

Ursus looked under the table at him.

"Be still, Homo! Come, don't dwell on it, you philosopher!"

But the wolf sat up, and looked towards the door, showing his teeth.

"What's wrong with you now?" said Ursus. And he caught hold of Homo by the skin of the neck.

Heedless of the wolf's growls, and wholly wrapped up in her own thoughts, and in the sound of Gwynplaine's voice, which left its after-taste within her, Dea was silent, and absorbed by that kind of ecstasy peculiar to the blind, which seems at times to give them a song to listen to in their souls, and to make up to them for the light which they lack, by some strain of ideal music. Blindness is a cavern, to which reaches the deep harmony of the Eternal.

While Ursus, addressing Homo, was looking down, Gwynplaine had raised his eyes.

He was about to drink a cup of tea, but did not drink it. He placed it on the table with the slow movement of a spring drawn back; his fingers remained open, his eyes fixed. He scarcely breathed.

A man was standing in the doorway, behind Dea. He was clad in black, with a hood. He wore a wig down to his eyebrows, and held in his hand an iron staff with a crown at each end. His staff was short and massive.

Imagine a Medusa thrusting her head between two branches in Paradise.

Ursus, who had heard some one enter and raised his head without loosing his hold of Homo, recognized the terrible personage.

He shook from head to foot, and whispered to Gwynplaine:

"It's the wapentake."

Gwynplaine recollected.

An exclamation of surprise was about to escape him, but he restrained it. The iron staff, with the crown at each end, was called the iron weapon. It was from this iron weapon, upon which the city officers of justice took the oath when they entered on their duties, that the old wapentakes of the English police derived their qualification.

Behind the man in the wig, the frightened landlord could just be perceived in the shadow.

Without saying a word, a personification of the *muta Themis* of the old charters, the man stretched his right arm over the radiant Dea, and touched Gwynplaine on the shoulder with the iron staff, at the same time pointing with his left thumb to the door of the Green Box behind him. These gestures, all the more imperious for their silence, meant, follow me.

"*Pro signo exeundi, sursum trahe,*" says the old Norman record.

He who was touched by the iron weapon had no right but the right of obedience. To that mute order there was no reply. The harsh penalties of the English law threatened the refractory. Gwynplaine felt a shock under the rigid touch of the law; then he sat as though petrified.

If, instead of having been merely grazed on the shoulder, he had been struck a violent blow on the head with the iron staff, he could not have been more stunned. He knew that the police officer summoned him to follow; but why! *That* he could not understand.

On his part Ursus, too, was thrown into the most painful agitation, but he saw through matters pretty distinctly. His thoughts ran on the jugglers and preachers, his competitors, on informations laid against the Green Box, on that delinquent the wolf, on his own affair with the three Bishopsgate commissioners, and who knows?—perhaps—but that would be too fearful—Gwynplaine's unbecoming and factious speeches touching the royal authority.

He trembled violently.

Dea was smiling.

Neither Gwynplaine nor Ursus pronounced a word. They had both the same thought: not to frighten Dea. It may have struck the wolf as well, for he ceased growling. True, Ursus did not loose him.

Homo, however, was a prudent wolf when occasion required. Who is there who has not remarked a kind of intelligent anxiety in animals? It may be that to the extent to which a wolf can understand mankind he felt that he was an outlaw.

Gwynplaine rose.

Resistance was impracticable, as Gwynplaine knew. He remembered Ursus's words, and there was no question possible.

He remained standing in front of the wapentake. The latter raised the iron staff from Gwynplaine's shoulder, and drawing it back, held it out straight in an attitude of command: a constable's attitude which was well understood in those days by the whole people, and which expressed the following order: "*Let this man, and no other, follow me. The rest remain where they are.   Silence!*"

No curious followers were allowed. In all times the police have had a taste for arrests of the kind. This description of seizure was termed sequestration of the person.

The wapentake turned round in one motion, like a piece of mechanism revolving on its own pivot, and with grave and magisterial step proceeded towards the door of the Green Box.

Gwynplaine looked at Ursus.

The latter went through a pantomime composed as follows : he shrugged his shoulders, placed both elbows close to his hips, with his hands out, and knitted his brows into chevrons, all which signifies,—we must submit to the unknown.

Gwynplaine looked at Dea.

She was in her dream. She was still smiling. He put the ends of his fingers to his lips, and sent her an unutterable kiss.

Ursus, relieved of some portion of his terror now that the wapentake's back was turned, seized the moment to whisper in Gwynplaine's ear :

"On your life, do not speak until you are questioned."

Gwynplaine, with the same care to make no noise as he would have taken in a sick room, took his hat and cloak from the hook on the partition, wrapped himself up to the eyes in the cloak, and pushed his hat over his forehead. Not having been to bed, he had his working clothes still on, and his leather collar round his neck. Once more he looked at Dea.   Having reached the door, the wapentake raised his staff and began to descend the steps; then Gwynplaine set out as if the man was dragging him by an invisible chain. Ursus watched Gwynplaine leave the Green Box. At that moment the wolf gave a low growl, but Ursus silenced him and whispered : "He is coming back."

In the yard, Master Nicless was stemming, with servile and imperious gestures, the cries of terror raised by Vinos and Fibi, as in great distress they watched Gwynplaine led away, and the mourning-colored garb and the iron staff of the wapentake.

The two girls were like petrifactions : they were in the attitude of stalactites.

Govicum, stunned, was looking open-mouthed out of a window.

The wapentake preceded Gwynplaine by a few steps, never turning round or looking at him, in that icy ease which is given by the knowledge that one is the law.

In death-like silence they both crossed the yard, went through the dark tap-room, and reached the street. A few passers-by had collected about the inn-door, and the justice of the quorum was there at the head of a squad of police. The idlers, stupefied, and without breathing a word, opened out and stood aside, with English discipline, at the sight of the constable's staff. The wapentake moved off in the direction of the narrow street then called the Little Strand, running by the Thames; and Gwynplaine, with the justice of the quorum's men in ranks on each side, like a double hedge, pale, without a motion except that of his steps, wrapped in his cloak as in a shroud, was leaving the inn farther and farther behind him as he followed the silent man, like a statue following a spectre.

CHAPTER III

LEX, REX, FEX

UNEXPLAINED arrest, which would greatly astonish an Englishman nowadays, was then a very usual proceeding of the police. Recourse was had to it, notwithstanding the Habeas Corpus Act, up to George II.'s time, especially in such delicate cases as were provided for by *lettres de cachet* in France; and one of the accusations against which Walpole had to defend himself was that he had caused or allowed Neuhoff to be arrested in that manner. The accusation was probably without foundation, for Neuhoff, King of Corsica, was put in prison by his creditors.

These silent captures of the person, very usual with the Holy Væhme in Germany, were admitted by German custom, which rules one half of the old English laws, and recommended in certain cases by Norman custom, which rules the other half. Justinian's chief of the palace police was called "*Silentiarius Imperialis.*" The English magistrates who practiced the captures in question relied upon numerous Norman texts:—*Canes latrant, sergentes silent.—Sergenter agere, id est tacere.*—They quoted Landulphus Sagax, paragraph 16:—*Facit Imperator silentium.*—They quoted the charter of King Philip in 1307:—*Multos tenebimus bastonerios qui, obmutescentes, sergentare valeant.*—They quoted the statutes of Henry I. of England, cap. 53:—*Surge signo jussus. Taciturnior esto. Hoc est esse in captione regis.*—They took advantage especially of the following prescription, held to form part of the ancient feudal franchises of England:—" *Sous les viscomtes sont les serjans de l'espée, lesquels doivent justicier vertueusement à l'espée tous ceux qui suient malveses compagnies, gens diffamez d'aucuns crimes, et gens fuites et forbannis . . . . et les doivent si vigoureusement et discrètement appréhender, que la bonne gent qui sont paisibles soient gardez paisiblement et que les malfeteurs soient espountés.*" To be thus arrested was to be seized "*à le*

70

glaive de l'espée." (*Vetus Consuetudo Normanniæ*, MS. part 1, sect. 1, ch. 11.) The jurisconsults referred besides " *in Charta Ludovici Hutuni pro Normannis,*" chapter *Servientes spathæ*. The *Servientes spathæ*, in the gradual approach of base Latin to our idioms, became *sergentes spadæ*.

These silent arrests were the contrary of the *Clameur de Haro*, and gave warning that it was advisable to hold one's tongue until such time as light should be thrown upon certain matters still in the dark.

They signified questions reserved, and showed in the operation of the police a certain amount of *raison d'état*.

The legal term "private" was applied to arrests of this description.

It was thus that Edward III., according to some chroniclers, caused Mortimer to be seized in the bed of his mother, Isabella of France. This again, we may take leave to doubt; for Mortimer sustained a siege in his town before being captured.

Warwick, the king-maker, delighted in practicing this mode of "attaching people."

Cromwell made use of it, especially in Connaught; and it was with this precaution of silence that Trailie Arcklo, a relation of the Earl of Ormond, was arrested at Kilmacaugh.

These captures of the body by the mere motion of justice, represented rather the summons to appear than the warrant of arrest. Sometimes they were but processes of inquiry, and even argued, by the silence imposed upon all, a certain consideration for the person seized.

For the mass of the people, little versed as they were in the estimate of such shades of difference, they had peculiar terrors.

It must not be forgotten that in 1705, and even much later, England was far from being what she is to-day. The general features of its constitution were confused and, at times, very oppressive. Daniel Defoe, who had himself had a taste of the pillory, characterizes the social order of England, somewhere in his writings, as "the iron hands of the law." There was not only the law, there was its arbitrary administration. We have but to recall Steele, ejected from Parliament; Locke, driven from his professorship; Hobbes and Gibbon, compelled to flight; Charles Churchill, Hume, and Priestley, persecuted; John Wilkes sent to the Tower. The task would be a long one, were we to count over the victims of the statute against seditious libel. The inquisition had, to some extent, spread its arrangements throughout Europe, and its police practice was taken as a guide. A monstrous attempt against all rights was possible in England. We have only to recall the *Gazetier Cuirassé*. In the midst of the eighteenth century, Louis XV. had writers, whose works displeased him, arrested in Piccadilly. It is true that George II. laid his hands on the Pretender in France, right in the middle of the hall at the opera. Those were two long arms! that of the King of France reaching London! that of the King of England, Paris! Such was the liberty of the period.

We may add, that they were fond of putting people to death privately in prisons, sleight-of-hand mingled with capital punishment; a hideous expedient, to which England is reverting at the present moment, thus giving to the world the strange spectacle of a great people, which, in its desire to take the better part, chooses the worse; and which, having before it the past on one side and progress on the other, mistakes its way, and takes night for day.

CHAPTER IV

URSUS PLAYS THE SPY ON THE POLICE

S we have already said, according to the very severe laws of the police of those days, the summons to follow the wapentake addressed to an individual, implied to all other persons present, the command not to stir.

Some curious idlers, however, were stubborn, and followed from afar off the *cortège* which had taken Gwynplaine into custody.

Ursus was of them.

He had been as nearly petrified as any one has a right to be. But Ursus, so often assailed by the surprises incident to a wandering life, and by the malice of chance, was, like a ship-of-war, prepared for action, and could call to the post of danger the whole crew—that is to say, the aid of all his intelligence.

He flung off his stupor, and began to think. He strove not to give way to emotion, but to stand face to face with circumstances.

To look fortune in the face is the duty of every one not an idiot; to seek not to understand, but to act.

Presently he asked himself: What could he do?

Gwynplaine being taken, Ursus was placed between two terrors—a fear for Gwynplaine, which instigated him to follow; and a fear for himself, which urged him to remain where he was.

Ursus had the intrepidity of a fly, and the impassibility of a sensitive plant. His agitation was not to be described. However, he took his resolution heroically, and decided to brave the law, and to follow the wapentake, so anxious was he concerning the fate of Gwynplaine.

His terror must have been great to prompt so much courage.

To what valiant acts will not fear drive a hare!

The chamois in despair jumps a precipice. To be terrified into imprudence is one of the forms of fear.

73

Gwynplaine had been carried off rather than arrested. The operation of the police had been executed so rapidly that the Fair field, generally little frequented at that hour of the morning, had scarcely taken cognizance of the circumstance.

Scarcely any one in the caravans had any idea that the wapentake had come to take Gwynplaine. Hence, the smallness of the crowd.

Gwynplaine, thanks to his cloak and his hat, which nearly concealed his face, could not be recognized by the passers-by.

Before he went out to follow Gwynplaine, Ursus took a precaution. He spoke to Master Nicless, to the boy Govicum, and to Fibi and Vinos, and insisted on their keeping absolute silence before Dea, who was ignorant of everything. That they should not utter a syllable that could make her suspect what had occurred; that they should make her understand that the cares of the management of the Green Box necessitated the absence of Gwynplaine and Ursus; that, besides, it would soon be the time of her daily siesta, and that before she awoke he and Gwynplaine would have returned; that all that had taken place had arisen from a mistake; that it would be very easy for Gwynplaine and himself to clear themselves before the magistrate and police; that a touch of the finger would put the matter straight, after which they should both return; above all, that no one should say a word on the subject to Dea. Having given these directions, he departed.

Ursus was able to follow Gwynplaine without being remarked. Though he kept at the greatest possible distance, he so managed as not to lose sight of him. Boldness in ambuscade is the bravery of the timid.

After all, notwithstanding the solemnity of the attendant circumstances, Gwynplaine might have been summoned before the magistrate for some unimportant infraction of the law.

Ursus assured himself that the question would be decided at once.

The solution of the mystery would be made under his very eyes by the direction taken by the *cortége* which took Gwynplaine from Tarrinzeau Field when it reached the entrance of the lanes of the Little Strand.

If it turned to the left, it would conduct Gwynplaine to the justice hall in Southwark. In that case there would be little to fear, some trifling municipal offense, an admonition from the magistrate, two or three shillings to pay, and Gwynplaine would be set at liberty, and the representation of " *Chaos Vanquished* " would take place in the evening as usual. In that case no one would know that anything unusual had happened.

If the *cortége* turned to the right, matters would be serious.

There were frightful places in that direction.

When the wapentake, leading the file of catchpoles between whom Gwynplaine walked, arrived at the small streets, Ursus watched them breathlessly. There are moments in which a man's whole being passes into his eyes.

Which way were they going to turn?

They turned to the right.

Ursus, staggering with terror, leaned against a wall that he might not fall.

There is no hypocrisy so great as the words which we say to ourselves, "*I wish to know the worst!*" At heart we do not wish it at all. We have a dreadful fear of knowing it. Agony is mingled with a dim effort not to see the end. We do not own it to ourselves, but we would draw back if we dared; and when we have advanced, we reproach ourselves for having done so.

Thus did Ursus. He shuddered as he thought:

"Here are things going wrong. I should have found it out soon enough. What business had I to follow Gwynplaine?"

Having made this reflection, man being but self-contradiction, he increased his pace, and, mastering his anxiety, hastened to get nearer the *cortége*, so as not to break, in the maze of small streets, the thread between Gwynplaine and himself.

The *cortége* of police could not move quickly on account of its solemnity.

The wapentake led it.

The justice of the quorum closed it.

This order compelled a certain deliberation of movement.

All the majesty possible in an official shone in the justice of the quorum. His costume held a middle place between the splendid robe of a doctor of music of Oxford, and the sober black habiliments of a doctor of divinity of Cambridge. He wore the dress of a gentleman under a long godebert, which is a mantle trimmed with the fur of the Norwegian hare. He was half gothic and half modern, wearing a wig like Lamoignon, and sleeves like Tristan l'Hermite. His great round eye watched Gwynplaine with the fixedness of an owl's.

He walked with a cadence. Never did honest man look fiercer.

Ursus, for a moment thrown out of his way in the tangled skein of streets, overtook, close to Saint Mary Overy, the *cortége*, which had fortunately been retarded in the church-yard by a fight between children and dogs, a common incident in the streets in those days. "*Dogs and boys*," says the old registers of police, placing the dogs before the boys.

A man being taken before a magistrate by the police was, after all, an every-day affair, and each one having his own business to attend to, the few who had followed soon dispersed. There remained but Ursus on the track of Gwynplaine.

They passed before two chapels opposite to each other, belonging

, the one to the Recreative Religionists, the other to the Hallelujah League, sects which flourished then, and which exist to the present day.

Then the *cortége* wound from street to street, making a zigzag, choosing by preference lanes not yet built on, roads where the grass grew, and deserted alleys.

At length it stopped.

It was in a little lane with no houses except two or three hovels. This narrow alley was composed of two walls, one on the left, low; the other on the right, high. The high wall was black, and built in the Saxon style with narrow holes, scorpions, and large square gratings over narrow loop-holes. There was no window on it, but here and there slits, old embrasures for cross bows and long bows. At the foot of this high wall was seen, like the hole at the bottom of a rat-trap, a little wicket gate, very elliptical in its arch.

This small door, encased in a full, heavy girding of stone, had a grated peep-hole, a heavy knocker, a large lock, hinges thick and knotted, a bristling of nails, an armor of plates, and hinges, so that altogether it was more of iron than of wood.

There was no one in the lane. No shops, no passengers; but in it there was heard a continual noise, as if the lane ran parallel to a torrent. There was a tumult of voices and of carriages. It seemed as if on the other side of the black edifice there must be a great street, doubtless the principal street of Southwark, one end of which ran into the Canterbury road, and the other on to London Bridge.

All the length of the lane, except the *cortége* which surrounded Gwynplaine, a watcher would have seen no other human face than the pale profile of Ursus hazarding a half advance from the shadow of the corner of the wall; looking, yet fearing to see. He had posted himself behind the wall at a turn of the lane.

The constables grouped themselves before the wicket. Gwynplaine was in the centre, the wapentake and his baton of iron being now behind him.

The justice of the quorum raised the knocker, and struck the door three times. The loop-hole opened.

The justice of the quorum said:

"By order of her Majesty."

The heavy door of oak and iron turned on its hinges, making a chilly opening, like the mouth of a cavern. A hideous depth yawned in the shadow.

Ursus saw Gwynplaine disappear within it.

CHAPTER V

HE wapentake entered behind Gwynplaine.

Then the justice of the quorum.

Then the constables.

The wicket was closed.

The heavy door swung to, closing hermetically on the stone sills, without any one seeing who had opened or shut it. It seemed as if the bolts re-entered their sockets of their own act. Some of these mechanisms, the inventions of ancient intimidation, still exist in old prisons; doors of which you saw no door-keeper. With them the entrance to a prison becomes like the entrance to a tomb.

This wicket was the lower door of Southwark Jail.

There was nothing in the harsh and worm-eaten aspect of this prison to soften its appropriate air of rigor.

Originally a pagan temple, built by the Catieuchlans for the Mogons, ancient English gods, it became a palace for Ethelwolfe and a fortress for Edward the Confessor; then it was elevated to the dignity of a prison, in 1199, by John Lackland. Such was Southwark Jail. This jail, at first intersected by a street, like Chenonceaux by a river, had been for a century or two a gate, that is to say, the gate of a suburb; the passage had then been walled up. There remain in England some prisons of this nature. In London, Newgate; at Canterbury, Westgate; at Edinburgh, Canongate. In France the Bastile was originally a gate.

Almost all the jails of England present the same appearance—a high wall without and a hive of cells within. Nothing could be more funereal than the appearance of those prisons, where spiders and justice spread their webs, and where John Howard, that ray of light, had not yet penetrated. Like the Old Gehenna of Brussels, they might well have have been designated Treurenberg—*the house of tears.*

78

Men felt before such buildings, at once so savage and inhospitable, the same distress that the ancient navigators suffered before the hell of slaves mentioned by Plautus, islands of creaking chains, *ferricrepiditæ insulæ*, when they passed near enough to hear the clank of the fetters.

Southwark Jail, an old place of exorcisms and torture, was originally used solely for the imprisonment of sorcerers, as was proved by two verses engraved on a defaced stone at the foot of the wicket:

> Sunt arreptitii, vexati dæmone multo
> Est energumenus, quem dæmon possidet unus.

Lines which draw a subtle delicate distinction between the demoniac and man possessed by a devil.

At the bottom of this inscription, nailed flat against the wall, was a stone ladder, which had been originally of wood, but which had been changed into stone by being buried in earth of petrifying quality at a place called Apsley Gowis, near Woburn Abbey.

The prison of Southwark, now demolished, opened on two streets, between which, as a gate, it formerly served as means of communication. It had two doors. In the large street a door, apparently used by the authorities; and in the lane the door of punishment, used by the rest of the living and by the dead also, because when a prisoner in the jail died, it was by that issue that his corpse was carried out. A liberation not to be despised.

Death is release into infinity.

It was by the gate of punishment that Gwynplaine had been taken into the prison.

The lane, as we have said, was nothing but a little passage, paved with flints, confined between two opposite walls. There is one of the same kind at Brussels called *Rue d'une Personne*. The walls were unequal in height. The high one was the prison; the low one, the cemetery—the enclosure for the mortuary remains of the jail—was not higher than the ordinary stature of a man. In it was a gate almost opposite the prison wicket. The dead had only to cross the street; the cemetery was but twenty paces from the jail. On the high wall was affixed a gallows; on the low one was sculptured a Death's head. Neither of these walls made its opposite neighbor more cheerful.

CHAPTER VI

NY one observing at that moment the other side of the prison —its façade—would have perceived the high street of Southwark, and might have remarked, stationed before the monumental and official entrance to the jail, a traveling carriage, recognized as such by its imperial. A few idlers surrounded the carriage. On it was a coat of arms, and a personage had been seen to descend from it and enter the prison. "Probably a magistrate," conjectured the crowd. Many of the English magistrates were noble, and almost all had the right of bearing arms. In France blazon and robe were almost contradictory terms. The Duke Saint-Simon says, in speaking of magistrates, "People of that class." In England a gentleman was not despised for being a judge.

There are traveling magistrates in England; they are called judges of circuit, and nothing was easier than to recognize the carriage as the vehicle of a judge on circuit. That which was less comprehensible was, that the supposed magistrate got down, not from the carriage itself, but from the box, a place which is not habitually occupied by the owner. Another unusual thing. People traveled at that period in England in two ways. By coach, at the rate of a shilling for five miles, and by post, paying three half-pence per mile, and twopence to the postilion after each stage. A private carriage, whose owner desired to travel by relays, paid as many shillings per horse per mile as the horseman paid pence. The carriage drawn up before the jail in Southwark had four horses and two postilions, which displayed princely state. Finally, that which excited and disconcerted conjectures to the utmost was the circumstance that the carriage was sedulously shut up. The blinds of the windows were closed up. The glasses in front were darkened by blinds; every opening by which the eye might have penetrated was

80

masked. From without, nothing within could be seen, and most likely
from within, nothing could be seen outside. However, it did not seem
probable that there was any one in the carriage.

Southwark being in Surrey, the prison was within the jurisdiction
of the sheriff of the county.

Such distinct jurisdictions were very frequent in England. Thus,
for example, the Tower of London was not supposed to be situated in
any county; that is to say, that, legally, it was considered to be in air.
The Tower recognized no authority of jurisdiction except in its own constable, who was qualified as *custos turris*. The Tower had its jurisdiction, its church, its court of justice, and its government apart. The

authority of its *custos* or constable extended, outside of London, over
twenty-one hamlets. As in Great Britain legal singularities engraft
one upon another, the office of the master gunner of England was
derived from the Tower of London.

Other legal customs seem still more whimsical. Thus, the English
Court of Admiralty consults and applies the laws of Rhodes and of
Oleron, a French island which was once English.

The sheriff of a county was a person of high consideration. He
was always an esquire, and sometimes a knight. He was called *specta-
bilis* in the old deeds, "a man to be looked at," a kind of intermediate
title between *illustris* and *clarissimus*,—less than the first, more than the
second. Long ago the sheriffs of the counties were chosen by the
people; but Edward II., and after him Henry VI., having claimed their
nomination for the crown, the office of sheriff became a royal emanation.

They all received their commissions from majesty, except the
sheriff of Westmoreland, whose office was hereditary, and the sheriffs
of London and Middlesex, who were elected by the livery in the common hall. Sheriffs of Wales and Chester possessed certain fiscal prerog-
atives. These appointments are all still in existence in England, but,
subjected little by little to the friction of manners and ideas, they have
lost their old aspects. It was the duty of the sheriff of the county to
escort and protect the judges on circuit. As we have two arms, he had
two officers; his right arm the under-sheriff, his left arm the justice of
the quorum. The justice of the quorum, assisted by the bailiff of the
hundred, termed the wapentake, apprehended, examined, and, under the
responsibility of the sheriff, imprisoned, for trial by the judges of circuit, thieves, murderers, rebels, vagabonds, and all sorts of felons.

The shade of difference between the under-sheriff and the justice
of the quorum, in their hierarchical service towards the sheriff, was
that the under-sheriff accompanied and the justice of the quorum
assisted.

The sheriff held two courts, one fixed and central, the county court,
and a movable court, the sheriff's turn. He thus represented both unity
and ubiquity. He might as judge be aided and informed on legal questions by the sergeant of the coif, called *sergens coifæ*, who is a sergeant-
at-law, and who wears under his black skull-cap a fillet of white Cam-
bray lawn.

The sheriff delivered the jails. When he arrived at a town in his
province, he had the right of summary trial of the prisoners, of which
he might cause either their release or their execution. This was called
a jail delivery. The sheriff presented bills of indictment to the twenty-
four members of the grand jury. If they approved, they wrote above,

billa vera; if the contrary, they wrote *ignoramus.* In the latter case the accusation was annulled, and the sheriff had the privilege of tearing up the bill. If during the deliberation a juror died, this legally acquitted the prisoner and made him innocent, and the sheriff, who had the privilege of arresting the accused, had also that of setting him at liberty.

That which made the sheriff singularly feared and respected was that he had the charge of executing all the orders of her majesty, a fearful latitude.

An arbitrary power lodges in such commissions.

The officers termed vergers, the coroners making part of the sheriff's *cortége,* and the clerks of the market as escort, with gentlemen on horseback and their servants in livery, made a handsome suite. The sheriff, says Chamberlayne, is the "life of justice, of law, and of the county."

In England an insensible demolition constantly pulverizes and dissevers laws and customs. You must understand in our day that neither the sheriff, the wapentake, nor the justice of the quorum could exercise their functions as they did then. There was in the England of the Past a certain confusion of powers, whose ill-defined attributes resulted in their overstepping their real bounds at times, a thing which would be impossible in the present day. The usurpation of power by police and justices has ceased. We believe that even the word wapentake has changed its meaning. It implied a magisterial function; now it signifies a territorial division : it specified the centurion; it now specifies the hundred (*centum*).

Moreover, in those days the sheriff of the county combined with something more and something less, and condensed in his own authority, which was at once royal and municipal, the two magistrates formerly called in France the civil lieutenant of Paris and the lieutenant of police. The civil lieutenant of Paris is pretty well described in an old police note : " The civil lieutenant had no dislike to domestic quarrels, because he always has the pickings."—(22d July, 1704). As to the lieutenant of police, he was a redoubtable person, multiple and vague. The best personification of him was René d'Argenson, who, as was said by Saint-Simon, displayed in his face the three judges of hell united.

The three judges of hell sat, as has already been seen, at Bishopsgate, London.

CHAPTER VII

WHEN Gwynplaine heard the wicket shut, creaking in all its bolts, he trembled. It seemed to him that the door which had just closed, was the communication between light and darkness; opening on one side on the living, human crowd, and on the other on a dead world; and now that everything illumined by the sun was behind him, that he had stepped over the boundary of life, and was standing without it, his heart contracted. What were they going to do with him? What did it all mean?

Where was he?

He saw nothing around him; he found himself in perfect darkness. The shutting of the door had momentarily blinded him. The window in the door had been closed as well. No loop-hole, no lamp. Such were the precautions of old times. It was forbidden to light the entrance to the jails, so that the new-comers should take no observations.

Gwynplaine extended his arms, and touched the wall on the right side and on the left. He was in a passage. Little by little a cavernous daylight, exuding, no one knows whence, and which floats about dark places, and to which the dilatation of the pupil adjusts itself slowly, enabled him to distinguish a feature here and there, and the corridor was vaguely sketched out before him.

Gwynplaine, who had never had a glimpse of penal severities, save in the exaggerations of Ursus, felt as though seized by a sort of vague gigantic hand. To be caught in the mysterious toils of the law is frightful. He who is brave in all other dangers, is disconcerted in the presence of justice. Why? Is it that the justice of man works in twilight, and the judge gropes his way? Gwynplaine remembered what Ursus had told him of the necessity for silence. He wished to see Dea

84

again; he felt some discretionary instinct, which urged him not to irritate. Sometimes to wish to be enlightened is to make matters worse; on the other hand, however, the weight of the adventure was so overwhelming, that he gave way at length and could not restrain a question.

"Gentlemen," said he, "whither are you taking me?"

They made no answer.

It was the law of silent capture, and the Norman text is formal: *A silentiariis ostio, præpositis introducti sunt.*

This silence froze Gwynplaine. Up to that moment he had believed himself to be firm: he was self-sufficing. To be self-sufficing is to be powerful. He had lived isolated from the world, and imagined that being alone he was unassailable; and now all at once he felt himself under the pressure of a hideous collective force. How was he to combat that horrible anonyma, the law? He felt faint under the perplexity; a fear of an unknown character had found a fissure in his armor; besides, he had not slept, he had not eaten, he had scarcely moistened his lips with a cup of tea. The whole night had been passed in a kind of delirium, and the fever was still on him. He was thirsty; perhaps hungry. The craving of the stomach disorders everything. Since the previous evening all kinds of incidents had assailed him. The emotions which had tormented had sustained him. Without the storm a sail would be a rag. But his was the excessive feebleness of the rag, which the wind inflates till it tears it. He felt himself sinking. Was he about to fall without consciousness on the pavement? To faint is the resource of a woman, and the humiliation of a man. He hardened himself, but he trembled. He felt as one losing his footing.

CHAPTER VIII

THEY began to move forward.

They advanced through the passage.

There was no preliminary registry, no place of record. The prisons in those times were not overburdened with documents. They were content to close round you without knowing why. To be a prison, and to hold prisoners, sufficed.

The procession was obliged to lengthen itself out, taking the form of the corridor. They walked almost in single file; first the wapentake, then Gwynplaine, then the justice of the quorum, then the constables, advancing in a group, and blocking up the passage behind Gwynplaine as with a bung. The passage narrowed. Now Gwynplaine touched the walls with both his elbows. In the roof, which was made of flints, dashed with cement, was a succession of granite arches jutting out, and still more contracting the passage. He had to stoop to pass under them. No speed was possible in that corridor. Any one trying to escape through it would have been compelled to move slowly. The passage twisted. All entrails are tortuous; those of a prison as well as those of a man. Here and there, sometimes to the right and sometimes to the left, spaces in the wall, square and closed by large iron gratings, gave glimpses of flights of stairs, some descending and some ascending.

They reached a closed door; it opened. They passed through, and it closed again. Then they came to a second door, which admitted them, then to a third, which also turned on its hinges. These doors seemed to open and shut of themselves. No one was to be seen. While the corridor contracted, the roof grew lower, until at length it was impossible to stand upright. Moisture exuded from the wall. Drops of water fell from the vault. The slabs that paved the corridor were clammy as an intestine. The diffused pallor that served as light be-

THE TORTURE-CHAMBER.

came more and more a pall. Air was deficient, and what was singularly ominous, the passage was a descent.

Close observation was necessary to perceive that there was such a descent. In darkness a gentle declivity is portentous. Nothing is more fearful than the vague evils to which we are led by imperceptible degrees.

It is awful to descend into unknown depths.

How long had they proceeded thus ? Gwynplaine could not tell.

Moments passed under such crushing agony seem immeasurably prolonged.

Suddenly they halted.

The darkness was intense.

The corridor widened somewhat. Gwynplaine heard close to him a noise of which only a Chinese gong could give an idea; something like a blow struck against the diaphragm of the abyss. It was the wapentake striking his wand against a sheet of iron.

That sheet of iron was a door.

Not a door on hinges, but a door which was raised and let down.

Something like a portcullis.

There was a sound of creaking in a groove, and Gwynplaine was suddenly face to face with a bit of square light. The sheet of metal had just been raised into a slit in the vault, like the door of a mouse-trap.

An opening had appeared.

The light was not daylight, but glimmer; but on the dilated eye-balls of Gwynplaine the pale and sudden ray struck like a flash of lightning.

It was some time before he could see anything. To see with dazzled eyes, is as difficult as to see in darkness.

At length, by degrees, the pupil of his eye became proportioned to the light, just as it had been proportioned to the darkness, and he was able to distinguish objects. The light, which at first had seemed too bright, settled into its proper hue and became livid. He cast a glance into the yawning space before him, and what he saw was terrible.

At his feet were about twenty steps, steep, narrow, worn, almost perpendicular, without balustrade on either side, a sort of stone ridge cut out from the side of a wall into stairs, entering and leading into a very deep cell. They reached to the bottom.

The cell was round, roofed by an ogee vault with a low arch, from the defective level in the imposts, a displacement common to cells under heavy edifices.

The kind of hole acting as a door, which the sheet of iron had just revealed, and on which the stairs abutted, was formed in the vault, so that the eye looked down from it as into a well.

The cell was large, and if it was the bottom of a well, it must have been a cyclopean one. The idea that the old word "*cul-de-basse-fosse*" awakens in the mind can only be applied to it if it be fancied to be a den of wild beasts.

The cell was neither flagged nor paved. The bottom was of that cold, moist earth peculiar to deep places.

In the midst of the cell, four low and disproportioned columns sustained a porch heavily ogival, of which the four mouldings united in the interior of the porch, something like the inside of a mitre. This porch, similar to the pinnacles under which sarcophagi were formerly placed, rose nearly to the top of the vault, and made a sort of central chamber in the cavern, if that could be called a chamber which had only pillars in place of walls.

From the key of the arch hung a brass lamp, round and barred like the window of a prison. This lamp threw around it—on the pillars, on the vault, on the circular wall which was seen dimly behind the pillars —a wan light, cut by bars of shadow.

This was the light which had at first dazzled Gwynplaine; now it threw out only a confused redness.

There was no other light in the cell—neither window, nor door, nor loop-hole.

Between the four pillars, exactly below the lamp, in the spot where there was most light, a pale and terrible form lay on the ground.

It was lying on its back; a head was visible, of which the eyes were shut; a body, of which the chest was a shapeless mass; four limbs belonging to the body, in the position of the cross of Saint Andrew, were drawn towards the four pillars by four chains fastened to each foot and each hand.

These chains were fastened to an iron ring at the base of each column. The form was held immovable, in the horrible position of being quartered, and had the icy look of a livid corpse.

It was naked. It was a man.

Gwynplaine, as if petrified, stood at the top of the stairs, looking down. Suddenly he heard a rattle in the throat.

The corpse was alive.

Close to the spectre, in one of the ogives of the porch, on each side of a great seat, which stood on a large flat stone, stood two men swathed in long black cloaks; and on the seat an old man was sitting, dressed in a red robe—wan, motionless, and ominous, holding a bunch of roses in his hand.

The bunch of roses would have enlightened any one less ignorant than Gwynplaine. The right of judging with a nosegay in his hand implied the holder to be a magistrate at once royal and municipal. The Lord Mayor of London still keeps up the custom. To assist the deliberations of the judges was the function of the earliest roses of the season.

The old man seated on the bench was the sheriff of the county of Surrey.

His was the majestic rigidity of a Roman dignitary.

The bench was the only seat in the cell.

By the side of it was a table covered with papers and books, on which lay the long, white wand of the sheriff. The men standing by the side of the sheriff were two doctors, one of medicine, the other of law; the latter recognizable by the sergeant's coif over his wig. Both wore black robes—one of the shape worn by judges, the other by doctors.

Men of these kinds wear mourning for the deaths of which they are the cause.

Behind the sheriff, at the edge of the flat stone under the seat, was crouched—with a writing-table near to him, a bundle of papers on his knees, and a sheet of parchment on the bundle—a secretary, in a round wig, with a pen in his hand, in the attitude of a man ready to write.

This secretary was of the class called keeper of the bag, as was shown by a bag at his feet.

These bags, in former times employed in law processes, were termed bags of justice.

With folded arms, leaning against a pillar, was a man entirely dressed in leather, the hangman's assistant.

These men seemed as if they had been fixed by enchantment in their funereal postures round the chained man. None of them spoke or moved.

There brooded over all a fearful calm.

What Gwynplaine saw was a torture chamber. There were many such in England.

The crypt of Beauchamp Tower long served this purpose, as did also the cell in the Lollards' prison. A place of this nature is still to be seen in London, called "the Vaults of Lady Place." In this last-mentioned chamber there is a grate for the purpose of heating the irons.

All the prisons of King John's time (and Southwark Jail was one) had their chambers of torture.

The scene which is about to follow was in those days a frequent one in England, and might, even, by criminal process be carried out to-day, since the same laws are still unrepealed. England offers the curious sight of a barbarous code living on the best terms with liberty. We confess that they make an excellent family party.

Some distrust, however, might not be undesirable. In the case of a crisis, a return to the penal code would not be impossible. English legislation is a tamed tiger with a velvet paw, but the claws are still there. Cut the claws of the law, and you will do well. Law almost ignores right. On one side is penalty, on the other humanity. Philosophers protest; but it will take some time yet before the justice of man is assimilated to the justice of God.

Respect for the law: that is the English phrase. In England they venerate so many laws, that they never repeal any. They save themselves from the consequences of their veneration by never putting them into execution. An old law falls into disuse like an old woman, and they never think of killing either one or the other. They cease to make use of them; that is all. Both are at liberty to consider themselves still young and beautiful. They may fancy that they are as they were. This politeness is called respect.

Norman custom is very wrinkled. That does not prevent many an English judge casting sheep's eyes at her. They stick amorously to an antiquated atrocity, so long as it is Norman. What can be more savage than the gibbet? In 1867 a man was sentenced to be cut into four quarters and offered to a woman—the Queen.

Still, torture was never practiced in England. History asserts this as a fact. The assurance of history is wonderful.

Matthew of Westminster mentions that the "Saxon law, very clement and kind," did not punish criminals by death; and adds that "it limited itself by cutting off the nose and scooping out the eyes." That was all!

Gwynplaine, scared and haggard, stood at the top' of the steps, trembling in every limb. He shuddered from head to foot. He tried to remember what crime he had committed. To the silence of the wapentake had succeeded the vision of torture to be endured. It was a step, indeed, forward; but a tragic one. He saw the dark enigma of the law under the power of which he felt himself increasing in obscurity.

The human form lying on the earth rattled in its throat again.

Gwynplaine felt some one touching him gently on his shoulder.

It was the wapentake.

Gwynplaine knew that meant that he was to descend.

He obeyed.

He descended the stairs step by step. They were very narrow, each eight or nine inches in height. There was no hand-rail. The descent required caution. Two steps behind Gwynplaine followed the wapentake, holding up his iron weapon; and at the same interval behind the wapentake, the justice of the quorum.

As he descended the steps, Gwynplaine felt an indescribable extinction of hope. There was death in each step. In each one that he descended there died a ray of the light within him. Growing paler and paler, he reached the bottom of the stairs.

The spectre lying chained to the four pillars still rattled in its throat.

A voice in the shadow said:

"Approach!"

It was the sheriff addressing Gwynplaine.

Gwynplaine took a step forward.

"Closer," said the sheriff.

The justice of the quorum murmured in the ear of Gwynplaine so gravely that there was solemnity in the whisper:

"You are before the sheriff of the county of Surrey."

Gwynplaine advanced towards the victim extended in the centre of the cell. The wapentake and the justice of the quorum remained where they were, allowing Gwynplaine to advance alone.

When Gwynplaine reached the spot under the porch, close to that miserable thing which he had hitherto perceived only from a distance, but which was a living man, his fear rose to terror. The man who was chained there was quite naked, except for that rag so hideously modest, which might be called the vineleaf of punishment, the *succingulum* of the Romans, and the *christipannus* of the Goths, of which the old Gallic jargon made *cripagne*. Christ wore but that shred on the cross.

The terror-stricken sufferer whom Gwynplaine now saw, seemed a man of about fifty or sixty years of age. He was bald. Grizzly hairs of beard bristled on his chin. His eyes were closed; his mouth open. Every tooth was to be seen. His thin and bony face was like a death's-head. His arms and legs were fastened by chains to the four stone pillars in the shape of the letter X. He had on his breast and belly a plate of iron, and on this iron five or six large stones were laid. His rattle was at times a sigh, at times a roar.

The sheriff, still holding his bunch of roses, took from the table with the hand which was free, his white wand, and standing up said:

"Obedience to her majesty."

Then he replaced the wand upon the table.

Then in words long-drawn as a knell, without a gesture, and immovable as the sufferer, the sheriff, raising his voice, said:

"Man, who liest here bound in chains, listen for the last time to the voice of justice; you have been taken from your dungeon and brought to this jail. Legally summoned in the usual forms, *formaliis verbis pressus;* not regarding lectures and communications which have been made, and which will now be repeated, to you; inspired by a bad and perverse spirit of tenacity, you have preserved silence, and refused to answer the judge. This is a detestable license, which constitutes, among deeds punishable by cashlit, the crime and misdemeanor of overseness."

The sergeant of the coif on the right of the sheriff interrupted him, and said, with an indifference indescribably lugubrious in its effect:

" *Overhernessa.* Laws of Alfred and of Godrun, chapter the sixth."

The sheriff resumed:

" The law is respected by all except by scoundrels who infest the woods where the hinds bear young."

Like one clock striking after another, the sergeant said:

" *Qui faciunt vastum in foresta ubi damæ solent founinare.*"

" He who refuses to answer the magistrate," said the sheriff, " is suspected of every vice. He is reputed capable of every evil."

The sergeant interposed:

" *Prodigus, devorator, profusus, salax, ruffianus, ebriosus, luxuriosus, simulator, consumptor patrimonii, elluo, ambro, et gluto.*"

" Every vice," said the sheriff, " means every crime. He who confesses nothing, confesses everything. He who holds his peace before the questions of the judge, is in fact a liar and a parricide."

" *Mendax et parricida,*" said the sergeant.

The sheriff said:

" Man, it is not permitted to absent one's self by silence. To pretend contumaciousness is a wound given to the law. It is like Diomede wounding a goddess. Taciturnity before a judge is a form of rebellion. Treason to justice is high treason. Nothing is more hateful or rash. He who resists interrogation, steals truth. The law has provided for this. For such cases, the English have always enjoyed the right of the foss, the fork, and chains."

" *Anglica Charta,* year 1088," said the sergeant.

Then with the same mechanical gravity, he added:

" *Ferrum, et fossam, et furcas cum aliis libertatibus.*"

The sheriff continued:

" Man! Forasmuch as you have not chosen to break silence, though of sound mind and having full knowledge in respect of the subject concerning which justice demands an answer, and forasmuch as you are diabolically refractory, you have necessarily been put to torture, and you have been, by the terms of the criminal statutes, tried by the ' *Peine forte et dure.*' This is what has been done to you, for the law requires that I should fully inform you. You have been brought to this dungeon. You have been stripped of your clothes. You have been laid on your back naked on the ground, your limbs have been stretched and tied to the four pillars of the law; a sheet of iron has been placed on your chest, and as many stones as you can bear have been heaped on your belly, 'and more,' says the law."

"*Plusque*," affirmed the sergeant.

The sheriff continued:

" In this situation, and before prolonging the torture, a second summons to answer and to speak has been made you by me, sheriff of the county of Surrey, and you have satanically kept silent, though under torture, chains, shackles, fetters, and irons."

"*Attachiamenta legalia*," said the sergeant.

" On your refusal and contumacy," said the sheriff, "it being right that the obstinacy of the law should equal the obstinacy of the criminal, the proof has been continued according to the edicts and texts. The first day you were given nothing to eat or drink."

"*Hoc est superjejunare*," said the sergeant.

There was silence, the awful hiss of a man's breathing was heard from under the heap of stones.

The sergeant-at-law completed his quotation.

" *Adde augmentum abstinentiæ ciborum diminutione. Consuetudo brittanica*, art. 504."

The two men, the sheriff and the sergeant, alternated. Nothing could be more dreary than their imperturbable monotony. The mournful voice responded to the ominous voice; it might be said that the priest and the deacon of punishment were celebrating the savage mass of the law.

The sheriff resumed:

" On the first day you were given nothing to eat or drink. On the second day you were given food, but nothing to drink. Between your teeth were thrust three mouthfuls of barley bread. On the third day they gave you to drink, but nothing to eat. They poured into your mouth at three different times, and in three different glasses, a pint of water taken from the common sewer of the prison. The fourth day is come. It is to-day. Now, if you do not answer, you will be left here till you die. Justice wills it."

The sergeant, ready with his reply, appeared.

" *Mors rei homagium est bonæ legi.*"

" And while you feel yourself dying miserably," resumed the sheriff, "no one will attend to you, even when the blood rushes from your throat, your chin, and your armpits, and every pore, from the mouth to the loins."

"*A throtabolla*," said the sergeant, "*et pabus et subhircis et a grugno usque ad crupponum.*"

The sheriff continued:

"Man, attend to me, because the consequences concern you. If you renounce your execrable silence, and if you confess, you will only be hanged, and you will have a right to the meldefeoh, which is a sum of money."

"*Damnum confitens*," said the sergeant, "*habeat le meldefeoh. Leges Inæ*, chapter the twentieth."

"Which sum," insisted the sheriff, "shall be paid in doitkins, suskins, and galihalpens, the only case in which this money is to pass, according to the terms of the statute of abolition, in the third of Henry V., and you will have the right and enjoyment of *scortum ante mortem*, and then be hanged on the gibbet. Such are the advantages of confession. Does it please you to answer to justice?"

The sheriff ceased, and waited.

The prisoner lay motionless.

The sheriff resumed:

"Man, silence is a refuge in which there is more risk than safety. The obstinate man is damnable and vicious. He who is silent before justice is a felon to the crown. Do not persist in this unfilial disobedience. Think of her Majesty. Do not oppose our gracious queen. When I speak to you, answer her; be a loyal subject.

The patient rattled in the throat.

The sheriff continued:

"So, after the seventy-two hours of the proof, here we are at the fourth day. Man, this is the decisive day. The fourth day has been fixed by the law for the confrontation."

"*Quarta die, frontem ad frontem adduce*," growled the sergeant.

"The wisdom of the law," continued the sheriff, "has chosen this last hour to hold what our ancestors called 'judgment by mortal cold,' seeing that it is the moment when men are believed on their yes or their no."

The sergeant on the right confirmed his words.

"*Judicium pro frodmortell, quod homines credendi sint per suum ya et per suum no.* Charter of King Adelstan, volume the first, page one hundred and sixty-three."

There was a moment's pause; then the sheriff bent his stern face towards the prisoner.

"Man, who art lying there on the ground——"

He paused.

"Man," he cried, "do you hear me?"

The man did not move.

"In the name of the law," said the sheriff, "open your eyes."

The man's lids remained closed.

The sheriff turned to the doctor, who was standing on his left:

"Doctor, give your diagnostic."

"*Probe, da diagnosticum,*" said the sergeant.

The doctor came down with magisterial stiffness, approached the man, leaned over him, put his ear close to the mouth of the sufferer, felt the pulse at the wrist, the armpit, and the thigh, then rose again.

"Well?" said the sheriff.

"He can still hear," said the doctor.

"Can he see?" inquired the sheriff.

The doctor answered, "He can see."

On a sign from the sheriff, the justice of the quorum and the wapentake advanced. The wapentake placed himself near the head of the patient. The justice of the quorum stood behind Gwynplaine.

The doctor retired a step behind the pillars.

Then the sheriff, raising the bunch of roses as a priest about to sprinkle holy water, called to the prisoner in a loud voice, and became awful.

"O, wretched man, speak! The law supplicates before she exterminates you. You, who feign to be mute, remember how mute is the tomb. You, who appear deaf, remember that damnation is more deaf. Think of the death which is worse than your present state. Repent: you are about to be left alone in this cell. Listen! you who are my likeness; for I am a man! Listen, my brother, because I am a Christian! Listen, my son, because I am an old man! Look at me; for I am the master of your sufferings, and I am about to become terrible. The terrors of the law make up the majesty of the judge. Believe, that I myself tremble before myself. My own power alarms me. Do not drive me to extremities. I am filled by the holy malice of chastisement. Feel, then, wretched man, the salutary and honest fear of justice, and obey me. The hour of confrontation is come, and you must answer. Do not harden yourself in resistance. Do not that which will be irrevocable. Think that your end belongs to me. Half man, half corpse, listen! At least, let it not be your determination to expire here, exhausted for hours, days, and weeks, by frightful agonies of hunger and foulness, under the weight of those stones, alone in this cell, deserted, forgotten, annihilated, left as food for the rats and the weasels, gnawed by creatures of darkness while the world comes and goes, buys and sells, whilst carriages roll in the streets above your head. Unless you would continue to draw painful breath without remission in the depths of this despair,—grinding your teeth, weeping, blaspheming,—without a doctor to appease the anguish of your wounds, without a priest to offer a divine draught of water to your soul. Oh! if only that you may not feel the frightful froth of the sepulchre ooze slowly from your lips, I adjure and conjure you to hear me. I call you to your own aid. Have pity on yourself. Do what is asked of you. Give way to justice. Open your eyes, and see if you recognize this man!"

The prisoner neither turned his head nor lifted his eyelids.

The sheriff cast a glance first at the justice of the quorum and then at the wapentake.

The justice of the quorum, taking Gwynplaine's hat and mantle, put his hands on his shoulders and placed him in the light by the side of the chained man. The face of Gwynplaine stood out clearly from the surrounding shadow, in its strange relief.

At the same time, the wapentake bent down, took the man's temples between his hands, turned the inert head towards Gwynplaine, and with his thumbs and his first fingers lifted the closed eyelids.

The prisoner saw Gwynplaine.

Then, raising his head voluntarily, and opening his eyes wide, he looked at him.

He quivered as much as a man can quiver with a mountain on his breast, and then cried out:

"'Tis he! Yes; 'tis he!"

And he burst into a horrible laugh.

"'Tis he!" he repeated.

Then his head fell back on the ground, and he closed his eyes again.

"Registrar, take that down," said the justice.

Gwynplaine, though terrified, had, up to that moment, preserved a calm exterior. The cry of the prisoner, "*'Tis he!*" overwhelmed him completely. The words, "*Registrar, take that down!*" froze him. It seemed to him that a scoundrel had dragged him to his fate without his being able to guess why, and that the man's unintelligible confession was closing round him like the clasp of an iron collar. He fancied himself side by side with him in the posts of the same pillory. Gwynplaine lost his footing in his terror, and protested. He began to stammer incoherent words in the deep distress of an innocent man, and quivering, terrified, lost, uttered the first random outcries that rose to his mind, and words of agony like aimless projectiles.

"It is not true. It was not me. I do not know the man. He

cannot know me, since I do not know him. I have my part to play this
evening. What do you want of me? I demand my liberty. Nor is
that all. Why have I been brought into this dungeon? Are there
laws no longer? You may as well say at once that there are no laws.

My Lord Judge, I repeat that it is not I. I am innocent of all that
can be said. I know I am. I wish to go away. This is not justice.
There is nothing between this man and me. You can find out. My
life is not hidden up. They came and took me away like a thief. Why
did they come like that? How could I know the man? I am a traveling mountebank, who plays farces at fairs and markets. I am the

Laughing Man. Plenty of people have been to see me. We are stay-
ing in Tarrinzeau Field. I have been earning an honest livelihood these
fifteen years. I am five-and-twenty. I lodge at the Tadcaster Inn. I
am called Gwynplaine. My lord, let me out. You should not take
advantage of the low estate of the unfortunate. Have compassion on a
man who has done no harm, who is without protection, and without
defense. You have before you a poor mountebank."

"I have before me," said the sheriff, "Lord Fermain Clancharlie,
Baron Clancharlie and Hunkerville, Marquis of Corleone in Sicily, and
a peer of England."

Rising, and offering his chair to Gwynplaine, the sheriff added:

"My lord, will your lordship deign to seat yourself?"

BOOK V

THE SEA AND FATE ARE MOVED BY THE SAME BREATH

CHAPTER I

THE DURABILITY OF FRAGILE THINGS

DESTINY sometimes proffers us a glass of madness to drink. A hand is thrust out of the mist, and suddenly hands us the mysterious cup in which is contained the latent intoxication.

Gwynplaine did not understand.

He looked behind him to see whom it was who had been addressed.

A sound may be too sharp to be perceptible to the ear; an emotion too acute conveys no meaning to the mind. There is a limit to comprehension as well as to hearing.

The wapentake and the justice of the quorum approached Gwynplaine, and took him by the arms. He felt himself placed in the chair which the sheriff had just vacated. He let it be done, without seeking an explanation.

When Gwynplaine was seated, the justice of the quorum and the wapentake retired a few steps, and stood upright and motionless, behind the seat.

Then the sheriff placed his bunch of roses on the stone table, put on spectacles which the secretary gave him, drew from the bundles of papers which covered the table a sheet of parchment, yellow, green, torn, and jagged in places, which seemed to have been folded in very small folds, and of which one side was covered with writing; standing under the light of the lamp, he held the sheet close to his eyes, and in his most solemn tone read as follows:

"In the name of the Father, the Son, and the Holy Ghost.

"This present day, the twenty-ninth of January, one thousand six hundred and ninetieth year of Our Lord.

"Has been wickedly deserted on the desert coast of Portland, with the intention of allowing him to perish of hunger, of cold, and of solitude, a child ten years old.

"That child was sold at the age of two years, by order of his most gracious majesty, King James the Second.

"That child is Lord Fermain Clancharlie, the only legitimate son of Lord Linnæus Clancharlie, Baron Clancharlie and Hunkerville, Marquis of Corleone in Sicily, a Peer of England, and of Ann Bradshaw, his wife, both deceased. That child is the inheritor of the estates and titles of his father. For this reason he was sold, mutilated, disfigured, and put out of the way by desire of his most gracious majesty.

"That child was brought up, and trained to be a mountebank at markets and fairs.

"He was sold at the age of two, after the death of the peer, his father, and ten pounds sterling were given to the king as his purchase-money, as well as for divers concessions, tolerations, and immunities.

"Lord Fermain Clancharlie, at the age of two years was bought by me, the undersigned, who write these lines, and mutilated and disfigured by a Fleming of Flanders, called Hardquanonne, who alone is acquainted with the secrets and modes of treatment of Doctor Conquest.

"The child was destined by us to be a laughing mask, *masca ridens.*

"With this intention Hardquanonne performed on him the operation, *Bucca fissa usque ad aures,* which stamps an everlasting laugh upon the face.

"The child, by means known only to Hardquanonne, was put to sleep and made insensible during its performance, knowing nothing of the operation which he underwent.

"He does not know that he is Lord Clancharlie.

"He answers to the name of Gwynplaine.

"This fact is the result of his youth, and the slight powers of memory he could have had when he was bought and sold, being then barely two years old.

"Hardquanonne is the only person who knows how to perform the operation *Bucca fissa*, and the said child is the only living subject upon which it has been essayed.

"The operation is so unique and singular, that though after long years this child should have come to be an old man instead of a child, and his black locks should have turned white, he would be immediately recognized by Hardquanonne.

"At the time that I am writing this, Hardquanonne, who has perfect knowledge of all the facts, and participated as principal therein, is detained in the prisons of his highness the Prince of Orange, commonly called King William III. Hardquanonne was apprehended and seized as being one of the band of Comprachicos or Cheylas. He is imprisoned in the dungeon of Chatham.

"It was in Switzerland, near the Lake of Geneva, between Lausanne and Vevey, in the very house in which his father and mother died, that the child was, in obedience with the orders of the king, sold and given up by the last servant of the deceased Lord Linnæus, which servant died soon after his master, so that this secret and delicate matter is now unknown to any one on earth, excepting Hardquanonne, who is in the dungeon of Chatham, and ourselves, now about to perish.

"We, the undersigned, brought up and kept, for eight years, for professional purposes the little lord bought by us of the king.

"To-day, flying from England to avoid Hardquanonne's ill-fortune, our fear of the penal indictments, prohibitions, and fulminations of parliament has induced us to desert, at night-fall, on the coast of Portland, the said child Gwynplaine, who is Lord Fermain Clancharlie.

"Now, we have sworn secrecy to the king, but not to God.

"To-night, at sea, overtaken by a violent tempest by the will of Providence, full of despair and distress, kneeling before Him who could save our lives, and may, perhaps, be willing to save our souls, having nothing more to hope from men, but everything to fear from God, having for only anchor and resource repentance of our bad actions, resigned to death, and content if Divine justice be satisfied, humble, penitent, and beating our breasts, we make this declaration, and confide and deliver it to the furious ocean to use as it best may according to the will of God. And may the Holy Virgin aid us, Amen. And we attach our signatures."

The sheriff interrupted, saying:

"Here are the signatures. All in different handwritings."

And he resumed:

"Doctor Gernardus Geestemunde.—Asuncion.—A cross, and at the side of it, Barbara Fermoy, from Tyrryf Isle, in the Hebrides;—Gaïz-

dorra, Captain ;—Giangirate ;—Jacques Quartourze, alias le Narbou-
nais ;—Luc-Pierre Capgaroupe, from the galleys of Mahon."

The sheriff, after a pause, resumed :

"A note written in the same hand as the text and the first signature."

And he read :

"Of the three men comprising the crew, the skipper having been
swept off by a wave, there remain but two, and we have signed, Gal-
deazun ;—Ave Maria, Thief."

The sheriff, interspersing his reading with his own observations,
continued ·

"At the bottom of the sheet is written :

"'At sea, on board of the *Matutina*, Biscay hooker, from the Gulf ·
de Pasages.'

"This sheet," added the sheriff, "is a legal document, bearing the
mark of King James the Second. On the margin of the declaration,
and in the same handwriting, there is this note :

"'The present declaration is written by us on the back of the royal
order, which was given us as our receipt when we bought the child.
Turn the leaf and the order will be seen.'"

The sheriff turned the parchment, and raised it in his right hand,
to expose it to the light.

A blank page was seen, if the word blank can be applied to a thing
so mouldy, and in the middle of the page three words were written, two
Latin words, *Jussu regis*, and a signature, *Jefferies*.

"*Jussu regis, Jefferies*," said the sheriff, passing from a grave voice
to a clear one.

Gwynplaine was as a man on whose head a tile falls from the
palace of dreams.

He began to speak, like one who speaks unconsciously :

"Gernardus, yes, the doctor. An old, sad-looking man. I was
afraid of him. Gaïzdorra, Captain, that means chief. There were
women, Asuncion, and the other. And then the Provençal. His name
was Capgaroupe. He used to drink out of a flat bottle on which there
was a name written in red."

"Behold it," said the sheriff.

He placed on the table something which the secretary had just
taken out of the bag.

It was a gourd, with handles like ears, covered with wicker. This
bottle had evidently seen service, and had sojourned in the water.
Shells and sea-weed adhered to it. It was encrusted and damascened
over with the rust of ocean. There was a ring of tar round its neck,

showing that it had been hermetically sealed. Now it was unsealed
and open. They had, however, replaced in the flask, a sort of bung
made of tarred oakum, which had been used to cork it.

"It was in this bottle," said the sheriff, "that the men about to
perish placed the declaration which I have just read. This message
addressed to justice has been faithfully delivered by the sea."

The sheriff increased the majesty of his tones, and continued :

"In the same way that Harrow Hill produces excellent wheat,
which is turned into fine flour for the royal table, so the sea renders
every service in its power to England, and when a nobleman is lost
finds, and restores him."

Then he resumed :

"On this flask, as you say, there is a name written in red."

He raised his voice, turning to the motionless prisoner :

"Your name, malefactor, is here. Such are the hidden channels by
which truth, swallowed up in the gulf of human actions, floats to the
surface."

The sheriff took the gourd, and turned to the light one of its sides,
which had, no doubt, been cleaned for the ends of justice. Between the
interstices of wicker was a narrow line of red reed, blackened here and
there by the action of water and of time.

The reed, notwithstanding some breakages, traced distinctly in the
wicker-work these twelve letters—Hardquanonne.

Then the sheriff, resuming that monotonous tone of voice which
resembles nothing else, and which may be termed a judicial accent,
turned towards the sufferer.

"Hardquanonne! when by us, the sheriff, this bottle, on which is
your name, was for the first time shown, exhibited, and presented to
you, you at once, and willingly, recognized it as having belonged to
you. Then, the parchment being read to you which was contained,
folded and enclosed within it, you would say no more; and in the hope,
doubtless, that the lost child would never be recovered, and that you
would escape punishment, you refused to answer. As the result of
your refusal, you have had applied to you the *peine forte et dure ;* and
the second reading of the said parchment, on which is written the
declaration and confession of your accomplices, was made to you—but
in vain.

"This is the fourth day, and that which is legally set apart for the
confrontation, and he who was deserted on the twenty-ninth of January, one thousand six hundred and ninety, having been brought into
your presence, your devilish hope has vanished, you have broken
silence, and recognized your victim."

The prisoner opened his eyes, lifted his head, and, with a voice strangely resonant of agony, but which had still an indescribable calm mingled with its hoarseness, pronounced in excruciating accents from under the mass of stones, words, to pronounce each of which he had to lift that which was like the slab of a tomb placed upon him. He spoke:

"I swore to keep the secret. I have kept it as long as I could. Men of dark lives are faithful, and hell has its honor. Now silence is useless. So be it! For this reason I speak. Well—yes; 'tis he! We did it between us—the king and I! The king, by his will; I, by my art!"

And looking at Gwynplaine:

"Now laugh forever!"

And he himself began to laugh.

This second laugh, wilder yet than the first, might have been taken for a sob.

The laugh ceased, and the man lay back. His eyelids closed.

The sheriff, who had allowed the prisoner to speak, resumed:

"All which is placed on record."

He gave the secretary time to write, and then said:

"Hardquanonne, by the terms of the law, after confrontation followed by identification; after the third reading of the declarations of your accomplices, since confirmed by your recognition and confession, and after your renewed avowal, you are about to be relieved from these irons, and placed at the good pleasure of her majesty to be hung as *plagiary.*"

"*Plagiary,*" said the sergeant of the coif. "That is to say, a buyer and seller of children. Law of the Visigoths, seventh book, third section, paragraph *Usurpaverit,* and Salic law, section the forty-first, paragraph the second, and law of the Frisons, section the twenty-first, *De Plagio;* and Alexander Nequam says:

"'*Qui pueros vendis, plagiarius est tibi nomen.*'"

The sheriff placed the parchment on the table, laid down his spectacles, took up the nosegay, and said:

"End of *la peine forte et dure.* Hardquanonne, thank her majesty."

By a sign, the justice of the quorum set in motion the man dressed in leather.

This man, who was the executioner's assistant, "groom of the gibbet," the old charters call him, went to the prisoner, took off the stones, one by one, from his chest, and lifted the plate of iron up, exposing the wretch's crushed sides. Then he freed his wrists and ankle-bones from the four chains that fastened him to the pillars.

The prisoner, released alike from stones and chains, lay flat on the ground, his eyes closed, his arms and legs apart, like a crucified man taken down from a cross.

"Hardquanonne," said the sheriff, "arise!"

The prisoner did not move.

The groom of the gibbet took up a hand and let it go; the hand fell back. The other hand, being raised, fell back likewise.

The groom of the gibbet seized one foot and then the other, and the heels feel back on the ground.

The fingers remained inert, and the toes motionless. The naked feet of an extended corpse seem, as it were, to bristle.

The doctor approached, and drawing from the pocket of his robe a little mirror of steel, put it to the open mouth of Hardquanonne. Then with his fingers he opened the eyelids. They did not close again. The glassy eyeballs remained fixed.

The doctor rose up and said :

" He is dead."

And he added:

" He laughed ; that killed him."

" 'Tis of little consequence," said the sheriff. " After confession, life or death is a mere formality."

Then, pointing to Hardquanonne by a gesture with the nosegay of roses, the sheriff gave the order to the wapentake :

" A corpse to be carried away to-night."

The wapentake acquiesced by a nod.

And the sheriff added :

" The cemetery of the jail is opposite."

The wapentake nodded again.

The sheriff, holding in his left hand the nosegay and in his right the white wand, placed himself opposite Gwynplaine, who was still seated, and made him a low bow ; then assuming another solemn attitude, he turned his head over his shoulder and looking Gwynplaine in the face, said :

" To you here present, we, Philip Denzill Parsons, knight, sheriff of the county of Surrey, assisted by Aubrey Dominick, Esq., our clerk and registrar, and by our usual officers, duly provided by the direct and special commands of her majesty, in virtue of our commission, and the rights and duties of our charge, and with authority from the Lord Chancellor of England, the affidavits having been drawn up and recorded, regard being had to the documents communicated by the Admiralty, after verification of attestations and signatures, after declarations read and heard, after confrontation made, all the statements and legal information having been completed, exhausted, and brought to a good and just issue, we signify and declare to you, in order that right may be done, that you are Fermain Clancharlie, Baron Clancharlie and Hunkerville, Marquis de Corleone in Sicily, and a peer of England; and God keep your lordship."

And he bowed to him.

The sergeant on the right, the doctor, the justice of the quorum, the wapentake, the secretary, all the attendants except the executioner, repeated his salutation still more respectfully, and bowed to the ground before Gwynplaine.

" Ah ! " said Gwynplaine ; " awake me ! "

And he stood up, pale as death.

" I come to awake you indeed," said a voice which had not yet been heard.

A man came out from behind the pillars. As no one had entered

the cell since the sheet of iron had given passage to the *cortege* of police, it was clear that this man had been there in the shadow before Gwynplaine had entered, that he had a regular right of attendance, and had been present by appointment and mission. The man was fat and pursy, and wore a court wig and a traveling cloak.

He was rather old than young, and very precise.

He saluted Gwynplaine with ease and respect—with the ease of a gentleman-in-waiting, and without the awkwardness of a judge.

"Yes," he said; "I have come to awaken you. For twenty-five years you have slept. You have been dreaming. It is time to awake. You believe yourself to be Gwynplaine; you are Clancharlie. You believe yourself to be one of the people; you belong to the peerage. You believe yourself to be of the lowest rank; you are of the highest. You believe yourself a player; you are a senator. You believe yourself poor; you are wealthy. You believe yourself to be of no account; you are important. Awake, my lord!"

Gwynplaine, in a low voice, in which a tremor of fear was to be distinguished, murmured:

"What does it all mean?"

"It means, my lord," said the fat man, "that I am called Barkilphedro; that I am an officer of the Admiralty; that this waif, the flask of Hardquanonne, was found on the beach, and was brought to be unsealed by me, according to the duty and prerogative of my office; that I opened it in the presence of two sworn jurors of the Jetsam Office, both members of parliament, William Blathwait, for the city of Bath, and Thomas Jervois, for Southampton; that the two jurors deciphered and attested the contents of the flask, and signed the necessary affidavit conjointly with me; that I made my report to her majesty, and by order of the queen all necessary and legal formalities were carried out with the discretion necessary in a matter so delicate; that the last form, the confrontation, has just been carried out; that you have 40,000*l.* a year; that you are a peer of the United Kingdom of Great Britain, a legislator and a judge, a supreme judge, a sovereign legislator, dressed in purple and ermine, equal to princes, like unto emperors; that you have on your brow the coronet of a peer, and that you are about to wed a duchess, the daughter of a king."

Under this transfiguration, overwhelming him like a series of thunder-bolts, Gwynplaine fainted.

CHAPTER II

THE WAIF KNOWS ITS OWN COURSE

ALL this had occurred owing to the circumstance of a soldier having found a bottle on the beach.

We will relate the facts.

In all facts there are wheels within wheels.

One day one of the four gunners composing the garrison of Calshor Castle picked up on the sand at low water a flask covered with wicker, which had been cast up by the tide. This flask, covered with mould, was corked by a tarred bung. The soldier carried the waif to the colonel of the castle, and the colonel sent it to the High Admiral of England. The Admiral meant the Admiralty; with waifs, the Admiralty meant Barkilphedro.

Barkilphedro, having uncorked and emptied the bottle, carried it to the queen. The queen immediately took the matter into consideration.

Two weighty counselors were instructed and consulted; viz., the Lord Chancellor, who is by law the guardian of the king's conscience, and the Lord Marshal, who is referee in Heraldry and in the pedigrees of the nobility. Thomas Howard, Duke of Norfolk, a Catholic peer, who is hereditary Earl Marshal of England, had sent word by his deputy

111

Earl Marshal, Henry Howard, Earl Bindon, that he would agree with
the Lord Chancellor. The Lord Chancellor was William Cowper. We
must not confound this chancellor with his namesake and contemporary
William Cowper, the anatomist and commentator on Bidloo, who published a treatise on muscles, in England, at the very time that Etienne
Abeille published a history of bones, in France. A surgeon is a very
different thing from a lord. Lord William Cowper is celebrated for
having, with reference to the affair of Talbot Yelverton, Viscount Longueville, propounded this opinion: That in the English constitution, the
restoration of a peer is more important than the restoration of a king.
The flask found at Calshor had awakened his interest at the highest
degree. The author of a maxim delights in opportunities to which it
may be applied. Here was a case of the restoration of a peer. Search
was made. Gwynplaine, by the inscription over his door, was soon
found. Neither was Hardquanonne dead. A prison rots a man, but
preserves him: if to keep is to preserve. People placed in Bastiles
were rarely removed. There is little more change in the dungeon than
in the tomb. Hardquanonne was still in the prison at Chatham. They
had only to put their hands on him. He was transferred from Chatham
to London. In the meantime, information was sought in Switzerland.
The facts were found to be correct. They obtained from the local
archives at Vevey, at Lausanne, the certificate of Lord Linnæus' marriage in exile, the certificate of his child's birth, the certificate of the
decease of the father and mother; and they had duplicates, duly authenticated, made to answer all necessary requirements.

All this was done with the most rigid secrecy, with what is called
royal promptitude, and with that mole-like silence recommended and
practiced by Bacon, and later on made law by Blackstone, for affairs
connected with the Chancellorship and the State, and in matters termed
parliamentary. The *jussu regis* and the signature *Jefferies* were authenticated. To those who have studied pathologically the cases of caprice
called "our good will and pleasure," this *jussu regis* is very simple.
Why should James II., whose credit required the concealment of such
acts, have allowed that to be written which endangered their success?
The answer is, cynicism—haughty indifference. Oh! you believe that
effrontery is confined to abandoned women? The *raison d'état* is
equally abandoned. *Et se cupit ante videri.* To commit a crime and
emblazon it,—there is the sum total of history. The king tattooes himself like the convict. Often when it would be to a man's greatest advantage to escape from the hands of the police, or the records of history, he
would seem to regret the escape, so great is the love of notoriety. Look
at my arm! Observe the design! *I* am Lacenaire! See, a temple of

love and a burning heart pierced through with an arrow! *Jussu regis.* It is I, James the Second. A man commits a bad action, and places his mark upon it. To fill up the measure of crime by effrontery, to denounce himself, to cling to his misdeeds, is the insolent bravado of the criminal. Christina seized Monaldeschi, had him confessed and assassinated, and said:

"I am the Queen of Sweden, in the palace of the King of France."

There is the tyrant who conceals himself, like Tiberius; and the tyrant who displays himself, like Philip II. One has the attributes of the scorpion, the other those rather of the leopard. James II. was of this latter variety. He had, we know, a gay and open countenance, differing so far from Philip. Philip was sullen; James jovial. Both were equally ferocious. James II. was an easy-minded tiger; like Philip II., his crimes lay light upon his conscience. He was a monster by the grace of God. Therefore he had nothing to dissimulate nor to extenuate, and his assassinations were by divine right. He, too, would not have minded leaving behind him those archives of Simancas, with all his misdeeds dated, classified, labeled, and put in order, each in its compartment, like poisons in the cabinet of a chemist. To set the sign-manual to crimes is right royal.

Every deed done is a draft drawn on the great invisible paymaster. A bill had just come due with the ominous endorsement, *Jussu regis.*

Queen Anne, in one particular unfeminine, seeing that she could keep a secret, demanded a confidential report of so grave a matter from the Lord Chancellor; one of the kind specified as "report to the royal ear." Reports of this kind have been common in all monarchies. At Vienna there was "a counselor of the ear"—an aulic dignitary. It was an ancient Carlovingian office—the *auricularius* of the old palatine deeds. He who whispers to the emperor.

William, Baron Cowper, Chancellor of England, whom the Queen believed in because he was short-sighted like herself, or even more so, had committed to writing a memorandum commencing thus:—"Two birds were subject to Solomon, a lapwing, the Hudbud, who could speak all languages, and an eagle, the Simourganka, who covered with the shadow of his wings a caravan of twenty thousand men. Thus, under another form, Providence," etc. The Lord Chancellor proved the fact that the heir to a peerage had been carried off, mutilated, and then restored. He did not blame James II., who was, after all, the Queen's father. He even went so far as to justify him. First, there are ancient monarchical maxims. *E senioratu eripimus. In roturagio cadat.* Secondly, there is a royal right of mutilation. Chamberlayne asserts the fact. *Corpora et bona nostrorum subjectorum nostra sunt,* said James I., of glorious and learned memory. The eyes of dukes of the blood royal have been plucked out for the good of the kingdom. Certain princes, too near to the throne, have been conveniently stifled between mattresses, the cause of death being given out as apoplexy. Now, to stifle is worse than to mutilate. The King of Tunis tore out the eyes of his father, Muley Assem, and his ambassadors have not been the less favorably received by the Emperor. Hence the king may order the suppression of a limb like the suppression of a state, etc. It is legal. But one law does not destroy another. "If a drowned man is cast up by the water, and is not dead, it is an act of God readjusting one of the king. If the heir be found, let the coronet be given back to him. Thus was it done for Lord Alla, King of Northumberland, who was also a mountebank. Thus should be done to Gwynplaine, who is also a king, seeing that he is a peer. The lowness of the occupation which he has been obliged to follow, under constraint of superior power, does not tarnish the blazon; as in the case of Abdolmumen, who was a king, although he had been a gardener; that of Joseph, who was a saint, although he had been a carpenter; that of Apollo, who was a god, although he had been a shepherd."

In short, the learned chancellor concluded by advising the re-instatement in all his estates and dignities, of Lord Fermain Clancharlie, miscalled Gwynplaine, on the sole condition that he should be confronted with the criminal Hardquanonne, and identified by the same. And on this point the chancellor, as constitutional keeper of the royal conscience, based the royal decision. The Lord Chancellor added in a proscript that if Hardquanonne refused to answer, he should be subjected to the *peine forte et dure,* until the period called the *frodmortell,* according to the statute of King Athelstane, which orders the confrontation to take place on the fourth day. In this there is a certain inconvenience, for if the prisoner dies on the second or third day the confrontation becomes difficult; still the law must be obeyed. The inconvenience of the law makes part and parcel of it. In the mind of the Lord Chancellor, however, the recognition of Gwynplaine by Hardquanonne was indubitable.

Anne, having been made aware of the deformity of Gwynplaine, and not wishing to wrong her sister, on whom had been bestowed the estates of Clancharlie, graciously decided that the Duchess Josiana should be espoused by the new lord,—that is to say, by Gwynplaine.

The re-instatement of Lord Fermain Clancharlie was, moreover, a very simple affair, the heir being legitimate, and in the direct line.

In cases of doubtful descent and of peerages in abeyance claimed by collaterals, the House of Lords must be consulted. This (to go no further back) was done in 1782, in the case of the barony of Sydney, claimed by Elizabeth Perry; in 1798, in that of the barony of Beaumont, claimed by Thomas Stapleton; in 1803, in that of the barony of Chandos, claimed by the Reverend Tymewell Brydges; in 1813, in that of the earldom of Banbury, claimed by General Knollys, etc., etc. But the present was no similar case. Here there was no pretense for litigation; the legitimacy was undoubted; the right clear and certain. There was no point to submit to the House, and the Queen, assisted by the Lord Chancellor, had power to recognize and admit the new peer.

Barkilphedro managed everything.

The affair, thanks to him, was kept so close, the secret was so hermetically sealed, that neither Josiana nor Lord David caught sight of the fearful abyss which was being dug under them. It was easy to deceive Josiana, intrenched as she was behind a rampart of pride. She was self-isolated. As to Lord David, they sent him to sea, off the coast of Flanders. He was going to lose his peerage, and had no suspicion of it. One circumstance is noteworthy.

It happened that at six leagues from the anchorage of the naval station commanded by Lord David, a captain called Halyburton broke through the French fleet. The Earl of Pembroke, President of the Council, proposed that this Captain Halyburton should be made vice-admiral. Anne struck out Halyburton's name, and put Lord David Dirry-Moir's in its place, that he might, when no longer a peer, have the satisfaction of being a vice-admiral.

Anne was well pleased. A hideous husband for her sister, and a fine step for Lord David. Mischief and kindness combined.

Her majesty was going to enjoy a comedy. Besides, she argued to herself that she was repairing an abuse of power committed by her august father. She was re-instating a member of the peerage. She was acting like a great queen; she was protecting innocence according to the will of God; the Providence in its holy and impenetrable ways, etc., etc. It is very sweet to do a just action which is disagreeable to those whom we do not like.

To know that the future husband of her sister was deformed, sufficed the queen. In what manner Gwynplaine was deformed, and by what kind of ugliness, Barkilphedro had not communicated to the queen, and Anne had not deigned to inquire. She was proudly and royally disdainful. Besides, what could it matter? The House of Lords could not but be grateful. The Lord Chancellor, its oracle, had approved. To restore a peer, is to restore the peerage. Royalty on this occasion had shown itself a good and scrupulous guardian of the privileges of the peerage. Whatever might be the face of the new lord, a face cannot be urged in objection to a right. Anne said all this to herself, or something like it, and went straight to her object, an object at once grand, woman-like, and regal; namely, to give herself a pleasure.

The queen was then at Windsor, a circumstance which placed a certain distance between the intrigues of the court and the public. Only such persons as were absolutely necessary to the plan were in the secret of what was taking place.

As to Barkilphedro, he was joyful, a circumstance which gave a lugubrious expression to his face.

If there be one thing in the world which can be more hideous than another, 'tis joy.

He had had the delight of being the first to taste the contents of Hardquanonne's flask. He seemed but little surprised, for astonishment is the attribute of a little mind. Besides, was it not all due to him, who had waited so long on duty at the gate of chance? Knowing how to wait, he had fairly won his reward.

This *nil admirari* was an expression of face. At heart we may admit that he was very much astonished. Any one who could have lifted the mask with which he covered his inmost heart even before God, would have discovered this: that at the very time Barkilphedro had begun to feel finally convinced that it would be impossible —even to him, the intimate and most infinitesimal enemy of Josiana— to find a vulnerable point in her lofty life. Hence an access of savage animosity lurked in his mind. He had reached the paroxysm which is called discouragement. He was all the more furious, because depairing. To gnaw one's chain!—how tragic and appropriate the expression! A villain gnawing at his own powerlessness!

Barkilphedro was perhaps just on the point of renouncing, not his desire to do evil to Josiana, but his hope of doing it; not the rage, but the effort. But how degrading to be thus baffled! To keep hate thenceforth in a case, like a dagger in a museum! How bitter the humiliation!

All at once to a certain goal—Chance, immense and universal, loves to bring such coincidences about—the flask of Hardquanonne came, driven from wave to wave, into Barkilphedro's hands. There is in the unknown an indescribable fealty which seems to be at the beck and call of evil. Barkilphedro, assisted by two chance witnesses, disinterested jurors of the Admiralty, uncorked the flask, found the parchment, unfolded, read it. What words could express his devilish delight!

It is strange to think that the sea, the wind, space, the ebb and flow of the tide, storms, calms, breezes, should have given themselves so much trouble to bestow happiness on a scoundrel. That co-operation had continued for fifteen years. Mysterious efforts! During fifteen years the ocean had never for an instant ceased from its labors. The waves transmitted from one to another the floating bottle. The shelving rocks had shunned the brittle glass; no crack had yawned in the flask; no friction had displaced the cork; the sea-weeds had not rotted the ozier; the shells had not eaten out the word "Hardquanonne;" the water had not penetrated into the waif; the mould had not rotted the parchment; the wet had not effaced the writing. What trouble the abyss must have taken! Thus that which Gernardus had flung into darkness, darkness had handed back to Barkilphedro. The message sent to God had reached the devil. Space had committed an abuse of confidence, and a lurking sarcasm which mingles with events had so arranged that it had complicated the loyal triumph of the lost child's becoming Lord Clancharlie with a venomous victory,—in doing a good action, it had mischievously placed justice at the service of iniquity. To save the victim of James II. was to give a prey to Barkilphedro. To re-instate Gwynplaine was to crush Josiana. Barkilphedro had succeeded; and it was for this that for so many years the waves, the surge, the squalls had buffeted, shaken, thrown, pushed, tormented, and respected this bubble of glass, which bore within it so many commingled fates. It was for this that there had been a cordial co-operation between the winds, the tides, and the tempests: a vast agitation of all prodigies for the pleasure of a scoundrel; the infinite co-operating with an earth-worm! Destiny is subject to such grim caprices.

Barkilphedro was struck by a flash of Titanic pride. He said to himself that it had all been done to fulfill his intention. He felt that he was the object and the instrument.

But he was wrong. Let us clear the character of chance.

Such was not the real meaning of the remarkable circumstance of which the hatred of Barkilphedro was to profit. Ocean had made itself father and mother to an orphan, had sent the hurricane against his executioners, had wrecked the vessel which had repulsed the child, had swallowed up the clasped hands of the storm-beaten sailors, refusing their supplications and accepting only their repentance; the tempest received a deposit from the hands of death. The strong vessel containing the crime was replaced by the fragile phial containing the reparation. The sea changed its character, and, like a panther turning nurse, began to rock the cradle, not of the child, but of his destiny, whilst he grew up ignorant of all that the depths of ocean were doing for him.

The waves to which this flask had been flung watching over that past which contained a future; the whirlwind breathing kindly on it; the currents directing the frail waif across the fathomless wastes of water; the caution exercised by sea-weed, the swells, the rocks; the vast froth of the abyss, taking under their protection an innocent child; the wave imperturbable as a conscience; chaos re-establishing order; the world-wide shadows ending in radiance; darkness employed to bring to light the star of truth; the exile consoled in his tomb; the heir given back to his inheritance; the crime of the king repaired; divine premeditation obeyed; the little, the weak, the deserted child with infinity for a guardian! All this Barkilphedro might have seen in the event on which he triumphed. This is what he did not see. He did not believe that it had all been done for Gwynplaine. He fancied that it had been effected for Barkilphedro, and that he was well worth the trouble. Thus it is ever with Satan.

Moreover, ere we feel astonished that a waif so fragile should have floated for fifteen years undamaged, we should seek to understand the tender care of the ocean. Fifteen years is nothing. On the 4th of October, 1867, on the coast of Morbihan, between the Isle de Groix, the extremity of the peninsula de Gavres, and the Rocher des Errants, the fishermen of Port Louis found a Roman amphora of the fourth century, covered with arabesques by the incrustations of the sea. That amphora had been floating fifteen hundred years.

Whatever appearance of indifference Barkilphedro tried to exhibit, his wonder had equaled his joy. Everything he could desire was there to his hand. All seemed ready made. The fragments of the event which was to satisfy his hate were spread out within his reach. He had nothing to do but to pick them up and fit them together—a repair which it was an amusement to execute. He was the artificer.

Gwynplaine! He knew the name. *Masca ridens.* Like every one else, he had been to see the Laughing Man. He had read the sign nailed up against the Tadcaster Inn, as one reads a play-bill that attracts a crowd. He had noted it. He remembered it directly in its most minute details; and, in any case, it was easy to compare them with the original. That notice, in the electrical summons which arose in his memory, appeared in the depths of his mind, and placed itself by the side of the parchment signed by the ship-wrecked crew, like an answer following a question, like the solution following an enigma; and the lines, "Here is to be seen Gwynplaine, deserted at the age of ten, on the 29th of January, 1690, on the coast at Portland"—suddenly appeared to his eyes in the splendor of an apocalypse. His vision was the light of *Mene, Tekel, Upharsin,* outside a booth. Here was the destruction of the edifice which made the existence of Josiana. A sudden earthquake. The lost child was found. There was a Lord Clancharlie. David Dirry-Moir was nobody. Peerage, riches, power, rank—all these things left Lord David and entered Gwynplaine. All the castles, parks, forests, town houses, palaces, domains, Josiana included, belonged to Gwynplaine. And what a climax for Josiana! What had she now before her? Illustrious and haughty, a player; beautiful, a monster. Who could have hoped for this? The truth was, that the joy of Barkilphedro had become enthusiastic. The most hateful combinations are surpassed by the infernal munificence of the unforeseen. When reality likes, it works masterpieces. Barkilphedro found that all his dreams had been nonsense; reality were better.

The change he was about to work would not have seemed less desirable had it been detrimental to him. Insects exist which are so savagely disinterested that they sting, knowing that to sting is to die. Barkilphedro was like such vermin.

But this time he had not the merit of being disinterested. Lord David Dirry-Moir owed him nothing, and Lord Fermain Clancharlie was about to owe him everything. From being a *protégé*, Barkilphedro was about to become a protector. Protector of whom? Of a peer of England. He was going to have a lord of his own, and a lord who would be his creature. Barkilphedro counted on giving him his first impressions. His peer would be the morganatic brother-in-law of the queen. His ugliness would please the queen in the same proportion as it displeased Josiana. Advancing by such favor, and assuming grave and modest airs, Barkilphedro might become a somebody. He had always been destined for the church. He had a vague longing to be a bishop.

Meanwhile he was happy.

Oh, what a great success! and what a deal of useful work had chance accomplished for him!

His vengeance—for he called it his vengeance—had been softly brought to him by the waves. He had not lain in ambush in vain.

He was the rock, Josiana was the waif, Josiana was about to be dashed against Barkilphedro, to his intense villainous ecstasy.

He was clever in the art of suggestion, which consists in making in the minds of others a little incision into which you put an idea of your own;—holding himself aloof, and without appearing to mix himself up in the matter, it was he who arranged that Josiana should go to the Green Box and see Gwynplaine. It could do no harm. The appearance of the mountebank, in his low estate, would be a good ingredient in the combination. Later on, it would season it.

He had quietly prepared everything beforehand. What he most desired was something unspeakably abrupt. The work on which he was engaged could only be expressed in these strange words: the construction of a thunder-bolt.

All preliminaries being complete, he had watched till all the necessary legal formalities had been accomplished. The secret had not oozed out, silence being an element of law.

The confrontation of Hardquanonne with Gwynplaine had taken place. Barkilphedro had been present. We have seen the result.

The same day a post-chaise belonging to the royal household was suddenly sent by her majesty to fetch Lady Josiana from London to Windsor, where the queen was at the time residing.

Josiana, for reasons of her own, would have been very glad to disobey, or at least to delay obedience, and put off her departure till next day; but court life does not permit of these objections. She was obliged to set out at once, and to leave her residence in London, Hunkerville House, for her residence at Windsor, Corleone Lodge.

The Duchess Josiana left London at the very moment that the wapentake appeared at the Tadcaster Inn to arrest Gwynplaine, and take him to the torture cell of Southwark.

When she arrived at Windsor, the Usher of the Black Rod, who guards the door of the presence chamber, informed her that her majesty was in audience with the Lord Chancellor and could not receive her until the next day; that, consequently, she was to remain at Corleone Lodge, at the orders of her majesty; and that she should receive the queen's commands direct, when her majesty awoke the next morning. Josiana entered her house feeling very spiteful, supped in a bad humor, had the spleen, dismissed every one except her page, then dismissed him, and went to bed while it was yet daylight.

When she arrived she had learnt that Lord David Dirry-Moir was expected at Windsor the next day, owing to his having, whilst at sea, received orders to return immediately and receive her majesty's commands.

CHAPTER III

AN AWAKENING

"No man could pass suddenly from Siberia into Senegal without losing consciousness."
—Humboldt.

HE swoon of a man, even of one the most firm and energetic, under the sudden shock of an unexpected stroke of good fortune, is nothing wonderful. A man is knocked down by the unforeseen blow, like an ox by the poleaxe. Francis d'Albescola, he who tore from the Turkish ports their iron chains, remained a whole day without consciousness when they made him pope. Now the stride from a cardinal to a pope is less than that from a mountebank to a peer of England.

No shock is so violent as a loss of equilibrium.

When Gwynplaine came to himself and opened his eyes, it was night. He was in an arm-chair, in the midst of a large chamber lined throughout with purple velvet, over walls, ceiling, and floor. The carpet was velvet. Standing near him, with uncovered head, was the fat man in the traveling cloak, who had emerged from behind the pillar in the cell at Southwark. Gwynplaine was alone in the chamber with him. From the chair, by extending his arms, he could reach two tables, each bearing a branch of six lighted wax candles. On one of these tables there were papers and a casket, on the other refreshments; a cold fowl, wine, and brandy, served on a silver-gilt salver.

Through the panes of a high window, reaching from the ceiling to the floor, a semicircle of pillars was to be seen, in the clear April night, encircling a court-yard with three gates, one very wide, and the other two, low. The carriage gate, of great size, was in the middle; on the right, that for equestrians, smaller; on the left, that for foot passengers, still less. These gates were formed of iron railings, with glittering

121

points. A tall piece of sculpture surmounted the central one. The
columns were probably in white marble, as well as the pavement of the
court, thus producing an effect like snow, and framed in its sheet of
flat flags was a mosaic, the pattern of which was vaguely marked in the

shadow. This mosaic, when seen by daylight, would no doubt have
disclosed to the sight, with much emblazonry and many colors, a
gigantic coat of arms, in the Florentine fashion. Zigzags of balustrades
rose and fell, indicating stairs of terraces. Over the court frowned an
immense pile of architecture, now shadowy and vague in the starlight.
Intervals of sky, full of stars, marked out clearly the outline of the

palace. An enormous roof could be seen, with the gable ends vaulted; garret windows, roofed over like visors; chimneys like towers; and entablatures covered with motionless gods and goddesses.

Beyond the colonnade there played in the shadow one of those

fairy fountains in which, as the water falls from basin to basin, it combines the beauty of rain with that of the cascade, and as if scattering the contents of a jewel-box, flings to the wind its diamonds and its pearls as though to divert the statues around. Long rows of windows ranged away, separated by panoplies in relievo, and by busts on small pedestals. On the pinnacles, trophies and morions with plumes cut in stone, alternated with statues of heathen deities.

In the chamber where Gwynplaine was, on the side opposite the window, was a fire-place as high as the ceiling, and on another, under a dais, one of those old specious feudal beds which were reached by a ladder, and where you might sleep lying across; the joint-stool of the bed was at its side; a row of arm-chairs by the walls, and a row of ordinary chairs, in front of them, completed the furniture. The ceiling was domed. A great wood fire in the French fashion blazed in the fireplace; by the richness of the flames, variegated of rose-color and green, a judge of such things would have seen that the wood was ash—a great luxury. The room was so large that the branches of candles failed to light it up. Here and there curtains over doors, falling and swaying, indicated communications with other rooms. The style of the room was altogether that of the reign of James I.,—a style square and massive, antiquated and magnificent. Like the carpet and the lining of the chamber, the dais, the baldaquin, the bed, the stool, the curtains, the mantel-piece, the coverings of the table, the sofas, the chairs, were all of purple velvet.

There was no gilding, except on the ceiling. Laid on it, at equal distance from the four angles, was a huge round shield of embossed metal, on which sparkled, in dazzling relief, various coats of arms; amongst the devices, on two blazons, side by side, were to be distinguished the cap of a baron and the coronet of a marquis; were they of brass, or of silver-gilt? You could not tell. They seemed to be of gold. And in the centre of this lordly ceiling, like a gloomy and magnificent sky, the gleaming escutcheon was as the dark splendor of a sun shining in the night.

The savage, in whom is embodied the free man, is nearly as restless in a palace as in a prison. This magnificent chamber was depressing. So much splendor produces fear. Who could be the inhabitant of this stately palace? To what colossus did all this grandeur appertain? Of what lion is this the lair? Gwynplaine, as yet but half awake, was heavy at heart.

"Where am I?" he said.

The man who was standing before him, answered:

"You are in your own house, my lord."

CHAPTER IV

IT takes time to rise to the surface.

Gwynplaine had been thrown into an abyss of stupefaction.

We do not gain our footing at once in unknown depths. There are routs of ideas, as there are routs of armies. The rally is not immediate. We feel as it were scattered; as though some strange evaporation of self were taking place. God is the arm. Chance is the sling. Man is the pebble. How are you to resist, once flung?

Gwynplaine, if we may coin the expression, ricocheted from one surprise to another. After the love letter of the duchess came the revelation in the Southwark dungeon.

In destiny, when wonders begin, prepare yourself for blow upon blow. The gloomy portals once open, prodigies pour in. A breach once made in the wall, and events rush upon us pell-mell. The marvelous never comes singly.

The marvelous is an obscurity. The shadow of this obscurity was over Gwynplaine. What was happening to him seemed unintelligible. He saw everything through the mist which a deep commotion leaves in the mind, like the dust caused by a falling ruin. The shock had been from top to bottom. Nothing was clear to him. However, light always returns by degrees. The dust settles. Moment by moment the density of astonishment decreases. Gwynplaine was like a man with his eyes open and fixed in a dream, as if trying to see what may be within it. He dispersed the mist. Then he re-shaped it. He had intermittances of wandering. He underwent that oscillation of the mind in the unforeseen, which alternately pushes us in the direction in which we understand, and then throws us back in that which is incomprehensible. Who has not at some time felt this pendulum in his brain?

125

By degrees his thoughts dilated in the darkness of the event, as the pupil of his eye had done in the underground shadows at Southwark. The difficulty was to succeed in putting a certain space between accumulated sensations. Before that combustion of hazy ideas called comprehension can take place, air must be admitted between the emotions. There, air was wanting. The event, so to speak, could not be breathed.

In entering that terrible cell at Southwark, Gwynplaine had expected the iron collar of a felon; they had placed on his head the coronet of a peer. How could this be? There had not been space of time enough between what Gwynplaine had feared and what had really occurred; it had succeeded too quickly,—his terror changing into other feelings too abruptly for comprehension. The contrasts were too tightly packed one against the other. Gwynplaine made an effort to withdraw his mind from the vise.

He was silent. This is the instinct of great stupefaction, which is more on the defensive than it is thought to be. Who says nothing is prepared for everything. A word of yours allowed to drop may be seized in some unknown system of wheels, and your utter destruction be compassed in its complex machinery.

The poor and weak live in terror of being crushed. The crowd ever expect to be trodden down. Gwynplaine had long been one of the crowd.

A singular state of human uneasiness can be expressed by the words: Let us see what will happen. Gwynplaine was in this state. You feel that you have not gained your equilibrium when an unexpected situation surges up under your feet. You watch for something which must produce a result. You are vaguely attentive. We will see what happens. What? You do not know. Whom? You watch.

The man with the paunch repeated, "You are in your own house, my lord."

Gwynplaine felt himself. In surprises, we first look to make sure that things exist; then, we feel ourselves, to make sure that we exist ourselves. It was certainly to him that the words were spoken; but he himself was somebody else. He no longer had his jacket on, or his esclavine of leather. He had a waistcoat of cloth of silver; and a satin coat, which he touched and found to be embroidered. He felt a heavy purse in his waistcoat pocket. A pair of velvet trunk hose covered his clown's tights. He wore shoes with high red heels. As they had brought him to this palace, so had they changed his dress.

The man resumed:

"Will your lordship deign to remember this: I am called Barkilphedro; I am clerk to the Admiralty. It was I who opened Hardquanonne's flask, and drew your destiny out of it. Thus, in the 'Arabian Nights,' a fisherman releases a giant from a bottle."

Gwynplaine fixed his eyes on the smiling face of the speaker.

Barkilphedro continued:

" Besides this palace, my lord, Hunkerville House, which is larger, is yours. You own Clancharlie Castle, from which you take your title, and which was a fortress in the time of Edward the Elder. You have nineteen bailiwicks belonging to you, with their villages and their inhabitants. This puts under your banner, as a landlord and a nobleman, about eighty thousand vassals and tenants. At Clancharlie you are a judge—judge of all, both of goods and of persons, and you hold your baron's court. The king has no right which you have not, except the privilege of coining money. The king, designated by the Norman law as chief signor, has justice, court, and coin. Coin is money. So that you, excepting in this last, are as much a king in your lordship as he is in his kingdom. You have the right, as a baron, to a gibbet with four pillars in England; and, as a marquis, to a scaffold with seven posts in Sicily: that of the mere lord having two pillars; that of a lord of the manor, three; and that of a duke, eight. You are styled prince in the ancient charters of Northumberland. You are related to the Viscounts Valentia in Ireland, whose name is Power, and to the Earls of Umfraville in Scotland, whose name is Angus. You are chief of a clan, like Campbell, Ardmannach, and Macallummore. You have eight barons' courts: Reculver, Baston, Hell-Kerters, Homble, Moricambe, Grundraith, Trenwardraith, and others. You have a right over the turf-cutting of Pillinmore, and over the alabaster quarries near Trent. Moreover, you own all the country of Penneth Chase; and you have a mountain with an ancient town on it. The town is called Vinecaunton; the mountain is called Moil-enlli. All which gives you an income of forty thousand pounds a year. That is to say, forty times the five-and-twenty thousand francs with which a Frenchman is satisfied."

Whilst Barkilphedro spoke, Gwynplaine, in a crescendo of stupor, remembered the past. Memory is a gulf that a word can move to its lowest depths. Gwynplaine knew all the words pronounced by Barkilphedro. They were written in the last lines of the two scrolls which lined the van in which his childhood had been passed, and, from so often letting his eyes wander over them mechanically, he knew them by heart. On reaching, a forsaken orphan, the traveling caravan at Weymouth, he had found the inventory of the inheritance which awaited him; and in the morning, when the poor little boy awoke, the first thing spelt by his careless and unconscious eyes was his own title and its possessions. It was a strange detail added to all his other surprises, that, during fifteen years, rolling from highway to highway, the clown of a traveling theatre, earning his bread day by day, picking up far-things, and living on crumbs, he should have traveled with the inventory of his fortune placarded over his misery.

Barkilphedro touched the casket on the table with his forefinger.

"My lord, this casket contains two thousand guineas which her gracious majesty the queen has sent you for your present wants."

Gwynplaine made a movement.

"That shall be for my Father Ursus," he said.

"So be it, my lord," said Barkilphedro. "Ursus, at the Tadcaster Inn. The Sergeant of the Coif, who accompanied us hither, and is about to return immediately, will carry them to him. Perhaps I may go to London myself. In that case I will take charge of it."

"I shall take them to him myself," said Gwynplaine.

Barkilphedro's smile disappeared, and he said:

"Impossible!"

There is an impressive inflection of voice which, as it were, under-lines the words. Barkilphedro's tone was thus emphasized; he paused, so as to put a full stop after the word he had just uttered. Then he continued, with the peculiar and respectful tone of a servant who feels that he is master:

"My lord, you are twenty-three miles from London, at Corleone Lodge, your court residence, contiguous to the Royal Castle of Wind-sor. You are here unknown to any one. You were brought here in a close carriage, which was awaiting you at the gate of the jail at South-wark. The servants who introduced you into this palace are ignorant who you are; but they know me, and that is sufficient. You may pos-sibly have been brought to these apartments by means of a private key which is in my possession. There are people in the house asleep, and it is not an hour to awaken them. Hence we have time for an explana-tion, which, nevertheless, will be short. I have been commissioned by her majesty——"

As he spoke, Barkilphedro began to turn over the leaves of some bundles of papers which were lying near the casket.

"My lord, here is your patent of peerage. Here is that of your Sicilian marquisate. These are the parchments and title-deeds of your eight baronies, with the seals of eleven kings, from Baldret, King of Kent, to James the Sixth of Scotland, and first of England and Scot-land united. Here are your letters of precedence. Here are your rent-rolls, and titles and descriptions of your fiefs, freeholds, dependencies, lands. and domains. That which you see above your head in the emblazonment on the ceiling are your two coronets: the circlet with pearls for the baron, and the circlet with strawberry leaves for the marquis.

"Here, in the wardrobe, is your peer's robe of red velvet, bordered

with ermine. To-day, only a few hours since, the Lord Chancellor and the Deputy Earl Marshal of England, informed of the result of your confrontation with the Comprachico Hardquanonne, have taken her majesty's commands. Her majesty has signed them, according to her royal will, which is the same as the law. All formalities have been complied with. To-morrow, and no later than to-morrow, you will take your seat in the House of Lords, where they have for some days been deliberating on a bill, presented by the Crown, having for its object the augmentation, by a hundred thousand pounds sterling yearly, of the allowance to the Duke of Cumberland, husband of the queen. You will be able to take part in the debate."

Barkilphedro paused, breathed slowly, and resumed:

"However, nothing is yet settled. A man cannot be made a peer of England without his own consent. All can be annulled and disappear, unless you acquiesce. An event nipped in the bud ere it ripens often occurs in state policy. My lord, up to this time silence has been preserved on what has occurred. The House of Lords will not be informed of the facts until to-morrow. Secrecy has been kept about the whole matter for reasons of state, which are of such importance, that the influential persons who alone are at this moment cognizant of your existence, and of your rights, will forget them immediately should reasons of state command their being forgotten. That which is in darkness may remain in darkness. It is easy to wipe you out; the more so as you have a brother, the natural son of your father and of a woman who afterwards, during the exile of your father, became mistress to King Charles II., which accounts for your brother's high position in court; for it is to this brother, bastard though he be, that your peerage would revert. Do you wish this? I cannot think so. Well, all depends on you. The queen must be obeyed. You will not quit the house till to-morrow in a royal carriage, and to go to the House of Lords. My lord, will you be a peer of England; yes or no? The queen has designs for you. She destines you for an alliance almost royal. Lord Fermain Clancharlie, this is the decisive moment. Destiny never opens one door without shutting another. After a certain step in advance, to step back is impossible. Whoso enters into transfiguration, leaves behind him evanescence. My lord, Gwynplaine is dead. Do you understand?"

Gwynplaine trembled from head to foot.

Then he recovered himself.

"Yes," he said.

Barkilphedro, smiling, bowed, placed the casket under his cloak, and left the room.

CHAPTER V

WE THINK WE REMEMBER; WE FORGET

HENCE arise those strange, visible changes which occur in the soul of man ?

Gwynplaine had been at the same moment raised to a summit and cast into an abyss.

His head swam with double giddiness. The giddiness of ascent and descent. A fatal combination.

He felt himself ascend, and felt not his fall.

It is appalling to see a new horizon.

A perspective affords suggestions,—not always good ones.

He had before him the fairy glade, a snare, perhaps, seen through opening clouds, and showing the blue depths of sky; so deep, that they are obscure.

He was on the mountain, whence he could see all the kingdoms of the earth. A mountain all the more terrible that it is a visionary one. Those who are on its apex are in a dream.

There where Satan tempted Jesus, how could a man struggle ?

Palaces, castles, power, opulence, all human happiness extending as far as eye could reach; a map of enjoyments spread out to the horizon; a sort of radiant geography of which he was the centre. A perilous mirage !

Imagine what must have been the haze of such a vision, not led up to, not attained to as by the gradual steps of a ladder, but reached without transition and without previous warning.

A man going to sleep in a mole's burrow, and awaking on the top of the Strasbourg steeple; such was the state of Gwynplaine.

Giddiness is a dangerous kind of glare, particularly that which bears you at once towards the day and towards the night, forming two whirlwinds, one opposed to the other.

He saw too much, and not enough.

He saw all, and nothing.

His state was what the author of this book has somewhere expressed as the blind man dazzled.

Gwynplaine, left by himself, began to walk with long strides. A bubbling precedes an explosion.

Notwithstanding his agitation, in this impossibility of keeping still, he meditated. His mind liquefied as it boiled. He began to recall things to his memory. It is surprising how we find that we have heard so clearly that to which we scarcely listened. The declaration of the shipwrecked men, read by the sheriff in the Southwark cell, came back to him clearly and intelligibly. He recalled every word, he saw under it his whole infancy.

Suddenly he stopped, his hands clasped behind his back, looking up to the ceiling—the sky—no matter what—whatever was above him.

"Quits!" he cried.

He felt like one whose head rises out of the water. It seemed to him that he saw everything—the past, the future, the present—in the accession of a sudden flash of light.

"Oh!" he cried, for there are cries in the depths of thought. "Oh! it was so, was it! I was a lord. All is discovered. They stole, betrayed, destroyed, abandoned, disinherited, murdered me! The corpse of my destiny floated fifteen years on the sea; all at once it touched the earth, and it started up, erect and living. I am reborn. I am born. I felt under my rags that the breast there palpitating was not that of a wretch; and when I looked on crowds of men, I felt that they were the flocks, and that I was not the dog, but the shepherd! Shepherds of the people, leaders of men, guides and masters, such were my fathers; and what they were I am! I am a gentleman, and I have a sword; I am a baron, and I have a casque; I am a marquis, and I have a plume; I am a peer, and I have a coronet. Lo! they deprived me of all this. I dwelt in light, they flung me into darkness. Those who proscribed the father, sold the son. When my father was dead, they took from beneath his head the stone of exile which he had placed for his pillow, and, tying it to my neck, they flung me into a sewer. Oh! those scoundrels who tortured my infancy! Yes, they rise and move in the depths of my memory. Yes; I see them again. I was that morsel of flesh pecked to pieces on a tomb by a flight of crows. I bled and cried under all those horrible shadows. Lo! it was there that they precipitated me, under the crush of those who come and go, under the trampling feet of men, under the undermost of the human race, lower than the serf, baser than the serving man, lower than the felon, lower than the slave, at the spot where Chaos becomes a sewer, in which I was engulfed. It is from thence that I come; it is from this that I rise; it is from this that I am risen. And here I am now. Quits!"

He sat down, he rose, clasped his head with his hands, began to pace the room again, and his tempestuous monologue continued within him.

"Where am I?—on the summit. Where is it that I have just alighted?—on the highest peak? This pinnacle, this grandeur, this dome of the world, this great power, is my home. This temple is in air. I am one of the gods. I live in inaccessible heights. This supremacy, which I looked up to from below, and from whence emanated such rays of glory that I shut my eyes; this ineffaceable peerage; this impregnable fortress of the fortunate, I enter. I am in it. I am of it. Ah, what a decisive turn of the wheel! I was below, I am on high—on high forever! Behold me a lord! I shall have a scarlet robe. I shall have an earl's coronet on my head. I shall assist at the coronation of kings. They will take the oath from my hands. I shall judge princes and ministers. I shall exist. From the depths into which I was thrown, I have rebounded to the zenith. I have palaces in town and country: houses, gardens, chases, forests, carriages, millions. I will give fêtes. I will make laws. I shall have the choice of joys and pleasures. And the vagabond Gwynplaine, who had not the right to gather a flower in the grass, may pluck the stars from heaven!"

Melancholy overshadowing of a soul's brightness! Thus it was that in Gwynplaine, who had been a hero, and perhaps had not ceased to be one, moral greatness gave way to material splendor. A lamentable transition! Virtue broken down by a troop of passing demons. A surprise made on the weak side of man's fortress. All the inferior circumstances called by men superior, ambition, the purblind desires of instinct, passions, covetousness, driven far from Gwynplaine by the wholesome restraints of misfortune, took tumultuous possession of his generous heart. And from what had this arisen? From the discovery of a parchment in a waif drifted by the sea. Conscience may be violated by a chance attack.

Gwynplaine drank in great draughts of pride, and it dulled his soul. Such is the poison of that fatal wine.

Giddiness invaded him. He more than consented to its approach. He welcomed it. This was the effect of previous and long-continued thirst. Are we an accomplice of the cup which deprives us of reason? He had always vaguely desired this. His eyes had always turned towards the great. To watch is to wish. The eaglet is not born in the eyrie for nothing.

Now, however, at moments, it seemed to him the simplest thing in the world that he should be a lord. A few hours only had passed, and yet the past of yesterday seemed so far off! Gwynplaine had fallen into the ambuscade of Better, who is the enemy of Good.

Unhappy is he of whom we say, how lucky he is!

Adversity is more easily resisted than prosperity. We rise more perfect from ill fortune than from good. There is a Charybdis in poverty, and a Scylla in riches. Those who remain erect under the thunder-bolt are prostrated by the flash. Thou who standest without shrinking on the verge of a precipice, fear lest thou be carried up on the innumerable wings of mists and dreams. The ascent which elevates will dwarf thee. An apotheosis has a sinister power of degradation.

It is not easy to understand what is good luck. Chance is nothing but a disguise. Nothing deceives so much as the face of fortune. Is she Providence? Is she Fatality?

A brightness may not be a brightness, because light is truth, and a gleam may be a deceit. You believe that it lights you; but no, it sets you on fire.

At night—a candle made of mean tallow becomes a star if placed in an opening in the darkness. The moth flies to it.

In what measure is the moth responsible?

The sight of the candle fascinates the moth as the eye of the serpent fascinates the bird.

Is it possible that the bird and the moth should resist the attraction? Is it possible that the leaf should resist the wind? Is it possible that the stone should refuse obedience to the laws of gravitation?

These are material questions, which are moral questions as well.

After he had received the letter of the duchess, Gwynplaine had recovered himself. The deep love in his nature had resisted it. But the storm having wearied itself on one side of the horizon, burst out on the other, for in destiny, as in nature, there are successive convulsions. The first shock loosens, the second uproots.

Alas! how do the oaks fall!

Thus he who, when a child of ten, stood alone on the shore of Portland, ready to give battle, who had looked steadfastly at all the combatants whom he had to encounter, the blast which bore away the vessel in which he had expected to embark, the gulf which had swallowed up the plank, the yawning abyss, of which the menace was its retrocession, the earth which refused him a shelter, the sky which refused him a star, solitude without pity, obscurity without notice, ocean, sky, all the violence of one infinite space, and all the mysterious enigmas of another; he who had neither trembled nor fainted before the mighty hostility of

the unknown; he, who still so young, had held his own with night, as
Hercules of old had held his own with death; he who in the unequal
struggle had thrown down this defiance, that he, a child, adopted a
child, that he encumbered himself with a load, when tired and ex-

hausted, thus rendering himself an easier prey to the attacks on his
weakness, and, as it were, himself unmuzzling the shadowy monsters in
ambush around him—he who, a precocious warrior, had immediately,
and from his first steps out of the cradle, struggled breast to breast
with destiny; he, whose disproportion with strife had not discouraged
from striving; he, who, perceiving in everything around him a fright-

ful occultation of the human race, had accepted that eclipse, and proudly continued his journey; he who had known how to endure cold, thirst, hunger, valiantly; he who, a pigmy in stature, had been a colossus in soul; this Gwynplaine, who had conquered the great terror of the abyss under its double form, Tempest and Misery, staggered under a breath—Vanity.

Thus, when she has exhausted distress, nakedness, storms, catastrophes, agonies on an unflinching man, Fatality begins to smile, and her victim, suddenly intoxicated, staggers.

The smile of Fatality! Can anything more terrible be imagined? It is the last resource of the pitiless trier of souls in his proof of man. The tiger, lurking in destiny, caresses man with a velvet paw. Sinister preparation, hideous gentleness in the monster!

Every self-observer has detected within himself mental weakness coincident with aggrandizement. A sudden growth disturbs the system, and produces fever.

In Gwynplaine's brain was the giddy whirlwind of a crowd of new circumstances; all the light and shade of a metamorphosis; inexpressibly strange confrontations; the shock of the past against the future. Two Gwynplaines, himself doubled; behind, an infant in rags, crawling through night—wandering, shivering, hungry, provoking laughter; in front, a brilliant nobleman—luxurious, proud, dazzling all London. He was casting off one form, and amalgamating himself with the other. He was casting the mountebank, and becoming the peer. Change of skin is sometimes change of soul. Now and then the past seemed like a dream. It was complex; bad and good. He thought of his father. It was a poignant anguish never to have known his father. He tried to picture him to himself. He thought of his brother, of whom he had just heard. Then he had a family! He, Gwynplaine! He lost himself in fantastic dreams. He saw visions of magnificence; unknown forms of solemn grandeur moved in mist before him. He heard flourishes of trumpets.

"And then," he said, "I shall be eloquent."

He pictured to himself a splendid entrance into the House of Lords. He should arrive full to the brim with new facts and ideas. What could he not tell them? What subjects he had accumulated! What an advantage to be in the midst of them, a man who had seen, touched, undergone, and suffered; who could cry aloud to them, "I have been near to everything, from which you are so far removed." He would hurl reality in the face of those patricians, crammed with illusions. They should tremble, for it would be the truth. They would applaud, for it would be grand. He would arise amongst those powerful men, more powerful than they. " I shall appear as a torch-bearer, to show them truth; and as a sword-bearer, to show them justice!" What a triumph !

And, building up these fantasies in his mind, clear and confused at the same time, he had attacks of delirium,—sinking on the first seat he came to; sometimes drowsy, sometimes starting up. He came and went, looked at the ceiling, examined the coronets, studied vaguely the hieroglyphics of the emblazonment, felt the velvet of the walls, moved the chairs, turned over the parchments, read the names, spelt out the titles, Buxton, Homble, Grundraith, Hunkerville, Clancharlie; compared the wax, the impression, felt the twist of silk appended to the royal privy seal, approached the window, listened to the splash of the fountain, contemplated the statues, counted, with the patience of a somnambulist, the columns of marble, and said:

" It is real."

Then he touched his satin clothes, and asked himself :

" Is it I ? Yes."

He was torn by an inward tempest.

In this whirlwind, did he feel faintness and fatigue ? Did he drink, eat, sleep ? If he did so, he was unconscious of the fact. In certain violent situations instinct satisfies itself, according to its requirements, unconsciously. Besides, his thoughts were less thoughts than mists. At the moment that the black flame of an irruption disgorges itself from depths full of boiling lava, has the crater any consciousness of the flocks which crop the grass at the foot of the mountain ?

The hours passed.

The dawn appeared, and brought the day. A bright ray penetrated the chamber, and at the same instant broke on the soul of Gwynplaine.

And Dea ! said the light.

BOOK VI

URSUS UNDER DIFFERENT ASPECTS

CHAPTER I

WHAT THE MISANTHROPE SAID

AFTER Ursus had seen Gwynplaine thrust within the gates of Southwark jail, he remained, haggard, in the corner from which he was watching. For a long time his ears were haunted by the grinding of the bolts and bars, which was like a howl of joy that one wretch more should be inclosed within them.

He waited. What for? He watched. What for? Such inexorable doors, once shut, do not re-open so soon. They are tongue-tied by their stagnation in darkness, and move with difficulty, especially when they have to give up a prisoner. Entrance is permitted. Exit is quite a

138

different matter. Ursus knew this. But waiting is a thing which we have not the power to give up at our own will. We wait in our own despite. What we do disengages an acquired force, which maintains its action when its object has ceased, which keeps possession of us and holds us, and obliges us for some time longer to continue that which has already lost its motive. Hence the useless watch, the inert position that we have all held at times, the loss of time which every thoughtful man gives mechanically to that which has disappeared. None escapes this law. We become stubborn in a sort of vague fury. We know not why we are in the place, but we remain there. That which we have begun actively, we continue passively, with an exhausting tenacity from which we emerge overwhelmed. Ursus, though differing from other men, was, as any other might have been, nailed to his post by that species of conscious reverie into which we are plunged by events all-important to us, and in which we are impotent. He scrutinized by turns those two black walls, now the high one, then the low; sometimes the door near which the ladder to the gibbet stood, then that surmounted by a death's head. It was as if he were caught in a vise, composed of a prison and a cemetery. This shunned and unpopular street was so deserted that he was unobserved.

At length he left the arch under which he had taken shelter, a kind of chance sentry-box, in which he had acted the watchman, and departed with slow steps. The day was declining, for his guard had been long. From time to time he turned his head and looked at the fearful wicket through which Gwynplaine had disappeared. His eyes were glassy and dull. He reached the end of the alley, entered another, then another, retracing almost unconsciously the road which he had taken some hours before. At intervals he turned, as if he could still see the door of the prison, though he was no longer in the street in which the jail was situated. Step by step he was approaching Tarrinzean Field. The lanes in the neighborhood of the fair-ground were deserted pathways between inclosed gardens. He walked along, his head bent down, by the hedges and ditches. All at once he halted, and drawing himself up, exclaimed, "So much the better!"

At the same time he struck his fist twice on his head and twice on his thigh, thus proving himself to be a sensible fellow, who saw things in their right light.

Then he began to growl inwardly, yet now and then raising his voice.

"It is all right! Oh, the scoundrel! the thief! the vagabond! the worthless fellow! the seditious scamp! It is his speeches about the government that have sent him there. He is a rebel. I was harboring a rebel. I am free of him, and lucky for me; he was compromising us. Thrust into prison! Oh, so much the better! What excellent laws! Ungrateful boy! I who brought him up! To give one's self so much trouble for this! Why should he want to speak and to reason? He mixed himself up in politics. The ass! As he handled pennies he babbled about the taxes, about the poor, about the people, about what was no business of his. He permitted himself to make reflections on pennies. He commented wickedly and maliciously on the copper money of the kingdom. He insulted the farthings of her Majesty. A farthing! Why, 'tis the same as the queen. A sacred effigy! Devil take it! a sacred effigy! Have we a queen, yes or no? Then respect her verdigris! Everything depends on the government: one ought to know that. I have experience, I have. I know something. They may say to me, But you give up politics, then? Politics, my friends, I care as much for them as for the rough hide of an ass. I received, one day, a blow from a baronet's cane. I said to myself, that is enough. I understand politics. The people have but a farthing, they give it; the queen takes it, the people thank her. Nothing can be more natural. It is for the peers to arrange the rest; their lordships, the lords spiritual and temporal. Oh! so Gwynplaine is locked up! So he is in prison. That is just as it should be. It is equitable, excellent, well-merited, and legitimate. It is his own fault. To criticise is forbidden. Are you a lord, you idiot? The constable has seized him, the justice of the quorum has carried him off, the sheriff has him in custody. At this moment he is probably being examined by a sergeant of the coif. They pluck out your crimes, those clever fellows! Imprisoned, my wag! So much the worse for him, so much the better for me! Faith, I am satisfied. I own frankly that fortune favors me. Of what folly was I guilty when I picked up that little boy and girl! We were so quiet before, Homo and I! What had they to do in my caravan, the little blackguards? Didn't I brood over them when they were young! Didn't I draw them along with my harness! Pretty foundlings, indeed; he as ugly as sin, and she blind of both eyes! Where was the use of depriving myself of everything for their sakes? The beggars grow up, forsooth, and make love to each other. The flirtations of the deformed! It was to that we had come. The toad and the mole; quite an idyl! That was what went on in my household. All which was sure to end by going before the justice. The toad talked politics! But now I am free of him. When the wapentake came I was at first a fool; one always doubts one's own good luck. I believed that I did not see what I did see; that it was impossible, that it was a nightmare, that a day-dream was playing me a trick. But no! Nothing could be truer. It is all clear. Gwyn-

plaine is really in prison. It is a stroke of Providence. Praise be to it!
He was the monster who, with the row he made, drew attention to my
establishment, and denounced my poor wolf. Be off, Gwynplaine; and,
see, I am rid of both! Two birds killed with one stone. Because Dea
will die, now that she can no longer see Gwynplaine. For she sees him,
the idiot! She will have no object in life. She will say, 'What am I
to do in the world?' Good-bye! To the devil with both of them. I
always hated the creatures! Die, Dea! Oh, I am quite comfortable!"

CHAPTER II

E returned to the Tadcaster Inn.

It struck half-past six. It was a little before twilight.

Master Nicless stood on his door-step.

He had not succeeded, since the morning, in extinguishing the terror which still showed on his scared face.

He perceived Ursus from afar.

"Well!" he cried.

"Well! what?"

"Is Gwynplaine coming back? It is full time. The public will soon be coming. Shall we have the performance of 'The Laughing Man' this evening?"

"I am the laughing man," said Ursus.

And he looked at the tavern-keeper with a loud chuckle.

Then he went up to the first floor, opened the window next to the sign of the inn, leant over towards the placard about Gwynplaine, the laughing man, and the bill of "*Chaos Vanquished;*" unnailed the one, tore down the other, put both under his arm, and descended.

Master Nicless followed him with his eyes.

"Why do you unhook that?"

Ursus burst into a second fit of laughter.

"Why do you laugh?" said the tavern-keeper.

"I am re-entering private life."

Master Nicless understood, and gave an order to his lieutenant, the boy Govicum, to announce to every one who should come that there would be no performance that evening. He took from the door the box made out of a cask, where they received the entrance money, and rolled it into a corner of the lower sitting-room.

A moment after, Ursus entered the Green Box.

142

He put the two signs away in a corner, and entered what he called the woman's wing.

Dea was asleep.

She was on her bed, dressed as usual, excepting that the body of her gown was loosened, as when she was taking her siesta.

Near her Vinos and Fibi were sitting—one on a stool, the other on the ground—musing. Notwithstanding the lateness of the hour, they had not dressed themselves in their goddesses' gauze, which was a sign of deep discouragement. They had remained in their drugget petticoats, and their dress of coarse cloth.

Ursus looked at Dea.

"She is rehearsing for a longer sleep," murmured he.

Then, addressing Fibi and Vinos:

"You both know all. The music is over. You may put your trumpets into the drawer. You did well not to equip yourselves as deities. You look ugly enough as you are, but you were quite right. Keep on your petticoats—no performance to-night, nor to-morrow, nor the day after to-morrow. No Gwynplaine. Gwynplaine is clean gone."

Then he looked at Dea again.

"What a blow to her this will be! It will be like blowing out a candle."

He inflated his cheeks.

"Puff! nothing more."

Then, with a little dry laugh:

"Losing Gwynplaine, she loses all. It would be just as if I were to lose Homo. It will be worse. She will feel more lonely than any one else could. The blind wade through more sorrow than we do."

He looked out of the window at the end of the room.

"How the days lengthen! It is not dark at seven o'clock. Nevertheless, we will light up."

He struck the steel and lighted the lamp which hung from the ceiling of the Green Box.

Then he leaned over Dea.

"She will catch cold; you have unlaced her bodice too low. There is a proverb:

'Though April skies be bright,
Keep all your wrappers tight.'"

Seeing a pin shining on the floor, he picked it up, and pinned up her sleeve. Then he paced the Green Box, gesticulating.

"I am in full possession of my faculties. I am lucid, quite lucid. I consider this occurrence quite proper, and I approve of what has

happened. When she awakes I will explain everything to her clearly.
The catastrophe will not be long in coming. No more Gwynplaine.
Good-night, Dea. How well all has been arranged! Gwynplaine in
prison, Dea in the cemetery, they will be *vis-à-vis!* A dance of death!
Two destinies going off the stage at once. Pack up the dresses. Fasten
the valise. For valise, read coffin. It was just what was best for them
both. Dea without eyes, Gwynplaine without a face. On high the
Almighty will restore sight to Dea and beauty to Gwynplaine. Death
puts things to rights. All will be well. Fibi, Vinos, hang up your
tambourines on the nail. Your talents for noise will go to rust; my
beauties, no more playing, no more trumpeting. *'Chaos Vanquished'* is
vanquished. 'The Laughing Man' is done for. 'Taratantara' is dead.
Dea sleeps on. She does well. If I were she I would never awake.
Oh! she will soon fall asleep again. A skylark like her takes very
little killing. This comes of meddling with politics. What a lesson!
Governments are rights. Gwynplaine to the sheriff. Dea to the
grave-digger. Parallel cases! Instructive symmetry! I hope the
tavern-keeper has barred the door. We are going to die to-night
quietly at home, between ourselves—not I, nor Homo, but Dea. As
for me, I shall continue to roll on in the caravan. I belong to the
meanderings of vagabond life. I shall dismiss these two women. I
shall not keep even one of them. I have a tendency to become an old
scoundrel. A maid-servant in the house of a libertine is like a loaf of
bread on the shelf. I decline the temptation. It is not becoming at my
age. *Turpe senilis amor.* I will follow my way alone with Homo.
How astonished Homo will be! Where is Gwynplaine? Where is Dea?
Old comrade, here we are once more alone together. Plague take it! I'm
delighted. Their bucolics were an incumbrance. Oh! that scamp
Gwynplaine, who is never coming back. He has left us stuck here. I
say, All right. And now 'tis Dea's turn. That won't be long. I like
things to be done with. I would not snap my fingers to stop her dying
—her dying! I tell you! See, she awakes!"

Dea opened her eyelids; many blind persons shut them when they
sleep. Her sweet unwitting face wore all its usual radiance.

"She smiles," whispered Ursus, "and I laugh. That is as it should
be."

Dea called:

"Fibi! Vinos! It must be the time for the performance. I think
I have been asleep a long time. Come and dress me."

Neither Fibi nor Vinos moved.

Meanwhile, the ineffable blind look of Dea's eyes met those of
Ursus. He started.

"Well!" he cried; "what are you about? Vinos! Fibi! Do you not hear your mistress? Are you deaf? Quick! the play is going to begin."

The two women looked at Ursus in stupefaction.

Ursus shouted:

"Do you not hear the audience coming in? Fibi, dress Dea. Vinos, take your tambourine."

Fibi was obedient. Vinos, passive. Together, they personified submission. Their master, Ursus, had always been to them an enigma. Never to be understood is a reason for being always obeyed. They simply thought he had gone mad, and did as they were told. Fibi took down the costume, and Vinos the tambourine.

Fibi began to dress Dea. Ursus let down the door-curtain of the women's room, and from behind the curtain continued:

"Look there, Gwynplaine! the court is already more than half full of people. They are in heaps in the passages. What a crowd! And you say that Fibi and Vinos look as if they did not see them. How stupid the gypsies are! What fools they are in Egypt! Don't lift the curtain from the door. Be decent. Dea is dressing."

He paused, and suddenly they heard an exclamation:

"How beautiful Dea is!"

It was the voice of Gwynplaine.

Fibi and Vinos started, and turned round. It was the voice of Gwynplaine, but in the mouth of Ursus.

Ursus, by a sign which he made through the door ajar, forbade the expression of any astonishment.

Then, again taking the voice of Gwynplaine:

"Angel!"

Then he replied in his own voice:

"Dea an angel! You are a fool, Gwynplaine. No mammifer can fly except the bats."

And he added:

"Look here, Gwynplaine! Let Homo loose; that will be more to the purpose."

And he descended the ladder of the Green Box very quickly, with the agile spring of Gwynplaine, imitating his step so that Dea could hear it.

In the court he addressed the boy, whom the occurrences of the day had made idle and inquisitive.

"Spread out both your hands," said he, in a loud voice.

And he poured a handful of pence into them.

Govicum was grateful for his munificence.

Ursus whispered in his ear:

"Boy, go into the yard; jump, dance, knock, bawl, whistle, coo, neigh, applaud, stamp your feet, burst out laughing, break something."

Master Nicless, saddened and humiliated at seeing the folks who had come to see "The Laughing Man" turned back and crowding towards other caravans, had shut the door of the inn. He had even given up the idea of selling any beer or spirits that evening, that he might have to answer no awkward questions; and, quite overcome by the sudden close of the performance, was looking, with his candle in his hand, into the court from the balcony above.

Ursus, taking the precaution of putting his voice between parentheses fashioned by adjusting the palms of his hands to his mouth, cried out to him:

"Sir! do as your boy is doing; yelp, bark, howl."

He re-ascended the steps of the Green Box, and said to the wolf:

"*Talk* as much as you can."

Then, raising his voice:

"What a crowd there is! We shall have a crammed performance."

In the meantime Vinos played the tambourine. Ursus went on:

"Dea is dressed. Now we can begin. I am sorry they have admitted so many spectators. How thickly packed they are! Look, Gwynplaine, what a mad mob it is. I will bet that to-day we shall take more money than we have ever done yet. Come, gypsies, play up, both of you. Come here. Fibi, take your clarion. Good. Vinos, drum on your tambourine. Fling it up and catch it again. Fibi, put yourself into the attitude of Fame. Young ladies, you have too much on. Take off those jackets. Replace stuff by gauze. The public like to see the female form exposed. Let the moralists thunder. A little indecency. Devil take it! What of that? Look voluptuous, and rush into wild melodies. Snort, blow, whistle, flourish, play the tambourine. What a number of people, my poor Gwynplaine!"

He interrupted himself.

"Gwynplaine, help me. Let down the platform." He spread out his pocket-handkerchief. "But first let me roar in my rag," and he blew his nose violently, as a ventriloquist ought. Having returned his handkerchief to his pocket, he drew the pegs out of the pulleys, which creaked as usual as the platform was let down.

"Gwynplaine, do not draw the curtain until the performance begins. We are not alone. You two come on in front. Music, ladies! tum, tum, tum. A pretty audience we have! the dregs of the people. Good heavens!"

The two gypsies, stupidly obedient, placed themselves in their usual corners of the platform. Then Ursus became wonderful. It was no longer a man, but a crowd. Obliged to make abundance out of emptiness, he called to aid his prodigious powers of ventriloquism. The whole orchestra of human and animal voices which was within him, he called into tumult at once.

He was legion. Any one with his eyes closed would have imagined that he was in a public place on some day of rejoicing, or in some sudden popular riot. A whirlwind of clamor proceeded from Ursus; he sang, he shouted, he talked, he coughed, he spat, he sneezed, took snuff, talked and responded, put questions and gave answers, all at once. The half-uttered syllables ran one into another. In the court, untenanted by a single spectator, were heard men, women, and children. It was a clear confusion of tumult. Strange laughter wound, vapor-like, through the noise, the chirping of birds, the swearing of cats, the wailings of children at the breast. The indistinct tones of drunken men were to be heard, and the growls of dogs under the feet of people who stamped on them. The cries came from far and near, from top to bottom, from the upper boxes to the pit. The whole was an uproar, the detail was a cry. Ursus clapped his hands, stamped his feet, threw his voice to the end of the court, and then made it come from underground. It was both stormy and familiar. It passed from a murmur to a noise, from a noise to a tumult, from a tumult to a tempest. He was himself, any, every, one else. Alone, and polyglot. As there are optical illusions, there are also auricular illusions. That which Proteus did to sight, Ursus did to hearing. Nothing could be more marvelous than his fac-simile to multitude. From time to time he opened the door of the women's apartment and looked at Dea. Dea was listening.

On his part the boy exerted himself to the utmost. Vinos and Fibi trumpeted conscientiously, and took turns with the tambourine. Master Nicless, the only spectator, quietly made himself the same explanation as they did, that Ursus was gone mad, which was, for that matter, but another sad item added to his misery. The good tavern-keeper growled out, what insanity! And he was serious, as a man might well be who has the fear of the law before him.

Govicum, delighted at being able to help in making a noise, exerted himself almost as much as Ursus. It amused him, and, moreover, it earned him pence.

Homo was pensive.

In the midst of the tumult Ursus now and then uttered such words as these:

"Just as usual, Gwynplaine. There is a cabal against us. Our rivals are undermining our success. Tumult is the seasoning of tri-

umph. Besides, there are too many people. They are uncomfortable.
The angles of their neighbors' elbows do not dispose them to good-
nature. I hope the benches will not give way. We shall be the victims of an incensed population. Oh! if our friend Tom-Jim-Jack were
only here! but he never comes now. Look at those heads rising one
above another. Those who are forced to stand don't look very well
pleased, though the great Galen pronounced it to be strengthening. We
will shorten the entertainment; as only '*Chaos Vanquished*' was announced in the playbill, we will not play '*Ursus Rursus.*' There will be
something gained in that. What an uproar! O blind turbulence of the
masses. They will do us some damage. However, they can't go on
like this. We should not be able to play. No one can catch a word of
the piece. I am going to address them. Gwynplaine, draw the curtain
a little aside.—Gentlemen——"

Here Ursus addressed himself with a shrill and feeble voice:

" Down with that old fool!"

Then he answered in his own voice:

" It seems that the mob insult me. Cicero is right; *plebs, fex urbis.*
Never mind, we will admonish the mob, though I shall have a great deal
of trouble to make myself heard. I will speak, notwithstanding. Man,
do your duty. Gwynplaine, look at that scold grinding her teeth down
there."

Ursus made a pause, in which he placed a gnashing of his teeth.
Homo, provoked, added a second, and Govicum a third.

Ursus went on:

" The women are worse than the men. The moment is unpropi-
tious, but it doesn't matter! Let us try the power of a speech; an eloquent speech is never out of place. Listen, Gwynplaine, to my attractive
exordium. Ladies and gentlemen, I am a bear. I take off my head to
address you. I humbly appeal to you for silence."

Ursus, lending a cry to the crowd, said:

" Grumphll!"

Then he continued:

" I respect my audience. Grumphll is an epiphonema as good as
any other welcome. You growlers. That you are all of the dregs of
the people, I do not doubt. That in no way diminishes my esteem for
you. A well-considered esteem. I have a profound respect for the bul-
lies who honor me with their custom. There are deformed folks amongst
you. They give me no offense. The lame and the humpbacked are
works of nature. The camel is gibbous. The bison's back is humped.
The badger's left legs are shorter than the right. That fact is decided
by Aristotle, in his treatise on the walking of animals. There are

those amongst you who have but two shirts, one on his back and the other at the pawnbroker's. I know that to be true. Albuquerque pawned his moustache, and St. Denis his glory. The Jews advanced money on the glory. Great examples. To have debts is to have something. I revere your beggardom.

Ursus cut short his speech; interrupting it in a deep bass voice by the shout:

• "Triple ass!"

And he answered in his politest accent:

"I admit it. I am a learned man. I do my best to apologize for it. I scientifically despise science. Ignorance is a reality on which we feed; science a reality on which we starve. In general one is obliged to choose between two things. To be learned and grow thin, or to browse and be an Ass. O gentlemen! browse! Science is not worth a mouthful of anything nice. I had rather eat a sirloin of beef than know what they call the psoas muscle. I have but one merit. A dry eye. Such as you see me, I have never wept. It must be owned that I have never been satisfied—never satisfied—not even with myself. I despise myself; but I submit this to the members of the opposition here present, —if Ursus is only a learned man, Gwynplaine is an artist."

He groaned again:

"Grumphll!"

And resumed:

"Grumphll again! it is an objection. All the same, I pass it over. Near Gwynplaine, gentlemen and ladies, is another artist, a valued and distinguished personage who accompanies us. His lordship Homo, formerly a wild dog, now a civilized wolf, and a faithful subject of her Majesty's. Homo is a mine of deep and superior talent. Be attentive and watch. You are going to see Homo play as well as Gwynplaine, and you must do honor to art. That is an attribute of great nations. Are you men of the woods? I admit the fact. In that case, *silvæ sint consule dignæ.* Two artists are well worth one consul. All right! Some one has flung a cabbage stalk at me, but did not hit me. That will not stop my speaking; on the contrary, a danger evaded makes folks garrulous, *Garrula pericula,* says Juvenal. My hearers! there are amongst you drunken men and drunken women. Very well. The men are unwholesome. The women are hideous. You have all sorts of excellent reasons for stowing yourselves away here on the benches of the pothouse. Want of work, idleness, the spare time between two robberies, porter, ale, stout, malt, brandy, gin, and the attraction of one sex for the other. What could be better? A wit prone to irony would find this a fair field. But I abstain. 'Tis luxury; so be it; but even an orgy should be kept within bounds. You are gay, but noisy. You imitate successfully the cries of beasts; but what would you say if, when you were making love to a lady, I passed my time in barking at you? It would disturb you, and so it disturbs us. I order you to hold your tongues. Art is as respectable as debauch. I speak to you civilly."

He apostrophized himself:

" May the fever strangle you, with your eyebrows like the beard of rye."

And he replied:

"Honorable gentlemen, let the rye alone. It is impious to insult the vegetables, by likening them either to human creatures or animals. Besides, the fever does not strangle. 'Tis a false metaphor. For pity's sake, keep silence. Allow me to tell you that you are slightly wanting in the repose which characterizes the true English gentleman. I see that some amongst you who have shoes out of which their toes are peeping, take advantage of the circumstance to rest their feet on the shoulders of those who are in front of them, causing the ladies to re- mark that the soles of shoes divide always at the part at which is the head of the metatarsal bones. Show more of your hands, and less of your feet. I perceive scamps who plunge their ingenious fists into the pockets of their foolish neighbors. Dear pickpockets, have a little modesty. Fight those next to you if you like; do not plunder them. You will vex them less by blackening an eye, than by lightening their purses of a penny. Break their noses if you like. The shop-keeper thinks more of his money than of his beauty. Barring this, accept my sympathies, for I am not pedantic enough to blame thieves. Evil exists. Every one endures it, every one inflicts it. No one is exempt from the vermin of his sins. That's what I keep saying. Have we not all our itch? I, myself, have made mistakes. *Plaudite, cives.*"

Ursus uttered a long groan, which he overpowered by these con- cluding words:

" My lords and gentlemen, I see that my address has unluckily dis- pleased you. I take leave of your hisses for a moment. I shall put on my head, and the performance is going to begin."

He dropped his oratorical tone, and resumed his usual voice.

"Close the curtain. Let me breathe. I have spoken like honey. I have spoken well. My words were like velvet; but they were useless. I called them my lords and gentlemen. What do you think of all this scum, Gwynplaine? How well may we estimate the ills which England has suffered for the last forty years through the ill-temper of these irritable and malicious spirits. The ancient Britons were warlike, these are melancholy and learned. They glory in despising the laws and

contemning royal authority. I have done all that human eloquence
can do. I have been prodigal of metonymics, as gracious as the bloom-
ing cheek of youth. Were they softened by them? I doubt it. What
can affect a people who eat so extraordinarily, who stupefy themselves

by tobacco so completely that their literary men often write their works
with a pipe in their mouths? Never mind. Let us begin the play."
    The rings of the curtain were heard being drawn over the rod.
The tambourines of the gypsies were still. Ursus took down his instrument, executed his prelude, and said, in a low tone:
    " Alas! Gwynplaine, how mysterious it is."

Then he flung himself down with the wolf.

When he had taken down his instrument, he had also taken from the nail a rough wig which he had, and which he had thrown on the stage in a corner within his reach. The performance of " *Chaos Vanquished* " took place as usual, minus only the effect of the blue light, and the brilliancy of the fairies. The wolf played his best. At the proper moment Dea made her appearance, and, in her voice so tremulous and heavenly, invoked Gwynplaine. She extended her arms, feeling for that head.

Ursus rushed at the wig, ruffled it, put it on, advanced softly, and holding his breath, his head bristled thus under the hand of Dea.

Then calling all his art to his aid, and copying Gwynplaine's voice, he sang with ineffable love the response of the monster to the call of the spirit. The imitation was so perfect that again the gypsies looked for Gwynplaine, frightened at hearing without seeing him.

Govicum, filled with astonishment, stamped, applauded, clapped his hands, producing an Olympian tumult, and himself laughed as if he had been a chorus of gods. This boy, it must be confessed, developed a rare talent for acting an audience.

Fibi and Vinos, being automatons of which Ursus pulled the strings, rattled their instruments, composed of copper and ass's skin, the usual sign of the performance being over and of the departure of the people.

Ursus arose, covered with perspiration. He said, in a low voice, to Homo :

"You see it was necessary to gain time. I think we have succeeded. I have not acquitted myself badly. I, who have as much reason as any one to go distracted. Gwynplaine may perhaps return to-morrow. It is useless to kill Dea directly. I can explain matters to you."

He took off his wig and wiped his forehead.

"I am a ventriloquist of genius," murmured he. "What talent I displayed! I have equaled Brabant, the engastrimythist of Francis I., of France. Dea is convinced that Gwynplaine is here."

"Ursus," said Dea, "where is Gwynplaine ? "

Ursus started and turned round. Dea was still standing at the back of the stage, alone under the lamp which hung from the ceiling. She was pale, with the pallor of a ghost.

She added, with an ineffable expression of despair :

"I know. He has left us. He is gone. I always knew that he had wings."

And raising her sightless eyes on high, she added :

"When shall I follow ? "

CHAPTER III

URSUS was stunned.

He had not sustained the illusion.

Was it the fault of ventriloquism? Certainly not. He had succeeded in deceiving Fibi and Vinos, who had eyes, although he had not deceived Dea, who was blind. It was because Fibi and Vinos saw with their eyes, while Dea saw with her heart. He could not utter a word. He thought to himself, *Bos in lingua.* The troubled man has an ox on his tongue.

In his complex emotions, humiliation was the first which dawned on him. Ursus, driven out of his last resource, pondered.

" I lavish my onomatopies in vain."

Then, like every dreamer, he reviled himself.

" What a frightful failure! I wore myself out in a pure loss of imitative harmony. But what is to be done next ? "

He looked at Dea. She was silent, and grew paler every moment, as she stood perfectly motionless. Her sightless eyes remained fixed in depths of thought.

Fortunately, something happened. Ursus saw Master Nicless in the yard, with a candle in his hand, beckoning to him.

Master Nicless had not assisted at the end of the phantom comedy played by Ursus. Some one had happened to knock at the door of the inn. Master Nicless had gone to open it. There had been two knocks, and twice Master Nicless had disappeared. Ursus, absorbed by his hundred-voiced monologue, had not observed his absence.

On the mute call of Master Nicless, Ursus descended.

He appoached the tavern-keeper. Ursus put his finger on his lips. Master Nicless put his finger on his lips.

The two looked at each other thus.

Each seemed to say to the other, "We will talk, but we will hold our tongues."

The tavern-keeper silently opened the door of the lower room of the tavern. Master Nicless entered. Ursus entered. There was no one there except these two. On the side looking on the street, both doors and window-shutters were closed.

The tavern-keeper pushed the door behind him, and shut it in the face of the inquisitive Govicum.

Master Nicless placed the candle on the table.

A low, whispering dialogue began.

"Master Ursus?"

"Master Nicless?"

"I understand at last."

"Nonsense!"

"You wished the poor blind girl to think that all was going on as usual."

"There is no law against my being a ventriloquist."

"You are a clever fellow."

"No."

"It is wonderful how you manage all that you wish to do."

"I tell you, it is not."

"Now, I have something to tell you."

"Is it about politics?"

"I don't know."

"Because in that case I could not listen to you."

"Look here; whilst you were playing actors and audience by yourself, some one knocked at the door of the tavern."

"Some one knocked at the door?"

"Yes."

"I don't like that."

"Nor I, either."

"And then?"

"And then I opened it."

"Who was it that knocked?"

"Some one who spoke to me."

"What did he say?"

"I listened to him."

"What did you answer?"

"Nothing. I came back to see you play."

"And——?"

"Some one knocked a second time."

"Who—the same person?"

"No, another."

"Some one else to speak to you ?"

"Some one who said nothing."

"I like that better."

"I do not."

"Explain yourself, Master Nicless."

"Guess who called the first time."

"I have no leisure to be an Œdipus."

"It was the proprietor of the circus."

"Over the way ?"

"Over the way."

"Whence comes all that fearful music.　Well ?"

"Well, Master Ursus, he makes you a proposal."

"A proposal ?"

"A proposal."

"Why ?"

"Because——"

"You have an advantage over me, Master Nicless; just now you solved my enigma, and now I cannot understand yours."

"The proprietor of the circus commissioned me to tell you that he had seen the *cortége* of police pass this morning, and that he, the proprietor of the circus, wishing to prove that he is your friend, offers to buy of you, for fifty pounds, ready money, your caravan, the green box, your two horses, your trumpets, with the women that blow them, your play, with the blind girl who sings in it, your wolf, and yourself."

Ursus smiled a haughty smile.

"Inn-keeper, tell the proprietor of the circus that Gwynplaine is coming back."

The inn-keeper took something from a chair in the darkness, and turning towards Ursus with both arms raised, dangled from one hand a cloak, and from the other a leather collar, a felt hat, and a jacket.

And Master Nicless said:

"The man who knocked the second time was connected with the police; he came in and left without saying a word, and brought these things."

Ursus recognized the collar, the jacket, the hat, and the cloak of Gwynplaine.

CHAPTER IV

MŒNIBUS SURDIS CAMPANA MUTA

RSUS smoothed the felt of the hat, touched the cloth of the cloak, the serge of the coat, the leather of the collar, and no longer able to doubt whose garments they were, with a gesture at once brief and imperative, and without saying a word, pointed to the door of the inn.

Master Nicless opened it.

Ursus rushed out of the tavern.

Master Nicless looked after him, and saw Ursus run as fast as his old legs would allow, in the direction taken that morning by the wapentake who carried off Gwynplaine.

A quarter of an hour afterwards, Ursus, out of breath, reached the little street in which stood the back wicket of the Southwark jail, which he had already watched so many hours. This alley was lonely enough at all hours, but if dreary during the day, it was portentous in the night. No one ventured through it after a certain hour. It seemed as though people feared that the walls should close in, and that if the prison or the cemetery took a fancy to embrace, they should be crushed in their clasp. Such are the effects of darkness. The pollard willows of the

156

ruelle Vauvert in Paris was thus ill-famed. It was said that during the night the stumps of those trees changed into great hands, and caught hold of the passers-by.

By instinct the Southwark folks shunned, as we have already men-

tioned, this alley between a prison and a church-yard. Formerly it had been barricaded during the night by an iron chain. Very uselessly; because the strongest chain which guarded the street was the terror it inspired.

Ursus entered it resolutely

What intention possessed him ! None.

He came into the alley to seek intelligence.

Was he going to knock at the gate of the jail? Certainly not. Such an expedient, at once fearful and vain, had no place in his brain. To attempt to introduce himself to demand an explanation. What folly! Prisons do not open to those who wish to enter, any more than to those who desire to get out. Their hinges never turn except by law. Ursus knew this. Why, then, had he come there? To see. To see what? Nothing. Who can tell? Even to be opposite the gate through which Gwynplaine had disappeared, was something.

Sometimes the blackest and most rugged of walls whispers, and some light escapes through a cranny. A vague glimmering is now and then to be perceived through solid and sombre piles of building. Even to examine the envelope of a fact may be to some purpose. The instinct of us all is to leave between the fact which interests us and ourselves but the thinnest possible cover. Therefore it was that Ursus returned to the alley in which the lower entrance to the prison was situated.

Just as he entered it he heard one stroke of the clock, then a second.

"Hold," thought he; "can it be midnight already?"

Mechanically he set himself to count.

"Three, four, five."

He mused.

"At what long intervals this clock strikes!—how slowly! Six; seven!"

Then he remarked:

"What a melancholy sound! Eight, nine! Ah! nothing can be more natural; it's dull work for a clock to live in a prison. Ten! Besides, there is the cemetery. This clock sounds the hour to the living, and eternity to the dead. Eleven! Alas! to strike the hour to him who is not free, is also to chronicle an eternity! Twelve!"

He paused.

"Yes, it is midnight."

The clock struck a thirteenth stroke.

Ursus shuddered.

"Thirteen!"

Then followed a fourteenth; then a fifteenth.

"What can this mean?"

The strokes continued at long intervals. Ursus listened.

"It is not the striking of a clock; it is the bell Muta. No wonder I said, How long it takes to strike midnight. This clock does not strike; it tolls. What fearful thing is about to take place?"

Formerly all prisons, and all monasteries, had a bell called Muta, reserved for melancholy occasions. La Muta (the mute) was a bell which struck very low, as if doing its best not to be heard.

Ursus had reached the corner which he had found so convenient for his watch, and whence he had been able, during a great part of the day, to keep his eye on the prison.

The strokes followed each other at lugubrious intervals.

A knell makes an ugly punctuation in space. It breaks the preoccupation of the mind into funereal paragraphs. A knell, like a man's death-rattle, notifies an agony. If in the houses about the neigborhood where a knell is tolled there are reveries straying in doubt, its sound cuts them into rigid fragments. A vague reverie is a sort of refuge. Some indefinable diffuseness in anguish allows now and then a ray of hope to pierce through it. A knell is precise and desolating. It concentrates this diffusion of thought, and precipitates the vapors in which anxiety seeks to remain in suspense. A knell speaks to each one in the sense of his own grief or of his own fear. Tragic bell! it concerns you. It is a warning to you. There is nothing so dreary as a monologue on which its cadence falls. The even returns of sound seem to show a purpose. What is it that this hammer, the bell, forges on the anvil of thought?

Ursus counted, vaguely and without motive, the tolling of the knell. Feeling that his thoughts were sliding from him, he made an effort not to let them slip into conjecture. Conjecture is an inclined plane, on which we slip too far to be to our own advantage. Still, what was the meaning of the bell?

He looked through the darkness in the direction in which he knew the gate of the prison to be.

Suddenly, in that very spot which looked like a dark hole, a redness showed. The redness grew larger, and became a light.

There was no uncertainty about it. It soon took a form and angles. The gate of the jail had just turned on its hinges. The glow painted the arch and the jambs of the door. It was a yawning rather than an opening. A prison does not open; it yawns—perhaps from ennui. Through the gate passed a man with a torch in his hand.

The bell rang on. Ursus felt his attention fascinated by two objects. He watched,—his ear the knell, his eye the torch. Behind the first man the gate, which had been ajar, enlarged the opening suddenly, and allowed egress to two other men; then to a fourth. This fourth was the wapentake, clearly visible in the light of the torch. In his grasp was his iron staff.

Following the wapentake, there filed and opened out below the gateway in order, two by two, with the rigidity of a series of walking posts, ranks of silent men.

This nocturnal procession stepped through the wicket in file, like a procession of penitents, without any solution of continuity, with a funereal care to make no noise, gravely—almost gently; a serpent issues from its hole with similar precautions.

The torch threw out their profiles and attitudes into relief. Fierce looks, sullen attitudes.

Ursus recognized the faces of the police who had that morning carried off Gwynplaine.

There was no doubt about it. They were the same. They were re-appearing.

Of course, Gwynplaine would also re-appear. They had led him to that place. They would bring him back.

It was all quite clear.

Ursus strained his eyes to the utmost. Would they set Gwynplaine at liberty?

The files of police flowed from the low arch very slowly, and, as it were, drop by drop. The toll of the bell was uninterrupted, and seemed to mark their steps. On leaving the prison, the procession turned their backs on Ursus, went to the right, into the bend of the street opposite to that in which he was posted.

A second torch shone under the gateway, announcing the end of the procession.

Ursus was now about to see what they were bringing with them. The prisoner. The man.

Ursus was soon, he thought, to see Gwynplaine.

That which they carried appeared.

It was a bier.

Four men carried a bier, covered with black cloth.

Behind them came a man, with a shovel on his shoulder.

A third lighted torch, held by a man reading a book, probably the chaplain, closed the procession.

The bier followed the ranks of the police, who had turned to the right.

Just at that moment the head of the procession stopped.

Ursus heard the grating of a key.

Opposite the prison, in the low wall which ran along the other side of the street, another opening was illuminated by a torch passing beneath it.

This gate, over which a death's head was placed, was that of the cemetery.

HARDQUANONNE'S BURIAL.

The wapentake passed through it, then the men, then the second torch. The procession decreased therein, like a reptile entering his retreat.

The files of police penetrated into that other darkness which was beyond the gate; then the bier; then the man with the spade; then the chaplain with his torch and his book, and the gate closed.

There was nothing left but a haze of light above the wall.

A muttering was heard. Then some dull sounds. Doubtless the chaplain and the grave-digger. The one throwing on the coffin some verses of Scripture, the other some clods of earth.

The muttering ceased; the heavy sounds ceased. A movement was made. The torches shone. The wapentake re-appeared, holding high his weapon, under the re-opened gate of the cemetery; then the chaplain with his book, and the grave-digger with his spade. The *cortège* re-appeared without the coffin.

The files of men crossed over in the same order, with the same taciturnity, and in the opposite direction. The gate of the cemetery closed. That of the prison opened. Its sepulchral architecture stood out against the light. The obscurity of the passage became vaguely visible. The solid and deep night of the jail was revealed to sight; then the whole vision disappeared in the depths of shadow.

The knell ceased. All was locked in silence. A sinister incarceration of shadows.

A vanished vision; nothing more.

A passage of spectres, which had disappeared.

The logical arrangement of surmises builds up something which at least resembles evidence. To the arrest of Gwynplaine, to the secret mode of his capture, to the return of his garments by the police officer, to the death bell of the prison to which he had been conducted, was now added, or rather adjusted,—portentous circumstance—a coffin carried to the grave.

"He is dead!" cried Ursus.

He sank down upon a stone.

"Dead! They have killed him! Gwynplaine! My child! My son!"

And he burst into passionate sobs.

CHAPTER V

RSUS, alas! had boasted that he had never wept. His reservoir of tears was full. Such plenitude as is accumulated drop on drop, sorrow on sorrow, through a long existence, is not to be poured out in a moment. Ursus wept long.

The first tear is a letting out of waters. He wept for Gwynplaine, for Dea, for himself, Ursus, for Homo. He wept like a child. He wept like an old man. He wept for everything at which he had ever laughed. He paid off arrears. Man is never nonsuited when he pleads his right to tears.

The corpse they had just buried was Hardquanonne's; but Ursus could not know that.

The hours crept on.

Day began to break. The pale clothing of the morning was spread out, dimly creased with shadow, over the bowling-green. The dawn lighted up the front of the Tadcaster Inn. Master Nicless had not gone to bed, because sometimes the same occurrence produces sleeplessness in many.

Troubles radiate in every direction. Throw a stone in the water, and count the splashes.

Master Nicless felt himself impeached. It is very disagreeable that such things should happen in one's house. Master Nicless, uneasy, and foreseeing misfortunes, meditated. He regretted having received such people into his house. Had he but known that they would end by getting him into mischief! But the question was how to get rid of them? He had given Ursus a lease. What a blessing if he could free himself from it. How should he set to work to drive them out?

Suddenly the door of the inn resounded with one of those tumult-

164

uous knocks which in England announces "Somebody." The gamut of knocking corresponds with the ladder of hierarchy.

It was not quite the knock of a lord; but it was the knock of a justice.

The trembling inn-keeper half opened his window. There was, indeed, the magistrate. Master Nicless perceived at the door a body of police, from the head of which two men detached themselves, one of whom was the justice of the quorum.

Master Nicless had seen the justice of the quorum that morning, and recognized him.

He did not know the other, who was a fat gentleman, with a waxen-colored face, a fashionable wig, and a traveling cloak.

Nicless was much afraid of the first of these persons, the justice of the quorum. Had he been of the court, he would have feared the other most, because it was Barkilphedro.

One of the subordinates knocked at the door again, violently.

The inn-keeper, with great drops of perspiration on his brow, from anxiety, opened it.

The justice of the quorum, in the tone of a man who is employed in matters of police, and who is well acquainted with various shades of vagrancy, raised his voice, and asked, severely, for—

" Master Ursus ! "

The host, cap in hand, replied :

" Your honor : he lives here."

" I know it," said the justice.

" No doubt, your honor."

" Tell him to come down."

" Your honor, he is not here."

" Where is he ? "

" I do not know."

" How is that ? "

" He has not come in."

" Then he must have gone out very early ? "

" No; but he went out very late."

" What vagabonds ! " replied the justice.

" Your honor," said Master Nicless, softly, " here he comes."

Ursus, indeed, had just come in sight, round a turn of the wall. He was returning to the inn. He had passed nearly the whole night between the jail, where at midday he had seen Gwynplaine, and the cemetery, where at midnight he had heard the grave filled up. He was pallid with two pallors—that of sorrow and of twilight.

Dawn, which is light in a chrysalis state, leaves even those forms which are in movement, in the uncertainty of night. Ursus, wan and indistinct, walked slowly, like a man in a dream.

In the wild distraction produced by agony of mind, he had left the inn with his head bare. He had not even found out that he had no hat on. His spare, gray locks fluttered in the wind. His open eyes appeared sightless. Often when awake we are asleep, and as often when asleep we are awake.

Ursus looked like a lunatic.

" Master Ursus," cried the inn-keeper, " come; their honors desire to speak to you."

Master Nicless, in his endeavor to soften matters down, let slip, although he would gladly have omitted, this plural, their honors—respectful to the group, but mortifying perhaps, to the chief, confounded therein, to some degree, with his subordinates.

Ursus started like a man falling off a bed, on which he was sound asleep.

"What is the matter?" said he.

He saw the police, and at the head of the police the justice.

A fresh and rude shock.

But a short time ago, the wapentake, now the justice of the quorum. He seemed to have been cast from one to the other, as ships by some reefs of which we have read in old stories.

The justice of the quorum made him a sign to enter the tavern.

Ursus obeyed.

Govicum, who had just got up, and who was sweeping the room, stopped his work, got into a corner behind the tables, put down his broom, and held his breath. He plunged his fingers into his hair, and scratched his head, a symptom which indicated attention to what was about to occur.

The justice of the quorum sat down on a form, before a table. Barkilphedro took a chair. Ursus and Master Nicless remained standing. The police officers, left outside, grouped themselves in front of the closed door.

The justice of the quorum fixed his eye, full of the law, upon Ursus. He said:

"You have a wolf."

Ursus answered:

"Not exactly."

"You have a wolf," continued the justice, emphasizing "wolf" with a decided accent.

Ursus answered:

"You see——"

And he was silent.

"A misdemeanor!" replied the justice.

Ursus hazarded an excuse:

"He is my servant."

The justice placed his hand flat on the table, with his fingers spread out, which is a very fine gesture of authority.

"Merry-andrew! to-morrow by this hour, you and your wolf must have left England. If not, the wolf will be seized, carried to the register office, and killed."

Ursus thought, "More murder!" but he breathed not a syllable, and was satisfied with trembling in every limb.

"You hear?" said the justice.

Ursus nodded.

The justice persisted:

"Killed."

There was silence.

"Strangled, or drowned."

The justice of the quorum watched Ursus.

"And yourself in prison."

Ursus murmured:

"Your worship!"

"Be off before to-morrow morning; if not, such is the order."

"Your worship!"

"What?"

"Must we leave England, he and I?"

"Yes."

"To-day?"

"To-day."

"What is to done?"

Master Nicless was happy. The magistrate, whom he had feared, had come to his aid. The police had acted as auxiliary to him, Nicless. They had delivered him from "such people." The means he had sought were brought to him. Ursus, whom he wanted to get rid of, was being driven away by the police, a superior authority. Nothing to object to. He was delighted. He interrupted:

"Your honor, that man——"

He pointed to Ursus with his finger.

"That man wants to know how he is to leave England to-day. Nothing can be easier. There are night and day at anchor on the Thames, both on this and on the other side of London Bridge, vessels that sail to the continent. They go from England to Denmark, to Holland, to Spain; not to France, on account of the war, but everywhere else. To-night several ships will sail, about one o'clock in the morning, which is the hour of high tide, and, amongst others, the *Vograat* of Rotterdam."

The justice of the quorum made a movement of his shoulder towards Ursus.

"Be it so. Leave by the first ship—by the *Vograat.*"

"Your worship," said Ursus.

"Well?"

" Your worship, if I had, as formerly, only my little box on wheels, it might be done. A boat would contain that, but——"

" But what ? "

" But now I have got the Green Box, which is a great caravan drawn by two horses, and however wide the ship might be, we could not get it into her."

" What is that to me?" said the justice. " The wolf will be killed."

Ursus shuddered, as if he were grasped by a hand of ice.

" Monsters !" he thought. " Murdering people is their way of settling matters."

The inn-keeper smiled, and addressed Ursus :

" Master Ursus, you can sell the Green Box."

Ursus looked at Nicless.

" Master Ursus, you have the offer."

" From whom ? "

" An offer for the caravan, an offer for the two horses, an offer for the two gypsy-women, an offer——"

" From whom ? " repeated Ursus.

" From the proprietor of the neighboring circus."

Ursus remembered it.

" It is true."

Master Nicless turned to the justice of the quorum.

" Your honor, the bargain can be completed to-day. The proprietor of the circus close by wishes to buy the caravan and the horses."

" The proprietor of the circus is right," said the justice ; " because he will soon require them. A caravan and horses will be useful to him. He, too, will depart to-day. The reverend gentlemen of the parish of Southwark have complained of the indecent riot in Tarrinzeau Field. The sheriff has taken his measures. To-night there will not be a single juggler's booth in the place. There must be an end of all these scandals. The honorable gentleman who deigns to be here present——"

The justice of the quorum interrupted his speech to salute Barkilphedro, who returned the bow.

" The honorable gentleman who deigns to be present, has just arrived from Windsor. He brings orders. Her Majesty has said, 'It must be swept away.'"

Ursus, during his long meditation all night, had not failed to put himself some questions. After all, he had only seen a bier. Could he be sure that it contained Gwynplaine? Other people might have died besides Gwynplaine. A coffin does not announce the name of the corpse, as it passes by. A funeral had followed the arrest of Gwynplaine. That proved nothing. *Post hoc, non propter hoc, etc.* Ursus had begun to doubt.

Hope burns and glimmers over misery like naphtha over water. Its hovering flame ever floats over human sorrow. Ursus had come to this conclusion, "It is probable that it was Gwynplaine whom they buried, but it is not certain. Who knows?—perhaps Gwynplaine is still alive."

Ursus bowed to the justice.

"Honorable judge, I will go away, we will go away, all will go away, by the *Vograat*, of Rotterdam, to-day. I will sell the Green Box, the horses, the trumpets, the gypsies. But I have a comrade, whom I cannot leave behind—Gwynplaine."

"Gwynplaine is dead," said a voice.

Ursus felt a cold sensation, such as is produced by a reptile crawling over the skin. It was Barkilphedro who had just spoken.

The last gleam was extinguished. No more doubt now. Gwynplaine was dead. A person in authority must know. This one looked ill-favored enough to do so.

Ursus bowed to him.

Master Nicless was a good-hearted man enough, but a dreadful coward. Once terrified, he became a brute. The greatest cruelty is that inspired by fear.

He growled out:

"This simplifies matters."

And he indulged, standing behind Ursus, in rubbing his hands, a peculiarity of the selfish, signifying, "I am well out of it," and suggestive of Pontius Pilate washing his hands.

Ursus, overwhelmed, bent down his head.

The sentence on Gwynplaine had been executed: Death. His sentence was pronounced: Exile. Nothing remained but to obey. He felt as in a dream.

Some one touched his arm. It was the other person, who was with the justice of the quorum. Ursus shuddered.

The voice which had said, "Gwynplaine is dead," whispered in his ear:

"Here are ten guineas, sent you by one who wishes you well."

And Barkilphedro placed a little purse on a table before Ursus. We must not forget the casket that Barkilphedro had taken with him.

Ten guineas out of two thousand! It was all that Barkilphedro could make up his mind to part with. In all conscience it was enough. If he had given more, he would have lost. He had taken the trouble of finding out a lord; and having sunk the shaft, it was but fair that the first proceeds of the mine should belong to him. Those who see meanness in the act are right, but they would be wrong to feel astonished. Barkilphedro loved money, especially money which was stolen. An

envious man is an avaricious one. Barkilphedro was not without his faults. The commission of crimes does not preclude the possession of vices. Tigers have their lice.

Besides, he belonged to the school of Bacon.

Barkilphedro turned towards the justice of the quorum, and said to him:

"Sir, be so good as to conclude this matter. I am in haste. A carriage and horses belonging to her Majesty await me. I must go full gallop to Windsor, for I must be there within two hours' time. I have intelligence to give and orders to take."

The justice of the quorum arose.

He went to the door, which was only latched, opened it, and, looking silently towards the police, beckoned to them authoritatively. They entered with that silence which heralds severity of action.

Master Nicless—satisfied with the rapid *dénouement* which cut short his difficulties—charmed to be out of the entangled skein, was afraid, when he saw the muster of officers, that they were going to apprehend Ursus in his house. Two arrests—one after the other—made in his house, first that of Gwynplaine, then that of Ursus, might be injurious to the inn. Customers dislike police raids.

Here, then, was a time for a respectful appeal, suppliant and generous. Master Nicless turned toward the justice of the quorum a smiling face, in which confidence was tempered by respect.

"Your honor, I venture to observe to your honor, that these honorable gentlemen, the police officers, might be dispensed with now that the wolf is about to be carried away from England, and that this man, Ursus, makes no resistance; and since your honor's orders are being punctually carried out, your honor will consider that the respectable business of the police, so necessary to the good of the kingdom, does great harm to an establishment, and that my house is innocent. The merry-andrews of the Green Box having been swept away, as her Majesty says, there is no longer any criminal here, as I do not suppose that the blind girl and the two women are criminals; therefore, I implore your honor to deign to shorten your august visit, and to dismiss these worthy gentlemen who have just entered, because there is nothing for them to do in my house; and, if your honor will permit me to prove the justice of my speech under the form of a humble question, I will prove the inutility of these revered gentlemen's presence by asking your honor, if the man, Ursus, obeys orders, and departs, who there can be to arrest here?"

"Yourself," said the justice.

A man does not argue with a sword which runs him through and through. Master Nicless subsided—he cared not on what, on a table, on a form, on anything that happened to be there—prostrate.

The justice raised his voice, so that if there were people outside, they might hear.

"Master Nicless Plumptree, keeper of this tavern, this is the last point to be settled. This mountebank and the wolf are vagabonds.

They are driven away. But the person most in fault is yourself. It is in your house, and with your consent, that the law has been violated ; and you, a man licensed, invested with a public responsibility, have established the scandal here. Master Nicless, your license is taken away ; you must pay the penalty, and go to prison."

The policemen surrounded the inn-keeper.

The justice continued, pointing out Govicum :

" Arrest that boy as an accomplice."

The hand of an officer fell upon the collar of Govicum, who looked at him inquisitively. The boy was not much alarmed, scarcely understanding the occurrence ; having already observed many things out of the way, he wondered if this were the end of the comedy.

The justice of the quorum forced his hat down on his head, crossed his hands on his stomach, which is the height of majesty, and added :

" It is decided, Master Nicless ; you are to be taken to prison, and put into jail, you and the boy ; and this house, the Tadcaster Inn, is to remain shut up, condemned and closed. For the sake of example. Upon which, you will follow us."

BOOK VII

THE TITANESS

CHAPTER I

THE AWAKENING

AND Dea!

It seemed to Gwynplaine, as he watched the break of day at Corleone Lodge, while the things we have related were occurring at the Tadcaster Inn, that the call came from without—but it came from within.

Who has not heard the deep clamors of the soul?

Moreover, the morning was dawning.

Aurora is a voice.

Of what use is the sun, if not to re-awaken that dark sleeper—the conscience?

Light and virtue are akin.

Whether the god be called Christ or Love, there is at times an hour when he is forgotten, even by the best. All of us, even the saints, require a voice to remind us, and the dawn speaks to us, like a sublime monitor. Conscience calls out before duty, as the cock crows before the dawn of day.

That chaos, the human heart, hears the *Fiat Lux!*

Gwynplaine—we will continue thus to call him; Clancharlie is a lord, Gwynplaine is a man—Gwynplaine felt as if brought back to life. It was time that the artery was bound up.

174

For awhile his virtue had spread its wings and flown away.

"And Dea!" he said.

Then he felt through his veins a generous transfusion. Something healthy and tumultuous rushed upon him. The violent irruption of good thoughts is like the return home of a man who has not his key, and who forces his own lock honestly. It is an escalade; but an escalade of good. It is a burglary; but a burglary of evil.

"Dea! Dea! Dea!" repeated he.

He strove to assure himself of his heart's strength. And he put the question with a loud voice—"Where are you?"

He almost wondered that no one answered him.

Then again, gazing on the walls and the ceiling, with wandering thoughts, through which reason returned.

"Where are you? Where am I?"

And in the chamber which was his cage, he began to walk again, to and fro, like a wild beast in captivity.

"Where am I? At Windsor; and you? in Southwark. Alas! this is the first time that there has been distance between us. Who has dug this gulf? I here, thou there. Oh! it cannot be; it shall not be! What is this that they have done to me?"

He stopped.

"Who talked to me of the queen? What do I know of such things? *I* changed! Why? Because I am a lord. Do you know what has happened, Dea? You are a lady. What has come to pass is astounding. My business now is to get back into my right road. Who is it who led me astray? There is a man who spoke to me mysteriously. I remember the words which he addressed to me: 'My lord, when one door opens another is shut. That which you have left behind is no longer yours.' In other words, you are a coward. That man, the miserable wretch! said that to me before I was well awake. He took advantage of my first moment of astonishment. I was as it were a prey to him. Where is he that I may insult him! He spoke to me with the evil smile of a demon. But see, I am myself again. That is well. They deceive themselves if they think that they can do what they like with Lord Clancharlie, a peer of England. Yes, with a peeress, who is Dea! Conditions! Shall I accept them! The queen. What is the queen to me, I never saw her. I am not a lord to be made a slave. I enter my position unfettered. Did they think they had unchained me for nothing? They have unmuzzled me. That is all. Dea! Ursus! we are together. That which you were, I was. That which I am, you are. Come. No. I will go to you directly—directly. I have already waited too long. What can they think, not seeing me return! That money! When I think I sent them that money! It was myself that they wanted. I remember the man said that I could not leave this place. We shall see that. Come! a carriage, a carriage! put to the horses. I am going to look for them. Where are the servants? I ought to have servants here since I am lord. I am master here. This is my house. I will twist off the bolts, I will break the locks, I will kick down the doors, I will run my sword through the body of any one who bars my passage. I should like to see who shall stop me. I have a wife, and she is Dea. I have a father, who is Ursus. My house is a palace, and I give it to Ursus. My name is a diadem, and I give it to Dea. Quick, directly, Dea, I am coming—yes, you may be sure that I shall soon stride across the intervening space!"

And raising the first piece of tapestry he came to, he rushed from the chamber impetuously.

He found himself in a corridor.

He went straight forward.

A second corridor opened out before him.

All the doors were open.

He walked on at random, from chamber to chamber, from passage to passage, seeking an exit.

CHAPTER II

N palaces after the Italian fashion, and Corleone Lodge was one, there were very few doors, but abundance of tapestry screens and curtained doorways.

In every palace of that date there was a wonderful labyrinth of chambers and corridors, where luxury ran riot; gilding, marble, carved wainscoting, Eastern silks; nooks and corners, some secret and dark as night, others light and pleasant as the day. There were attics, richly and brightly furnished; burnished recesses, shining with Dutch tiles and Portuguese azulejos. The tops of the high windows were converted into small rooms and glass attics, forming pretty habitable lanterns. The thickness of the walls was such that there were rooms within them. Here and there were closets, nominally wardrobes. They were called "The Little Rooms." It was within them that evil deeds were hatched.

When a Duke of Guise had to be killed, the pretty Présidente of Sylvecane abducted, or the cries of little girls brought thither by Lebel, smothered, such places were convenient for the purpose. They were labyrinthine chambers, impracticable to a stranger; scenes of abductions; unknown depths, receptacles of mysterious disappearances. In those elegant caverns princes and lords stored their plunder. In such a place the Count de Charolais hid Madame Courchamp, the wife of the Clerk of the Privy Council; Monsieur de Monthulé, the daughter of Haudry, the farmer of la Croix Saint Lenfroy; the Prince de Conti, the two beautiful baker women of l'Ile Adam; the Duke of Buckingham, poor Pennywell, etc. The deeds done there were such as were designated by the Roman law as committed *vi, clam, et precario*—by force, in secret, and for a short time. Once in, an occupant remained there till the master of the house decreed his or her release. They were gilded

177

oubliettes, savoring both of the cloister and the harem. Their staircases twisted, turned, ascended, and descended. A zig-zag of rooms, one running into another, led back to the starting point. A gallery terminated in a oratory. A confessional was grafted on to an alcove. Perhaps the architects of " the little rooms," building for royalty and aristocracy, took as models the ramifications of coral beds, and the openings in a sponge. The branches became a labyrinth. Pictures turning on false panels were exits and entrances. They were full of stage contrivances, and no wonder—considering the dramas that were played there! The floors of these hives reached from the cellars to the attics. Quaint madrepore inlaying every palace, from Versailles downwards, like cells of pigmies in dwelling-places of Titans. Passages, niches, alcoves, and secret recesses. All sorts of holes and corners, in which was stored away the meanness of the great.

These winding and narrow passages recalled games, blindfolded eyes, hands feeling in the dark, suppressed laughter, blind man's buff, hide and seek, while, at the same time, they suggested memories of the Atrides, of the Plantagenets, of the Medicis, of the brutal knights of Eltz, of Rizzio, of Monaldeschi; of naked swords, pursuing the fugitive flying from room to room.

The ancients, too, had mysterious retreats of the same kind, in which luxury was adapted to enormities. The pattern has been preserved underground in some sepulchres in Egypt, notably in the tomb of King Psammetichus, discovered by Passalacqua. The ancient poets have recorded the horrors of these suspicious buildings. *Error circumflexus. Locus implicitus gyris.*

Gwynplaine was in " the little rooms " of Corleone Lodge. He was burning to be off, to get outside, to see Dea again. The maze of passages and alcoves, with secret and bewildering doors, checked and retarded his progress. He strove to run, he was obliged to wander. He thought that he had but one door to thrust open, while he had a skein of doors to unravel. To one room succeeded another. Then a crossway, with rooms on every side.

Not a living creature was to be seen. He listened. Not a sound.

At times he thought that he must be returning towards his starting-point. Then, that he saw some one approaching. It was no one. It was only the reflection of himself in a mirror, dressed as a nobleman. *That* he?—Impossible! Then he recognized himself, but not at once.

He explored every passage that he came to.

He examined the quaint arrangements of the rambling building,
and their yet quainter fittings. Here, a cabinet, painted and carved in
a sentimental, but vicious style; there, an equivocal-looking chapel,
studded with enamels and mother-of-pearl, with miniatures on ivory
wrought out in relief, like those on old-fashioned snuff-boxes; there,

one of those pretty Florentine retreats, adapted to the hypochondriasis
of women, and even then called *boudoirs*. Everywhere—on the ceilings,
on the walls, and on the very floors—were representations, in velvet or
metal, of birds, of trees; of luxuriant vegetation, picked out in reliefs
of lace-work; tables covered with jet carvings, representing warriors,
queens, and tritons armed with the scaly terminations of a hydra. Cut

crystals combining prismatic effects with those of reflection. Mirrors repeated the light of precious stones, and sparkles glittered in the darkest corners. It was impossible to guess whether those many-sided, shining surfaces, where emerald green mingled with the golden hues of the rising sun, where floated a glimmer of ever-varying colors, like those on a pigeon's neck, were miniature mirrors, or enormous beryls. Everywhere was magnificence, at once refined and stupendous; if it was not the most diminutive of palaces, it was the most gigantic of jewel-cases. A house for Mab, or a jewel for Geo.

Gwynplaine sought an exit. He could not find one. Impossible to make out his way. There is nothing so confusing as wealth seen for the first time. Moreover, this was a labyrinth. At each step he was stopped by some magnificent object which appeared to retard his exit, and to be unwilling to let him pass. He was encompassed by a net of wonders. He felt himself bound and held back.

What a horrible palace! he thought

Restless, he wandered through the maze, asking himself what it all meant—whether he was in prison? chafing, thirsting for the fresh air. He repeated Dea! Dea! as if that word was the thread of the labyrinth, and must be held unbroken, to guide him out of it.

Now and then he shouted:

"Ho! Any one there?"

No one answered.

The rooms never came to an end. All was deserted, silent, splendid, sinister. It realized the fables of enchanted castles. Hidden pipes of hot air maintained a summer temperature in the building. It was as if some magician had caught up the month of June, and imprisoned it in a labyrinth. There were pleasant odors now and then, and he crossed currents of perfume, as though passing by invisible flowers. It was warm. Carpets everywhere. One might have walked about there, unclothed.

Gwynplaine looked out of the windows. The view from each one was different. From one he beheld gardens, sparkling with the freshness of a spring morning; from another, a plot decked with statues; from a third a patio in the Spanish style, a little square, flagged, mouldy, and cold. At times he saw a river—it was the Thames; sometimes a great tower—it was Windsor.

It was still so early that there were no signs of life without.

He stood still and listened.

"Oh! I will get out of this place," said he. "I will return to Dea! They shall not keep me here by force. Woe to him who bars my exit. What is that great tower yonder? If there was a giant, a hell-hound,

a minotaur, to keep the gates of this enchanted palace, I would anni-
hilate him. If an army, I would exterminate it. Dea! Dea!"

Suddenly he heard a gentle noise, very faint. It was like dropping
water. He was in a dark, narrow passage, closed, some few paces
farther on, by a curtain. He advanced to the curtain, pushed it aside,
entered. He leaped before he looked.

CHAPTER III

N octagon room, with a vaulted ceiling, without windows, but lighted by a skylight; walls, ceiling, and floors faced with peach-colored marble; a black marble canopy, like a pall, with twisted columns in the solid but pleasing Elizabethan style, over-shadowing a vase-like bath of the same black marble—this was what he saw before him. In the centre of the bath arose a slender jet of tepid and perfumed water, which, softly and slowly, was filling the tank. The bath was black to augment fairness into brilliancy.

It was the water which he had heard. A waste-pipe, placed at a certain height in the bath, prevented it from overflowing. Vapor was rising from the water; but not sufficiently to cause it to hang in drops on the marble. The slender jet of water was like a supple wand of steel, bending at the slightest current of air. There was no furniture, except a chair-bed with pillows, long enough for a woman to lie on at full length, and yet have room for a dog at her feet. The French, indeed, borrow their word *canapé* from *can-al-pie*. This sofa was of Spanish manufacture. In it silver took the place of wood-work. The cushions and coverings were of rich white silk.

On the other side of the bath, by the wall, was a lofty dressing-table of solid silver, furnished with every requisite for the table, having in its centre, and in imitation of a window, eight small Venetian mirrors, set in a silver frame. In a panel on the wall was a square opening, like a little window, which was closed by a door of solid silver. This door was fitted with hinges, like a shutter. On the shutter there glistened a chased and gilt royal crown. Over it, and affixed to the wall, was a bell, silver-gilt, if not of pure gold.

Opposite the entrance of the chamber, in which Gwynplaine stood

182

THE DUCHESS JOSIANA.

■

as if transfixed, there was an opening in the marble wall, extending to the ceiling, and closed by a high and broad curtain of silver tissue.

This curtain, of fairy-like tenuity, was transparent, and did not interrupt the view. Through the centre of this web, where one might expect a spider, Gwynplaine saw a more formidable object—a naked woman.

Yet not quite naked; for she was covered—covered from head to foot. Her dress was a long chemise; so long that it floated over her feet, like the dresses of angels in holy pictures; but so fine that it seemed liquid. More treacherous and more perilous was this covering than naked beauty could have been. History has registered the procession of princesses and of great ladies between files of monks; under pretext of naked feet and of humility, the Duchess de Montpensier showed herself to all Paris in a lace shift, a wax taper in her hand as a corrective.

The silver tissue, transparent as glass and fastened only at the ceiling, could be lifted aside. It separated the marble chamber, which was a bath-room, from the adjoining apartment, which was a bed-chamber. This tiny dormitory was as a grotto of mirrors. Venetian glasses, close together, mounted with gold mouldings, reflected on every side the bed in the centre of the room. On the bed, which, like the toilette-table, was of silver, lay the woman; she was asleep.

She was sleeping with her head thrown back, one foot peeping from its covering, like the Succuba, above whose heads dreams flap their wings.

Her lace pillow had fallen on the floor. Between her nakedness and the eye of the spectator were two obstacles—her chemise and the curtain of silver gauze; two transparencies. The room, rather an alcove than a chamber, was lighted with some reserve by the reflection from the bath-room. Perhaps the light was more modest than the woman.

The bed had neither columns, nor dais, nor top; so that the woman, when she opened her eyes, could see herself reflected a thousand times in the mirrors above her head.

The crumpled clothes bore evidence of troubled sleep. The beauty of the folds was proof of the quality of the material.

It was a period when a queen, thinking that she should be damned, pictured hell to herself as a bed with coarse sheets.

This fashion of sleeping partly undressed came from Italy, and was derived from the Romans. " *Sub clara nuda lacerna*," says Horace.

A dressing-gown, of curious silk, was thrown over the foot of the couch. It was apparently Chinese; for a great golden lizard was partly visible in between the folds.

Beyond the couch, and probably masking a door, was a large mirror, on which were painted peacocks and swans.

Shadow seemed to lose its nature in this apartment, and glistened. The spaces between the mirrors and the gold work were lined with that sparkling material called at Venice thread of glass—*i. e.*, spun glass.

At the head of the couch stood a reading-desk, on a movable pivot, with candles, and a book lying open, bearing this title, in large red letters: "*Alcoranus Mahumedis.*"

Gwynplaine saw none of these details. He had eyes only for the woman.

He was at once stupefied and filled with tumultuous emotions, states apparently incompatible, yet sometimes co-existent.

He recognized her.

Her eyes were closed, but her face was turned towards him. It was the duchess.

She, the mysterious being in whom all the splendors of the unknown were united; she who had occasioned him so many unavowable dreams; she who had written him so strange a letter! The only woman in the world of whom he could say, "She has seen me, and she desires me!"

He had dismissed the dreams from his mind; he had burned the letter. He had, as far as lay in his power, banished the remembrance of her from his thoughts and dreams. He no longer thought of her. He had forgotten her. . . . He saw her again! . . . .

Again he saw her, and saw her terrible in power. A woman naked is a woman armed.

His breath came in short catches. He felt as if he were in a storm-driven cloud. He looked. This woman before him! Was it possible? At the theatre, a duchess; here, a nereid, a nymph, a fairy. Always an apparition.

He tried to fly, but felt the futility of the attempt. His eyes were riveted on the vision, as though he were bound.

Was she a woman? Was she a maiden? Both. Messalina was, perhaps, present, though invisible, and smiled, while Diana kept watch.

Over all her beauty was the radiance of inaccessibility. No purity could compare with her chaste and haughty form. Certain snows, which have never been touched, give an idea of it—such as the sacred whiteness of the Jungfrau. That which was represented by that unconscious brow; by that rich, disheveled hair; by the drooping lids; by those blue veins, dimly visible; by the sculptured roundness of her bosom, her hips, and her knees, indicated by delicate pink undulations seen through the folds of her drapery, was the divinity of a queenly sleep. Immodesty was merged in splendor. She was as calm in her nakedness, as if she had the right to a godlike effrontery. She felt the security of an Olympian, who knew that she was daughter of the depths, and might say to the ocean, "Father!" And she exposed herself, unattainable and proud, to everything that should pass—to looks, to desires, to ravings, to dreams; as proud in her languor, on her boudoir couch, as Venus in the immensity of the sea-foam.

She had slept all night, and was prolonging her sleep into the daylight; her boldness, begun in shadow, continued in light.

Gwynplaine shuddered.

He admired her with an unhealthy and absorbing admiration, which ended in fear.

Misfortunes never come singly. Gwynplaine thought he had drained to the dregs the cup of his ill-luck. Now it was refilled. Who was it who was hurling all those unremitting thunder-bolts on his devoted head, and who had now thrown against him, as he stood trembling there, a sleeping goddess? What! was the dangerous and desirable object of his dream lurking all the while behind these successive glimpses of heaven? Did these favors of the mysterious tempter tend to inspire him with vague aspirations and confused ideas, and overwhelm him with an intoxicating series of realities proceeding from apparent impossibilities? Wherefore did all the shadows conspire against him, a wretched man; and what would become of him, with all those evil smiles of fortune beaming on him? Was his temptation pre-arranged? This woman, how and why was she there? No explanation! Why him? Why her? Was he made a peer of England expressly for this duchess? Who had brought them together? Who was the dupe? Who the victim? Whose simplicity was being abused? Was it God who was being deceived? All these undefined thoughts passed confusedly, like a flight of dark shadows, through his brain. That magical and malevolent abode, that strange and prison-like palace, was it also in the plot? Gwynplaine suffered a partial unconsciousness. Suppressed emotions threatened to strangle him. He was weighed down by an overwhelming force. His will became powerless. How could he resist? He was incoherent and entranced.

This time he felt he was becoming irremediably insane. His dark, headlong fall over the precipice of stupefaction continued.

But the woman slept on.

What aggravated the storm within him was, that he saw not the princess, not the duchess, not the lady; but the woman.

Deviations from right exist in man, in a latent state. There is an invisible tracing of vice, ready prepared in our organizations. Even when we are innocent, and apparently pure, it exists within us. To be stainless, is not to be faultless. Love is a law. Desire is a snare. There is a great difference between getting drunk once and habitual drunkenness. To desire a woman, is the former; to desire women, the latter.

Gwynplaine, losing all self-command, trembled.

What could he do against such a temptation? Here were no skillful effects of dress, no silken folds, no complex and coquettish adornments, no affected exaggeration of concealment or of exhibition, no cloud. It was nakedness in fearful simplicity—a sort of mysterious summons— the shameless audacity of Eden. The whole of the dark side of human nature was there. Eve worse than Satan; the human and the super- human commingled. A perplexing ecstasy, winding up in a brutal triumph of instinct over duty. The sovereign contour of beauty is imperious. When it leaves the ideal and condescends to be real, its proximity is fatal to man.

Now and then the duchess moved softly on the bed, with the vague movement of a cloud in the heavens, changing as a vapor changes its form. She undulated, composing and discomposing the charming curves of her body. Woman is as supple as water; and, like water, this one had an indescribable appearance of its being impossible to grasp her.

Absurd as it may appear, though he saw her present in the flesh before him, yet she seemed a chimera; and, palpable as she was, she seemed to him afar off. Scared and livid, he gazed on. He listened for her breathing, and fancied he heard only a phantom's respiration. He was attracted, though against his will. How arm himself against her— or against himself?

He had been prepared for everything except this danger. A savage door-keeper, a raging monster of a jailer—such were his expected an- tagonists. He looked for Cerberus, he saw Hebe.

A sleeping woman! What an opponent!

He closed his eyes. Too bright a dawn blinds the eyes. But through his closed eyelids there penetrated at once the woman's form— not so distinct, but beautiful as ever.

Fly! Easier said than done. He had already tried and failed. He was rooted to the ground, as if in dream. When we try to draw back, temptation clogs our feet, and glues them to the earth. We can still advance; but to retire is impossible. The invisible arms of sin rise from below and drag us down.

There is a common-place idea, accepted by every one, that feelings become blunted by experience. Nothing can be more untrue. You might as well say that by dropping nitric acid slowly on a sore it would heal and become sound, and that torture dulled the sufferings of Damiens. The truth is, that each fresh application intensifies the pain.

From one surprise after another, Gwynplaine had become desperate. That cup, his reason, under this new stupor, was overflowing. He felt within him a terrible awakening. Compass he no longer possessed. One idea only was before him—the woman. An indescribable happiness appeared, which threatened to overwhelm him. He could no longer decide for himself. There was an irresistible current and a reef. The reef was not a rock, but a siren. A magnet at the bottom of the abyss. He wished to tear himself away from this magnet—but how was he to carry out his wish? He had ceased to feel any basis of support. Who can foresee the fluctuations of the human mind! A man may be wrecked, as is a ship. Conscience is an anchor. It is a terrible thing, but, like the anchor, conscience may be carried away.

He had not even the chance of being repulsed on account of his terrible disfigurement. The woman had written to say that she loved him.

In every crisis there is a moment when the scale hesitates before kicking the beam. When we lean to the worst side of our nature, instead of strengthening our better qualities, the moral force which has been preserving the balance gives way, and down we go. Had this critical moment in Gwynplaine's life arrived?

How could he escape?

So it is she! the duchess! the woman! There she was in that lonely room,—asleep, far from succor, helpless, alone, at his mercy—yet he was in her power!

The duchess!

We have, perchance, observed a star in the distant firmament. We have admired it. It is so far off. What can there be to make us shudder in a fixed star? Well, one day—one night, rather—it moves. We perceive a trembling gleam around it. The star which we imagined to be immovable, is in motion. It is no longer a star, but a comet—the incendiary giant of the skies. The luminary moves on, grows bigger, shakes off a shower of sparks and fire, and becomes enormous. It advances towards us. Oh, horror! it is coming our way! The comet recognizes us, marks us for its own, and will not be turned aside. Irresistible attack of the heavens! What is it which is bearing down on us? An excess of light, which blinds us; an excess of life, which kills us. That proposal which the heavens make we refuse; that unfathomable love we reject. We close our eyes; we hide; we tear ourselves away; we imagine the danger is past. We open our eyes—the formidable star is still before us; but, no longer a star, it has become a world. A world unknown, a world of lava and ashes; the devastating prodigy of space. It fills the sky, allowing no compeers. The carbuncle of the firmament's depths, a diamond in the distance, when drawn close to us becomes a furnace. You are caught in its flames.

And the first sensation of burning is that of a heavenly warmth.

CHAPTER IV

SATAN

SUDDENLY the sleeper awoke. She sat up with a sudden and gracious dignity of movement, her fair silken tresses falling in soft disorder on her hips; her loosened night-dress disclosed her shoulder; she touched her pink toes with her little hand, and gazed for some moments on the naked foot, worthy to be worshiped by Pericles, and copied by Phidias. Then stretching herself, she yawned like a tigress in the rising sun.

Perhaps Gwynplaine breathed heavily, as we do when we endeavor to restrain our respiration.

"Is any one there?" said she.

She yawned as she spoke, and her very yawn was graceful.

Gwynplaine listened to the unfamiliar voice; the voice of a charmer, its accents exquisitely haughty, its caressing intonation softening its native arrogance.

Then rising on her knees,—there is an antique statue kneeling thus in the midst of a thousand transparent folds,—she drew the dressing-gown towards her, and springing from the couch, stood upright by it—nude; then, suddenly, with the swiftness of an arrow's flight, she was clothed. In the twinkling of an eye the silken robe was around her. The trailing sleeve concealed her hands; only the tips of her toes, with little pink nails like those of an infant, were left visible.

Having drawn from underneath the dressing-gown a mass of hair which had been imprisoned by it, she crossed behind the couch to the end of the room, and placed her ear to the painted mirror, which was, apparently, a door.

Tapping the glass with her finger, she called:

"Is any one there? Lord David! Are you come already? What time is it then? Is that you, Barkilphedro?"

191

She turned from the glass.

"No! it was not there. Is there any one in the bath-room? Will you answer? Of course not. No one could come that way."

Going to the silver lace curtain, she raised it with her foot, thrust it aside with her shoulder, and entered the marble room.

An agonized numbness fell upon Gwynplaine. No possibility of concealment. It was too late to fly. Moreover, he was no longer equal to the exertion. He wished that the earth might open and swallow him up. Anything to hide him.

She saw him.

She stared, immensely astonished, but without the slightest nervousness. Then, in a tone of mingled pleasure and contempt, she said:

"Why, it is Gwynplaine!"

Suddenly, with a rapid spring, for this cat was a panther, she flung herself on his neck. She clasped his head between her naked arms, from which the sleeves, in her eagerness, had fallen back.

Suddenly, pushing him back, and holding him by both shoulders with her small claw-like hands, she stood up face to face with him, and began to gaze at him with a strange expression.

It was a fatal glance she gave him with her Aldebaran-like eyes,— a glance at once equivocal and starlike. Gwynplaine watched the blue eye and the black eye, distracted by the double ray of heaven and of hell that shone in the orbs thus fixed on him. The man and the woman threw a malign dazzling reflection one on the other. Both were fascinated, he by her beauty, she by his deformity. Both were in a measure awe-stricken. Pressed down as by an overwhelming weight, he was speechless.

"Oh!" she cried. "How clever you are. You are come. You found out that I was obliged to leave London. You followed me. That was right. Your being here proves you to be a wonder."

The simultaneous return of self-possession acts like a flash of lightning. Gwynplaine, indistinctly warned by a vague, rude, but honest misgiving, drew back, but the pink nails clung to his shoulders and restrained him. Some inexorable power proclaimed its sway over him. He himself, a wild beast, was caged in a wild beast's den.

She continued:

"Anne, the fool, you know whom I mean—the Queen—ordered me to Windsor without giving any reason. When I arrived she was closeted with her idiot of a Chancellor. But how did you contrive to obtain access to me? That's what I call being a man—obstacles, indeed—there are no such things! You come at a call. You found things out. My name, the Duchess Josiana, you knew, I fancy. Who was it brought

you in? No doubt it was the page. Oh, he is clever! I will give him
a hundred guineas. Which way did you get in? Tell me! No! don't
tell me. I don't want to know. Explanations diminish interest. I prefer the marvelous, and you are hideous enough to be wonderful. You

have fallen from the highest heavens, or you have risen from the depths
of hell through the devil's trap-door. Nothing can be more natural.
The ceiling opened or the floor yawned. A descent in a cloud, or an
ascent in a mass of fire and brimstone, that is how you have traveled.
You have a right to enter like the gods. Agreed; you are my lover."

Gwynplaine was scared, and listened; his mind growing more

irresolute every moment. Now all was certain. Impossible to have
any further doubt. That letter! the woman confirmed its meaning.
Gwynplaine the lover and the beloved of a duchess! Mighty pride,
with its thousand baleful heads, stirred his wretched heart.

Vanity, that powerful agent within us, works us measureless evil.

The duchess went on:

"Since you are here, it is so decreed. I ask nothing more. There
is some one on high, or in hell, who brings us together. The betrothal
of Styx and Aurora! Unbridled ceremonies beyond all laws! The
very day I first saw you, I said, it is he! I recognize him. He is the
monster of my dreams. He shall be mine. We should give destiny a
helping hand. Therefore I wrote to you. One question, Gwynplaine,
do you believe in predestination? For my part, I have believed in it
since I read, in Cicero, Scipio's dream. Ah! I did not observe it.
Dressed like a gentleman! You in fine clothes! Why not? You are
a mountebank. All the more reason. A juggler is as good as a lord.
Moreover, what are lords? Clowns. You have a noble figure, you are
magnificently made. It is wonderful that you should be here. When
did you arrive? How long have you been here? Did you see me
naked? I am beautiful, am I not? I was going to take my bath. Oh!
how I love you! You read my letter! Did you read it yourself? Did
any one read it to you? Can you read? Probably you are ignorant.
I ask questions, but don't answer them. I don't like the sound of your
voice. It is soft. An extraordinary thing like you should snarl, and
not speak. You sing harmoniously. I hate it. It is the only thing
about you that I do not like. All the rest is terrible,—is grand. In
India you would be a god. Were you born with that frightful laugh on
your face? No! No doubt it is a penal brand. I do hope you have
committed some crime. Come to my arms."

She sank on the couch and made him sit beside her. They found
themselves close together unconsciously. What she said passed over
Gwynplaine like a mighty storm. He hardly understood the meaning
of her whirlwind of words. Her eyes were full of admiration. She
spoke tumultuously, frantically, with a voice broken and tender. Her
words were music; but their music was to Gwynplaine as a hurricane.
Again she fixed her gaze upon him and continued:

"I feel degraded in your presence, and oh! what happiness that
is. How insipid it is to be a grandee! I am noble, what can be more
tiresome? Disgrace is a comfort. I am so satiated with respect that I
long for contempt. We are all a little erratic, from Venus, Cleopatra,
Mesdames de Chevreuse and de Longueville, down to myself. I will
make a display of you, I declare. Here's a love affair which will be a

blow to my family, the Stuarts. Ah! I breathe again. I have discovered a secret. I am clear of royalty. To be free from its trammels is indeed deliverance. To break down, defy, make and destroy at will, that is true enjoyment. Listen, I love you."

She paused; then with a frightful smile, went on:

"I love you, not only because you are deformed; but because you are low. I love monsters, and I love mountebanks. A lover despised, mocked, grotesque, hideous, exposed to laughter on that pillory called a theatre, has for me an extraordinary attraction. It is tasting the fruit of hell. An infamous lover, how exquisite! To taste the apple, not of Paradise, but of hell; such is my temptation. It is for that I hunger and thirst. I am that Eve, the Eve of the depths. Probably you are, unknown to yourself, a devil. I am in love with a nightmare. You are a moving puppet, of which the strings are pulled by a spectre. You are the incarnation of infernal mirth. You are the master I require. I wanted a lover such as those of Medea and Canidia. I felt sure that some night would bring me such a one. You are all that I want. I am talking of a heap of things of which you probably know nothing. Gwynplaine, hitherto I have remained untouched; I give myself to you, pure as a burning ember. You evidently do not believe me; but if you only knew how little I care!"

Her words flowed like a volcanic eruption. Pierce Mount Etna, and you may obtain some idea of that jet of fiery eloquence.

Gwynplaine stammered:

"Madame——"

She placed her hand on his mouth.

"Silence," she said. "I am studying you. I am unbridled desire, immaculate. I am a vestal bacchante. No man has known me, and I might be the virgin pythoness at Delphos, and have under my naked foot the bronze tripod, where the priests lean their elbows on the skin of the python, whispering questions to the invisible god. My heart is of stone, but it is like those mysterious pebbles which the sea washes to the foot of the rock called Huntly Nabb, at the mouth of the Tees, and which if broken are found to contain a serpent. That serpent is my love. A love which is all-powerful, for it has brought you to me. An impossible distance was between us. I was in Sirius, and you were in Allioth. You have crossed the immeasurable space, and here you are. 'Tis well. Be silent. Take me."

She ceased; he trembled. Then she went on, smiling:

"You see, Gwynplaine, to dream is to create; to desire is to summon. To build up the chimera is to provoke the reality. The all-powerful and terrible mystery will not be defied. It produces result.

You are here. Do I dare to lose caste? Yes. Do I dare to be your
mistress? Your concubine? Your slave? Your chattel? Joyfully.
Gwynplaine, I am a woman. Woman is clay longing to become mire.
I want to despise myself. That lends a zest to pride. The alloy of
greatness is baseness. They combine in perfection. Despise me, you
who are despised. Nothing can be better. Degradation on degradation. What joy! I pluck the double blossom of ignominy. Trample
me under foot. You will only love me the more. I am sure of it. Do
you understand why I idolize you? Because I despise you. You are
so immeasurably below me that I place you on an altar. Bring
the highest and lowest depths together, and you have Chaos, and I
delight in Chaos. Chaos, the beginning and end of everything. What
is Chaos? A huge blot. Out of that blot God made light, and out of
that sink the world. You don't know how perverse I can be. Knead a
star in mud, and you will have my likeness."

Thus spoke the siren; the loosened robe revealing her virgin
bosom.

She went on:

"A wolf to all beside; a faithful dog to you. How astonished they
will all be! The astonishment of fools is amusing. I understand
myself. Am I a goddess? Amphitrite gave herself to the Cyclops.
Fluctivoma Amphitrite. Am I a fairy? Urgele gave herself to Bugryx,
a winged man, with eight webbed hands. Am I a princess? Marie
Stuart had Rizzio. Three beauties, three monsters. I am greater than
they, for you are lower than they. Gwynplaine, we were made for one
another. The monster that you are outwardly, I am within. Thence
my love for you. A caprice? Just so. What is a huricane but a
caprice? Our stars have a certain affinity. Together we are things of
night—you in your face, I in my mind. As your countenance is defaced, so is my mind. You, in your turn, create me. You come, and
my real soul shows itself. I did not know it. It is astonishing. Your
coming has evoked the hydra in me, who am a goddess. You reveal
my real nature. See how I resemble you. Look at me as if I were a
mirror. Your face is my mind. I did not know I was so terrible. I
am also, then, a monster. Oh! Gwynplaine, you do amuse me!"

She laughed a strange and childlike laugh; and, putting her mouth
close to his ear, whispered:

"Do you want to see a mad woman? look at me."

She poured her searching look into Gwynplaine. A look is a
philtre. Her loosened robe provoked a thousand dangerous feelings.
Blind, animal ecstasy was invading his mind, ecstasy combined with
agony.

Whilst she was speaking, though he felt her words like burning coals, his blood froze within his veins. He had not strength to utter a word.

She stopped, and looked at him.

"O, monster!" she cried. She grew wild.

Suddenly she seized his hands.

"Gwynplaine, I am the throne; you are the footstool. Let us join on the same level. Oh, how happy I am in my fall! I wish all the world could know how abject I am become. It would bow down all the lower. The more man abhors, the more does he cringe. It is human nature. Hostile, but reptile; dragon, but worm. Oh, I am as depraved as are the gods! They can never say that I am not a king's bastard. I act like a queen. Who was Rodope, but a queen loving Pteh, a man with a crocodile's head? She raised the third pyramid in his honor. Penthesilea loved the centaur, who, being now a star, is named Sagittarius. And what do you say about Anne of Austria? Mazarin was ugly enough! Now, you are not only ugly, you are deformed. Ugliness is mean, deformity is grand. Ugliness is the devil's grin behind beauty; deformity is the reverse of sublimity. It is the back view. Olympus has two aspects. One, by day, shows Apollo; the other, by night, shows Polyphemus. You! you are a Titan. You would be Behemoth in the forests, Leviathan in the deep, and Typhon in the sewer. You surpass everything. There is the trace of lightning in your deformity; your face has been battered by the thunder-bolt. The jagged contortion of forked lightning has imprinted its mark on your face. It struck you and passed on. A mighty and mysterious wrath has, in a fit of passion, cemented your spirit in a terrible and superhuman form. Hell is a penal furnace, where the iron called Fatality is raised to a white heat. You have been branded with it. To love you, is to understand grandeur. I enjoy that triumph. To be in love with Apollo, a fine effort, forsooth! Glory is to be measured by the astonishment it creates. I love you. I have dreamt of you night after night. This is my palace. You shall see my gardens. There are fresh springs under the shrubs; arbors for lovers; and beautiful groups of marble statuary by Bernini. Flowers! there are too many—during the spring the place is on fire with roses. Did I tell you that the queen is my sister? Do what you like with me. I am made for Jupiter to kiss my feet, and for Satan to spit in my face. Are you of any religion? I am a Papist. My father, James II., died in France, surrounded by Jesuits. I have never felt before as I feel now that I am near you. Oh, how I should like to pass the evening with you, in the midst of music, both reclining on the same cushion, under a purple awning, in a gilded gondola on the soft expanse of ocean. Insult me, beat me, kick me, cuff me, treat me like a brute! I adore you."

Caresses can roar. If you doubt it, observe the lion's. The woman was horrible, and yet full of grace. The effect was tragic. First he felt the claw, then the velvet of the paw. A feline attack, made up of advances and retreats. There was death as well as sport in this game of come and go. She idolized him, but arrogantly. The result was contagious frenzy. Fatal language, at once inexpressible, violent, and sweet. The insulter did not insult; the adorer outraged the object of adoration. She, who buffeted, deified him. Her tones imparted to her violent yet amorous words an indescribable Promethean grandeur.

According to Æschylus, in the orgies in honor of the great goddess, the women were smitten by this evil frenzy when they pursued the satyrs under the stars. Such paroxysms raged in the mysterious dances in the grove of Dodona. This woman was as if transfigured—if, indeed, we can term that transfiguration which is the antithesis of heaven. Her hair quivered like a mane ; her robe opened and closed. Nothing could be more attractive than that bosom, full of wild cries. The sunshine of the blue eye mingled with the fire of the black one. She was unearthly.

Gwynplaine, giving way, felt himself vanquished by the deep subtilty of this attack.

" I love you ! " she cried.

And she bit him with a kiss.

Homeric clouds were, perhaps, about to be required to encompass Gwynplaine and Josiana, as they did Jupiter and Juno. For Gwynplaine to be loved by a woman who could see, and who saw him; to feel on his deformed mouth the pressure of divine lips, was exquisite and maddening. Before this woman, full of enigmas, all else faded away in his mind. The remembrance of Dea struggled in the shadows with weak cries. There is an antique bas-relief representing the Sphynx devouring a Cupid. The wings of the sweet celestial are bleeding between the fierce, grinning fangs.

Did Gwynplaine love this woman ? Has man, like the globe, two poles ? Are we, on our inflexible axis, a moving sphere, a star when seen from afar, mud, when seen more closely, in which night alternates with day ? Has the heart two aspects—one on which its love is poured forth in light; the other in darkness ? Here a woman of light, there a woman of the sewer. Angels are necessary. Is it possible that demons are also essential ? Has the soul the wings of the bat ? Does twilight fall fatally for all ? Is sin an integral and inevitable part of our destiny? Must we accept evil as part and portion of our whole? Do we inherit sin as a debt? What awful subjects for thought!

Yet a voice tells us that weakness is a crime. Gwynplaine's feelings are not to be described. The flesh, life, terror, lust, an overwhelm-

ing intoxication of spirit, and all the shame possible to pride. Was he about to succumb?

She repeated, "I love you!" and flung her frenzied arms around him. Gwynplaine panted.

Suddenly, close at hand, there rang, clear and distinct, a little bell. It was the little bell inside the wall. The duchess, turning her head, said:

"What does she want of me?"

Quickly, with the noise of a spring door, the silver panel, with the golden crown chased on it, opened.

A compartment of a shaft, lined with royal blue velvet, appeared; and, on a golden salver, a letter.

The letter, broad and weighty, was placed so as to exhibit the seal, which was a large impression in red wax. The bell continued to tinkle. The open panel almost touched the couch where the duchess and Gwynplaine were sitting.

Leaning over, but still keeping her arm round his neck, she took the letter from the plate, and touched the panel.

The compartment closed in, and the bell ceased ringing.

The duchess broke the seal, and, opening the envelope, drew out two documents contained therein, and flung it on the floor at Gwynplaine's feet.

The impression of the broken seal was still decipherable, and Gwynplaine could distinguish a royal crown over the initial A.

The torn envelope lay open before him, so that he could read, "*To Her Grace the Duchess Josiana.*"

The envelope had contained both vellum and parchment. The former was a small, the latter a large, document. On the parchment was a large Chancery seal in green wax, called Lords' sealing-wax.

The face of the duchess, whose bosom was palpitating, and whose eyes were swimming with passion, became overspread with a slight expression of dissatisfaction.

"Ah!" she said. "What does she send me? A lot of papers! What a spoil-sport that woman is!"

Pushing aside the parchment, she opened the vellum.

"It is her handwriting. It is my sister's hand. It is quite provoking. Gwynplaine, I asked you if you could read. Can you?"

Gwynplaine nodded assent.

She stretched herself at full length on the couch, carefully drew her feet and arms under her robe, with a whimsical affectation of modesty, and, giving Gwynplaine the vellum, watched him with an impassioned look.

"Well! you are mine. Begin your duties, my beloved. Read me what the queen writes."

Gwynplaine took the vellum, unfolded it, and, in a voice tremulous with many emotions, began to read:

"MADAM,—

"We are graciously pleased to send to you herewith, sealed and signed by our trusty and well-beloved William Cowper, Lord High

Chancellor of England, a copy of a report, showing forth the very important fact that the legitimate son of Linnæus Lord Clancharlie has just been discovered and recognized, bearing the name of Gwynplaine, in the lowest rank of a wandering and vagabond life, among strollers and mountebanks. His false position dates from his earliest days. In accordance with the laws of the country, and in virtue of his hereditary rights, Lord Fermain Clancharlie, son of Lord Linnæus, will be this day admitted, and installed in his position in the House of Lords. Therefore, having regard to your welfare, and wishing to preserve for your use the property and estates of Lord Clancharlie of Hunkerville, we substitute him in the place of Lord David Dirry-Moir, and recommend him to your good graces. We have caused Lord Fermain to be conducted to Corleone Lodge. We will and command, as sister and as Queen, that the said Fermain Lord Clancharlie, hitherto called Gwynplaine, shall be your husband, and that you shall marry him. Such is our royal pleasure."

While Gwynplaine, in tremulous tones which varied at almost every word, was reading the document, the duchess, half risen from the couch, listened with fixed attention. When Gwynplaine finished, she snatched the letter from his hands.

"*Anne R.*," she murmured in a tone of abstraction.

Then picking up from the floor the parchment she had thrown down, she ran her eye over it. It was the confession of the shipwrecked crew of the *Matutina*, embodied in a report signed by the sheriff of Southwark and by the lord chancellor.

Having perused the report, she read the queen's letter over again. Then she said:

"Be it so."

And calmly pointing with her finger to the door of the gallery through which he had entered, she added:

"Begone."

Gwynplaine was petrified, and remained immovable. She repeated, in icy tones:

"Since you are my husband, begone."

Gwynplaine, speechless, and with eyes downcast like a criminal, remained motionless. She added:

"You have no right to be here; it is my lover's place."

Gwynplaine was like a man transfixed.

"Very well," said she, "I must go myself. So you are my husband. Nothing can be better. I hate you."

She rose, and with an indescribably haughty gesture of adieu, left the room. The curtain in the doorway of the gallery fell behind her.

CHAPTER V

THEY RECOGNIZE, BUT DO NOT KNOW, EACH OTHER

WYNPLAINE was alone.

Alone, and in presence of the tepid bath and the deserted couch.

The confusion in his mind had reached its culminating point. His thoughts no longer resembled thoughts. They overflowed and ran riot ; it was the anguish of a creature wrestling with perplexity. He felt as if he were awakening from a horrid nightmare. The entrance into unknown spheres is no simple matter.

From the time he had received the duchess's letter, brought by the page, a series of surprising adventures had befallen Gwynplaine, each one less intelligible than the other. Up to this time, though in a dream, he had seen things clearly. Now he could only grope his way. He no longer thought, nor even dreamed. He collapsed.

He sank down upon the couch which the duchess had vacated.

Suddenly, he heard a sound of footsteps, and those of a man. The noise came from the opposite side of the gallery to that by which the duchess had departed. The man approached, and his footsteps, though deadened by the carpet, were clear and distinct. Gwynplaine, in spite of his abstraction, listened.

Suddenly, beyond the silver web of curtain which the duchess had left partly open, a door, evidently concealed by the painted glass, opened wide, and there came floating into the room the refrain of an old French song, carolled at the top of a manly and joyous voice,

" Trois petits gorets sur leur fumier
Juraient comme de porteurs de chaise,

and a man entered. He wore a sword by his side, a magnificent naval uniform, covered with gold lace, and held in his hand a plumed hat with loops and cockade.

202

Gwynplaine sprang up erect as if moved by springs. He recognized the man, and was in turn recognized by him.

From their astonished lips came, simultaneously, this double exclamation :

" Gwynplaine ! "

" Tom-Jim-Jack ! "

The man with the plumed hat advanced towards Gwynplaine, who stood with folded arms.

" What are you doing here, Gwynplaine ? "

" And you, Tom-Jim-Jack, what are you doing here ? "

" Oh! I understand. Josiana! a caprice. A mountebank and a monster! The double attraction is too powerful to be resisted. You disguised yourself in order to get here, Gwynplaine ? "

" And you, too, Tom-Jim-Jack ? "

" Gwynplaine, what does this gentleman's dress mean ? "

" Tom-Jim-Jack, what does that officer's uniform mean ? "

" Gwynplaine, I answer no questions."

" Neither do I, Tom-Jim-Jack."

" Gwynplaine, my name is not Tom-Jim-Jack."

" Tom-Jim-Jack, my name is not Gwynplaine."

" Gwynplaine, I am here in my own house."

" I am here in my own house, Tom-Jim-Jack."

" I will not have you echo my words. You are ironical; but I've got a cane. An end to your jokes, you wretched fool."

Gwynplaine became ashy pale.

" You are a fool yourself, and you shall give me satisfaction for this insult."

" In your booth as much as you like, with fisticuffs."

" Here, and with swords ? "

" My friend, Gwynplaine, the sword is a weapon for gentlemen. With it I can only fight my equals. At fisticuffs we are equal; but not so with swords. At the Tadcaster Inn, Tom-Jim-Jack could box with Gwynplaine. At Windsor, the case is altered. Understand this; I am a rear-admiral."

" And I am a peer of England."

The man whom Gwynplaine recognized as Tom-Jim-Jack burst out laughing.

" Why not a king? Indeed, you are right. An actor plays every part. You'll tell me next that you are Theseus, Duke of Athens."

" I am a peer of England, and we are going to fight."

" Gwynplaine, this becomes tiresome. Don't play with one who can order you to be flogged. I am Lord David Dirry-Moir."

"And I am Lord Clancharlie."

Again Lord David burst out laughing.

"Well said! Gwynplaine is Lord Clancharlie. That is indeed the name the man must bear who is to win Josiana. Listen, I forgive you, and do you know the reason? It's because we are both lovers of the same woman."

The curtain of the door was lifted, and a voice exclaimed:

"You are the two husbands, my lords."

They turned.

"Barkilphedro!" cried Lord David.

It was indeed he; he bowed low to the two lords, with a smile on his face.

Some few paces behind him was a gentleman with a stern and dignified countenance, who carried in his hand a black wand. This gentleman advanced, and, bowing three times to Gwynplaine, said:

"I am the Usher of the Black Rod. I come to fetch your lordship, in obedience to Her Majesty's commands."

BOOK VIII

THE CAPITOL AND THINGS AROUND IT

CHAPTER I

ANALYSIS OF MAJESTIC MATTERS

IRRESISTIBLE Fate ever carrying him forward, which had now for so many hours showered its surprises on Gwynplaine, and which had transported him to Windsor, transferred him again to London.

Visionary realities succeeded each other without a moment's intermission. He could not escape from their influence. Freed from one, he met another. He had scarcely time to breathe.

Any one who has seen a juggler throwing

and catching balls can judge the nature of fate. Those rising and falling projectiles are like men tossed in the hands of Destiny—projectiles and playthings.

On the evening of the same day Gwynplaine was an actor in an extraordinary scene. He was seated on a bench covered with fleurs-de-lys; over his silken clothes he wore a robe of scarlet velvet, lined with white silk, with a cape of ermine, and on his shoulders two bands of ermine embroidered with gold. Around him were men of all ages, young and old, seated like him on benches covered with fleurs-de-lys, and dressed like him in ermine and purple. In front of him other men were kneeling, clothed in black silk gowns. Some of them were writing; opposite, and a short distance from him, he observed steps, a raised platform, a dais, a large escutcheon glittering between a lion and a unicorn, and at the top of the steps, on the platform under the dais, resting against the escutcheon, was a gilded chair with a crown over it. This was a throne.

The throne of Great Britain.

Gwynplaine, himself a peer of England, was in the House of Lords. How Gwynplaine's introduction to the House of Lords came about, we will now explain.

Throughout the day, from morning to night, from Windsor to London, from Corleone Lodge to Westminster Hall, he had step by step mounted higher in the social grade. At each step he grew giddier.

He had been conveyed from Windsor in a royal carriage with a peer's escort. There is not much difference between a guard of honor, and a prisoner's. On that day travelers on the London and Windsor road saw a galloping cavalcade of gentlemen pensioners of Her Majesty's household, escorting two carriages drawn at a rapid pace. In the first carriage sat the Usher of the Black Rod, his wand in his hand. In the second was to be seen a large hat with white plumes, throwing into shadow and hiding the face underneath it. Who was it who was being thus hurried on—a prince? a prisoner?

It was Gwynplaine.

It looked as if they were conducting some one to the Tower, unless, indeed, they were escorting him to the House of Lords. The queen had done things well. As it was for her future brother-in-law, she had provided an escort from her own household. The officer of the Usher of the Black Rod rode on horseback at the head of the cavalcade. The Usher of the Black Rod carried, on a cushion placed on a seat of the carriage, a black portfolio, stamped with the royal crown.

At Brentford, the last relay before London, the carriages and escort halted.

A four-horse carriage of tortoise-shell, with two postilions, a coach-man in a wig, and four footmen, was in waiting. The wheels, steps, springs, pole, and all the fittings of this carriage were gilt. The horses' harness was of silver.

This state coach was of an ancient and extraordinary shape, and would have been distinguished by its grandeur among the fifty-one celebrated carriages of which Roubo has left us drawings.

The Usher of the Black Rod and his officer alighted. The latter, having lifted the cushion, on which rested the royal portfolio, from the seat in the post-chaise, carried it on outstretched hands, and stood behind the Usher. He first opened the door of the empty carriage, then the door of that occupied by Gwynplaine, and, with downcast eyes, respectfully invited him to descend.

Gwynplaine left the chaise, and took his seat in the carriage.

The Usher carrying the rod, and the officer supporting the cushion, followed, and took their places on the low front seat provided for pages in old state coaches. The inside of the carriage was lined with white satin trimmed with Binche silk, with tufts and tassels of silver. The roof was painted with armorial bearings. The postilions of the chaises they were leaving were dressed in the royal livery. The attendants of the carriage they now entered wore a different but very magnificent livery.

Gwynplaine, in spite of his bewildered state in which he felt quite overcome, remarked the gorgeously-attired footmen, and asked the Usher of the Black Rod:

" Whose livery is that ! "

He answered:

" Yours, my lord."

The House of Lords was to sit that evening. *Curia erat serena,* run the old records. In England parliamentary work is by preference undertaken at night. It once happened that Sheridan began a speech at midnight and finished it at sunrise.

The two post-chaises returned to Windsor. Gwynplaine's carriage set out for London.

This ornamented four-horse carriage proceeded at a walk from Brentford to London, as befitted the dignity of the coachman. Gwynplaine's servitude to ceremony was beginning in the shape of his solemn-looking coachman. The delay was, moreover, apparently pre-arranged; and we shall see presently its probable motive.

Night was falling, though it was not quite dark, when the carriage stopped at the King's Gate, a large sunken door between two turrets, connecting Whitehall with Westminster. The escort of gentlemen pensioners formed a circle around the carriage. A footman jumped down from behind it and opened the door.

The Usher of the Black Rod, followed by the officer carrying the cushion, got out of the carriage, and addressed Gwynplaine:

"My lord, be pleased to alight. I beg your lordship to keep your hat on."

Gwynplaine wore under his traveling cloak the suit of black silk, which he had not changed since the previous evening. He had no sword. He left his cloak in the carriage. Under the arched way of the King's Gate there was a small side door, raised some few steps above the road. In ceremonial processions the greatest personage never walks first.

The Usher of the Black Rod, followed by his officer, walked first; Gwynplaine followed. They ascended the steps, and entered by the side door. Presently they were in a wide, circular room, with a pillar in the centre, the lower part of a turret. The room, being on the ground floor, was lighted by narrow windows in the pointed arches, which served but to make darkness visible. Twilight often lends solemnity to a scene. Obscurity is in itself majestic.

In this room, thirteen men, disposed in ranks, were standing; three in the front row, six in the second row, and four behind. In the front row one wore a crimson velvet gown; the other two, gowns of the same color, but of satin. All three had the arms of England embroidered on their shoulders. The second rank wore tunics of white silk, each one having a different coat of arms emblazoned in front. The last row were clad in black silk, and were thus distinguished. The first wore a blue cape. The second had a scarlet St. George embroidered in front. The third, two embroidered crimson crosses, in front and behind. The fourth had a collar of black sable fur. All were uncovered, wore wigs, and carried swords. Their faces were scarcely visible in the dim light, neither could they see Gwynplaine's face.

The Usher of the Black Rod, raising his wand, said:

"My Lord Fermain Clancharlie, Baron Clancharlie and Hunkerville, I, the Usher of the Black Rod, first officer of the presence chamber, hand your lordship over to Garter King-at-Arms."

The person clothed in velvet, quitting his place in the ranks, bowed to the ground before Gwynplaine, and said:

"My Lord Fermain Clancharlie, I am Garter, Principal King-at-Arms of England. I am the officer appointed and installed by his grace the Duke of Norfolk, hereditary Earl Marshal. I have sworn obedience to the king, peers, and knights of the garter. The day of my installation, when the Earl Marshal of England anointed me by pouring a goblet of wine on my head, I solemnly promised to be attentive to the nobility; to avoid bad company; to excuse, rather than accuse, gentlefolks; and to assist widows and virgins. It is I who have the charge of arranging the funeral ceremonies of peers, and the supervision

of their armorial bearings. I place myself at the orders of your lordship."

The first of those wearing satin tunics, having bowed deeply, said:

"My lord, I am Clarenceaux, Second King-at-Arms of England. I am the officer who arranges the obsequies of nobles below the rank of peers. I am at your lordship's disposal."

The other wearer of the satin tunic, bowed, and spoke thus:

"My lord, I am Norroy, Third King-at-Arms of England. Command me."

The second row, erect and without bowing, advanced a pace. The right-hand man said:

"My lord, we are the six Dukes-at-Arms of England. I am York."

Then each of the heralds, or Dukes-at-Arms, speaking in turn, proclaimed his title.

"I am Lancaster."

"I am Richmond."

"I am Chester."

"I am Somerset."

"I am Windsor."

The coats of arms embroidered on their breasts were those of the counties and towns from which they took their names.

The third rank, dressed in black, remained silent. Garter King-at-Arms, pointing them out to Gwynplaine, said:

"My lord, these are the four Pursuivants-at-Arms. Blue Mantle."

The man with the blue cape bowed.

"Rouge Dragon."

He with the St. George inclined his head. .

"Rouge Croix."

He with the scarlet crosses saluted.

"Portcullis."

He with the sable fur collar made his obeisance.

On a sign from the King-at-Arms, the first of the pursuivants, Blue Mantle, stepped forward and received from the officer of the Usher the cushion of silver cloth, and crown-emblazoned portfolio. And the King-at-Arms said to the Usher of the Black Rod:

"Proceed; I leave in your hands the introduction of his lordship!"

The observance of these customs, and also of others which will now be described, were the old ceremonies in use prior to the time of Henry VIII., and which Anne for some time attempted to revive. There is nothing like it in existence now. Nevertheless, the House of Lords thinks that it is unchangeable; and, if Conservatism exists anywhere, it is there.

It changes, nevertheless. *E pur si muove.*

For instance, what has become of the May-pole—which the citizens of London erected on the 1st of May, when the peers went down to the House? The last one was erected in 1713. Since then the May-pole has disappeared. Disuse.

Outwardly, unchangeable; inwardly, mutable. Take, for example, the title of Albemarle. It sounds eternal. Yet it has been through six different families—Odo, Mandeville, Bethune, Plantagenet, Beauchamp, Monck. Under the title of Leicester, five different names have been merged—Beaumont, Breose, Dudley, Sydney, Coke. Under Lincoln, six; under Pembroke, seven. The families change, under unchanging titles. A superficial historian believes in immutability. In reality it does not exist. Man can never be more than a wave; humanity is the ocean.

Aristocracy is proud of what women consider a reproach—age! Yet both cherish the same illusion, that they do not change.

It is probable the House of Lords will not recognize itself in the foregoing description, nor yet in that which follows, thus resembling the once pretty woman, who objects to having any wrinkles. The mirror is ever a scapegoat, yet its truths cannot be contested.

To portray exactly, constitutes the duty of an historian.

The King-at-Arms, turning to Gwynplaine, said :

"Be pleased to follow me, my lord."

And he added :

"You will be saluted. Your lordship, in returning the salute, will be pleased merely to raise the brim of your hat."

They moved off, in procession, towards a door at the far side of the room. The Usher of the Black Rod walked in front; then Blue Mantle, carrying the cushion; then the King-at-Arms; and after him came Gwynplaine, wearing his hat. The rest, kings-at-arms, heralds, and pursuivants, remained in the circular room.

Gwynplaine, preceded by the Usher of the Black Rod, and escorted by the King-at-Arms, passed from room to room, in a direction which it would now be impossible to trace, the old houses of parliament having been pulled down.

Amongst others, he crossed that Gothic state-chamber in which took place the last meeting of James II. and Monmouth, and whose walls witnessed the useless debasement of the cowardly nephew at the feet of his vindictive uncle. On the walls of this chamber hung, in chronological order, nine full-length portraits of former peers, with their dates—Lord Nansladron, 1305; Lord Baliol, 1306; Lord Benestede, 1314; Lord Cantilupe, 1356; Lord Montbegon, 1357; Lord Tibotot, 1373; Lord Zouch of Codnor, 1615; Lord Bella-Aqua, with no date; Lord Harren and Surrey, Count of Blois, also without date.

It being now dark, lamps were burning at intervals in the galleries. Brass chandeliers, with wax candles, illuminated the rooms, lighting them like the side aisles of a church.

None but officials were present.

In one room, which the procession crossed, stood, with heads respectfully lowered, the four clerks of the signet, and the Clerk of the Council.

In another room stood the distinguished Knight Banneret, Philip Sydenham, of Brympton, in Somersetshire. The Knight Banneret is a title conferred in time of war, under the unfurled royal standard.

In another room was the senior baronet of England, Sir Edmund Bacon, of Suffolk, heir of Sir Nicholas Bacon, styled, *Primus baronetorum Anglia.* Behind Sir Edmund was an armor-bearer with an arquebus, and an esquire carrying the arms of Ulster, the baronets being the hereditary defenders of the province of Ulster in Ireland.

In another room was the Chancellor of the Exchequer, with his four accountants, and the two deputies of the Lord Chamberlain, *appointed to cleave the tallies.*

At the entrance of a corridor covered with matting, which was the communication between the Lower and the Upper House, Gwynplaine was saluted by Sir Thomas Mansell, of Margam, Comptroller of the Queen's household and Member for Glamorgan; and at the exit from the corridor by a deputation of one for every two of the Barons of the Cinque Ports, four on the right and four on the left, the Cinque Ports being eight in number. William Hastings did obeisance for Hastings; Matthew Aylmor, for Dover; Josias Burchett, for Sandwich; Sir Philip Boteler, for Hythe; John Brewer, for New Rumney; Edward Southwell, for the town of Rye; James Hayes, for Winchelsea; George Nailor, for Seaford.

As Gwynplaine was about to return the salute, the King-at-Arms reminded him in a low voice of the etiquette.

"Only the brim of your hat, my lord."

Gwynplaine did as directed.

He now entered the so-called Painted Chamber, in which there was no painting, except a few of saints, and amongst them St. Edward, in the high arches of the long and deep-pointed windows, which were cut in two by a platform that formed the ceiling of Westminster Hall and the floor of the Painted Chamber.

On the far side of the wooden barrier which divided the room from end to end, stood the three Secretaries of State, men of mark. The functions of the first of these officials comprised the supervision of all affairs relating to the south of England, Ireland, the Colonies, France, Switzerland, Italy, Spain, Portugal, and Turkey. The second had charge of the north of England, and watched affairs in the Low Countries, Germany, Denmark, Sweden, Poland, and Russia. The third, a Scot, had charge of Scotland. The two first-mentioned were English:

one of them being the Honorable Robert Harley, Member for the
borough of New Radnor. A Scotch member, Mungo Graham, Esquire,
a relation of the Duke of Montrose, was present. All bowed, without
speaking, to Gwynplaine, who returned the salute by touching his hat.

The barrier-keeper lifted the wooden arm which, pivoting on a
hinge, formed the entrance to the far side of the Painted Chamber,
where stood the long table, covered with green cloth, reserved for peers.
A branch of lighted candles stood on the table. Gwynplaine, preceded
by the Usher of the Black Rod, Garter King-at-Arms, and Blue Mantle, penetrated into this privileged compartment. The barrier-keeper

closed the opening immediately Gwynplaine had passed. The King-at-Arms, having entered the precincts of the privileged compartment, halted.

The Painted Chamber was a spacious apartment. At the farther end, upright, beneath the royal escutcheon which was placed between the two windows, stood two old men, in red velvet robes, with two rows of ermine trimmed with gold lace on their shoulders, and wearing wigs, and hats with white plumes. Through the openings of their robes might be detected silk garments and sword hilts.

Motionless behind them stood a man dressed in black silk, holding on high a great mace of gold surmounted by a crowned lion.

It was the Mace-bearer of the Peers of England.

The lion is their crest. *Et les Lions ce sont les Barons et li Per*, runs the manuscript chronicle of Bertrand Duguesclin.

The King-at-Arms pointed out the two persons in velvet, and whispered to Gwynplaine:

"My lord, these are your equals. Be pleased to return their salute exactly as they make it. These two peers are barons, and have been named by the Lord Chancellor as your sponsors. They are very old, and almost blind. They will, themselves, introduce you to the House of Lords. The first is Charles Mildmay, Lord Fitzwalter, sixth on the roll of barons; the second is Augustus Arundel, Lord Arundel of Trerice, thirty-eighth on the roll of barons."

The King-at-Arms having advanced a step towards the two old men, proclaimed:

"Fermain Clancharlie, Baron Clancharlie, Baron Hunkerville, Marquis of Corleone, in Sicily, greets your lordships!"

The two peers raised their hats to the full extent of the arm, and then replaced them.

Gwynplaine did the same.

The Usher of the Black Rod stepped forward, followed by Blue Mantle and Garter King-at-Arms. The Mace-bearer took up his post in front of Gwynplaine, the two peers at his side, Lord Fitzwalter on the right, and Lord Arundel of Trerice on the left. Lord Arundel, the elder of the two, was very feeble. He died the following year, bequeathing to his grandson John, a minor, the title, which became extinct in 1768.

The procession, leaving the Painted Chamber, entered a gallery in which were rows of pilasters, and between the spaces were sentinels, alternately pike-men of England, and halberdiers of Scotland. The Scotch halberdiers were magnificent kilted soldiers, worthy to encounter later on, at Fontenoy, the French cavalry, and the royal cuirassiers, whom their colonel thus addressed: "*Messieurs les maitres, assurez vos chapeaux. Nous allons avoir l'honneur de charger.*"

The captain of these soldiers saluted Gwynplaine, and the peers,

his sponsors, with their swords. The men saluted with their pikes and halberds.

At the end of the gallery shone a large door, so magnificent that its two folds seemed to be masses of gold. On each side of the door, there stood, upright and motionless, men who were called door-keepers.

Just before you came to this door, the gallery widened out into a circular space. In this space was an arm-chair with an immense back, and on it, judging by his wig and from the amplitude of his robes, was a distinguished person. It was William Cowper, Lord Chancellor of England.

To be able to cap a royal infirmity with a similar one has its advantages. William Cowper was short-sighted. Anne had also defective sight, but in a lesser degree. The near-sightedness of William Cowper found favor in the eyes of the short-sighted queen, and induced her to appoint him Lord Chancellor, and Keeper of the Royal Conscience. William Cowper's upper-lip was thin, and his lower one thick—a sign of semi-good-nature.

This circular space was lighted by a lamp hung from the ceiling. The Lord Chancellor was sitting gravely in his large arm-chair; at his right was the Clerk of the Crown, and at his left the Clerk of the Parliaments.

Each of the clerks had before him an open register and an ink-horn.

Behind the Lord Chancellor was his mace-bearer, holding the mace with the crown on the top, besides the train-bearer and purse-bearer, in large wigs.

All these officers are still in existence. On a little stand, near the wool-sack, was a sword, with a gold hilt and sheath, and belt of crimson velvet.

Behind the Clerk of the Crown was an officer holding in his hands the coronation robe.

Behind the Clerk of the Parliaments another officer held a second robe, which was that of a peer.

The robes, both of scarlet velvet, lined with white silk, and having bands of ermine trimmed with gold lace over the shoulders, were similar, except that the ermine band was wider on the coronation robe.

The third officer, who was the librarian, carried on a square of Flanders leather, the red book, a little volume bound in red morocco, containing a list of the peers and commons, besides a few blank leaves and a pencil, which it was the custom to present to each new member on his entering the House.

Gwynplaine, between the two peers, his sponsors, brought up the procession, which stopped before the wool-sack.

The two peers, who introduced him, uncovered their heads, and Gwynplaine did likewise.

The King-at-Arms received from the hands of Blue Mantle the cushion of silver cloth, knelt down, and presented the black portfolio on the cushion to the Lord Chancellor.

The Lord Chancellor took the black portfolio, and handed it to the Clerk of the Parliament.

The Clerk received it ceremoniously, and then sat down.

The Clerk of the Parliament opened the portfolio, and arose.

The portfolio contained the two usual messages—the royal patent addressed to the House of Lords; and the writ of summons.

The Clerk read aloud these two messages, with respectful deliberation, standing.

The writ of summons, addressed to Fermain Lord Clancharlie, concluded with the accustomed formalities:

"We strictly enjoin you, on the faith and allegiance that you owe, to come and take your place in person among the prelates and peers sitting in our Parliament at Westminster, for the purpose of giving your advice, in all honor and conscience, on the business of the kingdom and of the Church."

The reading of the messages being concluded, the Lord Chancellor raised his voice:

"The message of the Crown has been read. Lord Clancharlie, does your lordship renounce transubstantiation, adoration of saints, and the mass?"

Gwynplaine bowed.

"The test has been administered," said the Lord Chancellor.

And the Clerk of the Parliament resumed:

"His lordship has taken the test."

The Lord Chancellor added:

"My Lord Clancharlie, you can take your seat."

"So be it," said the two sponsors.

The King-at-Arms rose, took the sword from the stand, and buckled it round Gwynplaine's waist.

"Ce faict," says the old Norman charter, "le pair prend son espée, et monte aux hauts siéges, et assiste a l'audience."

Gwynplaine heard a voice behind him, which said:

"I array your lordship in a peer's robe."

At the same time, the officer who spoke to him, who was holding the robe, placed it on him, and tied the black strings of the ermine cape round his neck.

Gwynplaine, the scarlet robe on his shoulders, and the golden sword by his side, was attired like the peers on his right and left.

The librarian presented to him the red book, and put it in the pocket of his waistcoat.

The King-at-Arms murmured in his ear:

"My lord, on entering, will bow to the royal chair."

The royal chair is the throne.

Meanwhile the two clerks were writing, each at his table—one on the register of the Crown; the other on the register of the House.

Then both—the Clerk of the Crown preceding the other—brought their books to the Lord Chancellor, who signed them. Having signed the two registers, the Lord Chancellor rose.

"Fermain Lord Clancharlie, Baron Clancharlie, Baron Hunkerville, Marquis of Corleone in Sicily, be you welcome among your peers, the lords spiritual and temporal, of Great Britain."

Gwynplaine's sponsors touched his shoulder.

He turned round.

The folds of the great gilded door at the end of the gallery opened.

It was the door of the House of Lords.

Thirty-six hours only had elapsed since Gwynplaine, surrounded by a different procession, had entered the iron door of Southwark jail.

What shadowy chimeras had passed, with terrible rapidity, through his brain! Chimeras which were hard facts; rapidity, which was a capture by assault!

CHAPTER II

IMPARTIALITY

HE creation of an equality with the king called Peerage, was, in barbarous epochs, a useful fiction. This rudimentary political expedient produced in France and England different results. In France, the peer was a mock king; in England, a real prince—less grand than in France, but more genuine: we might say less, but worse.

Peerage was born in France; the date is uncertain—under Charlemagne, says the legend; under Robert le Sage, says history; and history is not more to be relied on than legend. Favin writes:—"The King of France wished to attach to himself the great of his kingdom, by the magnificent title of peers, as if they were his equals."

Peerage soon thrust forth branches, and from France passed over to England.

The English peerage has been a great fact, and almost a mighty institution. It had for precedent the Saxon witenagemote. The Danish thane and the Norman vavassour commingled in the baron. Baron is the same as vir, which is translated into Spanish by *varon*, and which signifies, *par excellence*, "Man." As early as 1075, the barons made themselves felt by the king—and by what a king! By William the Conqueror. In 1086 they laid the foundation of feudality, and its basis was the "Doomsday Book." Under John Lackland came conflict. The French peerage took the high hand with Great Britain, and demanded that the King of England should appear at their Bar. Great was the indignation of the English barons. At the coronation of Philip Augustus, the King of England, as Duke of Normandy, carried the first square banner, and the Duke of Guyenne, the second. Against this king, a vassal of the foreigner, the War of the Barons burst forth. The barons imposed on the weak-minded King John, Magna Charta, from which

219

sprung the House of Lords. The pope took part with the king, and excommunicated the lords. The date was 1215, and the pope was Innocent III., who wrote the "*Veni, Sancte Spiritus,*" and who sent to John Lackland the four cardinal virtues in the shape of four gold rings. The Lords persisted. The duel continued through many generations. Pembroke struggled. 1248 was the year of "the provisions of Oxford." Twenty-four barons limited the king's powers, discussed him, and called a knight from each county to take part in the widened breach. Here was the dawn of the Commons. Later on, the Lords added two citizens from each city, and two burgesses from each borough. It arose from this, that up to the time of Elizabeth the peers were judges of the validity of elections to the House of Commons. From their jurisdiction sprang the proverb that the members returned ought to be without the three P's—*sine Prece, sine Pretio, sine Poculo.* This did not obviate rotten boroughs. In 1293, the Court of Peers in France had still the King of England under their jurisdiction; and Philippe le Bel cited Edward I. to appear before him. Edward I. was the king who ordered his son to boil him down after death, and to carry his bones to the wars. Under the follies of their kings the lords felt the necessity of fortifying parliament. They divided it into two chambers, the upper and the lower. The lords arrogantly kept the supremacy. "If it happens that any member of the Commons should be so bold as to speak to the prejudice of the House of Lords, he is called to the bar of the House to be reprimanded, and, occasionally, to be sent to the Tower." There is the same distinction in voting. In the House of Lords they vote one by one, beginning with the junior, called the puisne baron. Each peer answers "*Content,*" or "*non-Content.*" In the Commons they vote together, by "Aye," or "No," in a crowd. The Commons accuse, the peers judge. The peers, in their disdain of figures, delegated to the Commons who were to profit by it the superintendence of the Exchequer, thus named, according to some, after the table-cover, which was like a chess-board, and according to others, from the drawers of the old safe, where was kept, behind an iron grating, the treasure of the kings of England. The "Year-Book" dates from the end of the thirteenth century. In the War of the Roses the weight of the Lords was thrown, now on the side of John of Gaunt, Duke of Lancaster, now on the side of Edmund, Duke of York. Wat Tyler, the Lollards, Warwick, the King-maker, all that anarchy from which freedom is to spring, had for foundation, avowed or secret, the English feudal system. The Lords were usefully jealous of the Crown; for to be jealous is to be watchful. They circumscribed the royal initiative, diminished the category of cases of high treason, raised up pretended Richards against

Henry IV., appointed themselves arbitrators, judged the question of the three crowns between the Duke of York and Margaret of Anjou, and at need levied armies, and fought their battles of Shrewsbury, Tewkesbury, and St. Albans, sometimes winning, sometimes losing. Before this, in the thirteenth century, they had gained the battle of Lewes, and had driven from the kingdom the four brothers of the king, bastards of Queen Isabella by the Count de la Marche; all four usurers, who extorted money from Christians by means of the Jews; half princes, half sharpers—a thing common enough in more recent times, but not held in good odor in those days. Up to the fifteenth century the Norman Duke peeped out in the King of England, and the acts of Parliament were written in French. From the reign of Henry VII., by the will of the Lords, these were written in English. England, Briton under Uther Pendragon; Roman under Cæsar; Saxon under the Heptarchy; Danish under Harold; Norman after William, then became, thanks to the Lords, English. After that she became Anglican. To have one's religion at home is a great power. A foreign pope drags down the national life. A Mecca is an octopus, and devours it. In 1534, London bowed out Rome. The peerage adopted the reformed religion, and the Lords accepted Luther. Here we have the answer to the excommunication of 1215. It was agreeable to Henry VIII.; but, in other respects, the Lords were a trouble to him. As a bulldog to a bear, so was the House of Lords to Henry VIII. When Wolsey robbed the nation of Whitehall, and when Henry robbed Wolsey of it, who complained? Four Lords—Darcie, of Chichester; Saint John, of Bletsho; and (two Norman names) Mountjoie and Mounteagle. The king usurped. The peerage encroached. There is something in hereditary power which is incorruptible. Hence the insubordination of the Lords. Even in Elizabeth's reign the barons were restless. From this resulted the tortures at Durham. Elizabeth was as a farthingale over an executioneer's block. Elizabeth assembled Parliament as seldom as possible, and reduced the House of Lords to sixty-five members, amongst whom there was but one marquis (Winchester), and not a single duke. In France the kings felt the same jealousy and carried out the same elimination. Under Henry III. there were no more than eight dukedoms in the peerage, and it was to the great vexation of the king that the Baron de Mantes, the Baron de Coucy, the Baron de Coulommiers, the Baron de Chateauneuf-en-Thimerais, the Baron de la Fère-en-Tardenois, the Baron de Mortagne, and some others besides, maintained themselves as barons—peers of France. In England the crown saw the peerage diminish with pleasure. Under Anne, to quote but one example, the peerages become extinct since the twelfth century amounted to five hundred and sixty-five. The War of the Roses had begun the extermination of dukes, which the axe of Mary Tudor completed. This was, indeed, the decapitation of the nobility. To prune away the dukes was to cut off its head. Good policy, perhaps; but it is better to corrupt than to decapitate. James I. was of this opinion. He restored dukedoms. He made a duke of his favorite Villiers, who had made him a pig; * a transformation from the duke feudal to the duke courtier. This sowing was to bring forth a rank harvest: Charles II. was to make two of his mistresses duchesses—Barbara of Southampton and Louise de la Querouel of Portsmouth. Under Anne there were to be twenty-five dukes, of whom three were to be foreigners, Cumberland, Cambridge, and Schomberg. Did this court policy, invented by James I., succeed? No. The House of Peers was irritated by the effort to shackle it by intrigue. It was irritated against James I., it was irritated against Charles I., who, we may observe, may have had something to do with the death of his father, just as Marie de Medicis may have had something to do with the death of her husband. There was a rupture between Charles I. and the peerage. The lords who, under James I., had tried at their bar extortion, in the person of Bacon, under Charles I., tried treason, in the person of Strafford. They had condemned Bacon,—they condemned Strafford. One had lost his honor, the other lost his life. Charles I. was first beheaded in the person of Strafford. The Lords lent their aid to the Commons. The King convokes Parliament to Oxford, the revolution convokes it to London. Forty-four peers side with the King, twenty-two with the Republic. From this combination of the people with the Lords arose the Bill of Rights—a sketch of the French *Droits de l'homme*, a vague shadow flung back from the depths of futurity by the revolution of France on the revolution of England.

Such were the services of the peerage. Involuntary ones, we admit, and dearly purchased, because the said peerage is a huge parasite. But considerable services, nevertheless.

The despotic work of Louis XI., of Richelieu, and of Louis XIV., the creation of a sultan, leveling taken for true equality, the bastinado given by the sceptre, the common abasement of the people, all these Turkish tricks in France the peers prevented in England. The aristocracy was a wall, banking up the king on one side, sheltering the people on the other. They redeemed their arrogance towards the people by their insolence towards the king. Simon, Earl of Leicester, said to Henry III.: " *King, thou hast lied!*" The Lords curbed the crown, and grated against their kings in the tenderest point, that of

* Villiers called James I. "Your sowship."

venery. Every lord, passing through a royal park, had the right to kill a deer; in the house of the king the peer was at home; in the Tower of London the scale of allowance for the king was no more than that for a peer, viz., twelve pounds sterling per week. This was the House of Lords' doing.

Yet more. We owe to it the deposition of kings. The Lords ousted John Lackland, degraded Edward II., deposed Richard II., broke the power of Henry VI., and made Cromwell a possibility. What a Louis XIV. there was in Charles I.! Thanks to Cromwell, it remained latent. By the bye, we may here observe, that Cromwell himself, though no historian seems to have noticed the fact, aspired to the peerage. This was why he married Elizabeth Bouchier, descendant and heiress of a Cromwell, Lord Bouchier, whose peerage became extinct in 1471, and of a Bouchier, Lord Robesart, another peerage extinct in 1429. Carried on with the formidable increase of important events, he found the suppression of a king a shorter way to power than the recovery of a peerage. A ceremonial of the Lords, at times ominous, could reach even to the king. Two men-at-arms from the Tower, with their axes on their shoulders, between whom an accused peer stood at the bar of the house, might have been there in like attendance on the king as on any other nobleman. For five centuries the House of Lords acted on a system, and carried it out with determination. They had their days of idleness and weakness, as, for instance, that strange time when they allowed themselves to be seduced by the vessels loaded with cheeses, hams, and Greek wines sent them by Julius II. The English aristocracy was restless, haughty, ungovernable, watchful, and patriotically mistrustful. It was that aristocracy which, at the end of the seventeenth century, by act the tenth of the year 1694, deprived the borough of Stockbridge, in Hampshire, of the right of sending members to Parliament, and forced the Commons to declare null the election for that borough, stained by papistical fraud. It imposed the test on James, Duke of York, and, on his refusal to take it, excluded him from the throne. He reigned, notwithstanding; but the Lords wound up by calling him to account and banishing him. That aristocracy has had, in its long duration, some instinct of progress. It has always given out a certain quantity of appreciable light, except now towards its end, which is at hand. Under James II. it maintained in the Lower House the proportion of three hundred and forty-six burgesses against ninety-two knights. The sixteen barons, by courtesy, of the Cinque Ports were more than counterbalanced by the fifty citizens of the twenty-five cities. Though corrupt and egotistic, that aristocracy was, in some instances, singularly impartial. It is harshly judged. History

keeps all its compliments for the Commons. The justice of this is
doubtful. We consider the part played by the Lords a very great one.
Oligarchy is the independence of a barbarous state, but it is an independence. Take Poland, for instance, nominally a kingdom, really a republic. The peers of England held the throne in suspicion and guard-
ianship. Time after time they have made their power more felt than
that of the Commons. They gave check to the king. Thus, in that
remarkable year, 1694, the Triennial Parliament Bill, rejected by the
Commons, in consequence of the objections of William III., was passed by
the Lords. William III., in his irritation, deprived the Earl of Bath of
the governorship of Pendennis Castle, and Viscount Mordaunt of all
his offices. The House of Lords was the republic of Venice in the
heart of the royalty of England. To reduce the king to a doge was its
object; and, in proportion as it decreased the power of the crown, it
increased that of the people. Royalty knew this, and hated the peerage.
Each endeavored to lessen the other. What was thus lost by each was
proportionate profit to the people. Those two blind powers, monarchy
and oligarchy, could not see that they were working for the benefit of a
third, which was democracy. What a delight it was to the crown, in
the last century, to be able to hang a peer, Lord Ferrers!

However, they hung him with a silken rope. How polite!

"They would not have hung a peer of France," the Duke of Richelieu haughtily remarked. Granted. They would have beheaded him.
Still more polite!

Montmorency Tancarville signed himself *peer of France and England;* thus throwing the English peerage into the second rank. The
peers of France were higher and less powerful, holding to rank more
than to authority, and to precedence more than to domination. There
was between them and the Lords that shade of difference which sepa-
rates vanity from pride. With the peers of France, to take precedence
of foreign princes, of Spanish grandees, of Venetian patricians; to see
seated on the lower benches the Marshals of France, the Constable and
the Admiral of France, were he even Comte de Toulouse and son of
Louis XIV.; to draw a distinction between duchies in the male and
female line; to maintain the proper distance between a simple *comté,*
like Armagnac or Albret and a *comté pairie,* like Evreux; to wear by
right, at five-and-twenty, the blue ribbon of the golden fleece; to coun-
terbalance the Duke de la Tremoille, the most ancient peer of the
court, with the Duke Uzès, the most ancient peer of the parliament; to
claim as many pages and horses to their carriages as an elector; to be
called *monseigneur* by the first President; to discuss whether the Duke
de Maine dates his peerage as the Comte d'Eu, from 1458; to cross the

grand chamber diagonally, or by the side,—such things were grave matters. Grave matters with the Lords were the Navigation Act, the Test Act, the enrollment of Europe in the service of England, the command of the sea, the expulsion of the Stuarts, war with France. On one side, etiquette above all; on the other, empire above all. The peers of England had the substance, the peers of France the shadow.

To conclude, the House of Lords was a starting-point; towards civilization this is an immense thing. It had the honor to found a nation. It was the first incarnation of the unity of the people: English resistance, that obscure but all-powerful force, was born in the House of Lords. The barons, by a series of acts of violence against royalty, have paved the way for its eventual downfall. The House of Lords at the present day is somewhat sad and astonished at what it has unwillingly and unintentionally done, all the more that it is irrevocable.

What are concessions? Restitutions;—and nations know it.

"I grant," says the king.

"I get back my own," says the people.

The House of Lords believed that it was creating the privileges of the peerage, and it has produced the rights of the citizen. That vulture, aristocracy, has hatched the eagle's egg of liberty.

And now the egg is broken, the eagle is soaring, the vulture dying.

Aristocracy is at his last gasp; England is growing up.

Still, let us be just towards the aristocracy. It entered the scale against royalty, and was its counterpoise. It was an obstacle to despotism. It was a barrier.

Let us thank and bury it.

CHAPTER III

THE OLD HALL

EAR Westminster Abbey was an old Norman palace which was burnt in the time of Henry VIII. Its wings were spared. In one of them Edward VI. placed the House of Lords, in the other the House of Commons. Neither the two wings nor the two chambers are now in existence. The whole has been rebuilt.

We have already said, and we must repeat, that there is no resemblance between the House of Lords of the present day, and that of the past. In demolishing the ancient palace they somewhat demolished its ancient usages. The strokes of the pickaxe on the monument produce their counter-strokes on customs and charters. An old stone cannot fall without dragging down with it an old law. Place in a round room a parliament which has been hitherto held in a square room, and it will no longer be the same thing. A change in the shape of the shell changes the shape of the fish inside.

If you wish to preserve an old thing, human or divine, a code or a dogma, a nobility or a priesthood, never repair anything about it thoroughly, even its outside cover. Patch it up, nothing more. For instance, Jesuitism is a piece added to Catholicism. Treat edifices as you would treat institutions. Shadows should dwell in ruins. Worn-out powers are uneasy in chambers freshly decorated. Ruined palaces accord best with institutions in rags. To attempt to describe the House of Lords of other days would be to attempt to describe the unknown. History is night. In history there is no second tier. That which is no longer on the stage immediately fades into obscurity. The scene is shifted, and all is at once forgotten. The past has a synonym, the unknown.

The peers of England sat as a court of justice in Westminster

226

Hall, and as the higher legislative chamber in a chamber specially reserved for the purpose, called *The House of Lords.*

Besides the house of peers of England, which did not assemble as a court, unless convoked by the crown, two great English tribunals,

inferior to the house of peers, but superior to all other jurisdiction, sat in Westminster Hall. At the end of that hall they occupied adjoining compartments. The first was the Court of King's Bench, in which the king was supposed to preside; the second, the Court of Chancery, in which the Chancellor presided. The one was a court of justice, the other a court of mercy. It was the Chancellor who counseled the King to pardon; only rarely, though.

These two courts, which are still in existence, interpreted legislation, and reconstructed it somewhat, for the art of the judge is to carve
the code into jurisprudence; a task from which equity results as it best
may. Legislation was worked up and applied in the severity of the
great hall of Westminster, the rafters of which were of chestnut wood,
over which spiders could not spread their webs. There are enough of
them in all conscience in the laws.

To sit as a court, and to sit as a chamber, are two distinct things.
This double function constitutes supreme power. The Long Parliament, which began in November, 1640, felt the revolutionary necessity for this two-edged sword. So it declared that, as House of Lords,
it possessed judicial as well as legislative power.

This double power has been, from time immemorial, vested in the
House of Peers. We have just mentioned that as judges they occupied
Westminster Hall; as legislators, they had another chamber. This
other chamber, properly called the House of Lords, was oblong and
narrow. All the light in it came from four windows in deep embrasures, which received their light through the roof, and a bull's-eye,
composed of six panes with curtains, over the throne. At night there
was no other light than twelve half candelabra, fastened to the wall.
The chamber of Venice was darker still. A certain obscurity is pleasing to those owls of supreme power.

A high ceiling adorned with many-faced relievos and gilded cor-
nices, circled over the chamber where the Lords assembled. The Commons had but a flat ceiling. There is a meaning in all monarchical
buildings. At one end of the long chamber of the Lords was the door;
at the other, opposite to it, the throne. A few paces from the door, the
bar, a transverse barrier, and a sort of frontier, marked the spot where
the people ended, and the peerage began. To the right of the throne
was a fire-place with emblazoned pinnacles, and two bas-reliefs of marble, representing, one, the victory of Cuthwolf over the Britons, in 572;
the other, the geometrical plan of the borough of Dunstable, which had
four streets, parallel to the four quarters of the world. The throne was
approached by three steps. It was called the royal chair. On the two
walls, opposite each other, were displayed in successive pictures on a
huge piece of tapestry given to the Lords by Elizabeth, the adventures
of the Armada, from the time of its leaving Spain, until it was wrecked
on the coasts of Great Britain. The great hulls of the ships were
embroidered with threads of gold and silver, which had become blackened by time. Against this tapestry, cut at intervals by the candelabra
fastened in the wall, were placed, to the right of the throne, three rows
of benches for the bishops, and to the left three rows of benches for

the dukes, marquises, and earls, in tiers, and separated by gangways. On the three benches of the first section sat the dukes; on those of the second, the marquises; on those of the third, the earls. The viscounts' bench was placed across, opposite the throne, and behind, between the viscounts and the bar, were two benches for the barons.

On the highest bench to the right of the throne sat the two archbishops of Canterbury and York; on the middle bench, three bishops, London, Durham, and Winchester, and the other bishops on the lowest bench. There is between the Archbishop of Canterbury and the other bishops this considerable difference, that he is bishop "by divine providence," whilst the others are only so "by divine permission." On the right of the throne was a chair for the Prince of Wales, and on the left, folding chairs for the royal dukes, and behind the latter a raised seat for minor peers, who had not the privilege of voting. Plenty of fleurs-de-lis everywhere, and the great escutcheon of England over the four walls, above the peers, as well as above the king.

The sons of peers, and the heirs to peerages, assisted at the debates, standing behind the throne, between the dais and the wall. A large square space was left vacant between the tiers of benches placed along three sides of the chamber and the throne. In this space, which was covered with the state carpet, interwoven with the arms of Great Britain, were four wool-sacks—one in front of the throne, on which sat the Lord Chancellor, between the mace and the seal; one in front of the bishops, on which sat the judges, counselors of state, who had the right to sit, but not to vote; one in front of the dukes, marquises, and earls, on which sat the Secretaries of State; and one in front of the viscounts and barons, on which sat the Clerk of the Crown and the Clerk of the Parliament, and on which the two under-clerks wrote, kneeling.

In the middle of the space was a large covered table, heaped with bundles of papers, registers, and summonses, with magnificent inkstands of chased silver, and with high candlesticks at the four corners.

The peers took their seats in chronological order, each according to the date of the creation of his peerage. They ranked according to their titles, and within their grade of nobility according to seniority. At the bar stood the Usher of the Black Rod, his wand in his hand. Inside the door was the Deputy-Usher; and outside, the Crier of the Black Rod, whose duty it was to open the sittings of the Courts of Justice, with the cry, "*Oyez!*" in French, uttered thrice, with a solemn accent upon the first syllable. Near the Crier stood the Sergeant Mace-bearer of the Chancellor.

In royal ceremonies the temporal peers wore coronets on their heads, and the spiritual peers, mitres. The archbishops wore mitres, with a ducal coronet; and the bishops, who rank after viscounts, mitres, with a baron's coronet.

It is to be remarked, as a coincidence at once strange and instructive, that this square formed by the throne, the bishops, and the barons, with kneeling magistrates within it, was in form similar to the ancient parliament in France under the two first dynasties. The aspect of authority was the same in France as in England. Hincmar, in his treatise, "*De Ordinatione Sacri Palatii,*" described in 853, the sittings of the House of Lords at Westminster in the eighteenth century. Strange, indeed! a description given nine hundred years before the existence of the thing described.

But what is history! An echo of the past in the future; a reflex from the future on the past.

The assembly of Parliament was obligatory only once in every seven years.

The Lords deliberated in secret, with closed doors. The debates of the Commons were public. Publicity entails diminution of dignity.

The number of the Lords was unlimited. To create lords was the menace of royalty; a means of government.

At the beginning of the eighteenth century the House of Lords already contained a very large number of members. It has increased still further since that period. To dilute the aristocracy is politic. Elizabeth most probably erred in condensing the peerage into sixty-five lords. The less numerous, the more intense is a peerage. In assemblies, the more numerous the members, the fewer the heads. James II. understood this when he increased the Upper House to a hundred and eighty-eight lords; a hundred and eighty-six if we subtract from the peerages the two duchies of royal favorites, Portsmouth and Cleveland. Under Anne the total number of the lords, including bishops, was two hundred and seven. Not counting the Duke of Cumberland, husband of the Queen, there were twenty-five dukes, of whom the premier, Norfolk, did not take his seat, being a Catholic, and of whom the junior, Cambridge, the Elector of Hanover, did, although a foreigner. Winchester, termed first and sole Marquis of England—as Astorga was termed sole Marquis of Spain, was absent, being a Jacobite; so that there were only five marquises, of whom the premier was Lindsay, and the junior Lothian; seventy-nine earls, of whom Derby was premier, and Islay junior; nine viscounts, of whom Hereford was premier, and Lonsdale junior; and sixty-two barons, of whom Abergavenny was premier, and Hervey junior. Lord Hervey, the junior baron, was what was called the "Puisné of the House." Derby, of whom Oxford, Shrewsbury, and Kent took precedence, and who was therefore but the fourth under James II., became (under Anne) premier earl. Two Chancellor's names had disappeared from the list of barons—Verulam, under which designation history finds us Bacon; and Wem, under which it finds us Jefferies. Bacon and Jefferies! both names overshadowed, though by different crimes. In 1705, the twenty-six bishops were reduced to twenty-five, the See of Chester being vacant. Amongst the bishops some were peers of high rank, such as William Talbot, Bishop of Oxford, who was head of the Protestant branch of that family. Others were eminent Doctors, like John Sharp, Archbishop of York, formerly Dean of Norwich; the poet, Thomas Spratt, Bishop of Rochester, an apoplectic old man; and that Bishop of Lincoln, who was to die Archbishop of Canterbury, Wake, the adversary of Bossuet.

On important occasions, and when a message from the Crown to the House was expected, the whole of this august assembly—in robes, in wigs, in mitres, or plumes—formed in line, and displayed their rows of heads, in tiers, along the walls of the House, where the storm was vaguely to be seen exterminating the Armada—almost as much as to say, " The storm is at the orders of England."

THE whole ceremony of the investiture of Gwynplaine from his entry under the King's Gate to his taking the test under the nave window, was enacted in a sort of twilight.

Lord William Cowper had not permitted that he, as Lord Chancellor of England, should receive too many details of circumstances connected with the disfigurement of the young Lord Fermain Clancharlie, considering it below his dignity to know that a peer was not handsome; and feeling that his dignity would suffer if an inferior should venture to intrude on him information of such a nature. We know that a common fellow will take pleasure in saying: "that prince is humpbacked;" therefore, it is abusive to say that a lord is deformed. To the few words dropped on the subject by the queen the Lord Chancellor had contented himself with replying:

"The face of a peer is in his peerage!"

Ultimately, however, the affidavits he had read and certified enlightened him. Hence the precautions which he took. The face of the new lord, on his entrance into the House, might cause some sensation. This it was necessary to prevent; and the Lord Chancellor took his measures for the purpose. It is a fixed idea, and a rule of conduct in grave personages, to allow as little disturbance as possible. Dislike of incident is a part of their gravity. He felt the necessity of so ordering matters, that the admission of Gwynplaine should take place without any hitch, and like that of any other successor to the peerage.

It was for this reason that the Lord Chancellor directed that the reception of Lord Fermain Clancharlie should take place at the evening sitting. The Chancellor being the door-keeper—*Quodammodo ostiarus,*" says the Norman charter; "*Januarum cancellorumque potestas,*" says Tertullian—he can officiate outside the room on the threshold; and

232

Lord William Cowper had used his right by carrying out under the nave the formalities of the investiture of Lord Fermain Clancharlie. Moreover, he had brought forward the hour for the ceremonies; so that

the new peer actually made his entrance into the house before the house had assembled.

For the investiture of a peer on the threshold, and not in the chamber itself, there were precedents. The first hereditary baron, John de Beauchamp, of Holt Castle, created by patent by Richard II., in 1387, Baron Kidderminster, was thus installed. In renewing this precedent the Lord Chancellor was creating for himself a future cause for embarrassment, of which he felt the inconvenience less than two years afterwards on the entrance of Viscount Newhaven into the House of Lords.

Short-sighted as we have already stated him to be, Lord William Cowper scarcely perceived the deformity of Gwynplaine; while the two sponsors, being old and nearly blind, did not perceive it at all.

The Lord Chancellor had chosen them for that very reason.

More than this, the Lord Chancellor, having only seen the presence and stature of Gwynplaine, thought him a fine-looking man. When the door-keeper opened the folding doors to Gwynplaine there were but few peers in the house; and these few were nearly all old men. In assemblies the old members are the most punctual, just as towards women they are the most assiduous.

On the duke's benches there were but two, one white-headed, the other gray: Thomas Osborne, Duke of Leeds, and Schomberg, son of that Schomberg, German by birth, French by his marshal's bâton, and English by his peerage, who was banished by the edict of Nantes, and who, having fought against England as a Frenchman, fought against France as an Englishman. On the benches of the lords spiritual there sat only the Archbishop of Canterbury, Primate of England, above; and below, Dr. Simon Patrick, Bishop of Ely, in conversation with Evelyn Pierrepoint, Marquis of Dorchester, who was explaining to him the difference between a gabion considered singly and when used in the parapet of a field work, and between palisades and fraises; the former being a row of posts driven into the ground in front of the tents, for the purpose of protecting the camp; the latter sharp-pointed stakes set up under the wall of a fortress, to prevent the escalade of the besiegers and the desertion of the besieged; and the marquis was explaining further the method of placing fraises in the ditches of redoubts, half of each stake being buried and half exposed. Thomas Thynne, Viscount Weymouth, having approached the light of a chandelier, was examining a plan of his architect's for laying out his gardens at Longleat, in Wiltshire, in the Italian style,—as a lawn, broken up into plots, with squares of turf alternating with squares of red and yellow sand, of river shells, and of fine coal dust. On the viscounts' benches was a group of old peers, Essex, Ossulstone, Peregrine, Osborne, William Zulestein, Earl of Rochford, and amongst them, a few more youthful ones, of the faction which did not wear wigs, gathered round Price Devereux, Viscount Hereford, and discussing the question whether an infusion of Apalachian holly was tea. "Very nearly," said Osborne.—"Quite," said Essex. This discussion was attentively listened to by Paulet St. John, a cousin of Bolingbroke, of whom Voltaire was, later on, in some degree the pupil; for Voltaire's education, commenced by Père Porée, was finished by Bolingbroke. On the marquises' benches, Thomas de Grey, Marquis of Kent, Lord Chamberlain to the Queen, was informing Robert Bertie, Marquis of Lindsay, Lord Chamberlain of England, that the first prize in the great English lottery of 1694 had been won by two French refugees, Monsieur Le Coq, formerly councilor in the parliament of Paris, and Monsieur Ravenel, a gentleman of Brittany. The Earl of Wemyss was reading a book, entitled "*Pratique Curieuse des Oracles des Sybilles.*" John Campbell, Earl of Greenwich, famous for his long chin, his gayety, and his eighty-seven years, was writing to his mistress. Lord Chandos was trimming his nails.

The sitting which was about to take place, being a royal one, where the crown was to be represented by commissioners, two assistant door-keepers were placing in front of the throne a bench covered with purple velvet. On the second wool-sack sat the Master of the Rolls, *sacrorum scriniorum magister*, who had then for his residence the house formerly belonging to the converted Jews. Two under-clerks were kneeling, and turning over the leaves of the registers which lay on the fourth wool-sack. In the meantime the Lord Chancellor took his place on the first wool-sack. The members of the chamber took theirs, some sitting, others standing; when the Archbishop of Canterbury rose and read the prayer, and the sitting of the house began.

Gwynplaine had already been there for some time without attracting any notice. The second bench of barons, on which was his place, was close to the bar, so that he had had to take but a few steps to reach it. The two peers, his sponsors, sat, one on his right, the other on his left; thus almost concealing the presence of the new-comer.

No one having been furnished with any previous information, the Clerk of the Parliament had read in a low voice, and, as it were, mumbled through the different documents concerning the new peer, and the Lord Chancellor had proclaimed his admission in the midst of what is called, in the reports, "general inattention." Every one was talking. There buzzed through the House that cheerful hum of voices during which assemblies pass things which will not bear the light, and at which they wonder when they find out what they have done, too late.

Gwynplaine was seated in silence, with his head uncovered, between the two old peers, Lord Fitzwalter and Lord Arundel.

Let us add that Barkilphedro, like a spy as he was, had, in his official communications before the Lord Chancellor, attenuated to a certain extent the deformity of Lord Clancharlie, maintaining that Gwynplaine could at will suppress the grin and look serious. Besides, from an aristocratic point of view, what did it matter ! Lord Cowper, as a lawyer, had declared: " The restoration of a peer is of more importance than the restoration of a king!" It is a shame and an outrage for a lord to be deformed, but how does that affect his right? The right of being peer or king is superior to deformity or infirmity. Was not a wild beast's cry as hereditary as the peerage in the ancient family of the Comyns Earls of Buchan, extinct in 1347, so that it was by the tiger-yell that the Scotch peer was recognized? Did his blood-spotted face prevent Cæsar Borgia from being Duke de Valentinois? Did blindness prevent John of Luxemburg being King of Bohemia? Did a hump back prevent Richard III. from being King of England? Viewed aright, infirmity or deformity, accepted with haughty indifference, affirm and confirm grandeur. This is another aspect of the question, and not the least. As we have seen, nothing could oppose the admission of Gwynplaine, and the prudent precautions of the Lord Chancellor were superfluous from the point of view of aristocratic principle.

On entering, according to the instructions of the King-at-Arms— afterwards renewed by his sponsors—he had bowed to the throne.

Thus all was over. He was a peer.

That pinnacle, under the glory of which he had, all his life, seen his master, Ursus, bow himself down in fear—that prodigious pinnacle was under his feet.

He was in that place, so dark and yet so dazzling in England. Old peak of the feudal mountain, looked up to for six centuries by Europe and by history!

Terrible nimbus of a world of shadow! He had entered into the brightness of its glory, and his entrance was irrevocable.

He was there in his own sphere, seated on his throne, like the king on his.

He was there, and nothing in the future could obliterate the fact. The royal crown, which he saw under the dais, was brother to his coronet. He was a peer of that throne.

In the face of majesty he was peerage; less, but like.

Yesterday, what was he? A player. To-day, what was he? A prince.

Yesterday, nothing; to-day, everything.

It was a sudden confrontation of misery and power, meeting face to face, and resolving themselves at once into the two halves of a conscience. Two spectres, Adversity and Prosperity, were taking possession of the same soul, and each drawing that soul towards itself.

Oh, pathetic division of an intellect, of a will, of a brain, between two brothers who are enemies! the Phantom of Poverty and the Phantom of Wealth! Abel and Cain in the same man!

CHAPTER V

Y degrees the seats of the House filled as the lords arrived. The question was the vote for augmenting, by a hundred thousand pounds sterling, the annual income of George of Denmark, Duke of Cumberland, the queen's husband. Besides this, it was announced that several bills assented to by her majesty were to be brought back to the House by the Commissioners of the Crown empowered and charged to sanction them. This raised the sitting to a royal one. The peers all wore their robes over their usual court or ordinary dress. These robes, similar to that which had been thrown over Gwynplaine, were alike for all, excepting that the dukes had five bands of ermine, trimmed with gold; marquises, four; earls and viscounts, three; and barons, two. Most of the lords entered in groups. They had met in the corridors, and were continuing the conversations there begun. A few came in alone. The costumes of all were solemn; but neither their attitudes nor their words corresponded with them. On entering, each one bowed to the throne.

The peers flowed in. The series of great names marched past with scant ceremonial, the public not being present. Leicester entered and shook Lichfield's hand; then came Charles Mordaunt, Earl of Peterborough and Monmouth, the friend of Locke, under whose advice he had proposed the recoinage of money; then Charles Campbell, Earl of Loudoun, listening to Fulke Greville, Lord Brooke; then Dormer, Earl of Carnarvon; then Robert Sutton, Baron Lexington, son of that Lexington who recommended Charles II. to banish Gregorio Leti, the historiographer, who was so ill-advised as to try to become a historian; then Thomas Bellasys, Viscount Falconburg, a handsome old man; and the three cousins, Howard, Earl of Bindon, Bowes Howard, Earl of

Berkshire, and Stafford Howard, Earl of Stafford—all together; then John Lovelace, Baron Lovelace, which peerage became extinct in 1736, so that Richardson was enabled to introduce Lovelace in his book, and to create a type under the name. All these personages—celebrated each in his own way, either in politics or in war, and of whom many were an honor to England—were laughing and talking.

It was history, as it were, seen in undress.

In less than half an hour the House was nearly full. This was to be expected, as the sitting was a royal one. What was more unusual was the eagerness of the conversations. The House, so sleepy not long before, now hummed like a hive of bees.

The arrival of the peers who had come in late had woke them up. These lords had brought news. It was strange that the peers who had been there at the opening of the sitting knew nothing of what had occurred, while those who had not been there knew all about it.

Several lords had come from Windsor.

For some hours past the adventures of Gwynplaine had been the subject of conversation. A secret is a net; let one mesh drop, and the whole goes to pieces. In the morning, in consequence of the incidents related above, the whole story of a peer found on the stage, and of a mountebank become a lord, had burst forth at Windsor in Royal places. The princes had talked about it, and then the lackeys. From the Court the news soon reached the town. Events have a weight, and the mathematical rule of velocity, increasing in proportion to the squares of the distance, applies to them. They fall upon the public, and work themselves through it with the most astounding rapidity. At seven o'clock no one in London had caught wind of the story. By eight, Gwynplaine was the talk of the town. Only the lords who had been so punctual that they were present before the assembling of the House were ignorant of the circumstances, not having been in the town when the matter was talked of by every one, and having been in the House, where nothing had been perceived. Seated quietly on their benches, they were addressed by the eager new-comers.

" Well ! " said Francis Brown, Viscount Montacute, to the Marquis of Dorchester.

" What ? "

" Is it possible ? "

" What ? "

" The Laughing Man ! "

" Who is the Laughing Man ? "

" Don't you know the Laughing Man ? "

" No."

"He is a clown, a fellow performing at fairs. He has an extraordinary face, which people gave a penny to look at. A mountebank."

"Well, what then?"

"You have just installed him as a peer of England."

"You are the laughing man, my Lord Montacute!"

"I am not laughing, my Lord Dorchester."

Lord Montacute made a sign to the Clerk of the Parliament, who rose from his wool-sack, and confirmed to their lordships the fact of the admission of the new peer. Besides, he detailed the circumstances.

"How wonderful!" said Lord Dorchester. "I was talking to the Bishop of Ely all the while."

The young Earl of Annesley addressed old Lord Eure, who had but two years more to live, as he died in 1707.

"My Lord Eure."

"My Lord Annesley."

"Did you know Lord Linnæus Clancharlie ?"

"A man of by-gone days. Yes, I did."

"He died in Switzerland ? "

"Yes; we were relations."

"He was a republican under Cromwell, and remained a republican under Charles II.? "

"A republican ? Not at all! He was sulking. He had a personal quarrel with the king. I know from good authority that Lord Clancharlie would have returned to his allegiance, if they had given him the office of Chancellor, which Lord Hyde held."

"You astonish me, Lord Eure. I had heard that Lord Clancharlie was an honest politician."

"An honest politician ! does such a thing exist ! Young man, there is no such thing."

"And Cato ? "

"Oh, you believe in Cato, do you ? "

"And Aristides ? "

"They did well to exile him."

"And Thomas More ? "

"They did well to cut off his head."

"And in your opinion, Lord Clancharlie was a man as you describe. As for a man remaining in exile, why, it is simply ridiculous."

"He died there."

"An ambitious man disappointed ? "

"You ask if I knew him ? I should think so indeed. I was his dearest friend."

"Do you know, Lord Eure, that he married when in Switzerland ? "

"I am pretty sure of it."

"And that he had a lawful heir by that marriage ? "

"Yes ; who is dead."

"Who is living."

"Living ? "

"Living."

"Impossible ! "

"It is a fact—proved, authenticated, confirmed, registered."

"Then that son will inherit the Clancharlie peerage ? "

"He is not going to inherit it."

" Why ? "

" Because he has inherited it. It is done."

" Done ? "

" Turn your head, Lord Eure; he is sitting behind you, on the barons' benches.

Lord Eure turned, but Gwynplaine's face was concealed under his forest of hair.

" So," said the old man, who could see nothing but his hair, " he has already adopted the new fashion. He does not wear a wig."

Grantham accosted Colepepper.

" Some one is finely sold."

" Who is that ? "

" David Dirry-Moir."

" How is that ? "

" He is no longer a peer."

" How can that be ? "

And Henry Auverquerque, Earl of Grantham, told John Baron Colepepper the whole anecdote—how the waif-flask had been carried to the Admiralty, about the parchment of the Comprachicos, the *Jussu regis*, countersigned *Jefferies*, and the confrontation in the torture-cell at Southwark, the proof of all the facts acknowledged by the Lord Chancellor and by the Queen; the taking the test under the nave, and finally the admission of Lord Fermain Clancharlie at the commencement of the sitting. Both the lords endeavored to distinguish his face as he sat between Lord Fitzwalter and Lord Arundel, but with no better success than Lord Eure and Lord Annesley.

Gwynplaine, either by chance or by the arrangement of his sponsors, forewarned by the Lord Chancellor, was so placed in shadow as to escape their curiosity.

" Who is it ? Where is he ? "

Such was the exclamation of all the new-comers, but no one succeeded in making him out distinctly. Some, who had seen Gwynplaine in the Green Box, were exceedingly curious, but lost their labor; as it sometimes happens that a young lady is intrenched within a troop of dowagers, Gwynplaine was, as it were, enveloped in several layers of lords, old, infirm, and indifferent. Good livers, with the gout, are marvelously indifferent in stories about their neighbors.

There passed, from hand to hand, copies of a letter three lines in length, written, it was said, by the Duchess Josiana to the Queen, her sister, in answer to the injunction made by her Majesty, that she should espouse the new peer, the lawful heir of the Clancharlies, Lord Fermain. This letter was couched in the following terms:

" Madam :

" The arrangement will suit me just as well. I can have Lord David for my lover.

" (Signed) Josiana."

This note, whether a true copy or a forgery, was received by all with the greatest enthusiasm. A young lord, Charles Okehampton, Baron Mohun, who belonged to the wigless faction, read and re-read it with delight. Lewis de Duras, Earl of Faversham, an Englishman with a Frenchman's wit, looked at Mohun and smiled.

" That is a woman I should like to marry!" exclaimed Lord Mohun.

The lords around them overheard the following dialogue between Duras and Mohun.

" Marry the Duchess Josiana, Lord Mohun !"

" Why not ?"

" Plague take it."

" She would make one very happy!"

" She would make many very happy."

" But is it not always a question of many ?"

" Lord Mohun, you are right. With regard to women, we have always the leavings of others. Has any one ever had a beginning ?"

" Adam, perhaps."

" Not he."

" Then Satan."

" My dear lord," concluded Lewis de Duras, " Adam only lent his name. Poor dupe! He endorsed the human race. Man was begotten on the woman by the devil."

Hugh Cholmondeley, Earl of Cholmondeley, strong in points of law, was asked from the bishops' benches by Nathaniel Crew, who was doubly a peer, being a temporal peer, as Baron Crew, and a spiritual peer, as Bishop of Durham.

" Is it possible ?" said Crew.

" Is it regular ?" said Cholmondeley.

" The investiture of this peer was made outside the House," replied the Bishop; " but it is stated that there are precedents for it."

" Yes. Lord Beauchamp, under Richard II.; Lord Chenay, under Elizabeth."

" Lord Broghill, under Cromwell."

" Cromwell goes for nothing."

" What do you think of it all ?"

" Many different things."

"My Lord Cholmondeley, what will be the rank of this young Lord Clancharlie in the House?"

"My Lord Bishop, the interruption of the Republic having displaced ancient rights of precedence, Clancharlie now ranks in the peer-

age between Barnard and Somers, so that should each be called upon to speak in turn, Lord Clancharlie would be the eighth in rotation."

"Really! he, a mountebank from a public show!"

"The act, *per se*, does not astonish me, my Lord Bishop. We meet with such things. Still more wonderful circumstances occur! Was not the War of the Roses predicted by the sudden drying up of the river

Ouse, in Bedfordshire, on January 1st, 1399.   Now, if a river dries up, a peer may, quite as naturally, fall into a servile condition.   Ulysses, King of Ithaca, played all kinds of different parts.   Fermain Clancharlie remained a lord under his player's garb.   Sordid garments touch not the soul's nobility.   But taking the test and the investiture outside the sitting, though strictly legal, might give rise to objections.   I am of opinion that it will be necessary to look into the matter, to see if there be any ground to question the Lord Chancellor in Privy Council, later on.   We shall see in a week or two what is best to be done."

And the Bishop added:

" All the same.   It is an adventure such as has not occurred since Earl Gesbodus's time."

Gwynplaine, the Laughing Man ; the Tadcaster Inn ; the Green Box ; " *Chaos Vanquished ;* " Switzerland ; Chillon ; the Comprachicos ; exile ; mutilation ; the Republic ; Jefferies ; James II. ; the *jussu regis ;* the bottle opened at the Admiralty ; the father, Lord Linnæus ; the legitimate son, Lord Fermain ; the bastard son, Lord David ; the probable law suits ; the Duchess Josiana ; the Lord Chancellor ; the Queen —all these subjects of conversation ran from bench to bench.

Whispering is like a train of gunpowder.

They seized on every incident.   All the details of the occurrence caused an immense murmur through the house.   Gwynplaine, wandering in the depths of his reverie, heard the buzzing without knowing that he was the cause of it.   He was strangely attentive to the depths, not to the surface.   Excess of attention becomes isolation.

The buzz of conversation in the House impedes its usual business no more than the dust raised by a troop impedes its march.   The judges —who in the Upper House were mere assistants, without the privilege of speaking, except when questioned—had taken their places on the second wool-sack ; and the three Secretaries of State theirs on the third.

The heirs to peerages flowed into their compartment, at once without and within the House, at the back of the throne.

The peers in their minority were on their own benches.   In 1705 the number of these little lords amounted to no less than a dozen— Huntingdon, Lincoln, Dorset, Warwick, Bath, Barlington, Derwentwater,—destined to a tragical death,—Longueville, Lonsdale, Dudley, Ward, and Carterel : a troop of brats made up of eight earls, two viscounts, and two barons.

In the centre, on the three stages of benches, each lord had taken his seat.   Almost all the bishops were there.   The dukes mustered strong, beginning with Charles Seymour, Duke of Somerset ; and ending with George Augustus, Elector of Hanover, and Duke of Cambridge, junior in date of creation, and consequently junior in rank. All were in order, according to right of precedence: Cavendish, Duke of Devonshire, whose grandfather had sheltered Hobbs, at Hardwicke, when he was ninety-two; Lenox, Duke of Richmond; the three Fitzroys, the Duke of Southampton, the Duke of Grafton, and the Duke of Northumberland; Butler, Duke of Ormond; Somerset, Duke of Beaufort; Beauclerk, Duke of St. Albans; Paulet, Duke of Bolton; Osborne, Duke of Leeds; Wrottesley Russell, Duke of Bedford, whose motto and device was *che sara sara,* which expresses a determination to take things as they come; Sheffield, Duke of Buckingham; Manners, Duke of Rutland; and others. Neither Howard, Duke of Norfolk, nor Talbot, Duke of Shrewsbury, were present, being Catholics; nor Churchill, Duke of Marlborough, the French Malbrouck, who was at that time fighting the French and beating them. There were no Scotch dukes then—Queensberry, Montrose, and Roxburgh not being admitted till 1707.

CHAPTER VI

THE HIGH AND THE LOW

LL at once a bright light broke upon the House. Four door-keepers brought and placed on each side of the throne four high candelabra filled with wax-lights. The throne, thus illuminated, shone in a kind of purple light. It was empty, but august. The presence of the queen herself could not have added much majesty to it.

The Usher of the Black Rod entered with his wand, and announced:

"The Lords Commissioners of Her Majesty."

The hum of conversation immediately subsided.

A clerk, in a wig and gown, appeared at the great door, holding a cushion worked with *fleurs-de-lis*, on which lay parchment documents. These documents were bills. From each hung the *bille*, or *bulle*, by a silken string, from which laws are called bills in England, and bulls at Rome. Behind the clerk walked three men in peers' robes, and wearing plumed hats.

These were the Royal Commissioners. The first was the Lord High Treasurer of England, Godolphin; the second, the Lord President of the Council, Pembroke; the third, the Lord of the Privy Seal, Newcastle.

They walked one by one according to precedence, not of their rank, but of their commission—Godolphin first, Newcastle last, although a duke.

They reached the bench in front of the throne, to which they bowed, took off and replaced their hats, and sat down on the bench.

The Lord Chancellor turned towards the Usher of the Black Rod, and said:

"Order the Commons to the bar of the House."

246

The Usher of the Black Rod retired.

The clerk, who was one of the clerks of the House of Lords, placed on the table, between the four wool-sacks, the cushion on which lay the bills.

Then there came an interruption, which continued for some minutes. Two door-keepers placed before the bar a stool, with three steps. This stool was covered with crimson velvet, on which *fleurs-de-lis* were designed in gilt nails.

The great door, which had been closed, was re-opened; and a voice announced:

"The faithful Commons of England."

It was the Usher of the Black Rod announcing the other half of parliament.

The lords put on their hats.

The members of the House of Commons entered, preceded by their Speaker, all with uncovered heads.

They stopped at the bar. They were in their ordinary garb; for the most part dressed in black and wearing swords.

The Speaker, the Right Honorable John Smith, an esquire, member for the borough of Andover, got up on the stool which was at the centre of the bar. The Speaker of the Commons wore a robe of black satin, with large hanging sleeves, embroidered before and behind with brandenburgs of gold, and a wig smaller than that of the Lord Chancellor. He was majestic, but inferior.

The Commons, both Speaker and members, stood waiting, with uncovered heads, before the peers, who were seated, with their hats on.

Amongst the members of Commons might have been remarked the Chief Justice of Chester, Joseph Jekyll; the Queen's three Sergeants-at-Law—Hooper, Powys, and Parker; James Montagu, Solicitor-General; and the Attorney-General, Simon Harcourt. With the exception of a few baronets and knights, and nine lords by courtesy—Hartington, Windsor, Woodstock, Mordaunt, Granby, Scudamore, Fitzhardinge, Hyde, and Berkeley—sons of peers and heirs to peerages—all were of the people—a sort of gloomy and silent crowd.

When the noise made by the trampling of feet had ceased, the Crier of the Black Rod, standing by the door, exclaimed:

"Oyez!"

The Clerk of the Crown arose. He took, unfolded, and read the first of the documents on the cushion. It was a message from the Queen, naming three commissioners to represent her in Parliament, with power to sanction the bills.

"To wit——"

Here the Clerk raised his voice.

"Sidney Earl Godolphin."

The Clerk bowed to Lord Godolphin. Lord Godolphin raised his hat.

The Clerk continued:

"Thomas Herbert, Earl of Pembroke and Montgomery."

The Clerk bowed to Lord Pembroke. Lord Pembroke touched his hat.

The Clerk resumed:

"John Holles, Duke of Newcastle."

The Duke of Newcastle nodded.

The Clerk of the Crown resumed his seat.

The Clerk of the Parliaments arose. His under-clerk, who had been on his knees behind him, got up also. Both turned their faces to the throne, and their backs to the Commons.

There were five bills on the cushion. These five bills, voted by the Commons and agreed to by the Lords, awaited the royal sanction.

The Clerk of the Parliaments read the first bill.

It was a bill passed by the Commons, charging the country with the costs of the improvements made by the Queen to her residence at Hampton Court, amounting to a million sterling.

The reading over, the Clerk bowed low to the throne. The under-clerk bowed lower still; then, half turning his head towards the Commons, he said:

"The Queen accepts your benevolence—*et ainsi le veut.*"

The Clerk read the second bill.

It was a law condemning to imprisonment and fine whomsoever withdrew himself from the service of the train-bands. The train-bands were a militia, recruited from the middle and lower classes, serving gratis, which in Elizabeth's reign furnished, on the approach of the Armada, one hundred and eighty-five thousand foot-soldiers and forty thousand horse.

The two clerks made a fresh bow to the throne, after which, the under-clerk, again half turning his face to the Commons, said:

"*La Reine le veut.*"

The third bill was for increasing the tithes and prebends of the Bishopric of Lichfield and Coventry, which was one of the richest in England; for making an increased yearly allowance to the cathedral, for augmenting the number of its canons, and for increasing its deaneries and benefices, "to the benefit of our holy religion," as the preamble set forth.

The fourth bill added to the budget fresh taxes: one on marbled paper; one on hackney coaches, fixed at the number of eight hundred in London, and taxed at a sum equal to fifty-two francs yearly each; one on barristers, attorneys, and solicitors, at forty-eight francs a year a head; one on tanned skins, notwithstanding, said the preamble, the complaints of the workers in leather. One on soap, notwithstanding the petitions of the City of Exeter and of the whole of Devonshire, where great quantities of cloth and serge were manufactured; one on wine at four shillings; one on flour; one on barley and hops; and one renewing for four years—"the necessities of the State," said the preamble, "requiring to be attended to before the remonstrances of commerce"—tonnage-dues, varying from six francs per ton, for ships coming from the westward, to eighteen francs on those coming from the eastward. Finally, the bill, declaring the sums already levied for the current year insufficient, concluded by decreeing a poll-tax on each subject throughout the kingdom of four shillings per head, adding that a double tax would be levied on every one who did not take the fresh oath to Government.

The fifth bill forbade the admission into the hospital of any sick person who on entering did not deposit a pound sterling to pay for his funeral, in case of death. These last three bills, like the first two, were one after the other sanctioned and made law by a bow to the throne, and the four words pronounced by the under-clerk, "*la Reine le veut*," spoken over his shoulder to the Commons. Then the under-clerk knelt down again before the fourth wool-sack, and the Lord Chancellor said:

" *Soit fait comme il est désiré.*

This terminated the royal sitting. The Speaker, bent double before the Chancellor, descended from the stool, backwards, lifting up his robe behind him; the members of the House of Commons bowed to the ground, and as the Upper House resumed the business of the day, heedless of all these marks of respect, the Commons departed.

CHAPTER VII

STORMS OF MEN ARE WORSE THAN STORMS OF OCEANS

HE doors were closed again, the Usher of the Black Rod re-entered; the Lords Commissioners left the bench of State, took their places at the top of the dukes' benches, by right of their commission, and the Lord Chancellor addressed the House.

"My Lords, the House having deliberated for several days on the Bill which proposes to augment, by 100,000*l.* sterling the annual provision for his Royal Highness the Prince, her Majesty's Consort, and the debate having been exhausted and closed, the House will proceed to vote; the votes will be taken according to custom, beginning with the puisne Baron. Each Lord, on his name being called, will rise and answer *content*, or *non-content*, and will be at liberty to explain the motives of his vote, if he thinks fit to do so. Clerk, take the vote."

The Clerk of the House, standing up, opened a large folio, and spread it open on a gilded desk. This book was the list of the Peerage.

The puisne of the House of Lords at that time was John Hervey, created Baron and Peer in 1703, from whom is descended the Marquis of Bristol.

The Clerk called:

"My Lord John, Baron Hervey."

An old man in a fair wig arose, and said, "Content."

Then he sat down.

The Clerk registered his vote.

The Clerk continued:

"My Lord Francis Seymour, Baron Conway, of Killultagh."

"Content," murmured, half rising, an elegant young man, with a face like a page, who little thought that he was to be ancestor to the Marquises of Hertford.

250

"My Lord John Leveson, Baron Gower," continued the Clerk.

This Baron, from whom were to spring the Dukes of Sutherland, rose, and, as he reseated himself, said "Content."

The Clerk went on:

"My Lord Heneage Finch, Baron Guernsey."

The ancestor of the Earls of Aylesford, neither older nor less elegant than the ancestor of the Marquises of Hertford, justified his device, *aperto vivere voto*, by the proud tone in which he exclaimed, "Content."

Whilst he was resuming his seat, the Clerk called the fifth Baron.

"My Lord John, Baron Granville."

Rising and resuming his seat quickly, "Content," exclaimed Lord Granville, of Potheridge, whose peerage was to become extinct in 1709.

The Clerk passed to the sixth.

"My Lord Charles Montague, Baron Halifax."

"Content," said Lord Halifax, the bearer of a title which had become extinct in the Saville family, and was destined to become extinct again in that of Montague. Montague is distinct from Montagu and Montacute. And Lord Halifax added, "Prince George has an allowance as Her Majesty's Consort; he has another as Prince of Denmark; another as Duke of Cumberland; another as Lord High Admiral of England and Ireland; but he has not one as Commander-in-Chief. This is an injustice and a wrong which must be set right, in the interest of the English people."

Then Lord Halifax passed an eulogium on the Christian religion, abused popery, and voted the subsidy.

Lord Halifax sat down, and the Clerk resumed:

"My Lord Christopher, Baron Barnard."

Lord Barnard, from whom were to descend the Dukes of Cleveland, rose to answer to his name.

"Content."

He took some time in reseating himself, for he wore a lace band which was worth showing. For all that, Lord Barnard was a worthy gentleman and a brave officer.

While Lord Barnard was resuming his seat, the Clerk, who read by routine, hesitated for an instant; he readjusted his spectacles, and leaned over the register with renewed attention; then, lifting up his head, he said:

"My Lord Fermain Clancharlie, Baron Clancharlie and Hunkerville."

Gwynplaine arose.

"Non-content," said he.

Every face was turned towards him. Gwynplaine remained standing. The branches of candles, placed on each side of the throne, lighted up his features, and marked them against the darkness of the august chamber in the relief with which a mask might show against a background of smoke.

Gwynplaine had made that effort over himself which, it may be remembered, was possible to him in extremity. By a concentration of will equal to that which would be needed to cow a tiger, he had succeeded in obliterating for a moment the fatal grin upon his face. For an instant he no longer laughed. This effort could not last long. Rebellion against that which is our law or our fatality, must be short-lived; at times, the waters of the sea resist the power of gravitation, swell into a water-spout and become a mountain, but only on the condition of falling back again.

Such a struggle was Gwynplaine's. For an instant, which he felt to be a solemn one, by a prodigious intensity of will, but for not much longer than a flash of lightning lasts, he had thrown over his brow the dark veil of his soul—he held in suspense his incurable laugh. From that face upon which it had been carved, he had withdrawn the joy. Now it was nothing but terrible.

"Who is this man?" exclaimed all.

That forest of hair; those dark hollows under the brows; the deep gaze of eyes which they could not see; that head, on the wild outlines of which light and darkness mingled weirdly; were a wonder, indeed. It was beyond all understanding; much as they had heard of him, the sight of Gwynplaine was a terror. Even those who expected much found their expectations surpassed. It was as though on the mountain reserved for the gods, during the banquet on a serene evening, the whole of the all-powerful body being gathered together, the face of Prometheus, mangled by the vulture's beak, should have suddenly appeared before them, like a blood-colored moon on the horizon. Olympus looking on Caucasus! What a vision! Old and young, open-mouthed with surprise, fixed their eyes upon Gwynplaine.

An old man, respected by the whole House, who had seen many men and many things, and who was intended for a dukedom—Thomas, Earl of Wharton—rose in terror.

"What does all this mean?" he cried. "Who has brought this man into the House? Let him be put out."

And addressing Gwynplaine, haughtily:

"Who are you? Whence do you come?"

Gwynplaine answered:

"Out of the depths."

And, folding his arms, he looked at the lords.

"Who am I? I am wretchedness. My lords, I have a word to say to you."

A shudder ran through the House. Then all was silence. Gwynplaine continued:

"My lords, you are highly placed. It is well. We must believe that God has his reasons that it should be so. You have power, opulence, pleasure, the sun ever shining in your zenith; authority unbounded, enjoyment without a sting, and a total forgetfulness of others. So be it. But there is something below you—above you, it may be. My lords, I bring you news; news of the existence of mankind."

Assemblies are like children. A strange occurrence is as a Jack-in-the-box to them. It frightens them; but they like it. It is as if a spring were touched, and a devil jumps up. Mirabeau, who was also deformed, was a case in point in France.

Gwynplaine felt within himself, at that moment, a strange elevation. In addressing a body of men, one's foot seems to rest on them; to rest, as it were, on a pinnacle of souls—on human hearts, that quiver under one's heel. Gwynplaine was no longer the man who had been, only the night before, almost mean. The fumes of the sudden elevation which had disturbed him, had cleared off and become transparent, and in the state in which Gwynplaine had been seduced by a vanity, he now saw but a duty. That which had at first lessened, now elevated, him. He was illuminated by one of those great flashes which emanate from duty.

All round Gwynplaine arose cries of "Hear, hear!"

Meanwhile, rigid and superhuman, he succeeded in maintaining on his features that severe and sad contraction under which the laugh was fretting like a wild horse struggling to escape.

He resumed:

"I am he who cometh out of the depths. My lords, you are great and rich. There lies your danger. You profit by the night; but beware! The Dawn is all-powerful. You cannot prevail over it. It is coming. Nay! it is come. Within it is the day-spring of irresistible light. And who shall hinder that sling from hurling the sun into the sky? The sun I speak of is Right. You are Privilege. Tremble! The real master of the house is about to knock at the door. What is the father of Privilege? Chance. What is his son? Abuse. Neither Chance nor Abuse are abiding. For both a dark morrow is at hand! I am come to warn you. I am come to impeach your happiness. It is fashioned out of the misery of your neighbor. You have everything, and that everything is composed of the nothing of others. My lords, I am an advocate without hope, pleading a cause that is lost; but that cause God will gain on appeal. As for me, I am but a voice. Mankind is a mouth, of which I am the cry. You shall hear me! I am about to open before you, peers of England, the great assize of the people; of that sovereign who is the subject; of that criminal who is the judge. I am weighed down under the load of all that I have to say. Where am I to begin? I know not. I have gathered together, in the vast diffusion of suffering, my innumerable and scattered pleas. What am I to do with them now? They overwhelm me, and I must cast them to you in a confused mass. Did I foresee this? No. You are astonished. So I am. Yesterday, I was a mountebank. To-day, I am a peer. Deep play! Of whom! Of the Unknown. Let us all tremble. My lords, all the blue sky is for you. Of this immense universe you see but the sunshine. Believe me, it has its shadows. Amongst you I am called Lord Fermain Clancharlie; but my true name is one of poverty—Gwynplaine. I am a wretched thing carved out of the stuff of which the great are made, for such was the pleasure of a king. That is my history. Many amongst you knew my father. I knew him not. His connection with you was his feudal descent; his outlawry is the bond between him and me. What God willed was well. I was cast into the abyss. For what end! To search its depths. I am a diver, and I have brought back the pearl, truth. I speak, because I know. You shall hear me, my lords. I have seen, I have felt! Suffering is not a mere word, ye happy ones! Poverty I grew up in; winter has frozen me; hunger I have tasted; contempt I have suffered; pestilence I have undergone; shame I have drunk of. And I will vomit all these up before you, and this ejection of all misery shall sully your feet and flame about them. I hesitated before I allowed myself to be brought to the place where I now stand, because I have duties to others elsewhere, and my heart is not here. What passed within me has nothing to do with you. When the man, whom you call Usher of the Black Rod, came to seek me by order of the woman whom you call the Queen, the idea struck me for a moment that I would refuse to come. But it seemed to me that the hidden hand of God pressed me to the spot, and I obeyed. I felt that I must come amongst you. Why? Because of my rags of yesterday. It is to raise my voice among those who have eaten their fill that God mixed me up with the famished. Oh, have pity! Of this fatal world to which you believe yourselves to belong, you know nothing. Placed so high, you are out of it. But I will tell you what it is; I have had experience enough. I come from beneath the pressure of your feet. I can tell you your weight. Oh, you who are masters, do you know what you are? do you see what you are doing? No. Oh, it is dreadful! One night, one night of storm, a little deserted child, an orphan alone in the immeasurable creation, I made my entrance into that darkness which you call society. The first thing that I saw was the law, under the form of a gibbet; the second was riches, your riches, under the form of a woman dead of cold and hunger; the third, the future, under the form of a child left to die; the fourth, goodness, truth, and justice, under the figure of a vagabond, whose sole friend and companion was a wolf."

Just then, Gwynplaine, stricken by a sudden emotion, felt the sobs rising in his throat, causing him most unfortunately to burst into an uncontrollable fit of laughter.

The contagion was immediate. A cloud had hung over the assembly. It might have broken into terror; it broke into delight. Mad merriment seized the whole House. Nothing pleases the great chambers of sovereign man so much as buffoonery. It is their revenge upon their graver moments.

The laughter of kings is like the laughter of the gods. There is always a cruel point in it. The lords set to play. Sneers gave sting to their laughter. They clapped their hands around the speaker, and insulted him. A volley of merry exclamations assailed him like bright, but wounding hailstones.

" Bravo, Gwynplaine!"—"Bravo, Laughing Man!"—"Bravo, Snout of the Green Box!"—"Mask of Tarrinzeau Field!"—"You are going to give us a performance!"—"That's right; talk away!"—"There's a funny fellow!"—"How the beast does laugh, to be sure!"—"Good-day, pantaloon!"—"How d'ye do, my lord clown!"—"Go on with your speech!"—"That fellow a peer of England?"—"Go on!"—"No, no!" —"Yes, yes!"

The Lord Chancellor was much disturbed.

A deaf peer, James Butler, Duke of Ormond, placing his hand to his ear like an ear-trumpet, asked Charles Beauclerk, Duke of Saint Albans:

" How has he voted?"

" Non-content."

" By heavens!" said Ormond, " I can understand it, with such a face as his."

Do you think that you can ever recapture a crowd once it has escaped your grasp? And all assemblies are crowds alike. No, eloquence is a bit; if the bit breaks, the audience runs away, and rushes on till it has thrown the orator. Hearers naturally dislike the speaker, which is a fact not as clearly understood as it ought to be. Instinctively he pulls the reins, but that is a useless expedient. However, all orators try it, as Gwynplaine did.

He looked for a moment at those men who were laughing at him. Then he cried:

" So, you insult misery! Silence, Peers of England! Judges, listen to my pleading! Oh! I conjure you, have pity. Pity for whom? Pity for yourselves. Who is in danger? Yourselves! Do you not see that you are in a balance, and that there is in one scale your power, and in the other your responsibility? It is God who is weighing you. Oh, do not laugh. Think. The trembling of your consciences is the oscillation of the balance in which God is weighing your actions. You are not wicked; you are like other men, neither better nor worse. You believe yourselves to be gods, but be ill to-morrow, and see your divinity shivering in fever! We are worth one as much as the other. I address myself to honest men; there are such here. I address myself to lofty intellects; there are such here. I address myself to generous souls; there are such here. You are fathers, sons, and brothers; therefore you are often touched. He amongst you who has this morning watched the awaking of his little child, is a good man. Hearts are all alike. Humanity is nothing but a heart. Between those who oppress and those who are oppressed, there is but a difference of place. Your feet tread on the heads of men. The fault is not yours; it is that of the social Babel. The building is faulty, and out of the perpendicular. One floor bears down the other. Listen, and I will tell you what to do. Oh! as you are powerful, be brotherly. As you are great, be tender. If you only knew what I have seen! Alas! What gloom is there beneath! The people are in a dungeon. How many are condemned who are innocent! No daylight, no air, no virtue! They are without hope, and yet—there is the danger! they expect something. Realize all this misery. There are beings who live in death. There are little girls who at twelve begin by prostitution, and who end in old age at twenty. As to the severities of the criminal code, they are fearful. I speak somewhat at random, and do not pick my words. I say everything that comes into my head. No later than yesterday, I, who stand here, saw a man lying in chains, naked, with stones piled on his chest, expire in torture. Do you know of these things? No. If you knew what goes on, you would not dare to be happy. Who of you have been to Newcastle-upon-Tyne? There, in the mines, are men who chew coals to fill their stomachs and deceive hunger. Look here! in Lancashire, Ribblechester has sunk, by poverty, from a town to a village. I do not see that Prince George of Denmark requires a hundred thousand pounds extra. I should prefer receiving a poor sick man into the hospital, without compelling him to pay his funeral expenses in advance. In Carnarvon, and at Strathmore, as well as at Strathbickan, the exhaustion of the poor is horrible. At Strafford, they cannot drain the marsh, for want of money. The manufactories are shut up all over Lancashire. There is forced idleness everywhere. Do you know that the herring fishers at Harlech eat grass when the fishery fails? Do you know that at Burton-Lazars there are still lepers confined, on whom they fire if they leave their tan houses? At Ailesbury, a town of which one of you is lord, destitution is chronic. At Penkridge, in Coventry, where you have just endowed a cathedral and enriched a bishop, there are no beds in the cabins, and they dig holes in the earth, in which to put the little children to lie, so that instead of beginning life in the cradle, they begin it in the grave. I have seen these things! My lords, do you know who pays the taxes you vote? The dying! Alas! you deceive yourselves. You are going the wrong road. You augment the poverty of the poor to increase the riches of the rich. You should do the reverse. What! take from the worker to give to the idle, take from the tattered to give to the well-clad; take from the beggar to give to the prince! Oh, yes! I have old Republican blood in my veins. I have a horror of these things. How I execrate kings! And how shameless are the women! I have been told a sad story. How I hate Charles II.! A woman whom my father loved, gave herself to that king whilst my father was dying in exile. The prostitute! Charles II., James II.! After a scamp, a scoundrel. What is there in a king? A man, feeble and contemptible, subject to wants and infirmities. Of what good is a king? You cultivate that parasite, royalty; you make a serpent of that worm, a dragon of that insect. Oh, pity the poor! You increase the weight of the taxes for the profit of the throne. Look to the laws which you decree. Take heed of the suffering swarms which you crush. Cast your eyes down. Look at what is at your feet. O ye great, there are the little. Have pity! yes, have pity on yourselves; for the people is in its agony, and when the lower part of the trunk dies, the higher parts die too. Death spares no limb. When night comes no one can keep his corner of daylight. Are you selfish? then save others. The destruction of the vessel cannot be a matter of indifference to any passenger. There can be no wreck for some that is not wreck for all. Oh! believe it, the abyss yawns for all!"

The laughter increased and became irresistible.

For that matter, such extravagance as there was in his words was sufficient to amuse any assembly. To be comic without and tragic within, what suffering can be more humiliating? what pain deeper? Gwynplaine felt it. His words were an appeal in one direction, his face in the other. What a terrible position was his!

Suddenly, his voice rang out in strident bursts.

"How gay these men are! Be it so. Here is irony face to face with agony; a sneer mocking the death-rattle. They are all-powerful. Perhaps so; be it so. We shall see. Behold! I am one of them; but I am, also, one of you, O ye poor! A king sold me. A poor man sheltered me. Who mutilated me? A prince. Who healed and nourished me? A pauper. I am Lord Clancharlie; but I am still Gwynplaine. I take my place amongst the great; but I belong to the mean. I am amongst those who rejoice; but I am with those who suffer. Oh, this system of society is false! Some day will come that which is true. Then, there will be no more lords; and there shall be free and living

men. There will be no more masters; there will be fathers. Such is
the future. No more prostration; no more baseness; no more ignorance; no more human beasts of burden; no more courtiers; no more
toadies; no more kings; but Light! In the meantime, see me here. I
have a right, and I will use it. Is it a right? No, if I use it for myself.
Yes, if I use it for all. I will speak to you, my lords, being one of you.
O my brothers below, I will tell them of your nakedness. I will rise
up with a bundle of the people's rags in my hand. I will shake off
over the masters the misery of the slaves; and these favored and

arrogant ones shall no longer be able to escape the remembrance of the
wretched, nor the princes the itch of the poor; and so much the worse,
if it be the bite of vermin; and so much the better if it awake the lions
from their slumber."

Here Gwynplaine turned towards the kneeling under-clerks, who
were writing on the fourth wool-sack.

"Who are those fellows kneeling down? What are you doing?
Get up; you are men."

These words, suddenly addressed to inferiors whom a lord ought
not even to perceive, increased the merriment to the utmost.

They had cried, "Bravo!" Now, they shouted, "Hurrah!" From

clapping their hands, they proceeded to stamping their feet. One might have been back in the Green Box, only that there the laughter applauded Gwynplaine; here it exterminated him. The effort of ridicule is to kill. Men's laughter sometimes exerts all its power to murder.

The laughter proceeded to action. Sneering words rained down upon him. Humor is the folly of assemblies. Their ingenious and foolish ridicule shuns facts instead of studying them, and condemns questions instead of solving them. Any extraordinary occurrence is a point of interrogation; to laugh at it is like laughing at an enigma. But the Sphynx, which never laughs, is behind it.

Contradictory shouts arose:

"Enough! enough!—Encore! encore!"

William Farmer, Baron Leimpster, flung at Gwynplaine the insult cast by Rye Quiney at Shakespeare:

"*Histrio mima!*"

Lord Vaughan, a sententious man, twenty-ninth on the barons' bench, exclaimed:

"We must be back in the days when animals had the gift of speech. In the midst of human tongues the jaw of a beast has spoken."

"Listen to Balaam's ass," added Lord Yarmouth.

Lord Yarmouth presented that appearance of sagacity produced by a round nose and a crooked mouth.

"The rebel Linnæus is chastised in his tomb. The son is the punishment of the father," said John Hough, Bishop of Lichfield and Coventry, at whose prebendary Gwynplaine's attack had glanced.

"He lies!" said Lord Cholmondeley, the legislator so well read up in the law. "That which he calls torture is only the *peine forte et dure*, and a very good thing, too. Torture is not practiced in England."

Thomas Wentworth, Baron Raby, addressed the Chancellor:

"My Lord Chancellor, adjourn the House."

"No, no. Let him go on. He is amusing. Hurrah! hip! hip! hip!"

Thus shouted the young lords, their fun amounting to fury. Four of them especially were in the full exasperation of hilarity and hate. These were Laurence Hyde, Earl of Rochester; Thomas Tufton, Earl of Thanet; Viscount Hatton; and the Duke of Montagu.

"To your tricks, Gwynplaine!" cried Rochester.

"Put him out, put him out!" shouted Thanet.

Viscount Hatton drew from his pocket a penny, which he flung to Gwynplaine.

And John Campbell, Earl of Greenwich; Savage, Earl Rivers; Thompson, Baron Haversham; Warrington, Escrick, Rolleston, Rockingham, Carteret, Langdale, Barcester, Maynard, Hunsdon, Caërnarvon, Cavendish, Burlington, Robert Darcy, Earl of Holderness, Other Windsor, Earl of Plymouth, applauded.

There was a tumult as of pandemonium or of pantheon, in which the words of Gwynplaine were lost.

Amidst it all, there was heard but one word of Gwynplaine's: "Beware!"

Ralph, Duke of Montagu, recently down from Oxford, and still a beardless youth, descended from the bench of dukes, where he sat the nineteenth in order, and placed himself in front of Gwynplaine, with his arms folded. In a sword there is a spot which cuts sharpest, and in a voice an accent which insults most keenly. Montagu spoke with that accent, and sneering with his face close to that of Gwynplaine, shouted: "What are you talking about?"

"I am prophesying," said Gwynplaine.

The laughter exploded anew; and below this laughter, anger growled its continued bass. One of the minors, Lionel Cranfield Sackville, Earl of Dorset and Middlesex, stood up on his seat, not smiling, but grave as became a future legislator, and, without saying a word, looked at Gwynplaine with his fresh twelve-year-old face, and shrugged his shoulders. Whereat the Bishop of St. Asaph's whispered in the ear of the Bishop of St. David's, who was sitting beside him, as he pointed to Gwynplaine, "There is the fool;" then pointing to the child, "there is the sage."

A chaos of complaint rose from amidst the confusion of exclamations:

"Gorgon's face!"—"What does it all mean?"—"An insult to the House!"—"The fellow ought to be put out!"—"What a madman!"—"Shame! shame!"—"Adjourn the House!"—"No; let him finish his speech!"—"Talk away, you buffoon!"

Lord Lewis of Duras, with his arms a-kimbo, shouted:

"Ah! it does one good to laugh. My spleen is cured. I propose a vote of thanks in these terms: 'The House of Lords returns thanks to the Green Box.'"

Gwynplaine, it may be remembered, had dreamt of a different welcome.

A man who, climbing up a steep and crumbling acclivity of sand above a giddy precipice, has felt it giving way under his hands, his nails, his elbows, his knees, his feet; who—losing instead of gaining on his treacherous way, a prey to every terror of the danger, slipping back instead of ascending, increasing the certainty of his fall by his very efforts to gain the summit, and losing ground in every struggle for safety

—has felt the abyss approaching nearer and nearer, until the certainty of his coming fall into the yawning jaws open to receive him, has frozen the marrow of his bones;—that man has experienced the sensations of Gwynplaine.

He felt the ground he had ascended crumbling under him, and his audience was the precipice.

There is always some one to say the word which sums all up.

Lord Scarsdale translated the impression of the assembly in one exclamation:

"What is the monster doing here?"

Gwynplaine stood up, dismayed and indignant, in a sort of final convulsion. He looked at them all fixedly.

"What am I doing here? I have come to be a terror to you! I am a monster, do you say? No! I am the people! I am an exception? No! I am the rule; you are the exception! You are the chimera; I am the reality! I am the frightful man who laughs! Who laughs at what? At you, at himself, at everything! What is his laugh? Your crime and his torment! That crime he flings at your head! That punishment he spits in your face! I laugh, and that means I weep!"

He paused. There was less noise. The laughter continued, but it was more subdued. He may have fancied that he had regained a certain amount of attention. He breathed again, and resumed:

"This laugh which is on my face a king placed there. This laugh expresses the desolation of mankind. This laugh means hate, enforced silence, rage, despair. This laugh is the production of torture. This laugh is a forced laugh. If Satan were marked with this laugh, it would convict God. But the Eternal is not like them that perish. Being absolute, he is just; and God hates the acts of kings. Oh! you take me for an exception; but I am a symbol. Oh, all-powerful men, fools that you are! open your eyes. I am the incarnation of All. I represent humanity, such as its masters have made it. Mankind is mutilated. That which has been done to me has been done to it. In it, have been deformed right, justice, truth, reason, intelligence, as eyes, nostrils, and ears have been deformed in me; its heart has been made a sink of passion and pain, like mine, and, like mine, its features have been hidden in a mask of joy. Where God had placed his finger, the king set his sign-manual. Monstrous superposition! Bishops, peers, and princes, the people is a sea of suffering, smiling on the surface. My lords, I tell you that the people are as I am. To-day you oppress them; to-day you hoot at me. But the future is the ominous thaw, in which that which was as stone shall become wave. The appearance of solidity melts into liquid. A crack in the ice, and all is over. There will come an hour when convulsion shall break down your oppression; when an angry roar will reply to your jeers. Nay, that hour did come! Thou wert of it, O my Father! That hour of God did come, and was called the Republic! It was destroyed, but it will return. Meanwhile, remember that the line of kings armed with the sword was broken by Cromwell, armed with the axe. Tremble! Incorruptible solutions are at hand: the talons which were cut are growing again; the tongues which were torn out are floating away, they are turning to tongues of fire, and, scattered by the breath of darkness, are shouting through infinity; those who hunger are showing their idle teeth; false heavens, built over real hells, are tottering. The people are suffering—they are suffering; and that which is on high totters, and that which is below yawns. Darkness demands its change to light; the damned discuss the elect. Behold! it is the coming of the people, the ascent of mankind, the beginning of the end, the red dawn of the catastrophe! Yes, all these things are in this laugh of mine, at which you laugh to-day! London is one perpetual fête. Be it so. From one end to the other, England rings with acclamation. Well! but listen. All that you see is I. You have your fêtes—they are my laugh; you have your public rejoicings—they are my laugh; you have your weddings, consecrations, and coronations—they are my laugh. The births of your princes are my laugh. But above you is the thunder-bolt—it is my laugh."

How could they stand such nonsense? The laughter burst out afresh; and now it was overwhelming. Of all the lava which that crater, the human mouth, ejects, the most corrosive is joy. To inflict evil gayly is a contagion which no crowd can resist. All executions do not take place on the scaffold; and men, from the moment they are in a body, whether in mobs or in senates, have always a ready executioner amongst them, called sarcasm. There is no torture to be compared to that of the wretch condemned to execution by ridicule. This was Gwynplaine's fate. He was stoned with their jokes, and riddled by the scoffs shot at him. He stood there a mark for all. They sprang up; they cried "Encore;" they shook with laughter; they stamped their feet; they pulled each other's hands. The majesty of the place, the purple of the robes, the chaste ermine, the dignity of the wigs, had no effect. The lords laughed, the bishops laughed, the judges laughed, the old men's benches derided, the children's benches were in convulsions. The Archbishop of Canterbury nudged the Archbishop of York; Henry Compton, Bishop of London, brother of Lord Northampton, held his sides; the Lord Chancellor bent down his head, probably to conceal his inclination to laugh; and, at the bar, that statue of respect, the Usher of the Black Rod, was laughing also.

Gwynplaine, become pallid, had folded his arms; and, surrounded
by all those faces, young and old, in which had burst forth this grand
Homeric jubilee; in that whirlwind of clapping hands, of stamping
feet, and of hurrahs; in that mad buffoonery, of which he was the
centre; in that splendid overflow of hilarity; in the midst of that
unmeasured gayety, he felt that the sepulchre was within him. All was
over. He could no longer master the face which betrayed, nor the audience which insulted him.

That eternal and fatal law, by which the grotesque is linked with
the sublime—by which the laugh re-echoes the groan, parody rides
behind despair, and seeming is opposed to being—had never found
more terrible expression. Never had a light more sinister illumined
the depths of human darkness.

Gwynplaine was assisting at the final destruction of his destiny by
a burst of laughter. The irremediable was in this. Having fallen, we
can raise ourselves up; but, being pulverized, never. And the insult
of their sovereign mockery had reduced him to dust. From thenceforth nothing was possible. Everything is in accordance with the
scene. That which was triumph in the Green Box, was disgrace and
catastrophe in the House of Lords. What was applause there was insult
here. He felt something like the reverse side of his mask. On one
side of that mask he had the sympathy of the people, who welcomed
Gwynplaine; on the other, the contempt of the great, rejecting Lord
Fermain Clancharlie. On one side, attraction; on the other, repulsion;
both leading him towards the shadows. He felt himself, as it were,
struck from behind. Fate strikes treacherous blows. Everything will
be explained hereafter, but, in the meantime, destiny is a snare, and
man sinks into its pitfalls. He had expected to rise, and was welcomed
by laughter. Such apotheoses have lugubrious terminations. There is
a dreary expression—to be sobered; tragical wisdom born of drunkenness! In the midst of that tempest of gayety commingled with ferocity, Gwynplaine fell into a reverie.

An assembly in mad merriment drifts as chance directs, and loses
its compass when it gives itself to laughter. None knew whither they
were tending, or what they were doing.

The House was obliged to rise, adjourned by the Lord Chancellor,
"owing to extraordinary circumstances," to the next day. The peers
broke up. They bowed to the royal throne and departed. Echoes of
prolonged laughter were heard losing themselves in the corridors.

Assemblies, besides their official doors, have—under tapestry, under
projections, and under arches—all sorts of hidden doors, by which the
members escape like water through the cracks in a vase.

In a short time the chamber was deserted. This takes place quickly and almost imperceptibly, and those places, so lately full of voices, are suddenly given back to silence.

Reverie carries one far; and one comes by long dreaming to reach, as it were, another planet.

Gwynplaine suddenly awoke from such a dream. He was alone. The chamber was empty. He had not even observed that the House had been adjourned. All the peers had departed, even his sponsors. There only remained here and there some of the lower officers of the House, waiting for his lordship to depart before they put the covers on, and extinguished the lights.

Mechanically he placed his hat on his head, and, leaving his place, directed his steps to the great door opening into the gallery. As he was passing through the opening in the bar, a doorkeeper relieved him of his peer's robes. This he scarcely felt. In another instant, he was in the gallery.

The officials who remained observed with astonishment that the peer had gone out without bowing to the throne!

CHAPTER VIII

THERE was no one in the gallery.

Gwynplaine crossed the circular space, from whence they had removed the arm-chair and the tables, and where there now remained no trace of his investiture. Candelabra and lustres, placed at certain intervals, marked the way out. Thanks to this string of light, he retraced without difficulty, through the suite of saloons and galleries, the way which he had followed on his arrival with the King-at-Arms and the Usher of the Black Rod. He saw no one, except here and there some old lord with tardy steps, plodding along heavily in front of him.

Suddenly, in the silence of those great deserted rooms, bursts of indistinct exclamations reached him, a sort of nocturnal clatter unusual in such a place. He directed his steps to the place whence this noise proceeded, and found himself in a spacious hall, dimly lighted, which was one of the exits from the House of Lords. He saw a great glass door open, a flight of steps, footmen and links, a square outside, and a few coaches waiting at the bottom of the steps. This was the spot from which the noise which he had heard had proceeded.

Within the door, and under the hall lamp, was a noisy group in a storm of gestures and of voices. Gwynplaine approached in the gloom. They were quarreling. On one side there were ten or twelve young lords, who wanted to go out; on the other, a man with his hat on, like themselves, upright and with a haughty brow, who barred their passage.

Who was that man? Tom-Jim-Jack.

Some of these lords were still in their robes, others had thrown them off, and were in their usual attire. Tom-Jim-Jack wore a hat with plumes—not white, like the peers; but green tipped with orange.

267

He was embroidered and laced from head to foot, had flowing bows of ribbon and lace round his wrists and neck, and was feverishly fingering with his left hand the hilt of the sword which hung from his waist-belt, and on the billets and scabbard of which were embroidered an admiral's anchors.

It was he who was speaking and addressing the young lords; and Gwynplaine overheard the following:

"I have told you you are cowards. You wish me to withdraw my words. Be it so. You are not cowards; you are idiots. You all combined against one man. That was not cowardice. All right. Then it was stupidity. He spoke to you, and you did not understand him. Here, the old are hard of hearing, the young devoid of intelligence. I am one of your own order to quite sufficient extent to tell you the truth. This new-comer is strange, and he has uttered a heap of nonsense, I admit; but amidst all that nonsense there were some things which are true. His speech was confused, undigested, ill-delivered. Be it so. He repeated, 'You know, you know,' too often; but a man who was but yesterday a clown at a fair cannot be expected to speak like Aristotle or like Doctor Gilbert Burnet, Bishop of Salisbury. The vermin, the lions, the address to the under-clerks—all that was in bad taste. Zounds! who says it wasn't? It was a senseless and fragmentary and topsy-turvy harangue; but here and there came out facts which were true. It is no small thing to speak even as he did, seeing it is not his trade. I should like to see you do it. Yes; you! What he said about the lepers at Burton Lazars is an undeniable fact. Besides, he is not the first man who has talked nonsense. In fine, my lords, I do not like to see the many set upon one. Such is my humor; and I ask your lordships' permission to take offense. You have displeased me; I am angry. I am grateful to God for having drawn up from the depth of his low existence this peer of England, and for having given back his inheritance to the heir; and, without heeding whether it will or will not affect my own affairs, I consider it a beautiful sight to see an insect transformed into an eagle, and Gwynplaine into Lord Clancharlie. My lords, I forbid you holding any opinion but mine. I regret that Lord Lewis Duras should not be here. I should like to insult him. My lords, it is Fermain Clancharlie who has been the peer, and you who have been the mountebanks. As to his laugh, it is not his fault. You have laughed at that laugh; men should not laugh at misfortune. If you think that people cannot laugh at you as well, you are very much mistaken. You are ugly. You are badly dressed. My Lord Haversham, I saw your mistress the other day; she is hideous—a duchess, but a monkey. Gentlemen who laugh, I repeat that I should like to hear you try to say four words running! many men jabber; very few speak. You imagine you know something, because you have kept idle terms at Oxford or Cambridge, and because, before being peers of England on the benches of Westminster, you have been asses on the benches at Gonville and Caius. Here I am; and I choose to stare you in the face. You have just been impudent to this new peer. A monster, certainly; but a monster given up to beasts. I had rather be that man than you. I was present at the sitting, in my place as a possible heir to a peerage. I heard all. I have not the right to speak; but I have the right to be a gentleman. Your jeering airs annoyed me. When I am angry I would go up to Pendlehill, and pick the cloudberry which brings the thunder-bolt down on the gatherer. That is the reason why I have waited for you at the door. We must have a few words, for we have arrangements to make. Did it not strike you that you failed a little in respect towards myself? My lords, I entertain a firm determination to kill a few of you. All you who are here—Thomas Tufton, Earl of Thanet; Savage, Earl Rivers; Charles Spencer, Earl of Sunderland; Laurence Hyde, Earl of Rochester; you Barons, Gray of Rolleston, Cary Hunsdon, Escrick, Rockingham, little Carteret; Robert Darcy, Earl of Holderness; William, Viscount Hutton; and Ralph, Duke of Montagu; and any who choose, I, David Dirry-Moir, an officer of the fleet, summon, call, and command you to provide yourselves, in all haste, with seconds and umpires, and I will meet you face to face and hand to hand, to-night, at once, to-morrow, by day or night, by sun-light or by candle-light, where, when, or how you please, so long as there is two sword-lengths' space; and you will do well to look to the flints of your pistols and the edges of your rapiers, for it is my firm intention to cause vacancies in your peerages. Ogle Cavendish, take your measures, and think of your motto, *Cavendo tutus;* Marmaduke Langdale, you will do well, like your ancester, Grindold, to order a coffin to be brought with you. George Booth, Earl of Warrington, you will never again see the County Palatine of Chester, or your labyrinth like that of Crete, or the high towers of Dunham Massy! As to Lord Vaughan, he is young enough to talk impertinently, and too old to answer for it. I shall demand satisfaction for his words, of his nephew Richard Vaughan, Member of Parliament for the Borough of Merioneth. As for you, John Campbell, Earl of Greenwich, I will kill you as Achon killed Matas; but with a fair cut, and not from behind, it being my custom to present my heart and not my back to the point of the sword. I have spoken my mind, my lords. And so use witchcraft, if you like. Consult the fortune-tellers. Grease your skins with ointments and drugs to make them invulnerable; hang round your necks charms of the

devil or the virgin; I will fight you blest or curst, and I will not have
you searched to see if you are wearing any wizard's tokens.   On foot or
on horseback, on the high road if you wish it, in Piccadilly, or at
Charing Cross; and they shall take up the pavement for our meeting,
as they unpaved the court of the Louvre for the duel between Guise
and Bassompierre.   All of you!   Do you hear?   I mean to fight you
all.   Dormer, Earl of Caërnarvon, I will make you swallow my sword
up to the hilt, as Marolles did to Lisle Marivaux, and then we shall see,
my lords, whether you will laugh or not.   You, Burlington, who look
like a girl of seventeen, you shall choose between the lawn of your
house in Middlesex, and your beautiful garden at Londesborough, in
Yorkshire, to be buried in.   I beg to inform your lordships that it does
not suit me to allow your insolence in my presence.   I will chastise
you, my lords.   I take it ill that you should have ridiculed Lord Fermain Clancharlie.   He is worth more than you.   As Clancharlie, he has
nobility, which you have.   As Gwynplaine, he has intellect, which you
have not.   I make his cause my cause, insult to him insult to me, and
your ridicule my wrath.   We shall see who will come out of this affair
alive, because I challenge you to the death.   Do you understand?
With any arm, in any fashion, and you shall choose the death that
pleases you best; and since you are clowns as well as gentlemen, I proportion my defiance to your qualities, and I give you your choice of any
way in which a man can be killed, from the sword of the prince to the
fist of the blackguard."

To this furious onslaught of words, the whole group of young
noblemen answered by a smile.

"Agreed," they said.

"I choose pistols," said Burlington.

"I," said Escrick, "the ancient combat of the lists, with the mace
and the dagger."

"I," said Holderness, "the duel with two knives, long and short,
stripped to the waist, and breast to breast."

"Lord David," said the Earl of Thanet, "you are a Scot.   I choose
the claymore."

"I, the sword," said Rockingham.

"I," said Duke Ralph, "prefer the fists; 'tis noblest."

Gwynplaine came out from the shadow.   He directed his steps
towards him whom he had hitherto called Tom-Jim-Jack, but in whom
now, however, he began to perceive something more.

"I thank you," said he, "but this is my business."

Every head turned towards him.

Gwynplaine advanced.   He felt himself impelled towards the man whom he heard called Lord David; his defender, and perhaps something nearer. Lord David drew back.

"Oh!" said he. "It is you, is it? This is well-timed. I have a word for you as well. Just now you spoke of a woman, who, after having loved Lord Linnæus Clancharlie, loved Charles II."

"It is true."

"Sir, you insulted my mother."

"Your mother!" cried Gwynplaine. "In that case, as I guessed, we are——"

"Brothers," answered Lord David, and he struck Gwynplaine.

"We are brothers," said he; "so we can fight. One can only fight one's equal; who is one's equal if not one's brother? I will send you my seconds; to-morrow we will cut each other's throats."

BOOK IX

IN RUINS

CHAPTER I

IT IS THROUGH EXCESS OF GREATNESS THAT MAN REACHES EXCESS OF MISERY

AS midnight tolled from St. Paul's, a man who had just crossed London Bridge struck into the lanes of Southwark. There were no lamps lighted, it being at that time the custom in London, as in Paris, to extinguish the public lamps at eleven o'clock; that is, to put them out just as they became necessary. The streets were dark and deserted. When the lamps are out, men stay in. He whom we speak of advanced with hurried strides. He was strangely dressed for walking at such an hour. He wore a coat of embroidered silk, a sword by his side, a hat with white plumes, and no cloak. The watchmen, as they saw him pass, said, "It is a lord walking for a wager," and they moved out of his way with the respect due to a lord and to a better.

The man was Gwynplaine.

He was making his escape.

Where was he? He did not know. We have said that the soul has its cyclones; fearful whirlwinds, in which heaven, the sea, day, night, life, death, are all mingled in unintelligible horror. It can no longer breathe Truth; it is crushed by things in which it does not believe. Nothingness becomes hurricane. The firmament pales. Infinity is empty. The mind of the sufferer wanders away. He feels him-

self dying. He craves for a star. What did Gwynplaine feel ? a thirst;
a thirst to see Dea.

He felt but that. To reach the Green Box again, and the Tadcaster
Inn, with its sounds and light; full of the cordial laughter of the
people; to find Ursus and Homo, to see Dea again, to re-enter life.

Disillusion, like a bow, shoots its arrow, man, towards the True.

Gwynplaine hastened on. He approached Tarrinzeau Field. He walked
no longer now, he ran. His eyes pierced the darkness before him. His
glance preceded him, eargerly seeking the harbor on the horizon. What
a moment for him when he should see the lighted windows of Tadcaster Inn!

He reached the bowling-green. He turned the corner of the wall,
and saw before him, at the other end of the field, some distance off, the
inn—the only house, it may be remembered, in the field where the fair
was held.

He looked. There was no light; nothing but a black mass.

He shuddered. Then he said to himself that it was late, that the tavern was shut up, that it was very natural, that every one was asleep, that he had only to awaken Nicless or Govicum, that he must go up to the inn and knock at the door. He did so, running no longer now, but rushing.

He reached the inn, breathless. It is when, storm-beaten and struggling in the invisible convulsions of the soul until he knows not whether he is in life or in death, that all the delicacy of a man's affection for his loved ones, being yet unimpaired, proves a heart true. When all else is swallowed up, tenderness still floats unshattered.

He approached the inn with as little noise as possible. He recognized the nook, the old dog kennel, where Govicum used to sleep. In it, contiguous to the lower room, was a window opening on to the field. Gwynplaine tapped softly at the pane. It would be enough to awaken Govicum, he thought.

There was no sound in Govicum's room.

"At his age," said Gwynplaine, "a boy sleeps soundly."

With the back of his hand he knocked against the window gently. Nothing stirred.

He knocked louder twice. Still nothing stirred. Then, feeling somewhat uneasy, he went to the door of the inn and knocked. No one answered. He reflected, and began to feel a cold shudder come over him.

"Master Nicless is old, children sleep soundly, and old men heavily. Courage! louder!"

He had tapped, he had knocked, he had kicked the door; now he flung himself against it.

This recalled to him a distant memory of Weymouth, when, as a little child, he had carried Dea, an infant, in his arms.

He battered the door again violently, like a lord, which, alas! he was.

The house remained silent. He felt that he was losing his head. He no longer thought of caution. He shouted:

"Nicless! Govicum!"

At the same time he looked up at the windows, to see if any candle was lighted. But the inn was blank. Not a voice, not a sound, not a glimmer of light. He went to the gate and knocked at it, kicked against it, and shook it, crying out wildly:

"Ursus! Homo!"

The wolf did not bark.

A cold sweat stood in drops upon his brow. He cast his eyes around. The night was dark; but there were stars enough to render the fair-green visible. He saw—a melancholy sight to him—that every-thing on it had vanished.

There was not a single caravan. The circus was gone. Not a tent, not a booth, not a cart remained. The strollers, with their thousand

noisy cries, who had swarmed there, had given place to a black and sullen void.

All were gone.

The madness of anxiety took possession of him. What did this mean? What had happened? Was no one left? Could it be that life had crumbled away behind him? What had happened to them all?

Good heavens! Then he rushed like a tempest against the house. He struck the small door, the gate, the windows, the window-shutters, the walls with fists and feet, furious with terror and agony of mind.

He called Nicless, Govicum, Fibi, Vinos, Ursus, Homo. He tried every shout and every sound against this wall. At times he waited and listened; but the house remained mute and dead. Then, exasperated, he began again with blows, shouts, and repeated knockings, re-echoed all around. It might have been thunder trying to awake the grave.

There is a certain stage of fright in which a man becomes terrible. He who fears everything, fears nothing. He would strike the Sphynx. He defies the Unknown.

Gwynplaine renewed the noise in every possible form, stopping, resuming, unwearying in the shouts and appeals by which he assailed the tragic silence. He called a thousand times on the names of those who should have been there. He shrieked out every name except that of Dea, a precaution of which he could not have explained the reason himself, but which instinct inspired even in his distraction.

Having exhausted calls and cries, nothing was left but to break in. "I must enter the house," he said to himself; "but how?"

He broke a pane of glass in Govicum's room by thrusting his hand through it, tearing the flesh; he drew the bolt of the sash and opened the window. Perceiving that his sword was in the way, he tore it off angrily, scabbard, blade, and belt, and flung it on the pavement. Then he raised himself by the inequalities in the wall, and, though the window was narrow, he was able to pass through it. He entered the inn. Govicum's bed, dimly visible in its nook, was there; but Govicum was not in it. If Govicum was not in his bed, it was evident that Nicless could not be in his.

The whole house was dark. He felt in that shadowy interior the mysterious immobility of emptiness, and that vague fear which signifies —" There is no one here."

Gwynplaine, convulsed with anxiety, crossed the lower room, knocking against the tables, upsetting the earthenware, throwing down the benches, sweeping against the jugs, and, striding over the furniture, reached the door leading into the court, and broke it open with one blow from his knee, which sprung the lock. The door turned on its hinges. He looked into the court. The Green Box was no longer there.

THE THAMES.

CHAPTER II

WYNPLAINE left the house, and began to explore Tarrinzeau Field in every direction. He went to every place where,
the day before, the tents and caravans had stood. He
knocked at the stalls, though he knew well that they were
uninhabited. He struck everything that looked like a door or a window.
Not a voice arose from the darkness. Something like death had been
there.

The ant-hill had been razed. Some measures of police had apparently been carried out. There had been what, in our days, would be
called a razzia. Tarrinzeau Field was worse than a desert; it had been
scoured, and every corner of it scratched up, as it were, by pitiless
claws. The pocket of the unfortunate fair-green had been turned inside
out, and completely emptied.

Gwynplaine, after having searched every yard of ground, left the
green, struck into the crooked streets abutting on the site called East
Point, and directed his steps towards the Thames.

He had threaded his way through a net-work of lanes, bounded only
by walls and hedges, when he felt the fresh breeze from the water,
heard the dull lapping of the river, and suddenly saw a parapet in front
of him. It was the parapet of the Effroc stone.

This parapet bounded a block of the quay, which was very short
and very narrow. Under it the high wall, the Effroc stone, buried
itself perpendicularly in the dark water below.

Gwynplaine stopped at the parapet, and, leaning his elbows on it,
laid his head in his hands and set to thinking, with the water beneath
him.

Did he look at the water? No. At what then? At the shadow;
not the shadow without, but within him. In the melancholy night-

279

bound landscape, which he scarcely marked,—in the outer depths, which his eyes did not pierce, were the blurred sketches of masts and spars. Below the Effroc stone there was nothing on the river; but the quay sloped insensibly downwards till, some distance off, it met a pier, at which several vessels were lying, some of which had just arrived, others which were on the point of departure. These vessels communicated with the shore by little jetties, constructed for the purpose, some of stone, some of wood, or by movable gangways. All of them, whether moored to the jetties or at anchor, were wrapt in silence. There was neither voice nor movement on board, it being a good habit of sailors to sleep when they can, and awake only when wanted. If any of them were to sail during the night at high tide, the crews were not yet awake.

The hulls, like large black bubbles, and the rigging, like threads mingled with ladders, were barely visible. All was livid and confused. Here and there a red cresset pierced the haze.

Gwynplaine saw nothing of all this. What he was musing on was destiny.

He was in a dream—a vision—giddy in presence of an inexorable reality.

He fancied that he heard behind him something like an earthquake. It was the laughter of the Lords.

From that laughter he had just emerged. He had come out of it, having received a blow, and from whom?

From his own brother!

Flying from the laughter, carrying with him the blow, seeking refuge, a wounded bird, in his nest, rushing from hate and seeking love, what had he found?

Darkness.

No one.

Everything gone.

He compared that darkness to the dream he had indulged in.

What a crumbling away!

Gwynplaine had just reached that sinister bound—the void. The Green Box gone, was his universe vanished.

His soul had been closed up.

He reflected.

What could have happened? Where were they? They had evidently been carried away. Destiny had given him, Gwynplaine, a blow, which was greatness; its reaction had struck them another, which was annihilation. It was clear that he would never see them again. Precautions had been taken against that. They had scoured the fair-green, beginning by Nicless and Govicum, so that he should gain no clue through them. Inexorable dispersion! That fearful social system, at the same time that it had pulverized him in the House of Lords, had crushed them in their little cabin. They were lost; Dea was lost— lost to him forever. Powers of heaven! where was she? And he had not been there to defend her!

To have to make guesses as to the absent whom we love, is to put one's self to the torture. He inflicted this torture on himself. At every thought that he fathomed, at every supposition which he made, he felt within him a moan of agony.

Through a succession of bitter reflections he remembered a man who was evidently fatal to him, and who had called himself Barkil- phedro. That man had inscribed on his brain a dark sentence which re-appeared now, he had written it in such terrible ink that every letter had turned to fire; and Gwynplaine saw flaming at the bottom of his thought the enigmatical words, the meaning of which was at length solved : " *Destiny never opens one door without closing another.*"

All was over. The final shadows had gathered about him. In every man's fate there may be an end of the world for himself alone. It is called despair. The soul is full of falling stars.

This, then, was what he had come to.

A vapor had passed. He had been mingled with it. It had lain heavily on his eyes, it had disordered his brain. He had been out- wardly blinded, intoxicated within. This had lasted the time of a passing vapor. Then everything melted away, the vapor and his life. Awaking from the dream, he found himself alone.

All vanished, all gone, all lost. Night. Nothingness. Such was his horizon.

He was alone.

Alone has a synonyme, which is Dead. Despair is an accountant. It sets itself to find its total, it adds up everything, even to the far- things. It reproaches Heaven with its thunder-bolts and its pin-pricks. It seeks to find what it has to expect from fate. It argues, weighs, and calculates, outwardly cool, while the burning lava is still flowing on within.

Gwynplaine examined himself, and examined his fate.

The backward glance of thought; terrible recapitulation!

When at the top of a mountain, we look down the precipice; when at the bottom, we look up at heaven. And we say, I was there.

Gwynplaine was at the very bottom of misfortune. How sudden, too, had been his fall!

Such is the hideous swiftness of misfortune, although it is so heavy that we might fancy it slow. But no! It would likewise appear that snow, from its coldness, ought to be the paralysis of winter, and, from its whiteness, the immobility of the winding-sheet. Yet this is contradicted by the avalanche.

The avalanche is snow become a furnace. It remains frozen, but it devours. The avalanche had enveloped Gwynplaine. He had been torn like a rag, uprooted like a tree, precipitated like a stone. He recalled all the circumstances of his fall. He put himself questions and returned answers. Grief is an examination. There is no judge so searching as conscience conducting its own trial.

What amount of remorse was there in his despair? This he wished to find out, and dissected his conscience. Excruciating vivisection!

His absence had caused a catastrophe. Had this absence depended on him? In all that had happened, had he been a free agent? No! He had felt himself captive. What was that which had arrested and detained him—a prison? No. A chain? No. What then? Birdlime! He had sunk into the slough of greatness.

To whom has it not happened to be free in appearance, yet to feel that his wings are hampered?

There had been something like a snare spread for him. What is at first temptation ends by captivity.

Nevertheless (and his conscience pressed him on this point)—had he merely submitted to what had been offered him? No; he had accepted it.

Violence and surprise had been used with him in a certain measure, it was true; but he, in a certain measure, had given in. To have allowed himself to be carried off was not his fault; but to have allowed himself to be inebriated, was his weakness. There had been a moment—a decisive moment—when the question was proposed. This Barkilphedro had placed a dilemma before Gwynplaine, and had given him clear power to decide his fate by a word. Gwynplaine might have said "No." He had said "Yes."

From that "Yes," uttered in a moment of dizziness, everything had sprung. Gwynplaine realized this now in the bitter after-taste of that consent.

Nevertheless—for he debated with himself—was it then so great a wrong to take possession of his right, of his patrimony, of his heritage, of his house; and, as a patrician, of the rank of his ancestors; as an orphan of the name of his father? What had he accepted? A restitution. Made by whom? By Providence.

Then his mind revolted. Senseless acceptance! What a bargain had he struck! what a foolish exchange! He had trafficked with Providence at a loss. How now! For an income of 80,000*l.* a year; for seven or eight titles; for ten or twelve palaces; for houses in town, and castles in the country; for a hundred lackeys; for packs of hounds, and carriages, and armorial bearings; to be a judge and legislator; for a coronet and purple robes, like a king; to be a baron and a marquis; to be a peer of England, he had given the hut of Ursus and the smile of Dea. For shipwreck and destruction in the surging immensity of greatness, he had bartered happiness. For the ocean he had given the pearl. O madman! O fool! O dupe!

Yet, nevertheless,—and here the objection re-appeared on firmer ground,—in this fever of high fortune which had seized him, all had not been unwholesome. Perhaps there would have been selfishness in renunciation; perhaps he had done his duty in the acceptance. Suddenly transformed into a lord, what ought he to have done? The complication of events produces perplexity of mind. This had happened to him. Duty gave contrary orders. Duty on all sides at once, duty multiple and contradictory; this was the bewilderment which he had suffered. It was this that had paralyzed him, especially when he had not refused to take the journey from Corleone Lodge to the House of Lords. What we call rising in life is leaving the safe for the dangerous path. Which is, thenceforth, the straight line? Towards whom is our first duty? Is it towards those nearest to ourselves, or is it towards mankind generally? Do we not cease to belong to our own circumscribed circle, and become part of the great family of all? As we ascend, we feel an increased pressure on our virtue. The higher we rise, the greater is the strain. The increase of right is an increase of duty. We come to many cross-ways, phantom roads perchance, and we imagine that we see the finger of conscience pointing each one of them out to us. Which shall we take? Change our direction, remain where we are, advance, go back? What are we to do? That there should be cross-roads in conscience is strange enough; but responsibility may be a labyrinth.

And when a man contains an idea, when he is the incarnation of a fact,—when he is a symbolical man, at the same time that he is a man of flesh and blood,—is not the responsibility still more oppressive? Thence the care-laden docility and the dumb anxiety of Gwynplaine; thence his obedience when summoned to take his seat. A pensive man is often a passive man. He had heard what he fancied was the command of duty itself. Was not that entrance into a place where oppression could be discussed and resisted, the realization of one of his deepest aspirations? When he had been called upon to speak, he, the fearful human scantling, he, the living specimen of the despotic whims under which, for six thousand years, mankind has groaned in agony,—had he the right to refuse? Had he the right to withdraw his head from under the tongue of fire descending from on high to rest upon him?

In the obscure and giddy debate of conscience, what had he said to himself? This: "The people are a silence. I will be the mighty advocate of that silence; I will speak for the dumb; I will speak of the little to the great,—of the weak to the powerful. This is the purpose of my fate. God wills what he wills, and does it. It was a wonder that Hardquanonne's flask, in which was the metamorphosis of Gwynplaine into Lord Clancharlie, should have floated for fifteen years on the ocean, on the billows, in the surf, through the storms, and that all the raging of the sea did it no harm. But I can see the reason. There are destinies with secret springs. I have the key of mine, and know its enigma. I am predestined; I have a mission; I will be the poor man's lord; I will speak for the speechless with despair; I will translate inarticulate remonstrance; I will translate the mutterings, the groans, the murmurs, the voices of the crowd, their ill-spoken complaints, their unintelligible words, and those animal-like cries which ignorance and suffering put into men's mouths. The clamor of men is as inarticulate as the howling of the wind. They cry out, but they are not understood; so that cries become equivalent to silence, and silence with them means throwing down their arms. This forced disarmament calls for help. I will be their help; I will be the Denunciation; I will be the Word of the people. Thanks to me, they shall be understood. I will be the bleeding mouth from which the gag has been torn. I will tell everything. This will be great, indeed."

Yes; it is fine to speak for the dumb; but to speak to the deaf is sad. And that was his second part in the drama.

Alas! he had failed irremediably.

The elevation in which he had believed, the high fortune, had melted away like a mirage. And what a fall! To be drowned in a surge of laughter!

He had believed himself strong, he who, during so many years, had floated with observant mind on the wide sea of suffering; he who had brought back out of the great shadow so touching a cry. He had been flung against that huge rock, the frivolity of the fortunate. He believed himself an avenger; he was but a clown. He thought that he wielded the thunder-bolt; he did but tickle. In place of emotion, he met with mockery. He sobbed; they burst into gayety; and under that gayety, he had sunk fatally submerged.

And what had they laughed at? At his laugh.

So, that trace of a hateful act, of which he must keep the mark forever;—mutilation carved in everlasting gayety; the stigma of laughter, image of the sham contentment of nations under their oppressors: that mask of joy produced by torture; that abyss of grimace which he carried on his features; the scar which signified *Jussu regis*, the attestation of a crime committed by the king towards him, and the symbol of crime committed by royalty towards the people;—that it was which had triumphed over him—that it was which had overwhelmed him; so that the accusation against the executioner turned into sentence upon the victim. What a prodigious denial of justice! Royalty, having had satisfaction of his father, had had satisfaction of him! The evil that had been done had served as pretext and as motive for the evil which remained to be done. Against whom were the lords angered? Against the torturer? No. Against the tortured. Here is the throne; there, the people. Here, James II.; there, Gwynplaine. That confrontation, indeed, brought to light an outrage and a crime. What was the outrage? Complaint. What was the crime? Suffering. Let misery hide itself in silence, otherwise it becomes treason. And those men who had dragged Gwynplaine on the hurdle of sarcasm, were they wicked? No; but they, too, had their fatality: they were happy. They were executioners, ignorant of the fact. They were good-humored; they saw no use in Gwynplaine. He opened himself to them. He tore out his heart to show them, and they cried, "Go on with your play!" But, sharpest sting! he had laughed himself. The frightful chain which tied down his soul hindered his thoughts from rising to his face. His disfigurement reached even his senses; and, while his conscience was indignant, his face gave it the lie, and jested. Then all was over. He was the laughing man, the caryatid of the weeping world. He was an agony petrified in hilarity, carrying the weight of a universe of calamity, and walled up forever with the gayety, the ridicule, and the amusement of others; of all the Oppressed, of whom he was the Incarnation, he partook the hateful fate, to be a desolation not believed in; they jeered at his distress; to them he was but an extraordinary buffoon lifted out of some frightful condensation of misery, escaped from his prison, changed to a deity, risen from the dregs of the people to the foot of the throne, mingling with the stars, and who, having once amused the damned, now amused the elect. All that was in him of generosity, of enthusiasm, of eloquence, of heart, of soul, of fury, of anger, of love, of inexpressible grief, ended in—a burst of laughter! And he proved, as he had told the lords, that this was not the exception; but that it was the normal, ordinary, universal, unlimited, sovereign fact, so amalgamated with the routine of life, that they took no account of it. The hungry pauper laughs, the beggar laughs, the felon laughs, the prostitute laughs, the orphan laughs to gain his bread; the slave laughs, the soldier laughs, the people laugh. Society is so constituted, that every perdition, every indigence, every catastrophe, every fever, every ulcer, every agony, is resolved on the surface of the abyss into one frightful grin of joy. Now, he was that universal grin, and that grin was himself. The law of heaven, the unknown power which governs, had willed that a spectre visible and palpable, a spectre of flesh and bone, should be the synopsis of the monstrous parody which we call the world; and he was that spectre.

Immutable fate!

He had cried: "Pity for those who suffer." In vain! He had striven to awake pity—he had awakened horror. Such is the law of apparitions.

But while he was a spectre, he was also a man; here was the heart-rending complication. A spectre without, a man within. A man more than any other, perhaps, since his double fate was the synopsis of all humanity. And he felt that humanity was at once present in him, and absent from him. There was in his existence something insurmountable. What was he? A disinherited heir? No; for he was a lord. Was he a lord? No; for he was a rebel. He was the light-bearer; a terrible spoil-sport. He was not Satan, certainly; but he was Lucifer. His entrance, with his torch in his hand, was sinister.

Sinister for whom? for the sinister. Terrible to whom? to the terrible. Therefore, they rejected him. Enter their order? be accepted by them? Never. The obstacle which he carried in his face was frightful; but the obstacle which he carried in his ideas was still more insurmountable. His speech was to them more deformed than his face. He had no possible thought in common with the world of the great and powerful, in which he had by a freak of fate been born, and from which another freak of fate had driven him out. There was between men and his face a mask, and between society and his mind, a wall. In mixing, from infancy, a wandering mountebank, with that vast and tough substance which is called the crowd, in saturating himself with the attraction of the multitude, and impregnating himself with the great soul of mankind, he had lost, in the common sense of the whole of mankind, the particular sense of the reigning classes. On their heights, he was impossible. He had reached them wet with water from the well of Truth; the odor of the abyss was on him. He was repugnant to those princes perfumed with lies. To those who live on fiction, truth is disgusting; and he who thirsts for flattery vomits the real, when he has happened to drink it by mistake. That which Gwynplaine brought was not fit for their table. For what was it? Reason, wisdom, justice; and they rejected them with disgust.

There were bishops there. He brought God into their presence. Who was this intruder?

The two poles repel each other. They can never amalgamate, for transition is wanting. Hence the result—a cry of anger—when they were brought together in terrible juxtaposition: all misery concentrated in a man, face to face with all pride concentrated in a caste.

To accuse is useless. To state is sufficient. Gwynplaine, meditating on the limits of his destiny, proved the total uselessness of his effort. He proved the deafness of high places. The privileged have no hearing on the side next the disinherited. Is it their fault? Alas! no. It is their law. Forgive them! To be moved would be to abdicate. Of lords and princes expect nothing. He who is satisfied is inexorable. For those that have their fill, the hungry do not exist. The happy ignore and isolate themselves. On the threshold of their paradise, as on the threshold of hell, must be written, " Leave all hope behind."

Gwynplaine had met with the reception of a spectre entering the dwelling of the gods.

Here all that was within him rose in rebellion. No, he was no spectre, he was a man. He told them, he shouted to them, that he was Man.

He was not a phantom. He was palpitating flesh. He had a brain, and he thought; he had a heart, and he loved; he had a soul, and he hoped. Indeed, to have hoped overmuch was his whole crime.

Alas! he had exaggerated hope into believing in that thing at once so brilliant and so dark, which is called Society. He who was without had re-entered it.

It had at once, and at first sight, made him its three offers, and given him its three gifts—marriage, family, and caste. Marriage? He had seen prostitution on the threshold. Family? His brother had struck him, and was awaiting him the next day, sword in hand. Caste? It had burst into laughter in his face, at him, the patrician, at him, the wretch. It had rejected almost before it had admitted, him. So that his first three steps into the dense shadow of society had opened three gulfs beneath him.

And it was by a treacherous transfiguration that his disaster had begun; and catastrophe had approached him with the aspect of apotheosis!

Ascend! had signified Descend!

His fate was the reverse of Job's. It was through prosperity that adversity had reached him.

O tragical enigma of life! Behold what pitfalls! A child, he had wrestled against the night, and had been stronger than it; a man, he had wrestled against destiny, and had overcome it. Out of disfigurement he had created success; and out of misery, happiness. Of his exile he had made an asylum. A vagabond, he had wrestled against space; and, like the birds of the air, he had found his crumb of bread. Wild and solitary, he had wrestled against the crowd, and had made it his friend. An athlete, he had wrestled against that lion, the people; and he had tamed it. Indigent, he had wrestled against distress, he had faced the dull necessity of living, and from amalgamating with misery every joy of his heart, he had at length made riches out of poverty. He had believed himself the conqueror of life. Of a sudden he was attacked by fresh forces, reaching him from unknown depths; this time, with menaces no longer, but with smiles and caresses. Love, serpent-like and sensual, had appeared to him, who was filled with angelic love. The flesh had tempted him, who had lived on the ideal. He had heard words of voluptuousness like cries of rage; he had felt the clasp of a woman's arms, like the convolutions of a snake; to the illumination of truth had succeeded the fascination of falsehood; for it is not the flesh that is real, but the soul. The flesh is ashes, the soul is flame. For the little circle allied to him by the relationship of poverty and toil, which was his true and natural family, had been substituted the social family—his family in blood, but of tainted blood; and even before he had entered it, he found himself face to face with an intended fratricide. Alas! he had allowed himself to be thrown back into that society, of which Brantôme, whom he had not read, wrote: *The son has a right to challenge his father!* A fatal fortune had cried to him, "Thou art not of the crowd, thou art of the chosen!" and had opened the ceiling above his head like a trap in the sky, and had shot him up through this opening, causing him to appear, wild and unexpected, in the midst of princes and masters.

Then suddenly he saw around him, instead of the people who applauded him, the lords who cursed him. Mournful metamorphosis! Ignominious ennobling! Rude spoliation of all that had been his happiness! Pillage of his life by derision; Gwynplaine, Clancharlie, the lord, the mountebank, torn out of his old lot, out of his new lot, by the beaks of those eagles.

What availed it that he had commenced life by immediate victory over obstacle? Of what good had been his early triumphs? Alas! the fall must come, ere destiny be complete.

So, half against his will, half of it—because after he had done with the wapentake he had to do with Barkilphedro, and he had given a certain amount of consent to his abduction—he had left the real for the chimerical; the true for the false; Dea for Josiana; love for pride; lib-

erty for power; labor proud and poor, for opulence full of unknown responsibilities; the shade in which is God, for the lurid flames in which the devils dwell; Paradise for Olympus!

He had tasted the golden fruit. He was now spitting out the ashes to which it turned.

Lamentable result! Defeat, failure, fall into ruin, insolent expulsion of all his hopes, frustrated by ridicule! Immeasurable disillusion! and what was there for him in the future? If he looked forward to the morrow, what did he see? A drawn sword, the point of which was against his breast, and the hilt in the hand of his brother. He could see nothing but the hideous flash of that sword. Josiana and the House of Lords made up the background in a monstrous chiaroscuro full of tragic shadows.

And that brother seemed so brave and chivalrous! Alas! he had hardly seen the Tom-Jim-Jack, who had defended Gwynplaine, the Lord David, who had defended Lord Clancharlie; but he had had time to receive a blow from him and to love him.

He was crushed.

He felt it impossible to proceed further. Everything had crumbled about him. Besides, what was the good of it? All weariness dwells in the depths of despair.

The trial had been made. It could not be renewed.

Gwynplaine was like a gamester who has played all his trumps away, one after the other. He had allowed himself to be drawn to a fearful gambling table, without thinking what he was about; for, so subtle is the poison of illusion! he had staked Dea against Josiana, and had gained a monster; he had staked Ursus against a family, and had gained an insult; he had played his mountebank platform against his seat in the Lords; for the applause which was his, he had gained insult. His last card had fallen on that fatal green cloth, the deserted bowling-green. Gwynplaine had lost. Nothing remained but to pay. Pay up, wretched man!

The thunder-stricken lie still. Gwynplaine remained motionless. Anybody perceiving him from afar, in the shadow, stiff, and without movement, might have fancied that he saw an upright stone.

Hell, the serpent, and reverie are tortuous. Gwynplaine was descending the sepulchral spirals of the deepest thought.

He reflected on that world of which he had just caught a glimpse, with the icy contemplation of a last look. Marriage, but no love; family, but no brotherly affection; riches, but no conscience; beauty, but no modesty; justice, but no equity; order, but no equilibrium; authority, but no right; power, but no intelligence; splendor, but no light. Inexorable balance-sheet! He went throughout the supreme vision in which his mind had been plunged. He examined successively destiny, situation, society, and himself. What was destiny? A snare. Situation? Despair. Society? Hatred. And himself? A defeated man. In the depths of his soul he cried. Society is the step-mother, Nature is the mother. Society is the world of the body, Nature is the world of the soul. The one tends to the coffin, to the deal box in the grave, to the earth-worms, and ends there. The other tends to expanded wings, to transformation into the morning light, to ascent into the firmament, and there revives into new life.

By degrees a paroxysm came over him, like a sweeping surge. At the close of events there is always a last flash, in which all stands revealed once more. He who judges meets the accused face to face. Gwynplaine reviewed all that society and all that nature had done for him. How kind had nature been to him! How she, who is the soul, had succored him! All had been taken from him, even his features. The soul had given him all back—all, even his features; because there was on earth a heavenly blind girl made expressly for him, who saw not his ugliness, and who saw his beauty.

And it was from this that he had allowed himself to be separated; from that adorable girl, from his own adopted one, from her tenderness, from her divine blind gaze, the only gaze on earth that saw him, that he had strayed! Dea was his sister, because he felt between them the grand fraternity of above—the mystery which contains the whole of heaven. Dea, when he was a little child, was his virgin; because every child has his virgin, and at the commencement of life a marriage of souls is always consummated in the plenitude of innocence. Dea was his wife, for theirs was the same nest on the highest branch of the deep-rooted tree of Hymen. Dea was still more—she was his light, for without her all was void, and nothingness; and for him her head was crowned with rays. What would become of him without Dea? What could he do with all that was himself? Nothing in him could live without her. How, then, could he have lost sight of her for a moment? Oh, unfortunate man! He allowed distance to intervene between himself and his star; and, by the unknown and terrible laws of gravitation in such things, distance is immediate loss.

Where was she, the star? Dea! Dea! Dea! Dea! Alas! he had lost her light. Take away the star, and what is the sky? A black mass. But why, then, had all this befallen him? Oh, what happiness had been his! For him God had remade Eden. Too close was the resemblance, alas! even to allowing the serpent to enter; but this time it was the man who had been tempted. He had been drawn without, and then, by a frightful snare, had fallen into a chaos of murky laughter, which was hell. Oh, grief! Oh, grief! How frightful seemed all that had fascinated him! That Josiana, fearful creature!—half beast, half goddess! Gwynplaine was now on the reverse side of his elevation, and he saw the other aspect of that which had dazzled him. It was baleful! His peerage was deformed; his coronet was hideous; his purple robe, a funeral garment; those palaces, infected; those trophies, those statues, those armorial bearings, sinister; the unwholesome and treacherous air poisoned those who breathed it, and turned them mad. How brilliant the rags of the mountebank, Gwynplaine, appeared to him now! Alas! where was the Green Box, poverty, joy, the sweet wandering life—wandering together, like the swallows? They never left each other then; he saw her every minute, morning, evening. At table their knees, their elbows, touched; they drank from the same cup; the sun shone through the pane, but it was only the sun, and Dea was Love. At night they slept not far from each other; and the dream of Dea came and hovered over Gwynplaine, and the dream of Gwynplaine spread itself mysteriously above the head of Dea. When they awoke they could be never quite sure that they had not exchanged kisses in the azure mists of dreams. Dea was all innocence; Ursus, all wisdom. They wandered from town to town; and they had for provision and for stimulant the frank, loving gayety of the people. They were angel vagabonds, with enough of humanity to walk the earth and not enough of wings to fly away; and now all had disappeared! Where was it gone? Was it possible that it was all effaced? What wind from the tomb had swept over them? All was eclipsed! All was lost! Alas! power, irresistible and deaf to appeal, which weighs down the poor, flings its shadow over all, and is capable of anything. What had been done to them? And he had not been there to protect them, to fling himself in front of them, to defend them, as a lord, with his title, his peerage, and his sword; as a mountebank, with his fists and his nails! And here arose a bitter reflection, perhaps the most bitter of all. Well! no; he could not have defended them. It was he himself who had destroyed them; it was to save him, Lord Clancharlie, from them; it was to isolate his dignity from contact with them, that the infamous omnipotence of society had crushed them. The best way in which he could protect them would be to disappear, and then the cause of their persecution would cease. He out of the way, they would be allowed to remain in peace. Into what icy channel was his thought beginning to run! Oh! why had he allowed himself to be separated from Dea? Was not his first duty towards her? To serve and to defend the people? But Dea was the people. Dea was an orphan. She was blind; she represented humanity. Oh! what had they done to them? Cruel smart of regret! His absence had left the field free for the catastrophe. He would have shared their fate; either they would have been taken and carried away with him, or he would have been swallowed up with them. And, now, what would become of him without them? Gwynplaine without Dea. Was it possible? Without

Dea was to be without everything. It was all over now. The beloved group was forever buried in irreparable disappearance. All was spent. Besides, condemned and damned as Gwynplaine was, what was the good of further struggle? He had nothing more to expect either of men or of heaven. Dea! Dea! Where is Dea? Lost! What! lost? He who has lost his soul can regain it but through one outlet—death.

Gwynplaine, tragically distraught, placed his hand firmly on the parapet, as on a solution, and looked at the river.

It was his third night without sleep. Fever had come over him. His thoughts, which he believed to be clear, were blurred. He felt an imperative need of sleep. He remained for a few instants leaning over the water. Its darkness offered him a bed of boundless tranquillity in the infinity of shadow. Sinister temptation!

He took off his coat, which he folded and placed on the parapet; then, he unbuttoned his waistcoat. As he was about to take it off, his hand struck against something in the pocket. It was the red book which had been given him by the librarian of the House of Lords; he drew it from the pocket, examined it in the vague light of the night, and found a pencil in it, with which he wrote on the first blank that he found these two lines:

"I depart. Let my brother David take my place, and may he be happy!"

Then he signed, "FERMAIN CLANCHARLIE, peer of England."

He took off his waistcoat and placed it upon the coat; then his hat, which he placed upon the waistcoat. In the hat he laid the red book open at the page on which he had written. Seeing a stone lying on the ground, he picked it up and placed it in the hat.

Having done all this, he looked up into the deep shadow above him. Then his head sank slowly, as if drawn by an invisible thread towards the abyss.

There was a hole in the masonry near the base of the parapet; he placed his foot in it, so that his knee stood higher than the top, and

scarcely an effort was necessary to spring over it.   He clasped his
hands behind his back and leaned over.

"So be it," said he.

And he fixed his eyes on the deep waters.

Just then he felt a tongue licking his hands.

He shuddered, and turned round.

Homo was behind him.

CONCLUSION

THE NIGHT AND THE SEA

CHAPTER I

A WATCH-DOG MAY BE A GUARDIAN ANGEL

GWYNPLAINE uttered a cry.

"Is that you, wolf?"

Homo wagged his tail. His eyes sparkled in the darkness. He was looking earnestly at Gwynplaine.

Then he began to lick his hands again. For a moment Gwynplaine was like a drunken man, so great is the shock of Hope's mighty return.

Homo! What an apparition! During the last forty-eight hours he had exhausted what might be termed every variety of the thunder-bolt. But one was left to strike him—the thunder-bolt of joy. And it had just fallen upon him. Certainty, or at least the light which leads to it, regained; the sudden intervention of some mysterious clemency possessed, perhaps, by destiny; life saying, "Behold me!" in the darkest recess of the grave; the very moment in which all expectation has ceased bringing back health and deliverance; a place of safety discovered at the most critical instant in the midst of crumbling ruins; Homo was all this to Gwynplaine. The wolf appeared to him in a halo of light.

Meanwhile, Homo had turned round. He advanced a few steps, and then looked back to see if Gwynplaine was following him.

295

Gwynplaine was doing so. Homo wagged his tail, and went on.

The road taken by the wolf was the slope of the quay of the Effroc-stone. This slope shelved down to the Thames; and Gwynplaine, guided by Homo, descended it.

Homo turned his head now and then, to make sure that Gwynplaine was behind him.

In some situations of supreme importance nothing approaches so near an omniscient intelligence as the simple instinct of a faithful animal. An animal is a lucid somnambulist.

There are cases in which the dog feels that he should follow his master; others, in which he should precede him. Then the animal takes the direction of sense. His imperturbable scent is a confused power of vision in what is twilight to us. He feels a vague obligation to become a guide. Does he know that there is a dangerous pass, and that he can help his master to surmount it? Probably not. Perhaps he does. In any case, some one knows it for him. As we have already said, it often happens in life, that some mighty help which we have held to have come from below has, in reality, come from above. Who knows all the mysterious forms assumed by God?

What was this animal? Providence.

Having reached the river, the wolf led down the narrow tongue of land which bordered the Thames.

Without noise or bark he pushed forward on his silent way. Homo always followed his instinct, and did his duty; but with the pensive reserve of an outlaw.

Some fifty paces more, and he stopped. A wooden platform appeared on the right. At the bottom of this platform, which was a kind of wharf on piles, a black mass could be made out, which was a tolerably large vessel. On the deck of the vessel, near the prow, was a glimmer, like the last flicker of a night-light.

The wolf, having finally assured himself that Gwynplaine was there, bounded on to the wharf. It was a long platform, floored and tarred, supported by a net-work of joists, and under which flowed the river. Homo and Gwynplaine shortly reached the brink.

The ship moored to the wharf was a Dutch vessel, of the Japanese build, with two decks, fore and aft, and between them an open hold, reached by an upright ladder, in which the cargo was laden. There was thus a forecastle and an after-deck, as in our old river boats, and a space between them ballasted by the freight. The paper boats made by children are of a somewhat similar shape. Under the decks were the cabins, the doors of which opened into the hold and were lighted by glazed port-holes. In stowing the cargo a passage was left between the packages of which it consisted. These vessels had a mast on each deck. The foremast was called Paul, the mainmast Peter; the ship being sailed by these two masts, as the Church was guided by her two apostles. A gangway was thrown, like a Chinese bridge, from one deck to the other, over the centre of the hold. In bad weather, both flaps of the gangway were lowered, on the right and left, on hinges, thus making a roof over the hold; so that the ship, in heavy seas, was hermetically closed. These sloops, being of very massive construction, had a beam for a tiller, the strength of the rudder being necessarily proportioned to the height of the vessel. Three men, the skipper and two sailors, with a cabin-boy, sufficed to navigate these ponderous sea-going machines. The decks, fore and aft, were, as we have already said, without bulwarks. The great lumbering hull of this particular vessel was painted black, and on it, visible even in the night, stood out, in white letters, the words, *Vograat, Rotterdam.*

About that time many events had occurred at sea, and amongst others, the defeat of the Baron de Pointi's eight ships off Cape Carnero, which had driven the whole French fleet into refuge at Gibraltar; so that the Channel was swept of every man-of-war, and merchant vessels were able to sail backwards and forwards between London and Rotterdam, without a convoy.

The vessel on which was to be read the word *Vograat,* and which Gwynplaine was now close to, lay with her main-deck almost level with the wharf. But one step to descend, and Homo in a bound, and Gwynplaine in a stride, were on board.

The deck was clear, and no stir was perceptible. The passengers, if, as was likely, there were any, were already on board, the vessel being ready to sail, and the cargo stowed, as was apparent from the state of the hold, which was full of bales and cases. But they were, doubtless, lying asleep in the cabins below, as the passage was to take place during the night. In such cases the passengers do not appear on deck till they awake the following morning. As for the crew, they were probably having their supper in the men's cabin, whilst awaiting the hour fixed for sailing, which was now rapidly approaching. Hence the silence on the two decks connected by the gangway.

The wolf had almost run across the wharf; once on board, he slackened his pace into a discreet walk. He still wagged his tail—no longer joyfully, however; but with the sad and feeble wag of a dog troubled in his mind. Still preceding Gwynplaine, he passed along the after-deck, and across the gangway.

Gwynplaine, having reached the gangway, perceived a light in front of him. It was the same that he had seen from the shore. There was a lantern on the deck, close to the foremast, by the gleam of which was sketched in black, on the dim background of the night, what Gwynplaine recognized to be Ursus's old four-wheeled van.

This poor wooded tenement, cart and hut combined, in which his childhood had rolled along, was fastened to the bottom of the mast by thick ropes, of which the knots were visible at the wheels. Having been so long out of service, it had become dreadfully rickety; it leant over feebly on one side; it had become quite paralytic from disuse; and, moreover, it was suffering from that incurable malady—old age. Mouldy and out of shape, it tottered in decay. The materials of which it was built were all rotten. The iron was rusty, the leather torn, the wood-work worm-eaten. There were lines of cracks across the window in front, through which shone a ray from the lantern. The wheels were warped. The lining, the floor, and the axletrees seemed worn out with fatigue. Altogether, it presented an indescribable appearance of beggary and prostration. The shafts, stuck up, looked like two arms raised to heaven. The whole thing was in a state of dislocation. Beneath it was hanging Homo's chain.

Does it not seem that the law and the will of nature would have dictated Gwynplaine's headlong rush to throw himself upon life, happiness, love regained? So they would, except in some cases of deep terror such as his. But he who comes forth, shattered in nerve and uncertain of his way, from a series of catastrophes, each one like a fresh betrayal, is prudent even in his joy; hesitates, lest he should bear the fatality of which he has been the victim to those whom he loves; feels that some evil contagion may still hang about him, and advances towards happiness with wary steps. The gates of Paradise re-open; but before he enters he examines his ground.

Gwynplaine, staggering under the weight of his emotion, looked around him.

The wolf went and lay down silently by his chain.

CHAPTER II

BARKILPHEDRO, HAVING AIMED AT THE EAGLE, BRINGS DOWN THE DOVE

HE step of the little van was down—the door ajar—there was no one inside. The faint light which broke through the pane in front, sketched the interior of the caravan vaguely in melancholy chiaroscuro. The inscriptions of Ursus, glorifying the grandeur of Lords, showed distinctly on the worn-out boards, which were both the wall without and the wainscot within. On a nail, near the door, Gwynplaine saw his leather gorget and his cape hung up, as they hang up the clothes of a corpse in a dead-house. Just then he had neither waistcoat nor coat on.

Behind the van something was laid out on the deck at the foot of the mast, which was lighted by the lantern. It was a mattress, of which he could make out one corner. On this mattress some one was probably lying, for he could see a shadow move.

Some one was speaking. Concealed by the van, Gwynplaine listened.

It was Ursus's voice.

299

That voice, so harsh in its upper, so tender in its lower, pitch; that voice, which had so often upbraided Gwynplaine, and which had taught him so well, had lost the life and clearness of its tone. It was vague and low, and melted into a sigh at the end of every sentence. It bore but a confused resemblance to his natural and firm voice of old. It was the voice of one in whom happiness was dead. A voice may become a ghost.

Ursus seemed to be engaged in monologue rather than in conversation. We are already aware, however, that soliloquy was a habit with him. It was for that reason that he passed for a madman.

Gwynplaine held his breath, so as not to lose a word of what Ursus said, and this is what he heard:

"This is a very dangerous kind of craft, because there are no bulwarks to it. If we were to slip, there is nothing to prevent our going overboard. If we have bad weather, we shall have to take her below, and that will be dreadful. An awkward step, a fright, and we shall have a rupture of the aneurism. I have seen instances of it. O my God! what is to become of us? Is she asleep? Yes. She is asleep. Is she in a swoon? No. Her pulse is pretty strong. She is only asleep. Sleep is a reprieve. It is the happy blindness. What can I do to prevent people walking about here? Gentlemen, if there be anybody on deck, I beg of you to make no noise. Do not come near us, if you do not mind. You know a person in delicate health requires a little attention. She is feverish, you see. She is very young. 'Tis a little creature who is rather feverish. I put this mattress down here so that she may have a little air. I explain all this so that you should be careful. She fell down exhausted on the mattress as if she had fainted. But she is asleep. I do hope that no one will awake her. I address myself to the ladies, if there are any present. A young girl, it is pitiful! We are only poor mountebanks, but I beg a little kindness, and if there is anything to pay for not making a noise, I will pay it. I thank you, ladies and gentlemen. Is there any one there? No. I don't think there is. My talk is mere loss of breath. So much the better. Gentlemen, I thank you, if you are there; and I thank you still more if you are not. Her forehead is all in perspiration. Come, let us take our places in the galleys again. Put on the chain. Misery is come back. We are sinking again. A hand, the fearful hand which we cannot see, but the weight of which we feel ever upon us, has suddenly struck us back towards the dark point of our destiny. Be it so. We will bear up. Only I will not have her ill. I must seem a fool to talk aloud like this, when I am alone; but she must feel she has some one near her when she awakes. What shall I do if somebody awakes her suddenly? No noise, in the name of heaven! A sudden shock which would awake her suddenly, would be of no use. It will be a pity if anybody comes by. I believe that every one on board is asleep. Thanks be to Providence for that mercy. Well, and Homo? Where is he, I wonder? In all this confusion I forgot to tie him up. I do not know what I am doing. It is more than an hour since I have seen him. I suppose he has been to look for his supper somewhere ashore. I hope nothing has happened to him. Homo! Homo!"

Homo struck his tail softly on the planks of the deck.

"You are there. Oh! you are there! Thank God for that. If Homo had been lost, it would have been too much to bear. She has moved her arm. Perhaps she is going to awake. Quiet, Homo! The tide is turning. We shall sail directly. I think it will be a fine night. There is no wind: the flag droops. We shall have a good passage. I do not know what moon it is, but there is scarcely a stir in the clouds. There will be no swell. It will be a fine night. Her cheek is pale; it is only weakness! No, it is flushed; it is only the fever! Stay! It is rosy. She is well! I can no longer see clearly. My poor Homo, I no longer see distinctly. So we must begin life afresh. We must set to work again. There are only we two left, you see. We will work for her, both of us! She is our child. Ah! the vessel moves! We are off! Good-bye, London! Good-evening! good-night! To the devil with horrible London!"

He was right. He heard the dull sound of the unmooring as the vessel fell away from the wharf. Abaft on the poop a man, the skipper, no doubt, just come from below, was standing. He had slipped the hawser and was working the tiller. Looking only to the rudder, as befitted the combined phlegm of a Dutchman and a sailor, listening to nothing but the wind and the water, bending against the resistance of the tiller, as he worked it to port or starboard, he looked, in the gloom of the after-deck, like a phantom bearing a beam upon its shoulder. He was alone there. So long as they were in the river the other sailors were not required. In a few minutes the vessel was in the centre of the current, with which she drifted without rolling or pitching. The Thames, little disturbed by the ebb, was calm. Carried onwards by the tide, the vessel made rapid way. Behind her the black scenery of London was fading in the mist.

Ursus went on talking.

"Never mind, I will give her digitalis. I am afraid that delirium will supervene. She perspires in the palms of her hands. What sin can we have committed in the sight of God? How quickly has all this misery come upon us! Hideous rapidity of evil! A stone falls. It has claws. It is the hawk swooping on the lark. It is destiny. There you lie, my sweet child! One comes to London. One says: What a fine city! What fine buildings! Southwark is a magnificent suburb. One settles there. But now they are horrid places. What would you have me do there? I am going to leave. This is the 30th of April. I always distrusted the month of April. There are but two lucky days in April, the 5th and the 27th; and four unlucky ones—the 10th, the 20th, the 29th, and the 30th. This has been placed beyond doubt by the calculations of Cardan. I wish this day were over. Departure is a comfort. At dawn we shall be at Gravesend, and to-morrow evening at Rotterdam. Zounds! I will begin life again in the van. We will draw it, won't we, Homo?"

A light tapping announced the wolf's consent.

Ursus continued:

"If one could only get out of a grief, as one gets out of a city! Homo, we must yet be happy. Alas! there must always be the one who is no more. A shadow remains on those who survive. You know whom I mean, Homo. We were four, and now we are but three. Life is but a long loss of those whom we love. They leave behind them a train of sorrows. Destiny amazes us by a prolixity of unbearable suffering; who then can wonder that the old are garrulous? It is despair that makes the dotard, old fellow! Homo, the wind continues favorable. We can no longer see the dome of St. Paul's. We shall pass Greenwich presently. That will be six good miles over. Oh! I turn my back forever on those odious capitals, full of priests, of magistrates, and of people. I prefer looking at the leaves rustling in the woods. Her forehead is still in perspiration. I don't like those great violet veins in her arm. There is fever in them. Oh! all this is killing me. Sleep, my child. Yes; she sleeps."

Here a voice spoke: an ineffable voice, which seemed from afar, and appeared to come at once from the heights and the depths—a voice divinely fearful, the voice of Dea.

All that Gwynplaine had hitherto felt seemed nothing. His angel spoke. It seemed as though he heard words spoken from another world in a heaven-like trance.

The voice said:

"He did well to go. This world was not worthy of him. Only I must go with him. Father! I am not ill; I heard you speak just now. I am very well, quite well. I was asleep. Father, I am going to be happy."

"My child," said Ursus, in a voice of anguish; "what do you mean by that?"

The answer was:

" Father, do not be unhappy."

There was a pause, as if to take breath, and then these few words, pronounced slowly, reached Gwynplaine:

" Gwynplaine is no longer here. It is now that I am blind. I knew not what night was. Night is absence."

The voice stopped once more, and then continued :

" I always feared that he would fly away. I felt that he belonged to Heaven. He has taken flight suddenly. It was natural that it should end thus. The soul flies away like a bird. But the nest of the soul was in the height, where dwells the Great Loadstone, who draws all towards Him. I know where to find Gwynplaine. I have no doubt about the way. Father, it is yonder. Later on you will rejoin us, and Homo, too."

Homo, hearing his name pronounced, wagged his tail softly against the deck.

" Father ! " resumed the voice, " you understand that once Gwynplaine is no longer here, all is over. Even if I would remain, I could not, because one must breathe. We must not ask for that which is impossible. I was with Gwynplaine. It was quite natural, I lived. Now Gwynplaine is no more, I die. The two things are alike : either he must come, or I must go. Since he cannot come back, I am going to him. It is good to die. It is not at all difficult. Father, that which is extinguished here, shall be rekindled elsewhere. It is a heartache to live in this world. It cannot be that we shall always be unhappy. When we go to what you call the stars, we shall marry, we shall never part again, and we shall love, love, love ; and that is what is God."

" There, there, do not agitate yourself," said Ursus..

The voice continued :

" Well, for instance ; last year. In the spring of last year we were together, and we were happy. How different it is now ! I forget what little village we were in, but there were trees, and I heard the linnets singing. We came to London ; all was changed. This is no reproach, mind. When one comes to a fresh place, how is one to know anything about it ? Father, do you remember that one day there was a woman in the great box ; you said, ' It is a duchess.' I felt sad. I think it might have been better had we kept to the little towns. Gwynplaine has done right, withal. Now my turn has come. Besides, you have told me yourself, that when I was very little, my mother died, and that I was lying on the ground with the snow falling upon me, and that he, who was also very little then, and alone, like myself, picked me up, and that it was thus that I came to be alive ; so you cannot wonder that now I should feel it absolutely necessary to go and search the grave to see if Gwynplaine be in it.　　Because the only thing which exists in life, is the heart; and after life, the soul.　You take notice of what I say, father, do you not?　What is moving?　It seems as if we are in something that is moving, yet I do not hear the sound of the wheels."

After a pause the voice added:

"I cannot exactly make out the difference between yesterday and to-day.　I do not complain.　I do not know what has occurred; but something must have happened."

These words, uttered with deep and inconsolable sweetness, and with a sigh which Gwynplaine heard, wound up thus:

"I must go, unless he should return."

Ursus muttered gloomily:

"I do not believe in ghosts."

He went on:

"This is a ship.　You ask why the house moves; it is because we are on board a vessel.　Be calm; you must not talk so much.　Daughter, if you have any love for me, do not agitate yourself, it will make you feverish.　I am so old, I could not bear it if you were to have an illness.　Spare me! do not be ill!"

Again the voice spoke:

"What is the use of searching the earth, when we can only find in Heaven?"

Ursus replied, with a half attempt at authority:

"Be calm.　There are times when you have no sense at all.　I order you to rest.　After all, you cannot be expected to know what it is to rupture a blood-vessel.　I should be easy if you were easy.　My child, do something for me as well.　If he picked you up, I took you in. You will make me ill.　That is wrong.　You must calm yourself, and go to sleep.　All will come right.　I give you my word of honor, all will come right.　Besides, it is very fine weather.　The night might have been made on purpose.　To-morrow we shall be at Rotterdam, which is a city in Holland, at the mouth of the Meuse."

"Father," said the voice, "look here; when two beings have always been together from infancy, their state should not be disturbed, or death must come, and it cannot be otherwise.　I love you all the same, but I feel that I am no longer altogether with you, although I am as yet not altogether with him."

"Come! try to sleep," repeated Ursus.

The voice answered:

"I shall have sleep enough soon."

Ursus replied, in trembling tones:

"I tell you that we are going to Holland, to Rotterdam, which is a city."

"Father," continued the voice, "I am not ill; if you are anxious about that, you may rest easy. I have no fever. I am rather hot; it is nothing more."

Ursus stammered out:

"At the mouth of the Meuse——"

"I am quite well, father; but look here! I feel that I am going to die!"

"Do nothing so foolish," said Ursus.

And he added:

"Above all, God forbid that she should have a shock!"

There was a silence. Suddenly Ursus cried out:

"What are you doing? Why are you getting up? Lie down again, I implore of you."

Gwynplaine shivered, and stretched out his head.

CHAPTER III

E saw Dea. She had just raised herself up on the mattress. She had on a long white dress, carefully closed, and showing only the delicate form of her neck. The sleeves covered her arms, the folds, her feet. The branch-like tracery of blue veins, hot and swollen with fever, were visible on her hands. She was shivering and rocking, rather than reeling, to and fro, like a reed. The lantern threw up its glancing light on her beautiful face. Her loosened hair floated over her shoulders. No tears fell on her cheeks. In her eyes there was fire, and darkness. She was pale, with that paleness which is like the transparency of a divine life in an earthly face. Her fragile and exquisite form was, as it were, blended and interfused with the folds of her robe. She wavered like the flicker of a flame, while, at the same time, she was dwindling into shadow. Her eyes, opened wide, were resplendent. She was as one just freed from the sepulchre; a soul standing in the dawn.

Ursus, whose back only was visible to Gwynplaine, raised his arms in terror.

"Oh! my child! Oh! heavens! she is delirious. Delirium is what I feared worst of all. She must have no shock, for that might kill her; yet nothing but a shock can prevent her going mad. Dead or mad! what a situation! O God! what can I do? My child, lie down again."

Meanwhile, Dea spoke. Her voice was almost indistinct, as if a cloud already interposed between her and earth.

"Father, you are wrong. I am not in the least delirious. I hear all you say to me, distinctly. You tell me that there is a great crowd of people, that they are waiting, and that I must play to-night. I am quite willing. You see that I have my reason; but I do not know what

306

to do, since I am dead, and Gwynplaine is dead. I am coming all the
same. I am ready to play. Here I am; but Gwynplaine is no longer
here."

"Come, my child," said Ursus, "do as I bid you. Lie down again."

"He is no longer here, no longer here. Oh! how dark it is!"

"Dark," muttered Ursus. "This is the first time she has ever
uttered that word!"

Gwynplaine, with as little noise as he could help making as he
crept, mounted the step of the caravan, entered it, took from the nail
the cape and the collar, put the collar round his neck, and redescended

from the van, still concealed by the projection of the cabin, the rigging, and the mast.

Dea continued murmuring. She moved her lips, and by degrees the murmur became a melody. In broken pauses, and with the interrupted cadences of delirium, her voice broke into the mysterious appeal she had so often addressed to Gwynplaine in " *Chaos Vanquished.*" She sang, and her voice was low and uncertain as the murmur of the bee:

> " Noche, quita te de alli !
> El alba canta" . . . *

She stopped.

"No, it is not true. I am not dead. What was I saying? Alas! I am alive. I am alive. He is dead. I am below. He is above. He is gone. I remain. I shall hear his voice no more, nor his footstep. God, who had given us a little Paradise on earth, has taken it away. Gwynplaine, it is over. I shall never feel you near me again. Never! And his voice! I shall never hear his voice again. And she sang:

> " Es menester a cielos ir —
> Deja, quiero,
> A tu negro
> Caparazon." †

She stretched out her hand, as if she sought something in space on which she might rest.

Gwynplaine, rising by the side of Ursus, who had suddenly become as though petrified, knelt down before her.

" Never," said Dea, "never shall I hear him again."

She began, wandering, to sing again:

> Deja, quiero,
> A tu negro
> Caparazon."

Then she heard a voice—even the beloved voice—answering:

> " O ven ! ama !
> Eres alma,
> Soy corazon." ‡

---

* " Depart, O night ! sings the dawn."

† " We must go to heaven.
  Take off, I entreat thee,
  Thy black cloak."

‡ " O come and love !
  Thou art the soul,
  I am the heart."

And at the same instant Dea felt under her hand the head of Gwynplaine. She uttered an indescribable cry.

"Gwynplaine!"

A light, as of a star, shone over her pale face, and she tottered. Gwynplaine received her in his arms.

"Alive!" cried Ursus.

Dea repeated, "Gwynplaine."

And with her head bowed against Gwynplaine's cheek, she whispered faintly:

"You have come down to me again; I thank you, Gwynplaine."

And seated on his knee, she lifted up her head. Wrapt in his embrace, she turned her sweet face towards him, and fixed on him those eyes so full of light and shadow, as though she could see him.

"It is you," she said.

Gwynplaine covered her sobs with kisses. There are words which are at once words, cries, and sobs, in which all ecstasy and all grief are mingled and burst forth together. They have no meaning, and yet tell all.

"Yes! it is! It is I, Gwynplaine, of whom you are the soul. Do you hear me? I, of whom you are the child, the wife, the star, the breath of life. I, to whom you are eternity. It is I. I am here. I hold you in my arms. I am alive. I am yours. Oh! when I think that in a moment all would have been over—one minute more, but for Homo! I will tell you everything. How near is despair to joy! Dea, we live! Dea, forgive me. Yes. Yours forever. You are right. Touch my forehead. Make sure that it is I. If you only knew—but nothing can separate us now. I rise out of hell, and ascend into heaven. Am I not with you? You said that I descended. Not so; I re-ascend. Once more with you! Forever! I tell you forever. Together! We are together! Who would have believed it? We have found each other again. All our troubles are past. Before us now there is nothing but enchantment. We will renew our happy life, and we will shut the door so fast that misfortune shall never enter again. I will tell you all. You will be astonished. The vessel has sailed. No one can prevent that now. We are on our voyage, and at liberty. We are going to Holland. We will marry. I have no fear about gaining a livelihood. What can hinder it? There is nothing to fear. I adore you!"

"Not so quick," stammered Ursus.

Dea, trembling, and with the rapture of an angelic touch, passed her hand over Gwynplaine's profile. He overheard her say to herself:

"It is thus that God is made."

Then she touched his clothes.

" The esclavine," she said, "the cape. Nothing changed. All as it was before."

Ursus, stupefied, delighted, smiling, drowned in tears, looked at them, and addressed an aside to himself:

" I don't understand it in the least. I am a stupid idiot—I, who saw him carried to the grave! I cry, and I laugh. That is all I know. I am as great a fool as if I were in love myself. But that is just what I am. I am in love with them both. Old fool! Too much emotion. Too much emotion. It is what I was afraid of. No, it is that I wished for. Gwynplaine, be careful of her. Yes, let them kiss! it is no affair of mine. I am but a spectator. What I feel is droll. I am the parasite of their happiness, and I am nourished by it."

While Ursus was talking to himself, Gwynplaine exclaimed:

" Dea, you are too beautiful! I don't know where my wits were gone these last few days. Truly, there is but you on earth. I see you again, but as yet I can hardly believe it. In this ship! But tell me, how did it all happen? To what a state have they reduced you. But where is the Green Box? They have robbed you. They have driven you away. It is infamous. Oh! I will avenge you. I will avenge you, Dea. They shall answer for it. I am a peer of England."

Ursus, as if stricken by a planet full in his breast, drew back, and looked at Gwynplaine attentively.

" It is clear that he is not dead; but can he have gone mad?" and he listened to him doubtfully.

Gwynplaine resumed:

" Be easy, Dea; I will carry my complaint to the House of Lords."

Ursus looked at him again, and struck his forehead with the tip of his forefinger. Then making up his mind:

" It is all one to me," he said. "It will be all right, all the same. Be as mad as you like, my Gwynplaine. It is one of the rights of man. As for me, I am happy; but how came all this about?"

The vessel continued to sail smoothly and fast. The night grew darker and darker. The mists, which came inland from the ocean, were invading the zenith, from which no wind blew them away. Only a few large stars were visible, and they disappeared one after another, so that soon there were none at all, and the whole sky was dark, infinite, and soft. The river broadened until the banks on each side were nothing but two thin brown lines mingling with the gloom. Out of all this shadow rose a profound peace. Gwynplaine, half seated, held Dea in his embrace. They spoke, they cried, they babbled, they murmured in a mad dialogue of joy. How are we to paint thee, O joy!

" My life!"

"My heaven!"

"My love!"

"My whole happiness!"

"Gwynplaine!"

"Dea, I am drunk. Let me kiss your feet."

"Is it you, then, for certain?"

"I have so much to say to you now that I do not know where to begin."

"One kiss!"

"O, my wife!"

"Gwynplaine, do not tell me that I am beautiful. It is you who are handsome."

"I have found you again. I hold you to my heart. This is true. You are mine. I do not dream. Is it possible? Yes, it is. I recover possession of life. If you only knew! I have met with all sorts of adventures. Dea!"

"Gwynplaine, I love you!"

And Ursus murmured:

"Mine is the joy of a grandfather."

Homo, having come from under the van, was going from one to the other discreetly, exacting no attention, licking them left and right—now Ursus's thick shoes, now Gwynplaine's cape, now Dea's dress, now the mattress. This was his way of giving his blessing.

They had passed Chatham and the mouth of the Medway. They were approaching the sea. The shadowy serenity of the atmosphere was such that the passage down the Thames was being made without trouble: no manœuvre was needful, nor was any sailor called on deck. At the other end of the vessel the skipper, still alone, was steering. There was only this man aft. At the bow the lantern lighted up the happy group of beings who, from the depths of misery, had suddenly been raised to happiness by a meeting so unhoped-for.

CHAPTER IV

NAY; ON HIGH!

SUDDENLY Dea, disengaging herself from Gwynplaine's embrace, arose. She pressed both her hands against her heart, as if to still its throbbings.

"What is wrong with me?" said she. "There is something the matter. Joy is suffocating. No, it is nothing! That is lucky. Your re-appearance, O my Gwynplaine, has given me a blow—a blow of happiness. All this heaven of joy which you have put into my heart has intoxicated me. You being absent, I felt myself dying. The true life which was leaving me you have brought back. I felt as if something was being torn away within me. It is the shadows that have been torn away, and I feel life dawn in my brain—a glowing life, a life of fever and delight. This life which you have just given me is wonderful. It is so heavenly, that it makes me suffer somewhat. It seems as though my soul is enlarged and can scarcely be contained in my body. This life of seraphim, this plenitude, flows into my brain, and penetrates it. I feel like a beating of wings within my breast. I feel strangely, but happy. Gwynplaine, you have been my resurrection."

She flushed, became pale, then flushed again, and fell.

"Alas!" said Ursus, "you have killed her."

Gwynplaine stretched his arms towards Dea. Extremity of anguish coming upon extremity of ecstasy, what a shock! He would himself have fallen, had he not had to support her.

"Dea!" he cried, shuddering, "what is the matter?"

"Nothing," said she; "I love you!"

She lay in his arms, lifeless, like a piece of linen; her hands were hanging down helplessly.

Gwynplaine and Ursus placed Dea on the mattress. She said, feebly:

" I cannot breathe lying down."

They lifted her up.

Ursus said :

" Fetch a pillow."

She replied :

" What for ? I have Gwynplaine."

She laid her head on Gwynplaine's shoulder, who was sitting behind, and supporting her, his eyes wild with grief.

" Oh," said she, " how happy I am ! "

Ursus took her wrist, and counted the pulsation of the artery. He did not shake his head. He said nothing, nor expressed his thought except by the rapid movement of his eyelids, which were opening and closing convulsively, as if to prevent a flood of tears from bursting out.

" What is the matter ? " asked Gwynplaine.

Ursus placed his ear against Dea's left side.

Gwynplaine repeated his question eagerly, fearful of the answer.

Ursus looked at Gwynplaine, then at Dea. He was livid. He said :

" We ought to be parallel with Canterbury. The distance from here to Gravesend cannot be very great. We shall have fine weather all night. We need fear no attack at sea, because the fleets are all on the coast of Spain. We shall have a good passage."

Dea, bent, and growing paler and paler, clutched her robe convulsively. She heaved a sigh of inexpressible sadness, and murmured :

" I know what this is; I am dying ! "

Gwynplaine rose in terror. Ursus held Dea.

" Die ! You die ! No; it shall not be ! You cannot die ! Die now ! Die at once ! It is impossible ! God is not ferociously cruel— to give you and to take you back in the same moment. No ; such a thing cannot be. It would make one doubt in Him. Then, indeed, would everything be a snare—the earth, the sky, the cradles of infants, the human heart, love, the stars. God would be a traitor, and man a dupe. There would be nothing in which to believe. It would be an insult to the creation. Everything would be an abyss. You know not what you say, Dea. You shall live ! I command you to live ! You must obey me ! I am your husband and your master, I forbid you to leave me ! Oh, heavens ! Oh, wretched Man ! No, it cannot be ; I to remain in the world after you ! Why, it is as monstrous as that there should be no sun ! Dea ! Dea ! recover ! It is but a moment of passing pain. One feels a shudder at times, and thinks no more about it. It is absolutely necessary that you should get well and cease to suffer. *You* die ! What have I done to you ? The very thought of it drives me mad.

We belong to each other, and we love each other. You have no reason for going! It would be unjust! Have I committed crimes? Besides, you have forgiven me. Oh, you would not make me desperate—have me become a villain, a madman, drive me to perdition? Dea, I entreat you! I conjure you! I supplicate you! Do not die!"

And clenching his hands in his hair, agonized with fear, stifled with tears, he threw himself at her feet.

"My Gwynplaine," said Dea, "it is no fault of mine."

There then rose to her lips a red froth, which Ursus wiped away with the fold of her robe, before Gwynplaine, who was prostrate at her feet, could see it.

Gwynplaine took her feet in his hands, and implored her in all kinds of confused words.

"I tell you, I will not have it! *You* die? I have no strength left to bear it. Die? Yes; but both of us together—not otherwise. *You* die, my Dea? I will never consent to it! My divinity! my love! Do you understand that I am with you? I swear that you shall live! Oh, but you cannot have thought what would become of me after you were gone. If you had an idea of the necessity which you are to me, you would see that it is absolutely impossible! Dea! you see I have but you! The most extraordinary things have happened to me. You will hardly believe that I have just explored the whole of life in a few hours! I have found out one thing—that there is nothing in it! You exist! if you did not, the universe would have no meaning. Stay with me! Have pity on me! Since you love me, live on! If I have just found you again, it is to keep you! Wait a little longer; you cannot leave me like this, now that we have been together but a few minutes! Do not be impatient! Oh, Heaven, how I suffer! You are not angry with me, are you? You know that I could not help going when the wapentake came for me. You will breathe more easily presently, you will see. Dea, all has been put right. We are going to be happy. Do not drive me to despair, Dea! I have done nothing to you!"

These words were not spoken, but sobbed out. They rose from his breast—now in a lament which might have attracted the dove, now in a roar which might have made lions recoil.

Dea answered him in a voice growing weaker and weaker, and pausing at nearly every word.

"Alas! it is of no use, my beloved! I see that you are doing all you can. An hour ago I wanted to die; now I do not. Gwynplaine—my adored Gwynplaine! how happy we have been! God placed you in my life, and He takes me out of yours. You see, I am going. You will remember the Green Box, won't you; and poor blind little Dea?

You will remember my song? Do not forget the sound of my voice,
and the way in which I said, 'I love you!' I will come back and tell
it to you again, in the night while you are asleep. Yes, we found each
other again; but it was too much joy. It was to end at once. It is

decreed that I am to go first. I love my father, Ursus, and my brother,
Homo, very dearly. You are all so good. There is no air here. Open
the window. My Gwynplaine, I did not tell you, but I was jealous of
a woman who came one day. You do not even know of whom I speak.
Is it not so? Cover my arms, I am rather cold. And Fibi and Vinos,
where are they? One comes to love everybody. One feels a friendship

for all those who have been mixed up in one's happiness. We have a kindly feeling towards them for having been present in our joys. Why has it all passed away? I have not clearly understood what has happened during the last two days. Now I am dying. Leave me in my dress. When I put it on I foresaw that it would be my shroud. I wish to keep it on. Gwynplaine's kisses are upon it. Oh, what would I not have given to have lived on! What a happy life we led in our poor caravan! How we sang! How I listened to the applause! What joy it was never to be separated from each other! It seemed to me that I was living in a cloud with you: I knew one day from another, although I was blind. I knew that it was morning, because I heard Gwynplaine; I felt that it was night, because I dreamed of Gwynplaine. I felt that I was wrapped up in something, which was his soul. We adored each other so sweetly. It is all fading away; and there will be no more songs. Alas! that I cannot live on! You will think of me, my beloved!"

Her voice was growing fainter. The ominous waning, which was death, was stealing away her breath. She folded her thumbs within her fingers, a sign that her last moments were approaching. It seemed as though the first uncertain words of an angel just created, were blended with the last failing accents of the dying girl.

She murmured:

"You will think of me, won't you? It would be very sad to be dead, and to be remembered by no one. I have been wayward at times; I beg pardon of you all. I am sure that, if God had so willed it, we might yet have been happy, my Gwynplaine; for we take up but very little room, and we might have earned our bread together in another land. But God has willed it otherwise. I cannot make out in the least why I am dying. I never complained of being blind, so that I cannot have offended any one. I should never have asked for anything, but always to be blind as I was, by your side. Oh, how sad it is to have to part!"

Her words were more and more inarticulate, evaporating into each other, as if they were being blown away. She had become almost inaudible.

"Gwynplaine," she resumed, "you will think of me, won't you? I shall crave it when I am dead."

And she added:

"Oh, keep me with you!"

Then, after a pause, she said:

"Come to me as soon as you can. I shall be very unhappy without you, even in heaven. Do not leave me long alone, my sweet Gwynplaine ! My Paradise was here. Above there is only heaven ! Oh ! I cannot breathe ! My beloved ! My beloved ! My beloved !"

"Mercy !" cried Gwynplaine.

"Farewell !" murmured Dea.

And he pressed his mouth to her beautiful icy hands. For a mo-

ment it seemed as if she had ceased to breathe. Then she raised herself on her elbows, and an intense splendor flashed across her eyes, and through an ineffable smile her voice rang out clearly :

"Light !" she cried. "I see !"

And she expired. She fell back rigid and motionless on the mattress.

"Dead !" said Ursus.

And the poor old man, as if crushed by his despair, bowed his bald

head and buried his swollen face in the folds of the gown which covered
Dea's feet. He lay there in a swoon.

Then Gwynplaine became awful.

He arose, lifted his eyes, and gazed into the vast gloom above him.

Seen by none on earth, but looked down upon, perhaps, as he stood
in the darkness, by some invisible presence, he stretched his hands on
high, and said :

"I come ! "

And he strode across the deck, towards the side of the vessel, as if
beckoned by a vision.

A few paces off was the abyss. He walked slowly, never casting
down his eyes. A smile came upon his face, such as Dea's had just
worn. He advanced straight before him, as if watching something.
In his eyes was a light like the reflection of a soul perceived from
afar off.

He cried out, "Yes !" At every step he was approaching nearer
to the side of the vessel.

His gait was rigid, his arms were lifted up, his head was thrown
back, his eyelids were fixed. His movement was ghost-like.

He advanced without haste and without hesitation, with fatal precision, as though there were before him no yawning gulf and open
grave.

He murmured :

"Be easy. I follow you. I understand the sign that you are
making me."

His eyes were fixed upon a certain spot in the sky, where the
shadow was deepest. The smile was still upon his face.

The sky was perfectly black ; there was no star visible in it, and
yet he evidently saw one.

He crossed the deck.

A few stiff and ominous steps, and he had reached the very edge.

"I come," said he ; "Dea, behold, I come ! "

One step more, there was no bulwark ; the void was before him ; he strode into it.

He fell.

The night was thick and dull, the water deep. It swallowed him up. He disappeared calmly and silently. None saw or heard him. The ship sailed on, and the river flowed.

Shortly afterwards the ship reached the sea.

When Ursus returned to consciousness, he found that Gwynplaine was no longer with him, and he saw Homo by the edge of the deck baying in the shadow and looking down upon the water.

On the last page of the manuscript is the following note :

" Finished August 23, 1868, at half-past ten o'clock in the morning, at Brussels, No. 4 Place des Barricades."

This work, most of which was written in Guernsey, was begun at Brussels, July 21, 1866, and finished at Brussels, August 23, 1868.

THE END

Lightning Source UK Ltd.
Milton Keynes UK
UKHW022205270223
417761UK00005B/265